ARABIAN WINDS

Linda Chaikin

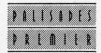

MULTNOMAH BOOKS
SISTERS, OREGON

ARABIAN WINDS
published by Palisades
a part of the Questar publishing family

© 1997 by Linda Chaikin

International Standard Book Number: 1-57673-105-7

Cover illustration by JoAnn Wistling
Cover design by Catherine Bergstrom
Edited by Janet Kobobel Grant

Printed in the United States of America

Scripture quotations are from: *The New King James Version* (NKJV)
© 1984 by Thomas Nelson, Inc.

The King James Version (KJV)

For information:
QUESTAR PUBLISHERS, INC., PO BOX 1720, SISTERS, OREGON 97759

LIBRARY OF CONGRESS CATALOGING-IN-PUBLICATION DATA
Chaikin, L. L., 1943-   Arabian winds/by Linda Chaikin.   p. cm.
      ISBN 1-57673-105-7 (alk. paper) 1. World War, 1914–1918—Medical care—Fiction
2. World War, 1914–1918—Egypt—Fiction.   I. Title
PS3553.H2427A89 1997   96-53685
813'.54–dc21   CIP

97 98 99 00 01 02 03 — 10 9 8 7 6 5 4 3 2 1

ARABIAN WINDS

To Steve,
ture love seeks the very best,
and your love and support have made this possible.
Linda

HISTORICAL PRELUDE

THE SUMMER OF 1914 the world stood on a precipice, waiting for the verdict to be handed down by Europe's ruling lords and kings. The elite had taken it upon themselves to sentence a generation to the whirlwinds of death, that their leaders might seize the kingdoms of the world. Godless ambition added to pride caused the clouds of war to gather. Soon millions of young soldiers would be sacrificed in trenches across Europe and in the burning sands of the Arabian desert.

It was the last hour of youthful silence, a moment in time that hovered in the pale light before the moon turned to blood. Soon the ground would be soaked with sweat and tears and would weep as a woman in travail—not in birth pangs, but as a much-grieved death angel who must open her arms wide to receive fallen sons in the long sleep.

That summer was the end of many things and the beginning of a lament ushered in by the tramp of marching armies. Soon now the kings of Earth would unleash the Guns of August into the Great War, the beginning of sorrows.

Yet hope lived in the good-bye kiss of the girl the soldier left behind—or in the service of the young women like British nurse Allison Wescott. She would eventually follow the British and

Australian soldiers into the Arabian desert and Jerusalem under General Allenby. There she would find the wounded, delirious with pain and fever, and Major Bret Holden, who had much to explain...

PART 1

Arabian Desert

1914

1

NURSE ALLISON WESCOTT KNEW LITTLE OF THE FUTURE. She was on a four-day leave from the medical missionary compound at Zeitoun in Cairo, Egypt, and the burden on her mind was not war and bittersweet romance but whether or not she dare walk barefoot across the hut floor. Mindful of an influx of desert scorpions, she grimaced as she reached for her slippers, carefully turned them over, and shook them, and put them on before investigating an eerie sound that had awakened her from sleep.

She stood tensely alert in one of the twelve "vacation" huts located between the Turkish controlled town of Aleppo in the Arabian Desert and Baghdad. Contemplating the origin of that sound, Allison shivered despite the suffocating heat. A desert rat, perhaps? Her long, flame–colored tresses glimmered like spun silk in the light of the large white moon. She did not bother to light the oil lamp, for the open window permitted light from the Arabian Desert sand and the moon to illuminate the room.

She paused to listen again to that scarcely audible noise that had awakened her only minutes ago. The rising wind, hot and dry, which shifted the dunes, sent fine grains of sand scattering across the outer courtyard.

Then she remembered Major Karl Reuter. Only hours ago the

mysterious German officer had been found dead by the Arab water boy. Apparently Major Reuter had met with an accident. Now Allison remembered what it was that had disturbed her about the death: Was it truly an accident?

Yesterday Allison and some twenty archaeology enthusiasts from all parts of Egypt and Palestine had arrived at this cluster of huts a mile from the British consulate in Aleppo. The huts, once used as barracks for Turkish soldiers of the Ottoman Empire, had been vacated after the revolution in Turkey when the soldiers were transferred to Baghdad. It was through the enterprising efforts of German Baroness Helga Kruger that the Ottoman government in Constantinople had given permission for the Cairo Archaeological Club to renovate the huts and make them into something of a tourist "dwelling" for the enthusiasts. As the baroness had pointed out, a number of tourists were arriving each year to see Egypt with its sphinxes and pyramids, and some remained in the area for a season to see more of Arabia.

Every summer, for as far back as Allison could remember, the Archaeological Club held a holiday near Aleppo in cooperation with the British Museum, working at the Carchemish Digs near the Berlin-Baghdad Railway being constructed under the auspices of Germany's Kaiser Wilhelm. During these yearly summer holidays, the renovated huts were opened to accommodate the club members and their friends. The summer of 1914 was no exception, and the archaeology lovers and serious history students from Cairo had arrived for what many privately believed would be their last holiday until the war clouds were dispersed from Europe. Even though the distant thunder of war could be heard, the British Society in Cairo remained certain the Ottoman Empire, which now controlled Arabia and Palestine, including Jerusalem, would not enter the war. Life for the British in Egypt would remain much the same, with the continuation of its self-satisfying culture of polo, dinner parties, and tea clubs.

The weather, as always in July, had been miserably hot. Allison wondered why the club had waited until the worst month to have its archaeology holiday. Most British with any sense of style went to the breezy Mediterranean Sea at the Gulf of Akaba and rode horses along the shore as small blue waves rolled to the beach.

This year, members of the club had arrived for the most part in a good mood. All, of course, except for retired Major-General Rex Blaine, who had accompanied his amiable wife, Sarah. General Blaine always jokingly found fault with something, usually the heat. "The flies are as thick as one of the ten plagues," he would complain with jocularity.

Then, with shocking suddenness, tragedy had struck the club as one of their own turned up dead—an accident.

It had all begun when Allison's cousin, Neal Bristow, from the Carchemish Digs, who had been hired by the baroness to hold lectures and take the group by camel on an expedition tour out to the Hittite site, did not arrive as expected. He was to have joined his sister, Leah, who was this year's club hostess. Then the water boy had stumbled upon the dead body of Major Karl Reuter among the dunes near what the British called "Arabian Well."

The boy had found the man at sundown as the glorious desert twilight was coming down like a curtain, and the club members were converging on the compound's courtyard to enjoy the Turkish lamb kabobs that the baroness had arranged as a picnic beneath the stars. She had invited other guests as well, including the British consul and his wife, and a few Turkish officials.

Before Major Reuter's death, Allison had noticed the German officer arrive. He was a quiet, unsmiling man who was said to be supervising the building of the Baghdad Railway.

Allison shuddered. She had seen the body, a dark figure in formidable German uniform, carried to the back hut adjacent to her own.

Earlier in the day, when the club members were arriving for the outdoor dinner, it was believed Major Reuter was in his hut and would be joining them. And now he was dead. It seemed to her he had been a rather mysterious man, and she wondered with a prickle of her skin how he had died. No one seemed to know. The Turkish official, a friend of Baroness Kruger, had wired German intelligence in Constantinople and was now waiting for an officer, a Colonel Brent Holman from the German secret police, to look into the incident.

"How did he die, do you suppose?" asked Sarah Blaine, a petite woman with big brown eyes. Allison noted that Sarah's question had seemed to upset cousin Leah. Like the rest, the paleness in Leah's complexion showed her to be more troubled than she would let on. A German officer's death would not be passed over lightly by headquarters at Baghdad, but Leah seemed to be more troubled than the situation warranted.

Dour-faced Professor Blackstone, from the Cairo Archaeological School, had emptied his glass with a little too much zest and answered Sarah Blaine's question with a hint of impatience. "He must have been bitten by a desert viper, my dear Sarah."

There was silence, and Sarah's husband, Rex Blaine, the retired major-general, looked about at the others. A smirk unexpectedly appeared on his hard mouth as he must have guessed everyone's unspoken fears. "What else could it have been?"

Yes, thought Allison, with a sense of foreboding, *what else indeed?*

General Blaine's question did little to help the moment, as the fire flickered in the outdoor brazier where the lamb sizzled and filled the breeze with what was to Allison a sickening aroma. Her appetite had completely gone.

"The vipers are quite deadly," agreed Professor Blackstone. "We all know that. The victim dies within minutes. He must have been bitten when he went out to his pack horse to retrieve his bag."

Dies within minutes . . .

"Minutes is time enough to call out for help," Allison had said. She had looked about at the others to see their reactions, but the faces of those present were as tense and noncommittal as Leah's. Leah had not looked at Allison when she spoke, and Allison had gathered by this that Leah was worried about her elder brother, Neal, and his absence.

Leah had stood, saying to Baroness Kruger that the dreadful incident had ruined her desire to partake of supper, and would the baroness mind too dreadfully if Leah retired early to her hut. She would wait for Neal there. "I'm quite sure he'll have arrived by morning," she had said in an attempt at optimism.

Allison also had retired early and supperless to her hut and had taken a long time to turn sleepy. But now she was wide awake again, and with small prospect of getting back to sleep, she concentrated instead on the noise that had awakened her. The sound she had mistaken for a desert rat or the wind made her all the more tense.

Allison's thoughts ran into the barricade of cousin Neal's delayed arrival. Was he still at the archaeological digs at Jerablus, by the Euphrates River? It wasn't lost on Allison how Leah had pretended before the others that she wasn't worried about Neal. Allison had hoped to speak with Leah alone before she retired, but her cousin had avoided her.

"Maybe he decided to wait a day longer and come down with T.E. Lawrence and Woolly of the British Museum," Leah had said with a toss of her beautiful glossy hair. "You know how archaeologists are, always dramatically excited over some new find of Hittite pottery."

"Yes," drawled General Rex Blaine with a malicious twinkle, "if the Germans working on the railway don't confiscate their finds from beneath their studious noses." His casual mention of the Berlin-Baghdad Railway workers had seemed to bring an uneasy moment to the entire group, especially Baroness Helga Kruger, who was the German buyer for the Berlin Museum. While the baroness had been the one to arrange for the archaeological holiday, Allison was also aware that the darling of the social set in Arabia was a buyer for Kaiser Wilhelm.

The sound that woke her minutes ago must have been the wind, decided Allison. It blew, smelling and whispering of the warm, mysterious secrets of the desert: the shade of a Bedouin tent; a date palm oasis; and the vast, empty silence of Arabia stretching far beyond the white dunes. All this, while the purple-black sky throbbed with the same intense white stars that the Lord had bidden Abraham to look upon when he had promised him many descendants.

She tensed. The sound came again, clearer now. She wouldn't have heard it if her window hadn't been open. *It wasn't the wind,* she thought, *because the wind does not make stealthy footsteps.*

Her soft slippers enabled her to cross the room silently so she could peer out the window without attracting attention. The wooden huts were all alike, each consisting of a small room with a front and back door. Baroness Kruger had arranged for carpentry work to be done, and now each hut had its own primitive bathroom with a round tin tub, and a back porch with a line where clothing could be hung up to dry in the desert heat and wind.

Allison had taken no more than a few steps when she stopped, listening. She held her breath, straining to hear. There it was again. The clicking sound of metal as someone tried to open a door lock. Her door? And to think this was happening while she sat complacently in bed remembering the recent death of Major Reuter.

As a nurse, Allison had seen death many times in Cairo. But now even she shivered, contemplating the hut next to her own and its silent occupant laid out on the bed waiting for the intelligence officer to arrive from Baghdad.

A gust of warm wind rattled the window blind and sent the timbers creaking. Suddenly she understood, or thought she did. With a catch in her breath she realized someone was not trying to get inside her room at all; the person was trying to enter the hut containing Major Reuter's body.

For a moment it seemed to Allison that her heart had stopped beating. In the next moment she was at the small window that faced the major's hut. As the cotton curtains fluttered, she could peer across the small desert yard. The moonlight had not yet fallen on this section of the compound, and the three or four steps leading up to the small back porch were in shadows. Yet she could see someone standing at the door working at the lock. In an eerie moment, the person's head turned in the direction of her window, and with a start she recognized Leah.

Allison backed away a step at a time. She felt her heart must be as audible as a drumbeat. Leah Bristow, her cousin. Whatever possessed her?

Now that she thought about it, just what did she know about her cousin? Allison hesitated; then, her fingers trembling, she managed to softly slide back the bolt on her back door so it wouldn't make a sound. She stepped out onto the small back porch and closed her door.

For another moment she stood poised, looking through the darkness at the other hut. The sandy yard that ran lengthwise between her bungalow and the German major's was bare of shrubs and empty, except for unseen desert insects that crept about in the cooler night. She imagined the large, fuzzy spiders called wind spiders because they could run so swiftly; lizards; and deadly scorpions. Had it been a scorpion sting or a viper that suddenly took Major Reuter's life?

A shiver ran along her skin. Leah was no longer on the porch. Perhaps she had returned to her own hut. Then a tiny flicker of amber light brightened the main room as though someone had struck a match.

Allison came down the wooden steps, tightly clutching her wrapper. On either side of her, the line of similar huts was bright with moonlight, and the sand and rock glistened gray-white. Like ink blotches, the shadows from the desert palms that walled the compound swayed eerily across the sand. Farther back, behind the trees, the ground sloped away into a gully-like dry watercourse. Beyond, it rose upward again to stretch out toward the hills of the Arabian desert and the fathomless black sky.

The wind had risen in the last hour, and sand was driven into smooth little mounds on the steps and piled up against the huts like miniature dunes. The sand covered everything, forming a gritty carpet that crunched beneath Allison's slippers. That sound, though hardly noticeable, seemed to Allison to trumpet her approach in the hot quiet of that uneasy hour when everyone else was asleep—or should be.

With a nervous sense of being watched, she looked back toward the other huts. Their windows were like empty black eye sockets staring at her.

She climbed the steps to the porch of Major Reuter's hut and found the door ajar. Then Leah was inside....

Entering with a whispering movement, Allison heard a faltering footstep from the bedroom where the Major's body lay stretched on the bed. As though disturbed by Allison's presence, the wind sent the timbers creaking, setting her heart racing again.

"It's me, Allison," she whispered.

Silence. Then a swift movement. The tiny flame went out. Expecting Leah to respond, Allison heard only the wind blowing grains of sand against the side of the hut. She began to fear. It was Leah, wasn't it?

In the moment of uncertain silence that entangled Allison, she had second thoughts. Perhaps the golden hair she had seen had not belonged to her cousin but to someone else—someone other than Leah—but she was the only blonde in the archaeology club....

No, thought Allison, *there was someone else, someone I had never seen before.* She had thought her a newcomer.

A light footstep came from behind Allison, not from where she thought Leah was. Fear springing up Allison's spine, she tried to whirl just as a strong hand clamped over her mouth, followed by a cold pistol barrel pressed against her neck. Rigid with shock, she heard the curt whisper in her hair. "Don't make a sound."

A wordless prayer gripped her heart. An indefinable noise came from the darkness on the other side of the room, so faint that she could hardly hear it above the thumping of her heart. Her hand brushed against the smooth binding of a book on a table. As she recoiled, it fell to the floor with a startling thud that shattered the tense silence.

In the moment of uncertainty, the front door suddenly flew open, and she heard footsteps as someone fled. A frustrated breath came from her assailant, who flung Allison aside and crashed his way through objects of furniture that lay in his path.

Allison fell against a small table with rickety legs, and for a precarious moment she tried desperately to cling to it as she went down, hitting her head against something hard. She lay on the floor for a moment or two in the sweltering darkness. When she finally tried to sit up, she felt dizzy and uncertain. Her head still aching, she reached shaking fingers to the side of her temple, trying to remember the layout of the room, for they were all identical.

Slowly her dizziness eased, and her vision could make out the room in the moonlight. She stood, becoming aware of something else: the room had been ransacked. The furniture stood in disarray. It only could have been done before Leah arrived, since she hadn't had time to do it herself.

I would have heard her. I wasn't more than five minutes behind her.

Nor was it likely to have been done by the intruder who had crept up behind Allison, for he must have entered just seconds after she did.

The dry palm branches outside on the tree by the bathroom window rattled. Allison swallowed. Sweat trickled down her sides. *Dear God*, she prayed silently. *Someone else could still be in here!*

In that instant, she heard the bathroom door open. Sheer, cold panic gripped her with icy fingers as she heard the floorboards creak. Allison backed away, screaming as loudly as she could, her legs bumping against a toppled chair. She fell. The intruder brushed against her as he moved through the back door, out across the porch, and down the steps into the night.

Alone, she heard the wind sending the door creaking to and fro on its unoiled hinges, then someone entered through the front door and groped his way to the electric light switch.

Allison sheltered her eyes from the harsh amber light of the single bulb in the low ceiling. The main room, sparsely furnished and as unbecomingly utilitarian as her own, slowly came to life. On the bed in the corner lay the corpse of Major Reuter covered with a blanket. And in the doorway stood a rugged and darkly handsome German officer.

Allison blinked, pale and shaken, and stared at him.

2

THE CONTENTS OF A SCARRED CHEST OF DRAWERS had been dumped onto the floor. Papers from a satchel were also scattered in disarray, and clothing was strewn across a chair. Something caught Allison's eye: a stack of bright green luxurious towels and washcloths, with an unopened bar of perfumed soap—obviously the touch of Baroness Kruger—sat undisturbed on a stool by an open, empty closet.

The bare wooden floor with gaps between the planks was scattered with the inevitable grains of sand and something else that crawled away between the boards—a large, hairy spider.

Allison shivered, for she could never get used to them, and then realized the spider was the least of her worries. Her eyes narrowed against the painful light and lifted slowly from the floorboards to the German officer in the doorway.

Allison scrutinized the intimidating uniform with its cold Iron Cross, the brass, the black-and-crimson band that went around the collar, the duck-bill cap pulled low, and the polished black boots with the trousers tucked into them and blousing to the knee. The German wore a saber and a dark brown leather shoulder holster, but the revolver was drawn and pointed steadily at Allison.

A sick feeling of despair crept through her soul. The exceptionally good-looking man behind the uniform merged with all the ruthlessness it represented, but he was more than a mere soldier carrying out blind orders; he wore the uniform of a colonel in the dreaded secret police.

Her gaze shifted from the glinting gun barrel to the most riveting, midnight-blue eyes she had ever seen. His hair was very dark, and he had a small scar on his chin that added to his ruthless good looks.

In a low, harsh whisper that brought her a fresh attack of panic, he demanded something in German. She had no idea what he had said and tried to guess.

"I—I can't speak German. I'm Nurse Allison Wescott from Cairo. I—um, thought I saw a burglar and came to see who it was, and—and then you came through the back door... "

There was a brief pause as his alert gaze flicked over her. Then she was startled when his accent altered, becoming a deliberate, dry British tone. He clipped, "You came to confront a burglar without a weapon, dressed for bed?" He leaned his shoulder into the open doorway, still holding the gun. "You're very brave, Fräulein. Maybe too curious and too brave. You will forgive me if I don't believe you?"

She flushed, and her gaze wavered, coming to rest absently on the book she'd knocked from the table. Any other man, especially a British officer, would have come at once to help her to her feet, to ask if she were hurt, to apologize for flinging her into the table. The German colonel flicked his revolver in an abrupt gesture.

"Get up, Fräulein."

Allison managed to do so with more dignity than she had supposed she could muster. His undisguised arrogance brought out the will to defy him. She wasn't about to cower or faint. Instead, she met his level, penetrating gaze.

"Your nationality," he demanded.

"I've told you already."

"Answer again!"

She couldn't help herself; her brow lifted. "British," she clipped in return. "What else did you expect?"

It was quite probably dangerous to provoke his rage, but the little dig had come to her tongue too easily. She expected to see him puff up with dignity and threaten to shoot; instead, she was taken off guard when the shadow of a cynical smile touched his mouth.

"God save the king." He gave a sharp nod of his head in mock homage for King Edward. "May I say, *Fräulein*, that your king is most wise to send the innocent to do his spy work. Who would suspect a charming cherub with a tangle of flame curls? A dark brow arched as his gaze swept her dishabille. "Do you always tiptoe about in silk pajamas? I might have put a hole clean through your heart tonight. A dreadful waste—besides, one death in an evening is enough, don't you think?" He nodded toward the stiffening corpse.

She felt a red heat flare in her cheeks and drew her wrapper more tightly about her. The arrogant beast. "I am not a spy for England, Colonel. But one death is quite enough, yes. I am pleased that as a German soldier you look upon life as a worthy commodity. It is more than your Kaiser will honor us with."

He regarded her for a moment, almost curiously, but did not press the issue. "Sit down. 'Please'."

She did so because her knees were weak and she would be foolish to goad him further. He stood looking about the ransacked room. Unwillingly her eyes traced the masculine line of his chin and jaw, tense with restrained anger. Despite the suffocating heat, she felt a shiver.

He reached over, drew shut the door, and bolted it. He checked the two small windows, drawing them shut and fastening them, pulling the curtains across. The room grew instantly hotter. She felt the sweat on her forehead and moved cautiously to brush away a long strand of hair that was glued to her throat, afraid he would think she was reaching for a weapon.

She continued to watch him, aware of his muscle and stature that alerted feminine interest to the man in a uniform she would normally find distasteful. He walked across the room to the bathroom door, pushed it open slowly, and switched on the light. His cobalt blue eyes returned to her, and she thought they softened slightly. "Wait here. And don't be foolish and try to run. You can't get far."

"I've no reason to run," she said with false poise as he went to close and lock the back door she had left ajar. Allison sat stiffly, listening as he searched the bathroom in a way that would leave nothing unturned.

She heard him rummaging through drawers and throwing things about in haste. What was he was looking for? Had Leah already found it? If she had, Allison couldn't betray her now. Allison must bear the brunt of the officer's accusations until she could talk to her cousin alone and discover what this was all about. Whatever the colonel expected to find in Major Reuter's belongings must have something to do with German intelligence.

She stood from the chair softly and eased herself to the doorway of the bedroom. The colonel was lifting the small rug to search the wooden planks of the floor. Not finding what he wanted, he set the rug back down and stood, looking about. His gaze fell on her in the doorway, and his eyes narrowed beneath sooty lashes.

"If you wonder why I have not chased after him, it's because he had little time to find what he came here for—unless he knew precisely where to look. That is a possibility I'm not dismissing, *Fräulein*. But I need not worry about catching him at the moment. Through you, I will learn who he is and where he has gone. And if he was not successful, what he sought may still be here. So now you will sit still and keep silent while I search."

She realized he thought Leah was a man. It occurred to Allison she might mention the third intruder, the one who had arrived before Leah. Instead, she refrained. She had no reason to trust this German intelligence officer from Baghdad.

He went straight to the empty satchel. She expected him to examine the strewn papers first, but instead he deftly removed the satchel's outer casing and searched briefly then tossed it aside. She watched as he sorted swiftly through the papers.

She could see by his tense expression that he hadn't found what he wanted. He searched the bureau and under the mattress, leaving nothing undone.

Allison sat silently, watching as he looked in every conceivable place. She turned her head away as he searched the body, the clothes, and the boots. Then, apparently satisfied, he walked in a cool and precise German stride to the major's desk and resumed tossing things about as though in a desperate hurry.

When the careful search was completed, he stopped and looked suspiciously at her. She braced herself for what she believed would be far worse questioning as he returned without the item he wanted. She brushed her hair back and sat up straighter.

She expected him to explode into a rage, but now smooth and calm, he appeared to accept that he had failed to find what he was looking for. She became curious as he thoughtfully leaned his shoulder into the wall and apparently debated with himself over whatever was stirring about in his mind. He seemed to have forgotten all about her.

It was suffocatingly hot, and she looked longingly toward the window beside her.

"Do not open it," he said, proving he had not forgotten her at all. He watched her lazily as he removed his German jacket and tossed it on the back of the chair. He loosened the shirt at his neck while he scanned her with an intense appraisal. She turned her head away, fanning herself with a piece of paper from the table. He walked up quietly and plucked it from her with a half smile, then held it toward the light.

Allison, studying his face as he bent over the light, was furious with herself for even noticing his far too appealing appearance. Evidently the sheet was not of interest, for he let it flutter. He looked down at her with a trace of a smile.

"What are you doing here?"

"I'm here on holiday from Cairo. I came with friends."

"Charming. A delightful little vacation spot, *Fräulein*, he commented drly."

She ignored him. "I'm here as a member of the Cairo Archaeological Club. I think you already know that."

"What is your name and occupation?"

"I think you know that as well."

He scrutinized her, one hand on a hip. "The questions. Answer them," he stated in a soft tone.

She drew in a breath, averting her eyes. "Nurse Allison Wescott. My father is a governor-general, so you'd best watch out. Any foul play with me, and your government will hear about it. You'll be court-martialed."

He actually laughed. The warm, blue-black eyes flickered, taking her in. "What if I told you I have valid reason to consider you a Turkish spy?"

She sucked in her breath. "Absurd! If I were a spy in Aleppo, Colonel, I'd do a bit better job now, wouldn't I?"

His eyes twinkled. "Would you, Nurse Wescott? Perhaps it's your job to throw me off guard."

"You already know my name and occupation. So why do you still—"

He lifted a brow, amused. "You think it is unreasonable that I believe you are a spy from Constantinople?"

"Why, yes! I'm full-blooded English and proud of it."

He scanned her. "Interesting, perhaps, to some. Yet I have heard that English women lack the warmth of German women. I'm profoundly curious to know if this could be true?"

She stared straight ahead. "I cannot account for what you may have heard, but it is just as well with me you think so, Colonel."

His smile was disarming. "A pity. You had best understand the seriousness of the charge. I could take you back a prisoner to Constantinople unless you come forth with the truth."

Stunned, she stared at him and saw a flicker of blue fire in his narrowing gaze. He walked toward her, his dark head held arrogantly. He stopped, hands on hips, and studied her face. For the first time in her life Allison wanted to slap a man. She dare not, not this German officer. She had no doubt he could make good his threat and render her life utterly miserable until her father could go through governmental routes to get her released.

Suddenly, she felt faint and lowered her head.

He stood looking down at her for a moment with a slight frown and said gently: "Pull yourself together, *Fräulein*. What are you doing here, taking such mammoth risks?"

"I told you. I heard a noise."

He folded his arms and looked toward Major Reuter. "Did you know him?" he inquired.

Her mouth was dry, and she swallowed several times. "No. I didn't come here out of romantic sorrow to weep over the dead, if that's what you think."

"I assure you, it didn't enter my mind. How did he die?"

"I—I don't know."

She was deciding that this colonel was an utterly unlikable man who utterly reeked with arrogance.

He paced. "Who attended Major Reuter when he was brought in from where the horses and mules were kept?"

"I believe it was the Turkish official. A local doctor was called in, but there was no chance of helping the major. He was already dead."

"You are certain of that, *Fräulein?*"

"Why, yes—". She stopped. She wasn't, but why should she tell him?

"You are not certain," he said wryly.

She lifted her chin. "No."

"Then did you check the cause of his death?"

"If you mean, did I attend him at any time, Colonel, no, I did not. I just learned of the matter toward dinner. Afterward, when we knew what had happened, a number of the women in our club, including myself, decided our appetites had fled, and we retired early."

He watched her with keen interest, a shadow of a smile on his mouth. "A green-eyed, auburn-haired British spy perhaps...?"

She flushed. "I am a nurse, Colonel, as I have already told you."

"So you did, *Fräulein.* You heard nothing of gossip? How he might have died so unexpectedly?"

Allison moved uneasily in the chair. "There was some talk of a viper bite," she admitted.

"Since you're a nurse you should be able to tell me."

She stared at him, and in the moment of uncomfortable silence, only the wind could be heard. Allison didn't move and felt the sweat stand out above her lip. She glanced across the room to the shadowed bed.

"A nurse timid over a dead body?" he asled softly. "Rather odd, but interesting."

"It isn't that."

"Then what is it?"

She looked at him half-accusing. "Can't you find out from the Turkish official? He would have the medical papers. He's staying at the home of a German friend of yours—Baroness Kruger. He and others from Aleppo, including," she added meaningfully, "the British consul and his wife."

His mouth turned down. "You will permit me to distrust the Turkish dogs?"

"Yet you will trust me?" she inquired with feigned surprise.

"I merely order your opinion in the matter. Perhaps I already know and am testing your claim to be a nurse. You will look at Major Reuter now. You will give me your professional diagnosis, Nurse Wescott—unless you wish to accompany me back to Baghdad a prisoner." He smiled pleasantly.

She stood, coolly meeting his stare. "I will need a light. But I can offer little information even if I look at him."

"Nevertheless, you will do as I ask. You know there would be fang marks. Since he was fully dressed in uniform with his boots on, you need not look below his knees." He gestured his head. "Come, we'll have a look. You're not squeamish?"

She stood stiffly. "I told you, Colonel; I'm a nurse."

"Quickly then."

She walked ahead of him and stopped. "There's not enough light."

His eyes narrowed. He lit a lantern and brought it to the bed, watching her steadily. Allison was expressionless as she cooperated, and only once did she feel the unprofessional desire to gag, certain the response was enhanced by the colonel's penetrating gaze.

"There is evidence of fang marks," she said in a low, hoarse whisper.

"Where?"

"Here, on his left wrist. It's surrounded by a dark purple area."

He leaned over and carefully studied the mark as if to convince himself, then flipped the blanket back over the corpse. He stood, arms folded, in speculative silence.

Allison walked away, longing for a breath of fresh air. "You see, Colonel, he wasn't murdered as you say. Perhaps he leaned over to pick something up from the sand by the rocks and, in a flash, the viper struck," she challenged, hoping to catch him off guard.

"That reasoning won't hold, *Fräulein*. After he was bitten, why didn't he draw his revolver to kill the viper, which would also alert others to his condition? Neither did he use his knife to bleed out the poison. You're saying he just sat there and waited to die?"

Those had been her very thoughts when Sarah Blaine had brought it up. She turned her back. "He was in shock," she countered. "A viper bite will do that to some people. They have no time to react. It must have been so for Major Reuter."

"You will permit me to reject such arguments. I knew Karl—" He stopped abruptly. She turned her head cautiously and looked at him, wondering not at what he had said, but why he would not care to admit it. Of course he would know the major since they both had come from Baghdad.

He ignored her alert gaze and said smoothy: "If I had the time or the inclination, I could remove his boot and show you another scar—a viper bite that he doctored himself and survived. Why did he not do the same now?"

"I don't know. But you're wasting your time questioning me. I had nothing to do with this unfortunate incident."

She stood weakly, holding to the edge of a table, and was startled when she felt his hand on her arm. She looked at him quickly, and grew confused by the concern that glinted in his eyes.

"You'd better sit down."

"I'd rather not, Colonel," she said stiffly. "Please get on with it."

He reached inside his jacket and pulled out a leather billfold and snapped it open. She had a glimpse of his photograph and little else before he flipped it closed and replaced it. "I am Colonel Brent Holman, recently arrived in Baghdad from Berlin. My primary orders have been delayed while I investigate the death of Major Reuter."

"I see nothing to investigate," she tried smoothly.

"No? I suppose our mysterious viper also decided to ransack his hut?"

She ignored that and shrugged. "A Bedouin, perhaps, looking for trinkets."

"Whoever tore this place apart was looking for more than trinkets, and you probably know what they wanted," he suggested wryly.

"No, I do not. I only arrived yesterday."

"You are a nurse at what hospital in Cairo?"

"Not a hospital. A ship. The *Mercy*. We voyage the White Nile from Alexandria to the Sudan."

Aware of his gaze, her sea-green eyes glanced away.

"The *Mercy*," he repeated, nothing in his voice.

"It is privately owned, Colonel Holman. It belongs to my aunt. She, too, is a nurse and has served on the Nile for thirty years."

"So…instead of a green-eyed auburn-haired spy, I've caught a ministering angel, is that it? And you came to Aleppo with the archaeological club on holiday?"

She raised her head, feeling the heat in her cheeks. "Yes, that's right. With friends of my parents."

"Members of the club also?"

"Yes. Retired General Rex Blaine and his wife, Sarah. They'll soon be leaving to settle in Capetown."

"Instead of England? Odd."

"Not odd. He's bought a ranch there. He's weary of army life. But you can ask them personally, Colonel."

"Who was in this room that you came to meet before he escaped? Or did you come to stop the intruder yourself?"

Allison sank into the chair, gripping the arms beneath her sweating palms. "I heard something that awakened me. My hut is just next door, and my window was open. I knew this was Major Reuter's room and that it had been locked by the Turkish official until your arrival from Baghdad—"

She stopped. *How did he get here so soon?*

At her sudden alertness, his eyes narrowed. "So! You took advantage of my absence to break in!"

He was trying to sidetrack her! Allison remained calm. "I've no reason to break in."

"I found you here."

"The door was already unlocked. I told you, I saw someone breaking in from my window."

"You saw who it was?" he asked too quietly.

She avoided his eyes and fanned herself. "I didn't see the intruder's face."

"That isn't what I asked, *Fräulein*. Did you recognize who it was?"

"Why do you persist in questioning me like this? Why don't you search for the intruders who were here before me? Before either of us arrived?"

"Intruders? More than one?"

She hesitated, wondering if she should tell him about her experience in the hut after he had chased Leah—if it had been Leah. Now, she wasn't certain.

She drew in a breath. "I don't know. As I said, Colonel, I heard a noise, and it woke me up. I assume it did, because what else could it have been? I got up and looked out my window and saw—" She stopped. He looked at her. She went on smoothly: "I saw someone on the back porch who appeared to be tampering with the door. So I—I came to see who it was."

She swallowed and stared back evenly. How could she tell him it was a woman? It might give Leah away. And she must say nothing until she had at least spoken with Leah.

"You're lying to me," he stated evenly, yet gently. "What were you looking for?"

"Looking for?"

His eyes narrowed with restrained impatience. "Yes. The real reason you're here—you did not find it, and yet you must have known what to look for."

Then Leah had probably been searching for something. But what?

"And you came. A woman alone. Without a weapon."

"I admit it was foolish, but—" She bit her lip when his smile unmasked her.

"You thought it safe because you recognized the intruder and felt curious enough to see what he was up to in the dead of night. Fortunately, you ran into me instead."

She averted her eyes. "Fortunately?"

The corner of his mouth turned. "Ah, so the innocent *Fräulein* is not so careless after all."

"I know what my eyes have seen, Colonel; that the hut was ransacked. I know nothing more. I don't even know what it is you want— or what the intruder was doing here. But I assume—" She stopped.

His brows lifted. "Yes? I wait breathlessly. What do you assume, *Fräulein?*"

"The same thing you do. Someone—I am not sure who—had a good reason to come here tonight. What it was they searched for, I cannot tell you. However, this delay in questioning me allows the real suspect to escape."

But if it really had been Leah who broke in, this delay gave her cousin time to prepare her story for the German authorities. And as long as Colonel Holman suspected Allison, she could shield Leah.

Allison stole a brief glance, noting the cleft in his chin, the handsome curve of his jaw line, and that up close his eyes were not quite as icy as they first appeared. Her gaze moved away when he noticed her scrutiny and gave her a knowing sideglance.

"You must be honest with me. It is important to the British as well as the Germans that you cooperate."

Just why it should be of interest to the British he didn't say, and she suspected he was merely suggesting this to deceive her.

"I've no cause to be uncooperative, Colonel Holman, since England and Germany are not at war, despite your cynicism."

His smile was wry. "Who was it you thought you saw breaking in tonight?"

She remained calm and avoided direct eye contact. "I've already told you. I don't know who it was. Perhaps you are not telling me the truth either, Colonel Holman."

He lifted his head with a jerk as though taken by surprise. He recovered smoothly. "It is your duty to tell me, a member of the secret police, everything."

Allison refused to be cowed. "I don't know anything, Colonel."

"You may regret you've not cooperated, *Fräulein*. I could see you are held for lengthy questioning here in Aleppo. I may have you transported to Constantinople. I could have you placed under arrest for months. And while your government may complain, you *Fräulein*, will be keeping unpleasant and lonely company with the rats. Is that what you want?"

Her eyes met his evenly, and she masked a shudder. "Nothing the German police might do would surprise me, Colonel Holman."

He was silent for a time, watching her, looking tired and grim, as though he had wearied of their exchange. "Go to your hut, softly. "Stay there until morning. Otherwise, I will take you to h quarters tonight for your own safety."

She believed he meant it. She stood shakily, pale in the light. For a brief moment she thought she saw something like regret in his eyes before he turned away.

"As you wish, Colonel," she said, aware her voice also revealed regret.

She had walked to the back door when he said, "Wait."

She did so, wondering with dread whether or not he had changed his mind.

As she turned, he walked up and handed her a revolver, an oddly gentle half-smile on his face.

"It will help you sleep. I wouldn't want my main witness to unexpectedly meet with the same death as Major Reuter. You still have much to answer for, Nurse Wescott."

Amazed, she looked down at the revolver in his hand, wondering if he actually intended her to have it.

He laid it in her hand. "Good night, *Fräulein*. I will see you again under less…stressful circumstances, I hope."

Confused, she said nothing.

"Go. Before I change my mind," he ordered softly.

She turned and hurried down the steps and across the moonlit yard to her own hut.

he said
ad-

3

IT MUST HAVE BEEN NEARING TWO in the morning when Allison entered her dark hut. The moon was well above the hills, and its clear light, intensified by the glittering wastes of desert sand, lent an eerie luminous effect to the darkness of the little hut.

She stood still for a moment in the open doorway, uncertain whether she wanted to enter and close the door. An odd sensation traveled up her back as she gazed about the room, so much like the one she had just left.

Strange, thought Allison, fingering the heavy pistol, *how Colonel Holman gave this to me.* If he believed her a suspect in Karl Reuter's death, why trust her with a gun? For all he knew she might already possess one. *He behaved oddly,* she thought, *in more ways than one.*

Familiar shapes in the room, the bed and her luggage sitting on the floor, stood darkly outlined. A wandering breath of wind soughed under the eaves and whispered its way across the roof, scattering sand and making her think of footsteps.

A moment later came a stealthy creak of hinges. The light from the open doorway of the bathroom moved against the wall, a shadow blotted the gleaming brightness, and a whispered voice breathed, "Allison, I thought you would never get back!"

Allison nearly collapsed against the door as all of her nervous energy seemed to have been spent, her hand falling limply to her side with the revolver. "Leah—"

"Close the door. Hurry! The secret police won't look for me here."

Allison pulled it shut, thrusting the bolt in place. As she pulled herself together emotionally, she groped her way past a chair to the table with a half-empty box of matches beside the oil lamp. "Don't light that! Use the candle," rasped Leah.

Allison lit a match with unsteady fingers. A little flame flared up, and she held it to the half-burned, squat candle on a metal saucer.

Her eyes narrowed against the flame, sought out her cousin, and fell with a start to the short, polished pistol barrel in Leah's hand. Her cousin, in her twenties, was an attractive, athletic blonde. But no vestige of prettiness was left in the face that stared back at Allison now. Little remained there except desperation. Leah's blue eyes were granite hard and unwavering. "Where did you get that gun?" demanded Leah. "Did you bring it from Cairo?"

"The German colonel from Baghdad gave it to me. Don't ask me why. He was as cold and ruthless as one would expect from that sort. But he seemed to think I was at risk." She tried to smile. "He wants me alive for the next four days for more questioning. Sort of like setting a guard around the fatted calf."

Leah swallowed and did not return the smile, nor did she lower her revolver. "Did he know who I was?"

"I don't think so."

Leah hesitated, lowered the gun, and shoved it into her jacket pocket apologetically. "I'm sorry. I can't take any chances. There are few I can trust."

She came forward into the room, drawing the bathroom door shut behind her, and whispered, "I didn't mean to leave you there to face him alone. Understand, I had no choice. You shouldn't have followed me like that. You should have known—" She stopped, letting out an exasperated breath.

"That you had ample reason to prowl about at midnight? You chose a fine time to play detective! And in the hut of a high-ranking German official at that."

Leah showed no apology or intimidation. Her blue eyes burned. "I could wish it were as school-girlish as you make it sound. Unfortunately, those days are gone forever. This is deadly serious. Do I seem foolish enough to go there without a good reason? Oh, I'm sorry, Allison! I don't mean to sound so impatient."

"I want you to know I just got the third degree from that German colonel."

"You didn't say anything about me?"

"No, and—"

"You're certain you said nothing?" Leah interrupted with a harsh whisper.

"I just told you I didn't. And is this my thanks, a gun pointed at me by a cousin I haven't seen in three years?"

Leah gave a sharp sigh. "I saw the Colonel arrive an hour ago. Who is he, did he say?"

"Colonel Holman."

"I've heard of him. He's tough and ruthless. It looks as though you survived, but I am sorry you had to go through it."

So she knew who Colonel Holman was. But none of this made the least bit of sense.

"Why did you follow me?" Leah demanded.

"Good heavens, why wouldn't I?"

"You had no cause."

"No cause? To look out my window and see my cousin burglarizing Major Reuter's hut?" she asked incredulously.

"Burglarize? What made you think that?"

"What else would I think?" asked Allison, fighting back frustration. She was more shaken than she would let on. Leah was the one who had always been blessed with a personality that remained cool under stress.

"What brought you to the window?" asked Leah suspiciously. "I was as quiet as a puttering rat."

"Rats," quipped Allison, "are not quiet. And neither were you. Anyway, my window was wide open and faced the back porch of Major Reuter's hut. A sound woke me, and I went to look and saw you, at least I saw your hair. I assumed it was you, though I admit when I called to you in the hut and you didn't answer, you gave me an awful scare."

Leah walked over to check the bolted door, as though the act were a habitual one, and came back. "I couldn't answer," she whispered. "I'm glad you didn't use my name. Unfortunately it was a mistake to give yours, because—"

She stopped, and Allison saw the muscle in her cheek twitch with tension.

Because what? wondered Allison, but for the moment Leah was asking the questions.

"Then I wasn't very smart if I awoke you," said Leah. "I thought I was being exceedingly careful. If you heard me, then perhaps they did, too."

"They? Who are 'they'? The German intelligence officer from Baghdad?"

"I wasn't speaking of Colonel Holman," came Leah's tense voice, and she looked about the room as if expecting someone to emerge from the shadows. "Anyway, he didn't come from Baghdad the way the Turkish official thought. Neal had mentioned something about Colonel Holman arriving at the railway near the Carchemish Digs last week. Neal had already left the digs when I drove down here to wait for him. He should have been here by now."

Allison remained riveted on the information Leah had just given her about Colonel Holman's presence at the archaeological digs for the past week. What did it mean?

"Why are you so interested in the death of Major Reuter?"

Leah studied her thoughtfully, as if trying to come to some urgent decision.

"Look, Leah, something dreadful is going on with you and Neal, and as family I think I ought to know what it is. If you're in trouble out at the digs, either of you, I want to help if I can."

Leah looked at her blankly. "The digs?"

"Archaeology. If Neal sold an item to Baroness Kruger he shouldn't have and the British Museum is up in arms about it, maybe I can do something to help."

"Trouble out at the digs...sold something we shouldn't have..." Leah gave a short, hysterical giggle, then stopped just as quickly. "Dear heaven, I wish it were little more than that."

"My father will be arriving from Bombay in a few weeks. Maybe he can do something. He's high up in government and has many friends. You can trust me. If you think you can't, I would be very disappointed. It's true we've never been close, but I've always felt we were, well, friends anyway. And if you'd like to explain—"

"It was all a mistake on my part," rushed Leah, "a personal matter, and a foolish one. Well, I suppose I could tell you. You see, I did something unwise last year when I visited Baghdad on business for the museum. I met Major Reuter, and we began this rather ridiculous little romance. It ended badly, and I confess I got burned. He had a photograph of me in his wallet. And I wanted to get it back before the intelligence officer found it. It could prove, well, embarrassing to me and my work at the digs..."

Her voice seemed suddenly to fail her, and she took a few steps to the nearest chair and sat down abruptly, as though her legs could no longer support her. Then she helped herself to a pitcher of stale, warm lemonade left over from that afternoon.

"That's all there is to it," she said tiredly.

Allison watched her and for a minute Allison stood fingering the warm metal of the revolver in her pocket. "You lie very badly, Leah," she said quietly. "I've a feeling you'd never laid eyes on Major Karl Reuter before he arrived. And I see I can forget all about a minor mishap out at the digs. This is much bigger. I'm not a complete ninny, you know. If Reuter had anything of yours in his wallet, it wasn't a photograph signed 'Yours truly.' But if that's what you want me to think, then why did you come here to my hut, looking pale and as frightened as though you had bumped into a ghost?"

Leah said nothing but stared at the candle flame.

"You might have returned to your own room," said Allison softly. "You could have insisted you never left it when Colonel Holman came to question you. It's your word against mine, even if I had told him it was you I followed, which I'm not about to do. Obviously, you managed to slip away from him. A pretty fine trick in itself considering the manner of man we're up against. I'd rather face a hunter with two rifles. He came back not knowing who it was he had chased."

"I can't go back to my room. He'll look for me there. And so will the other side."

"The other side?"

Leah looked at Allison worriedly. "What did you tell Holman?"

"Only that I followed someone breaking into the hut."

"He's too clever to believe that."

"So I gather. But there was little else he could do about it tonight. I needed to talk to you to find out what's going on. I'm so confused at the moment that I wouldn't have contradicted you had you insisted you were sound asleep when all this was going on. The truth is,"

Allison said wearily, "I wasn't sure it was you."

Leah looked at her tensely. "What do you mean?"

Allison frowned slightly, remembering. "I saw your hair from my window. In the moonlight it showed like a halo. Later I remembered another blonde in the club. She came up with Dr. Blackstone. I think they've got a little romance going, but don't say I said so. It's supposed to be a hush-hush sort of thing. He's much older than she."

Allison said all this deliberately to give her cousin time to adjust, to think, to make the decision to either trust her or withdraw into secrecy. She wouldn't insist on Leah telling her anything. She would wait until Neal arrived.

Allison walked to the open window and looked out, feeling the wind. The stars gleamed, and the yard was in mysterious desert shadows. She felt as if she ought to close the window regardless of the heat and draw the curtains closed, as Colonel Holman had done in Major Reuter's hut.

"You're right," said Leah. "I came here because I'm desperate. I need help."

Allison smiled bravely. "What's a family for except to help in desperate situations? And if I hadn't already decided to stand on your side and Neal's—because I think he's involved in this in some way—I wouldn't have trailed after you tonight. I admit I'd rather face a viper than Colonel Holman again. So I'm all ears. What's it about, Leah?"

"Would you mind if I closed the windows first? It'll be like an oven in here, but we mustn't take a chance."

"My very thought," said Allison, and she went to latch a window, pulling down the blind. Leah closed the other window, checked both doors again to see if they were bolted, then came to sit on the edge of the rumpled bed.

Allison plugged in the small metal fan and drew up a scarred chair with its out-of-place lush upholstery in a hideous chartreuse. *Baroness Kruger might know a good deal about archaeology, but she obviously knows nothing about interior decorating,* thought Allison with a rueful grimace. She had noticed that same color in the towels in Major Reuter's hut. The memory of the corpse lying on the bed, and the ruthless blue-black stare of the intelligence officer, quickly sobered her, and she turned her full attention to her cousin.

Leah was watching her tensely, looking like anything but a woman taking dangerous risks and being chased by a German intelligence officer. She sat on the mattress, her eyes bright with youth, her long blond hair falling in waves about her shoulders.

"This is hardly the time for it, but you'll forgive me if I can't take chances. I must know more about you first, before I can share the truth."

"Know about me? Your own cousin?" Allison smiled.

Leah gave a brief shrug. "It's been rather a long time since you told me about what you're doing in Cairo. I've some family catching up to do. Tell me first what you're about. Your work, that is. You've an appreciation for archaeology, but you're not exactly into it are you?"

"No. I'm a nurse, remember? I graduated two years ago from nursing school in London. A school appropriately named after a favorite heroine, Florence Nightingale." She smiled. "A creative name for the school, don't you think? Anyway, after schooling I felt called by God—I'm sure you find that phrasing odd—to attend Oswald Chambers Bible Training School in London. I only went there for a year, but it was a good year. I met some delightful and dedicated people. But the finest friends were Mr. Chambers and his wife, Biddy. I was there when their baby daughter, Kathleen, was born. It was like a big family, a very special one. And it was one of the happiest years I've spent in London away from home."

Leah was listening, but Allison could see her eyes kept traveling toward the windows. "Yes, I remember all that," whispered Leah. "You wrote Neal about it. Said you were learning so much about prayer and waiting for God."

"Yes…"

"Neal always did seem more comfortable talking about God than I did," said Leah. "You know how I grew up. My mum and dad were quite antagonistic toward things Christian. Anyway, go on."

"Let's see…I came home to Cairo when my sabbatical at the BTC in London was up and I spent a few months with Father traveling on government business to India. Then a letter arrived from Aunt Lydia asking me to join her in medical mission work on the Nile. You know about the hospital boat, the *Mercy*?"

"I've heard of the work Lydia does. Neal speaks of her sometimes. He's always respected the 'dear old saint,' as he calls her. Says she has more courage at sixty than some Englishmen confronting the thought of war."

Allison smiled thinking of the maiden aunt who had taken her under her wing and had insisted Allison had chosen the right calling—nursing—even when she had second thoughts. She had fainted once when helping Aunt Lydia amputate the arm of a *fellahin*, an Egyptian peasant who grew cotton along the Nile.

"Neal is right," Allison said softly. "Aunt Lydia is a grand woman. Of course, Neal thinks so highly of her because she practically raised him after your parents died." She looked at Leah, masking her sadness. "I wish she could have raised you, too."

Leah shrugged her straight, somewhat athletic shoulders. "I never blamed her. She couldn't take us both. Anyway, I didn't mind India. And although Uncle George was a tough, straight-laced military man, I did get to spend all my Christmases in Cairo with the rest of you." She sighed, as though her troubled mind traveled a long-forgotten, friendly path. "Those were good times, weren't they? Too bad we all grew apart in our college years."

"Yes," said Allison quietly, and wondered again why the family had decided to send Leah to India to be raised by Uncle George, a brigadier, and to give Neal to Aunt Lydia. Logic would seem to argue for the opposite.

"Lydia always favored Neal," said Leah, as if reading her thoughts. "Said he looked like his father—the proverbial tall, blond, and handsome. No one seemed to like Dad's choice of a wife much, did they?" She gave a small but curt laugh.

"I never knew your mother. I often wondered why she never came to the gatherings when we were children. They always said she hated Cairo."

Leah shrugged.

Allison rebuked herself. *I should have stayed closer to Leah. I should have tried harder, but my own life seemed to drag me down a different path, one with heartaches of its own.* But she wouldn't think of Nevile now…

"Oh, well," said Leah. "Tell me more about recently. So you've been working with Lydia on the medical boat? I suppose you love the work or you wouldn't be doing it."

"I feel it's more rewarding than anything else I might have done with my nursing skills. It's demanding, wonderful at times, horrid most of the time, and dreadfully heart-rending when there's so little actually to be done for the dying and diseased. The Lord knows we do our best, but there is so much we just can't do, especially for the children and the old." She smiled. "But while it keeps me awake many nights, I wouldn't give it up even to marry Prince Charming. I'll grow old like Aunt Lydia and die single I suppose, but I believe it will have been worth it. I intend to stay in Egypt, although Aunt Lydia is making grand plans of following the Nile all the way to

Ethiopia. It will be quite a trip. And some students from Oswald Chambers' school may go with us. Several are interested in preaching, and one is looking into foreign missions. Aunt Lydia wants to build a David Livingston-style hut and translate Scripture into some tribal dialect."

"Sounds hard and emotionally draining."

"Usually is," said Allison softly, studying her cousin's pale, tense face. "But we know that no circumstance will ever separate us from Christ's love and care. Do you mind if I speak of these things?" she asked.

Leah raised a capable square hand and shook her head. "No, not at all. I respect you. I suppose all that talk about God's concern was a hint that he could care for me as well. But I'm not ready for that. If you don't mind, I'll share my burdens with you instead."

Allison smiled. "I'm all yours. Now that I've brought you up to date, what about these troubles of yours?"

Leah ran her fingers through her long hair, pushing it back from her face. She turned her face toward the humming, chattering fan for a moment, searching for a breeze.

"So how did you get interested in archaeology?" Leah asked.

Allison drew in a breath and answered. "Through Neal. He wrote such interesting letters from the various digs in Arabia, especially Carchemish. And when Neal got involved in biblical archaeology, that was even more interesting. It happened that Mother had friends in the Cairo Archaeological Club—General Rex Blaine and his wife, Sarah. They're like godparents to me. Do you know them? Anyway, I became involved in the club through them, and one thing led to another."

"General Blaine is a friend of your mother?"

Allison wondered at her response. "Yes, he knew my father in Khartoum when Father was in foreign service. General Blaine is retired now. He and Sarah make all the social clubs in Cairo, with friends among the other foreign ambassadors and officials. Of course, with the tension going on now with Germany, being invited to dine with German officials isn't as popular as it was even six months ago. But the various officials in Cairo—German, French, Turkish, and all the others—know each other and have developed friendships through the years. We can all still get together over an Egyptian meal and Turkish coffee and laugh."

Leah smiled briefly, but she did not laugh.

Allison became more serious. "I know what you mean. I'm not one to company with them myself. And after tonight, I don't think I'll ever want to again."

"War will come, Allison. As surely as we sit here now. And millions will die. The little tête-à-tête between ambassadors in British Egypt isn't as harmless and warm and friendly as you may believe."

Allison searched Leah's face and saw the gravity. "You speak of General Blaine?"

"I speak of all of them—all the retired military 'chums,' as they're wont to call each other. You'll find there's a vein in every one of them that will turn venomous under the right set of circumstances. Not that I'm singling out General Blaine, mind you. I don't even know him."

"Yes, I understand. He and Sarah have been family friends for years. Mother and Sarah are close. And General Blaine and my father have traveled together."

Leah nodded her understanding and indifferent approval. Then she glanced searchingly about the hot enclosure as though to make certain no one was listening. Allison's uneasy gaze followed hers, lingering on the door that led into the darkened bathroom, across which lay the long shadow of the tall set of drawers. The heavy mat blinds over the two windows hung still and wilted in the heat, and the candlelight flickered on the low ceiling. All at once the silence in the hut was forbidding. Allison had the sudden and disturbing fancy that the sweltering silent night and the hot sand dunes shifting in the wind had crept closer about the outer walls to listen.

"Don't you think we should leave on the bathroom light?" said Allison in a low voice. "The bolts, as you know, are flimsy to say the least. And if anyone should come sneaking about, they'll think twice before they try to meddle knowing the light from the window falls on the back porch."

Allison went to pull the string that turned on the bare yellow bulb, closed the door, and returned. Leah had risen from the bed and was pacing.

"I wouldn't involve you, but there's no choice left to me. Neal should have been here by now. And while he may yet arrive before dawn, there's a chance he won't…" She looked at Allison evenly. "That he can't."

Allison's stomach knotted. "What do you mean 'can't'?"

"I mean that he may know they're on to him. And he would have made straight for Jerusalem as planned, knowing I understood. I'm to join him as soon as I can. There's a vehicle hidden a few hours from here, and neither the Turks nor the Germans are likely to know about it."

Allison swallowed. "Go on. Why? Why couldn't he come?"

"He's either made a run for it, or they got to him the way they got to Karl Reuter. I'm sorry," she said when Allison stared up at her, her face pale in the flickering candlelight. "But we won't rush to conclusions. I'm merely outlining the worst that might have happened. You must know the way things are."

"But why? Why would Neal be in such trouble?"

"Karl Reuter's death wasn't an accident," Leah said quietly but firmly.

That was what Colonel Holman had said. "What makes you think so? I mean, why couldn't he just have gotten bitten by a poisonous viper? It happens often enough around here. You know it as well as I."

Leah leaned forward and said, "Listen carefully. He wasn't the real Major Reuter. He was a British agent. He was doing surveillance work in Constantinople until matters became too dangerous. Someone else took his place there; I don't know who. Reuter came to Baghdad to pass on information to Neal."

Allison was stunned. "You mean he wasn't a German officer? He was working for England?"

Leah nodded. "The other side must have found out, because they murdered him last night before he could meet with Neal to pass the information."

Allison's teeth chattered. "What information?"

"I wish I knew."

"So cousin Neal really isn't in archaeology, but British intelligence?"

"Something like that," Leah whispered. "It's too long and involved to explain now."

"And you?" Allison asked uneasily.

"I'm involved as well, but I'm a small fry compared to the others. I take my orders from Neal. And Neal takes them from someone else; I don't know who. Someone higher up. They thought a woman would get by without detection; so I was sent ahead of Neal as the initial contact for Major Reuter. If I was here, then Reuter was to know that everything was to proceed as planned. Had Neal arrived yesterday as expected, he was to lead the club to the Carchemish Digs, and Karl Reuter was to meet with him."

Leah's white face was strained. "But someone got to Reuter before I could warn him that Neil wasn't here. You saw what happened.

Someone knows a great deal, and in the end, Karl must have known it. He—he tried to warn me. I admit I'm scared, Allison. If Neal doesn't show, I'm the only one left. And whoever killed Karl is still here."

Allison stared at her. This couldn't be real. But Leah's steady gaze convinced her it was. Leah was indeed frightened—and the British agent posing as Major Karl Reuter was dead. Allison pulled herself together, hoping to encourage Leah. Steadily, but with a slight quaver Allison couldn't control, she said, "Neal may be all right, just delayed."

"That's possible."

"He's tough; you know it as well as I. And if he found out somehow that they were on to him, he wouldn't show."

Leah stood and paced. "That's just it. I don't know for sure, but I can't take chances. The information is too important. Our plans were that if anything went wrong and Neal was stopped, I could expect to hear from another contact, someone higher up."

Allison wrung her sweating hands and glanced toward the bolted, shadowy door. "You have no idea who it was?"

"No. It could be anyone. It could be a member of the club, someone in Aleppo, a woman, a man," she gestured, "British, Turkish, German—usually the one we least suspect."

"So—so that's why you broke into the hut, to try to locate the information?"

Leah looked at her, as though cautious again. "The real information wouldn't be there."

"I don't understand," said Allison, getting to her feet. "If it wasn't there, then why was the hut ransacked? Why would you risk yourself?"

Leah sat for a moment or two, looking about her and listening to the wind. Then, looking at Allison, Leah said softly, "I have to take a chance with you. I trust you—not because you're my cousin, though that helps. But you're genuine in so many things. I really think you would die for your country as well as for your God. I mean that as a compliment."

Allison swallowed, then tried to smile wryly. "I'd rather live for them—if you don't mind."

"Listen, Allison, I need your help. Will you?"

"Of course. I'll do what I can," she said without hesitation. "I couldn't look myself in the mirror each morning if I didn't."

Leah smiled for the first time. "I was counting on that."

Allison sat down again, and leaning forward, her elbows on her knees, she listened in silence as Leah began in a low voice. "The reason I went to Karl's hut tonight was because I suspected he knew they were on to him, but it was too late to escape. He would have had no more than a few minutes. But he would have left a sign for Neal. We worked that much out long ago. It's standard practice. So I had to try."

Allison rubbed her arms and looked about the shadows. "If I were the enemy, I wouldn't have waited to rummage his things in the hut. I'd have searched the body and gotten what I came for before the Arab boy found him at the well."

Leah smiled wearily. "It seldom works that way. There are safeguards. No one is entrusted with more than a portion of any critical secret, and that person would not carry it with him in written form. Neal knows more than I. And his contact knows another part that Neal doesn't. Each of us knows bits and pieces. We rarely ever write anything except for brief, one-line codes we've worked out between us."

"That makes sense, but wouldn't the enemy agent have known as much? Wouldn't he have found any code left for you? The hut was rummaged through before you got there. Whoever murdered him must have found the message." Her eyes clung to Leah's. "Someone was there before you, because after Holman chased after you, I was there in the dark—and so was someone else. I was never so scared in my life. Then the sound of Holman's returning interrupted—thank God! And whoever it was slipped out the back porch." She shuddered, imagining a dark, faceless void that could be anyone. "He must have found it and left."

Leah didn't answer immediately and looked down at her fingernails. "Whoever murdered Neal's contact hasn't left. He's still here. Though he rummaged through Reuter's things, he didn't find the code Karl left me. I have it."

Allison didn't know whether to feel patriotic relief or to allow her fears for Leah to overwhelm her. "But how? You were only there a minute."

"About four minutes."

"But someone must have spent twenty minutes searching and tearing the hut apart. How is it that you found it?"

"Because I knew exactly what to look for, something that anyone else would have ignored. Most people could pass right by it and think nothing. When I got there I lit a match—went straight to the desk to look. It wasn't there but on the floor. I, too, thought I heard a footstep before you entered—I had just enough time to pick up the message when I heard you give a muffled cry. I fled—and Holman came after me. But I didn't keep running. I slipped under the back porch, below the steps. There's a space there. It's dark and probably crawling with spiders and scorpions, but it was my best chance."

"Then you—you must have heard the real murderer's footsteps leaving the porch before Colonel Holman came through the front door and turned on the light."

"Yes."

"Did you see who it was?"

"Too dark. I didn't dare move. I heard steps fade away in the sand. I waited perhaps ten minutes, then crept softly across the yard between Karl's hut and yours. I waited for you until you arrived about twenty minutes later."

Allison swallowed, and silence engulfed them. As though in agreement, they listened to the wind blowing against the hut, the wood creaking and covering the sound of any footsteps that might be moving outside in the night.

"Then you have what you wanted?" whispered Allison. "But if you struck the match, you were probably seen. And—and he must have seen you pick up something from the floor. That footstep you heard might have meant your death."

Leah nodded, white in the candlelight. "It's probably true that your presence caused enough confusion that I was able to escape. Even Holman, coming when he did, seems to have frightened him, though they must both be on the same side."

"What is it you want me to do? Get through to the British consul?" asked Allison.

"No, not yet. My orders are to wait here for a new contact."

"But you can't wait here. If someone saw you tonight, your life is in danger."

"Whoever it was didn't see me come in here—nor does Holman know. And he won't come snooping around your hut now that he's already questioned you. This is as safe a place as I can find until my contact arrives. It will give me time to think about the message that Karl left in his hut. And Neal may come yet. Even if he doesn't find me in my hut, he knows you're here and that I'd likely tell you where to find me. No," she said gravely, "I must wait this out for a few days."

"They'll ask about you in the morning. Holman is bound to

demand you be brought to him for questioning. If you just up and disappear—"

"He'll need to send one of his men to search for me at the digs. The delay will set him on the wrong trail. He'll think that's where I've gone. They all will. And that's a good excuse for my absence. You'll tell them I went in search of Neal. And whoever murdered Karl will think the same. He knows I picked up something from the floor, and he'll be determined to get it. He'll go to the digs, too."

Allison nodded, but her unease grew as the candlelight flickered. "It will be difficult to keep you hidden here, but I think I can manage."

"In the meantime," said Leah, "you'll go on as though nothing has happened. You're here on holiday, and you intend to get the recreation and learning you came for, even if a German officer was accidentally bitten by a poisonous viper. And that's all it was as far as you're concerned. No one is likely to expect a young British nurse to grieve over a German's death. As for Colonel Holman, you'll behave as though his treatment of you was what you would expect from his sort. But you will fare better if your actions tell him you're not to be intimidated.

"Your father's in British foreign service. You have friends in high places. The British consul and his wife are both here. And so are family friends, General Blaine and his wife. You'll behave as normally as you can. You'll pretend to be concerned over my absence and Neal's, of course. You may even insist that not enough is being done to locate us. But in the interval, you'll behave as normally as possible. Go on the archaeology hikes, attend the talks. See what you can pick up in bits and pieces of conversation from the others in the club."

Allison nodded. "What about General Blaine and Sarah. Can I let them in on this?"

"Never! You're not to breath a word of this to anyone, no matter how much you think you can trust them. No one else except Neal—and the new contact."

"How will we know who the contact is?"

"We won't until he gives a sign. You can be certain it's no one in the club, or in Aleppo. He won't have arrived yet. It's too soon."

"He's coming from Cairo intelligence?"

"Yes, but you needn't concern yourself with that." Getting up from the bed, Leah went to the small table next to the lamp, picked up Allison's Bible, and returned to Allison who watched, curiously pleased over Leah's unexpected interest.

Leah opened it to the Old Testament and retrieved a folded piece of paper. Allison didn't recall having left it there and leaned over to see what it was. In the candlelight she saw one word had been written in a masculine hand: "HITTITEebg."

Leah looked at her gravely. "I didn't think anyone would find it here if something happened to me before you came back."

"You mean that's the whole message?" she whispered.

Leah nodded. "Not something one would suspect or find unusual in a gathering such as this. But it actually contains several pieces of information. It is printed, in black ink, all in upper case except the last three letters, and written in the third quadrant of the page. He may have been using a code that can be applied to a single word. Karl wrote it and left it on the dresser. It reveals that he knew he had been spotted and that he has hidden the information he was to give to Neal."

The moon had set, and the hut was now swaddled in darkness. The candlelight cast swaying shadows on the ceiling.

"It's saying something more," whispered Leah, "but I don't know what it is yet. Neal would know. I must think!"

"It could have something to do with archaeology," said Allison.

"Yes, but what? And the answer could be right before our noses!"

"Now we must guess what it is. If only Neal would arrive."

Leah latched hold of Allison's arm tightly enough to cause her to wince. "You were in that hut tonight longer than I was. You sat there in the light for a good twenty minutes. Think, Allison. Was there anything at all that might remind you of the Hittite civilization or the Old Testament?"

Allison stood and paced, trying to remember. But though she thought long and hard, sitting down and closing her eyes while trying to picture everything in the hut, nothing significant would come to mind, except the virile good looks of the mysterious German colonel.

"All I see is Colonel Holman searching, with everything scattered about—and the corpse of Karl Reuter."

Leah placed the paper back inside the Bible and set it down on the bed. "Maybe it will come to you yet. In the meantime, I'll do my own hard thinking. If it were impossible to understand, Karl would have risked more by writing another word or two. Because he didn't, I know he expected me to understand. And the horrid thing is, I don't!" She threw her hands over her head, her long blond hair swaying in despair. "I should never have volunteered for this. It's all gone wrong."

"That isn't true. You retrieved the code word, didn't you? You made it safely to my hut, and you've even gotten me to help. We've just begun. A night's sleep will help; the best thing either of us can do is go to bed. Morning will come fast. And if I'm to show the countenance of a tourist during breakfast, I'd better get some rest. That reminds me, I shall have a dreadful time sneaking food in here. And I'll need to make it clear to the serving man I don't want him making up the bed."

"I'd forgotten that—"

"I'll think of something. If nothing else, when you hear him coming to the back door, dive under the bed. That's one place they never sweep," she said with a light attempt at humor.

Leah's mouth turned, but her eyes were haunted. "I'll remember that," she said. "It may be better if you don't go to breakfast until after he leaves. You can do your devotional reading while he's cleaning. No one will think anything of it since they all know about your work on the medical missionary boat. It fits the expectations of you as a young medical missionary."

"Yes, and I hope that everything else I'm doing does, too."

4

ALLISON HAD RISEN EARLY AND DRESSED comfortably in blue chambray cotton. She had drawn her lush hair back from her face for coolness and was now seated at one of the long dining tables with General Blaine and his wife. Tension gnawed at her insides, but she tried to mask it.

Baroness Helga Kruger, who kept lavish homes for entertaining foreign dignitaries and their wives in both Cairo and Aleppo, rose and made an announcement. Her German accent was not heavy but charmed her hearers.

She referred briefly to the tragic death of Major Karl Reuter and then reminded everyone of her assistant's previous warning that the location of the expedition huts could be dangerous due to the number of desert vipers and scorpions. Everyone was to be especially cautious, and no one, under any circumstances, was to hike to any ruins in or near the huts without a Turkish guide. Anyone doing so would temporarily be suspended from membership and called in for questioning by the Turkish authorities.

"Well, Sarah," said General Blaine in a low voice, "that's the end of your jaunt out to the digs."

"Nonsense," she replied. "She didn't say we couldn't go by car. Besides, she's overreacting, if you ask me."

The baroness's assistant then stood and informed the group that Major Reuter's body was being taken into Aleppo that day for burial. Colonel Holman of the Baghdad German police would be asking a few questions of the club members during the next several days. "Our friends, the Turkish officials here in Aleppo, are requesting that club members cooperate fully."

A babble of low-toned conversation broke out around the tables. Allison hoped her tension didn't show, and she glanced across the dining room to where Helga Kruger sat near the screened window. Except for her commendable interest in archaeology, the baroness was not the sort of woman that especially interested Allison. But after last night and the information Leah had given her, no one in the club was above suspicion—and particularly the German woman in her late forties. Allison tried to recall the bits and pieces of information about Helga that had come her way the last several years. Baroness Kruger was the widow of a Berlin financier who had done much military contracting for Kaiser Wilhelm's government. The baron had been killed in a train accident on the Berlin-Baghdad Railway in the mountainous territory of Bulgaria. Helga, relatively young and attractive, had never remarried, but had collected, so Sarah Blaine had told Allison, a huge fortune from military defense.

With an interest in archaeology and Palestine, Baroness Kruger had first gone to Constantinople where she entered the social scene, then moved to Cairo where she came to be known as one of the most socially powerful of the Europeans. For the last several years she had been deeply involved in buying Hittite sculptures and inscriptions for the Cairo Museum. She was competing with the representatives of the British Museum in Carchemish and elsewhere in Arabia. Neal had once mentioned in a letter to Allison that the baroness was a "friendly nemesis." And although an elegant woman of fashion, she was often seen being driven about the desert by her

Turkish driver and bodyguard, wearing trousers and boots and sporting a revolver. Yet when it came to archaeology, she embraced the club members of many countries and assumed a motherly attitude toward the younger women and men in the club.

She traveled with a Turkish maid who styled Baroness Kruger's hair and applied her makeup for her. As a result, she appeared attractive on this bright, hot morning while several other women in the party looked as if they were already wilted from the heat. They fanned their haggard faces with beaded fans from Cairo. While the other women in the club were dressed casually for the wilderness environment, today Helga wore a simple but stunning pale-green linen dress with a high neckline studded with flecks of emeralds.

Looking at Baroness Kruger now, Allison decided there was more to Helga than her elegantly arranged blue-black hair and the fortune her husband had left her. The mouth, carefully painted with lipstick, had a somewhat bitter twist to it that no amount of makeup could hide. *What does she have to be bitter about?* wondered Allison. *The death of her husband? Some secret pain?*

"A charming piece of baggage," whispered General Blaine. "I wonder if she ever gives credit to her poor hubby when she drapes those emeralds and diamonds about her neck each morning? I heard she was a young dancer in a Berlin tavern when he picked her up and made her his elegant missus."

"Rex!" Sarah Blaine mildly rebuked him.

The pudgy major-general, who had retired from what was called the "F and P," Foreign and Political Department in India, gave Allison a wink to show his remark was meant to be harmless after all and gave her hand a fatherly pat. He then turned his attention back to his wife. "Well, you can't blame me, Sarah. Being a god-uncle to my angelic little Allison, I'm biased indeed when it comes to a shining example of what character ought to be. Now Allison here could wear emeralds and linen in the middle of the Arabian desert, and I'd believe in it."

Allison laughed. "I don't own any emeralds, Rex. And if I did, I wouldn't wear them on an expedition." She smiled at the older couple, who had been friends of her parents since before she was born. Nothing General Blaine said scandalized her, for he was always jovial and she took everything he said as coming from an affable personality.

"It looks as though you've been up late," he said. "Trouble sleeping in these wretched huts?" He looked at her curiously. "Maybe we three ought to return to Cairo."

"Oh, I wouldn't think of it," Allison assured him. There was a pause as if he waited for her to explain her mood this morning. It was on the tip of her tongue to tell him why she was in a downcast mood and what had happened the night before in all its hideous vividness. But Leah's haunted face came to mind, and the warning she had given not to breathe a word of anything to anyone. While Allison completely trusted General Blaine and Sarah, she skirted the issue with a little yawn and looked around the table at what was for breakfast.

"You should have slept in," said Sarah. "Did that Arab boy come banging on your door to make the bed? I told him to go away when he came to ours. It was dreadful!"

"What you need, dear girl, is a swig of this," said the general, and poured Allison a cup of *qahwa*, a special blend of supreme Turkish coffee. "The baroness, who is a self-proclaimed expert in all things Turkish, has arranged for the coffee to be served in style," he said lightly. "There's *saada*, without sugar, *ariha,* little sugar, *mazbut*, medium sugar, and *ziyada*, syrupy."

Allison smiled. "I'll settle for strong and black this time. Sarah, how can you drink that syrupy brew as though you're enjoying it?"

"And on an empty stomach," groaned Rex.

"And offend the baroness by not doing so?" whispered the sprightly Sarah, a tiny woman with delicate gray at her temples. General Blaine affectionately called her his "Wee Sparrow."

Sarah leaned toward Allison, whom she looked upon as a niece since she and the general had no children of their own, and whispered with wide eyes, "This was the first time she has ever spoken to me, and she suggested I try it. I'd drink petrol if it meant she would notice me at last."

"I notice you, love. That's all that really matters," interjected Rex.

"Who do you think she's having at her Cairo home this Christmas holiday?" she asked Allison.

"Listen to her!" jested Rex. "She's dying to let you know and pretends she's calm. Tell her, Sarah dear, before you burst. The pharaoh himself. Aren't you impressed, Allison?"

Allison smiled as Sarah wrinkled her nose at her husband. "Pharaoh indeed, but he might as well be. The prince of Cairo, that's who," she told Allison. "And this time I'm going to get an invitation to the Christmas party if it kills me."

"Such spoiled, snobbish inclinations you have, Sarah," said General Blaine. "Well, go ahead and wrangle to get the invitation. And while you gaze starry-eyed at the prince of Cairo, I'll collect a few Turkish cigars from her all-male get-together in the library. I hear she collects cigars and even smokes them…"

"Rex," said Sarah in a half-scolding voice, "you're positively houndish!"

"She doesn't actually smoke cigars, does she?" said Allison in a low, laughing voice.

"She does indeed," said Rex, but he gave Allison a wink when Sarah glared at him. Allison recognized the too-sweet dislike in General Blaine's voice when he spoke of the baroness. As a retired officer in the British military, his scorn for what he called "the war-hungry

German Empire" was well known to others, including the baroness.

"Rex, how can you?" hissed Sarah. "If she heard you, I'd *never* get an invitation."

"The end of the world as we know it, of course," he moaned in good humor. "Then, for love of dear Sarah, I shall quite behave myself." He reached across the table for the serving plate of *ayish,* bread stuffed with beaten rice and cream, and *gibna,* cheese served warm and melted. He heaped two servings on his plate.

"About this old-bone-digging holiday each year: the weather is atrocious, and the people positively ghoulish in their interest in dead things, but the food is tremendous," he confided in Allison.

She laughed. "I've wondered why you didn't stay in Cairo, seeing how you loathe hiking out to the digs with Sarah and me."

"And now you know the truth. I came because I heard the baroness was in charge of the menu."

"He's a positive glutton, aren't you, darling?" said Sarah. "But I love you just the same."

"After twenty years?" he teased. "And now that I've injured my back I've a good excuse to stay close to the hut. The blue bead must not be working after all."

"The blue bead?" asked Allison.

"Tell her, Sarah. I'm going to eat while I have the chance."

"Didn't you know?" said Sarah. "Blue beads ward off the evil eye. The Arabs have them for their camels and donkeys, and even their houses have a blue painted strip. Look—isn't it a charming turquoise?"

Allison looked uneasily at the blue bead on the silver chain around Sarah's neck, but Sarah seemed to think it harmless.

"It's sweet, isn't it?" said Sarah. "Rex bought it for me in the village last night. I was wondering where he had gone."

"Anything for my love. I'm totally sacrificial."

"Such nonsense," said Allison. "Not your dedication, Rex," she hastened. "I mean the notion that a blue bead can ward off evil. You don't believe that, do you?" she asked Sarah.

Sarah shrugged and lifted her *ayish* to take a bite.

"Evil is more subtle and personal," said Allison. "Satan doesn't tremble at anything except—"

"Now, now," interrupted General Blaine, lifting a square hand. "This isn't Sunday morning, my dear. There'll be no preaching until I finish my breakfast. But maybe Major Reuter should have carried a blue bead. Might have saved him from that viper bite."

"Rex, I don't think you should make a joke about death," said Sarah. "It was a dreadful thing to happen, even if he was—was—"

"She's too generous. I'll finish her sentence for her. A soldier of Kaiser Wilhelm II," said Rex.

"I don't see how it could have been a viper," mused Allison, sipping her Turkish coffee.

"Why not?" said Sarah, interested, but General Blaine interrupted.

"Don't tell me you think he was murdered, too?" he said to Allison.

"Too? You mean you do?" she inquired rather surprised.

"Heavens, no! Though I can see why a number of British fellows might want to do him in—and that odious and arrogant colonel from Baghdad. What is his name? Oh yes, Holman." He glanced about. "We haven't met the charming fellow yet."

"Rex, do lower your voice," begged Sarah. "This isn't exactly British territory, you know."

"Of course it isn't. It's Turkish. A pity, too."

"So you think it was an accident?" asked Sarah.

"It's as clear as they come, dear."

"Then I wish you'd explain it. It's horrible, I think."

"Horrible, yes, but quite understandable to one who knows

these desert critters. Take the cobra, for instance," he suggested.

"You can have it," said Sarah, shivering. "Don't you ever bring one of those things home for your odd collection of creatures."

"Of all reptiles," he continued, "the cobra is perhaps the best known, and a spitting cobra is most remarkable of all. When the cobra strikes, it aims at its victim's eyes. It can spit its venom from its front teeth for distances up to three meters."

Allison wanted to glance around the floor, and Sarah pushed away her half-eaten plate of food. "Really, Rex, this whole matter is tasteless and disgusting after the man's death."

"Sorry, Sarah dear. Here, Allison, hand me that bowl of oranges."

Allison thought of the bruise on the arm of the British agent masquerading as Major Karl Reuter. That, plus the fang marks, certainly hadn't come from ten feet away, but she dare not mention it now, lest they wonder how she had seen the wound. She remembered something else about cobras she had learned in her medical training that General Blaine hadn't mentioned. A cobra, when it bites, uses a chewing action which destroys its fang marks, making it more difficult for a physician to know what manner of reptile has bitten his patient.

She changed the subject. "So you won't be coming with us on the hike to the digs because of your back?"

"A nurse's heart to the rescue. It's about time one of you asked me how I felt. It's all Sarah's fault. She brought a trunk of clothes, enough for a month. And guess who had to carry it for a half mile when our Mercedes broke down?"

"Oh, no, the car isn't working?" asked Allison. "I was hoping Sarah and I could use it to drive out to the Carchemish Digs. The club hasn't planned a trip until Thursday, and I'm worried about cousin Neal."

"Another no-show," said General Blaine.

Another? thought Allison.

Rex looked at his wife, who was still ashen after his discourse on the spitting cobra. "Then you and Allison can borrow a vehicle from the British consul. I'll see what can I do after breakfast."

Allison finished her meal in silence, wondering how she might smuggle something to Leah.

"Are you coming, Allison?" asked Sarah.

"Oh, yes, the morning lecture. I'd forgotten about it. Who's to speak now that Neal is late, do you know?"

"Helga's assistant, the Turk," said General Blaine.

"His name is Jemal," Sarah said. "A perfectly nice fellow. It should be interesting."

"Brought some Hittite things," said the General.

Allison froze. Hittite things...? "I'll be a little late," she mentioned casually. "Save me a good seat, will you? I've forgotten my sun hat."

"We'll save you the best seat in the house," said Rex. "Come along, Sarah, lead me to the lecture. I'm in the mood for a doze."

When they had left and the others were drifting out of the dining hall in a murmur of low chatter, Allison glanced about. Seeing no one watching her, she quickly gathered fruit and bread and stuffed them inside her knapsack.

On her way back to the hut, she stopped to look behind her, haunted by the notion that she was being watched by unseen eyes. Except for a few of the visitors on their way to the lecture, the glittering sweep of the sand-blanketed grounds was empty. The morning sunlight shimmered off the sand and heated the rocks and buildings like a furnace.

She stood in the bowl-like yard with its half-circle of huts. All the windows looked down on her, and she could imagine Colonel Holman in one of those huts now, searching for incriminating evidence against a member of the club. As General Blaine had said, the colonel hoped to pin the death of his comrade on one of them. It was the way of the German secret police. Was he looking at her now through the window? Or had he accompanied the Turkish officials into Aleppo for the burial of what he believed to be the remains of Major Karl Reuter? She felt a pang when she thought of the agent's true British family. Would they ever be told how he had met his death? And that he was buried somewhere in Arabia as a German soldier of the Kaiser? Probably not, she thought dismally. Only God knew where he was, who he was, and who had murdered him.

She shuddered and quickened her steps when a voice called, "Allison?"

Baroness Helga Kruger walked toward her, wearing a wide-brimmed Australian hat, a rather unusual sight, considering the labors her maid must have gone through to do her hair in such stunning form. This was one of the few times Allison had actually spoken with the woman.

Beneath the shadow of the hat, Helga's face, showing tiny lines of age, was taut. "Aren't you coming to hear Jemal?"

"Why, yes, I'd forgotten my hat, that's all."

"I can't imagine what has detained your cousin, Neal," she mused, a small frown between her brows. "He was to arrive yesterday."

Allison had the strange idea that Helga was waiting for her response and was curious what it would be. "Don't you think someone should be sent to check on him? Anything might have happened. Trouble with his motor vehicle perhaps," she added ambiguously.

"I'm told Colonel Holman is on his way in that direction. He left earlier this morning. Unfortunately he left before I could speak with him."

Colonel Holman! thought Allison. *So he isn't here searching the huts.*

Helga glanced about. "Have you seen Leah? I noticed she didn't come to breakfast. When I knocked on her hut door this morning, no one answered. Most unusual for your cousin. She is quite professional."

Caution, Allison warned herself. The deep dark eyes alertly watched her. "I talked with her yesterday," said Allison truthfully. "She was worried about Neal. I'm sure she'll show up when she can."

"She has the tour to lead tomorrow to Aleppo. I hope she hasn't forgotten. It's so unusual for Leah." Helga gazed off across the grounds toward Leah's hut that was situated so that the cooler early morning shadows shrouded it mysteriously. "I'll try knocking again. If she doesn't answer this time, I think I shall use the master key."

So she had a master key. The "master key" would work in each lock. There was nothing unusual about that, thought Allison, looking at the key ring that flashed in the sunlight, since the baroness had bought the compound from the Turkish officials in Aleppo.

"I fear the accident that took Major Reuter's life has upset her," stated Helga.

"It's upset us all."

Helga turned a frank gaze upon her. "I cannot help thinking they knew each other."

"I don't see how that's possible, since Major Reuter came from Constantinople." Allison shifted her knapsack to her other arm and glanced about casually, as though expecting someone to join them.

"I suppose you're right. I'd forgotten. He said he had been in Baghdad for two weeks. I admit I was surprised he knew of our meeting and wished to attend. I didn't realize our club was becoming so well known."

"The meeting was in the Cairo paper," said Allison easily, adding, so as not to appear entirely closed to Helga's vague suggestion, "but I see what you mean; Baghdad is rather far, isn't it? Did he say he read about it in the paper there?"

"I had no time to inquire. He spoke to my assistant when he arrived." Helga turned to walk on without giving Allison time to answer, then stopped suddenly. "Did you know someone broke into the major's hut last night? The Arab boy found the lock broken this morning. He said the major's belongings had been scattered about the hut."

Allison felt as though she were under the even stare of a python. Believing that Helga knew Colonel Holman had spoken with her last night, she admitted: "Yes, so Colonel Holman told me. Quite odd, wasn't it?"

Helga's expression flickered with subdued satisfaction. A meticulously plucked brow lifted. "He left for the Carchemish Digs before either I or Jemal spoke with him about the matter. Then you saw him before he left? He told you about it? Curious that you would know." Allison looked at her wondering how to slip out of her own noose. Helga went on smoothly: "Then he knows. That is good. It means he will return to look into the matter. It was dreadful enough we met with an accident, but if news gets out we had a burglary, it will generate bad publicity for the club. I mean—why would any of us wish to rummage through his belongings like that?"

"Maybe it was just a petty thief who thought he might find a few things to sell at the bazaar in Aleppo."

"Most likely that's what it was. But none of my servants are thieves," she stated flatly.

"I didn't mean to imply—"

"I hope whoever broke in was only that. A petty thief."

"What else could it have been?" asked Allison bluntly.

Helga looked at her with fathomless dark eyes. "I'm sure I don't know, except that items a thief would usually take were all there. Jemal informs me nothing was missing."

"Of course your assistant would not know for certain, unless he knew everything the major had brought with him, and that isn't likely."

"Yes. You are right. We must wait until Colonel Holman returns."

Allison hoped the baroness didn't notice the flush that she felt warming her cheeks. Under Helga's level gaze, Allison turned to look toward her hut. "I shall be anxious to know if you hear anything about Neal. I'm still hoping he'll arrive this morning. You'll let me know right away?"

"Yes, and you will want to know about Leah as well."

"Yes, certainly. If you'll excuse me, I need to hurry. General Blaine and his wife are saving me a seat at the lecture."

"I'm sure you'll enjoy it."

"Yes, I'm sure I will. Thank you." Allison was hurrying on when Helga called, "If you have a copy of Woolly's book on archaeology, you will want to bring it with you since Jemal will refer to some of Woolly's notes on the Hittites."

There was that word again. But the baroness could not possibly be using it in the way Leah had informed her last night. There was nothing uncommon about referring to the Hittites since the British Museum was exploring their ancient civilization at Jerablus.

"I don't have Woolly's book," Allison confessed. "I couldn't find a copy to buy before I left Cairo. There seems to have been a run on them. The book dealer was reordering from London when I left."

The baroness looked distracted as she stared across at Leah's vacant hut. She murmured something about getting more books for her own bookstore in Cairo from Constantinople, then walked briskly across the grounds. Allison looked after her uneasily, then turned and made for her own hut.

The baroness was suspicious. How much did she know? Perhaps

more importantly, did her national loyalties lie with the territorial ambitions of Kaiser Wilhelm? She was of German blood, but that was not enough cause to suspect her. It was unjust to brand every ex-patriot as a spy for Berlin. General Blaine had said she was loyal to the Kaiser, but while Allison thought affectionately of the general, it was true that he was so staunchly anti-German that his remarks bordered on being vicious.

For the first time, Allison wondered what made his tongue so adder-like when it came to the baroness. When she had an opportunity, she might ask Sarah.

Allison entered the hut, bolted the door, and turned to the desk where Leah sat busily at work with pencil and paper. She looked up, the lines of weariness visible on her face. "If only I'd had a minute longer in that hut," she sighed with exasperation and tapped the edge of the stubby pencil against the table. "'HITTITEebg.' What was he telling me to look for?"

"I wish I could be of more help. As it is, I've robbed the dining table. Here, nothing much to boast about, I'm afraid. Just some bread, cheese, and an orange. Sorry, no coffee," she added as Leah's hopeful gaze flew to her hand. "I'll try for coffee at lunch."

As Leah peeled the orange, deep in thought, Allison stood watching her. "You're trying too hard. Maybe you should let it go. Take a nap. You didn't sleep last night. I heard you walking about."

"There's no time to nap. If only Neal were here, he would know more what to look for."

"And if he doesn't come at all?" whispered Allison. "How long can we manage to hide you like this? The baroness was on her way to your hut. You didn't show at breakfast, and everyone is beginning to ask."

Leah looked at her worriedly. "What of Colonel Holman? Did he go inside my hut?"

"No, which seems unusual, seeing how ruthless he was in dealing with me last night. Helga says he's gone to Carchemish. It's terribly suspicious that Neal hasn't shown up and neither of you has led the club since Major Reuter met with his accident."

"Whatever happens, I'll need to know what Karl meant by this word first. And you'll need to keep convincing them there's nothing more on your mind than attending the expedition. Tomorrow is the excursion into Aleppo. You'll need to go and put up a good front."

The thought made Allison uneasy. "I hate to leave you here like this. If they decide to search, the baroness has a key to all the huts."

"Why would she search? She has no reason to suspect I'm here. And Holman has already questioned you."

"I'm not so sure she isn't suspicious. She behaved oddly just now. The way she watched me and asked leading questions made me think she might be working with Holman. What do you know about Helga?"

Leah shrugged. "You know the type. Wealthy, widowed, and bored. She has lots of money to play with. And unlike some women who prefer a round of parties, the baroness is educated and interested in political dialogue. As I've said, she knows Neal and has bought pieces for the Cairo Museum. Naturally she would be suspicious this morning. Karl's hut was broken into, no one knows where I am, and Neal hasn't shown himself."

"I suppose. She said Holman left early. Don't you think his behavior is strange?"

"What do you mean?"

Allison was thoughtful. "He thinks his colleague was murdered. So why would he leave before questioning the others in the club? Once we leave for British Cairo, he won't be able to interrogate anyone since he'll have no further jurisdiction."

"Yes, I see what you mean. I would have expected him to stay too, unless…"

"Unless what?" asked Allison, alert.

Leah sighed. "I don't know…"

"Do you think he suspects Neal? He may have gone to the digs to search for him."

"Neal is just one of the reasons he would go there." Leah glanced toward the door, then back at Allison. "We've long suspected the Berlin-Baghdad Railway is being built to haul German troops into Arabia, although the Kaiser denies this. Holman will meet with his contacts at the railway headquarters. I suspect he'll wire his superiors in Constantinople and inform them of Karl's death."

"But what if they wire back and say the real Karl Reuter is still in Constantinople? What if Major Reuter himself wires back!"

"That's part of the risk we take. I'm sure our side would have taken care of that possibility."

Allison recognized the tension in Leah's voice. She wasn't sure at all. And that put even more pressure on her to come up with the coded word's meaning.

"Tell me again what you saw in Major Reuter's hut," pressed Leah.

"I've told you everything. There was nothing but his satchel of papers, his clothing—and that's just it," she insisted. "If the clue is something he hid in his clothing, you'll never know what it is."

"No, Reuter was too careful. He would know I wouldn't have time to search his things. The paper was on his desk in plain sight, and he would make anything else visible as well, but just as unlikely to draw attention from the enemy." She stood restlessly. "Think, Allison! Are you quite certain you saw nothing else while sitting in that chair under Holman's questioning?"

Allison walked to the small window and drew aside the curtain, thinking, as she had tried to do all morning. Even at breakfast, while General Blaine and Sarah chatted, her mind had revisited that dreadful room. Yet all she saw in her memory was Colonel Brent Holman, his riveting blue stare and his arrogant stance, as he insisted she had stolen important information from Karl Reuter.

She let the curtain fall back into place. "I must go. Helga has left your hut and is walking back toward the main building. I don't want her to catch me just coming out. I've taken too long to get my hat." She snatched it from the peg and opened the door, letting in a path of sunlight. "I'll keep thinking. And I'll be back after lunch."

Leah smiled unexpectedly but tiredly. "Get that coffee this time, will you?"

"I promise," Allison responded.

She stepped out, turned the key in the lock, and waited a second until she heard Leah slide the bolt into place. Even if the baroness made up some excuse to use her master key while she was away, she couldn't get inside. But Allison would need to do some explaining of how she managed to bolt the door from the outside!

She was coming down the steps, strapping on her hat, when a man's voice spoke from the side of the hut. "So there you are. I've been looking for you."

Her heart jumped to her throat, and she turned rigid.

David.

5

ALLISON LOOKED AT HIM DAZED, so surprised was she to see the young Jewish activist she had met in London at Oswald Chambers Bible Training College. He stood below the porch in the hot sand, wearing khaki knee-pants, leather boots, and the traditional, helmet-like expedition hat made of canvas. She hardly recognized him out of London dress and noted that he also sported a rifle slung over his shoulder. A kitbag sat at his feet, containing his clothing. He obviously intended to stay awhile.

"David," she breathed. "I thought you left London when I did, that you had gone home to South Africa. What on earth are you doing here?"

He grinned. "On 'Earth,' where would a Jew feel more at home than in Palestine, I ask you?"

"This is Aleppo," she stated. "You are not in Jerusalem. And the Turks are questioning anyone who even hints of knowing David Ben-Gurion."

He shrugged his heavy shoulders with a determination she had come to recognize. "Well, then I'm safe for the moment. I haven't met Ben-Gurion yet."

She caught the meaning to the word *yet*. Then he had made up his mind, she thought. His politics had convinced him to involve himself on the side of the Zionist Movement in Jerusalem.

"You're risking your life, you know," she said quietly.

His brown eyes turned serious. "Some things are worth the risk. A homeland is one of them." He smiled again. "But we've waited nearly two thousand years. I can wait a few more weeks. I came to see you. I heard in Cairo you were here." His eyes laughed at her. "Still into your biblical archaeology, are you?"

She came down the steps, and they walked slowly toward the main buildings. "What were you doing in Cairo? Did you go by to see my family? They would have enjoyed meeting you. I told them how you braved the BTC to argue religion and politics with Oswald Chambers and some of the students."

"Ah, Daniel in the lion's den," he jested. "And like him, I came out without a scratch."

She smiled. David had a pleasant way about him, even as he aired his doubts that Jesus was the promised Jewish Messiah. Many of the Christian students, as well as Chambers, had warmly befriended him, and the friendship deepened during the two months in which David had come to the large house turned into a college by Oswald Chambers and his wife, Biddie. Allison would never forget the rainy Christmas Eve when he had arrived with Wade Findlay, another BTC student. David had appeared the traditional activist, ready to argue into the late hours of the night to prove his new friends wrong. When Chambers had not wished to argue but had befriended the young man who was away from his home in South Africa, David had been content to leave the topic of Jesus and discuss the idea of a national homeland for the Jews in Palestine. He had met Lord Balfour, so David told them, and Chaim Weizman. And David planned to contact Zionists who were living and working in Jerusalem. David Ben-Gurion was the head of a Jerusalem group that was trying to gain some semblance of independence from the Turks. David's dream was to join them.

"So you're going to Jerusalem?" she asked.

"I'm convinced our time has come. I've a plan to meet a friend here first. Perhaps you know him. He's done some work in archaeology as well; minor stuff, so he says. He's never one to boast. I met him in London at a Zionist meeting."

"He's Jewish?"

"No, he's as British as they come, but he's on our side." He grinned. "He can wax more eloquent than I when it comes to touting reasons for a Jewish homeland. He was at the meetings, I think, just to look us over for future harvesting."

"Harvesting?"

"The war. It's coming, you know."

A cloud settled over her emotions. A war would ruin the medical-missionary work with Aunt Lydia aboard the *Mercy*. "War isn't inevitable," she insisted.

"Don't be a desert ostrich. There's no stopping the ambitions of Germany. 'It's Germany's time,' as they say. They are flat on the side of Austria and her move to annex Serbia. And if the Russian czar Nicholas intervenes on behalf of Serbia, it'll be the excuse the kaiser is looking for to join Austria and declare war, not only on Serbia and Russia, but also on France and England. And Arabia will be in the thick of the battle."

Allison feared he was right. "Why Arabia? Because of the oil reserves?"

"That has a lot to do with it." He lowered his voice. "Why else would they be building the railway from Baghdad to Palestine? Access to oil and troop movements."

"Yes, but Turkey controls Arabia, and they're unlikely to side with the kaiser but rather with England. And not everyone agrees that war is inevitable," she protested. "Why, even now the heads of government are negotiating, trying to work out peace over the Balkan war."

"The kaiser doesn't want peace," he said with a touch of scorn. "Austria annexing Bosnia was just the beginning. The kaiser and his war minister have been preparing for years, building masses of weapons in secret, including some of the biggest guns ever—howitzers, with shells that can flatten a city." David scowled to himself. "I say they have St. Petersburg in mind. While the rest of Europe dozes like an old man in the sun, Germany's army of reserves, numbering two million, is preparing for battle at a day's notice."

He looked at her and gave an apologetic smile. "There I go again. If I were smart I wouldn't always talk war when I see you, would I?"

She smiled and said nothing. "By the way," he said, "that reminds me. I've brought you a letter. You see? There are other reasons I've come. Here, from your other admirer, Wade Findlay."

She laughed. "So you came all the way to Arabia to play postman, did you? I hardly believe it, but thanks just the same." She took the letter and placed it unopened in her kitbag.

"Aren't you going to read it?" he teased. "A love letter from your greatest admirer—no, I shouldn't say greatest."

She pretended she hadn't noticed his intent. "Never mind about Wade. So tell me about this friend of yours you've come here to meet. Who is he?"

"Bret Holden."

Startled, she looked at him. "What did you say?"

"Bret Holden," he repeated. "Why?"

She shook her head, relieved. "No reason. I thought you said someone else."

"Bret is expecting me, though I have a way of showing up unexpectedly and dropping my bag on someone's doorstep. What I have to talk to him about may gain me a warm welcome."

She looked at him and noted that his tanned face had grown

grave. The determination she had come to recognize was visible in his eyes.

"Sounds rather mysterious," she said quietly.

He shrugged. "I heard in Cairo that this club is the biggest in Arabia."

"It is the biggest," Allison responded, letting him change the subject. "Several experts are here this year. I don't know everyone," she admitted. "There are some new faces. If anyone would know where to find your friend, it would be the secretary of the club, Baroness Helga Kruger."

"Ah yes, the wealthy German widow."

"You know her?" she asked curiously.

"No. Heard of her. Who hasn't?"

"I'll introduce you to her at lunch. You are staying?"

"Until tomorrow. If Bret's not here, I'll drive on up to the Carchemish Digs at Jerablus. He's a friend of the archaeologist Woolly and his assistant, T. E. Lawrence."

Woolly and Lawrence, along with Neal and Leah, worked for the British Museum at Carchemish.

"Neal is at Carchemish, too, isn't he?" he asked blandly.

At the mention of her cousin, her concerns came back to plague her. She watched David with subdued caution. She would like to tell him about Leah; yet it would be unwise without first asking her.

"Yes, Neal was to have been here to lecture on the newest finds," she explained. "He's been delayed."

"Nothing serious?"

"We—I don't know. He may come in today." She looked at him sideways as they walked slowly toward the lecture hut. "This friend of yours, Bret Holden, the one you met at the Zionist meetings in London, what makes you think he's here?"

He shrugged. "I was told rather hush in Cairo that I might find him if I inquired from Neal at the digs. I stopped here first, thinking I might save time since they might be with the club, and because I knew you were here." He watched her. "I've missed you."

She made no reply. While David was attractive and she admired his dedication to help establish a Jewish colony in Jerusalem, she was even more concerned about his coming to recognize the Messiah. She hadn't said anything to him, but David's name was written in a journal Oswald Chambers gave her as a going away present when she left his school in London.

"Be totally his!" Chambers had told her in that simple and sweet way that said so much of the man's own relationship with Christ.

David's name was written down with several others for whom she prayed each Sunday afternoon when she gave herself to Bible reading and rest. How could she help him see that it was possible to remain a Jew and believe in Y'shua? He had several times used the argument that "Jesus is for the Goyim, the Gentiles."

No, any romantic interest must not grow, she told herself firmly. David must remain only a friend. Anyway, there was Wade Findlay, she reminded herself, a young man she had met at Chambers' college.

"Have you heard of Bret Holden before?" David asked.

She tried to place the name. It sounded a little like "Holman," but in thinking of the ruthless German colonel, she dismissed the idea.

"No, but that isn't to say Professor Holden isn't here. As I've said, there are several new faces this year, including a professor from Constantinople."

He frowned. "If I don't find him, I'll drive on to Jerablus. He's likely to be poking around the Hittite palace there. Bret is especially interested in anything Hittite," he said.

There was that word again, but did it mean anything coming

from David? What had Leah told her—it would be left to the agent trying to get in touch with her or Neal to make the first contact. He would disclose himself in such a way as not to breed suspicion from curious onlookers. David certainly didn't seem like an agent, but who was Bret Holden? Was he a true professor, or was it a cover? She must mention this possibility to Leah. As for David, who would suspect a Jew interested in Zionism to work primarily for the British government?

But she knew David. At least, she told herself she did, and he did not seem the type to be Neal's superior in the British intelligence. His political fires were smoldering in the cause for a Jewish homeland, and his spirit found no rest in any cause that did not benefit the rallying call of, "Next year in Jerusalem."

"Neal is my cousin," she stated. "I didn't know you knew him. You never mentioned him at BTC. And I don't recall having told you about him, or his line of work for the museum."

"Oh, didn't I?" he said casually. "Well, I've never met him personally. Bret told me about him. Said he was a Hittite expert."

Everything pointed to David being the new contact sent in an emergency to see Leah. But if that were so, why had he been in London? And why had he involved himself in the Zionist meetings? Had he gone there as a spy seeking contacts to aid the British in Arabia should war actually break out? It was also strange that the man named Bret Holden had attended those meetings, and as David hinted, was there "harvesting" for the future war needs.

Allison remained silent, wondering if she dare mention Leah and that she waited in secret to make contact with the agent who would take the place of the murdered Major Karl Reuter. But to blurt it out with so little to go on was foolish. She trusted David, and she admitted that when she first saw him she had felt a wave of relief, for she had thought that here was a man to whom both she and Leah could turn for help. But she must say nothing until she talked with Leah after lunch.

She took David's arm and edged him forward. "We're late. Let's hurry. So Bret Holden knows my cousin Neal?"

"Bret said they met two years ago in Constantinople. Neal was there about a Hittite sculpture piece at the museum. Come to think of it, it had something to do with the Baroness Kruger and her work for the Turkish museum. There was a dispute over who should have the piece. Neal claimed she had swiped it away from the digs without his knowing. Lawrence especially was upset about it."

"Don't look now, but here comes Helga," whispered Allison. "And David, I'd appreciate it if you wouldn't let it be known why you're here. Say you came to see me, would you?"

He looked at her, a hint of surprise in his brown eyes. As Baroness Kruger walked toward them, he smiled and gave a wink. "Don't worry."

"A new visitor, Allison? I don't think we've met." Helga turned her steady dark eyes on David and extended a firm, bejeweled, feminine hand. "I'm Baroness Kruger, secretary to the Archaeological Club. You've come up from Cairo?"

David could be all charm when he chose to be and he was now, bending over her hand as though he himself were a German count dressed in regal splendor. "Professor David Goldstein—from New York. I'm on tour."

Professor! Allison tried to mask her unease over David's pretense.

"Splendid. You've come with credentials, of course?" came Helga's smooth voice.

Now what? thought Allison. But David smiled, outwardly unaffected by the baroness's icy greeting and her obvious skepticism.

"I never travel without my papers, Baroness, but I confess I didn't expect to be digging them out now—in the middle of the grounds.

We're already late for the lecture. Your assistant is speaking, isn't he? Professor Jemal Pasha of Cairo University? If you insist—"

"I would not insist. The height of rudeness, Professor Goldstein. It can wait for a more convenient time. You understand the embarrassing pressure put upon me by the Turkish officials of Aleppo. Anyone with a Jewish name is immediately suspected of Zionist 'temperament.'"

"And sure to stir up trouble, yes?"

Her eyes flickered at his casual insolence. "The Turkish officials have insisted we limit membership to our club to—to—"

"The fair race. Yes, I understand, Baroness, and I wouldn't want to embarrass you by insisting I be admitted to the club because of my credentials. I was here merely to see an old friend before passing on to Cairo." He gestured his chestnut-colored head toward Allison. "Nurse Allison Wescott. We met in London."

Allison's gaze had dropped, and she felt the warm color of indignation rise in her face over the baroness's blatant anti-Semitism. But meeting David's eyes, she saw he understood and did not wish to make a point of it.

"In that case, you're quite welcome to stay, Professor Goldstein. Nevertheless, friend of Allison's or not, we will need to see your papers. You understand, of course. It isn't my ruling."

"Your good intentions are quite understood, Baroness."

Although Helga turned her gaze on Allison and smiled, her eyes did not. "The real reason I've come is to let you know that your cousin Leah is not in her hut. And it appears she left in a hurry. She took nothing with her, not even a change of clothing. Her things have been ransacked. Someone broke into her hut the same way they did Major Reuter's. Very odd. The question is, why?"

Allison masked a shiver of alarm. Whoever murdered Karl Reuter had seen Leah pick up that piece of paper from the floor, and now he had searched her hut.

"I think I should contact the Turkish police at once," said Helga.

"What's this?" asked David, looking from Helga to Allison. "A burglar in the club? Now this is something to talk about. Looking for rare pieces to sell perhaps?"

"I hardly think so," said Helga coolly.

"We've had a death," explained Allison.

"An accident," insisted Helga. "A German officer from Baghdad, Major Karl Reuter. The burglary—if it is that—has nothing to do with the accident."

Allison watched David's response to the major's name, hoping to see a faint glimmer of recognition, linking them as friendly agents. If he had been sent to replace the supposed Karl Reuter, he would know about the major's death.

"What kind of accident?"

"A victim of the cobra," said Helga, looking about the desert absently. "I was asking Allison earlier if her cousin Leah might have taken his death hard and gone back to the expedition house at Jerablus, especially since Neal hasn't shown up either."

"If she has gone back," hastened Allison, "she'll meet up with Colonel Holman."

"Yes, I hadn't thought of that. Yet none of the servants mentioned seeing Leah leave. That she didn't take her clothing is suspicious. So I went to check the vehicle she arrived in." Her dark eyes flickered smugly. "It's still parked under the acacia tree. So she can hardly have left. She must be here somewhere."

Allison remained expressionless.

"I'm on my way now to speak to the security man," Helga said. "A second viper bite does seem out of the ordinary coming so soon after the first one, doesn't it?"

"Yes," murmured Allison, "it would be odd indeed."

Helga looked at her, and her expression changed. "About that archaeology book by Woolly," she said thoughtfully. "The one on the Hittites. I'm afraid I won't be able to loan it to you after all. I remembered on my way to Leah's hut that I'd lent it to Major Reuter when he first arrived. He was admiring my library and asked for it specifically. Said he had so much reading to do before listening to this year's lecturers. He was looking forward to the excursion out to the digs. Unfortunately, he didn't have time to enjoy it."

Allison blinked. She was remembering something she had seen in the hut. The book she had knocked to the floor, simply and appropriately titled, *The Hittites*.

Her heart began to beat faster. Of course. Major Reuter could have left his message for Leah in the Hittite book.

It was David who spoke. "Woolly's book on the Hittite discovery? It's quite excellent. Matter of fact, I brought along a copy." He looked at Allison. "I'll lend you mine."

"That would be good of you," said Helga. "Everything in Major Reuter's hut is being held for investigation until his death is cleared as an accident."

So the book was still in the hut.

Helga had turned and walked away, bent on finding the private security guard she had hired for the club meeting. Soon there would be a full-fledged search for Leah, and who knew where it would lead? Allison couldn't take the chance that her hut would be searched. Leah must escape, but how could she get hold of that book from Major Reuter's hut first?

Allison had another thought. What if the murderer realized the item he was looking for was not with Leah but remained in the hut?

"Something wrong, Allison?" asked David quietly.

"I'm worried about Neal's absence. It isn't like him to be irresponsible. He knew he had this morning's lecture."

"He may have been held up at Carchemish for some reason. No

use jumping to the worst conclusions. And Leah may have gone there to find him."

"I wish it were as simple as that," she said in a low voice.

"What's this? You don't think so? Something going on I don't know about?"

"David, did you say you were driving up to Jerablus to meet Professor Holden?"

"Yes, I was thinking of leaving in the morning if he isn't here. And from the warm welcome of 'her majesty,' I can see I won't be invited to take a hut."

"I'd like to ride up with you, if you would let me."

"Sure, we'll leave now if you want. I've a motorbike." He took her in cautiously. "Think you can ride in back?"

"I could, but there's no need. Baroness Kruger mentioned Leah's Mercedes parked near here. It will get us there more quickly."

"What about the keys?"

Leah had them, of course, but Allison knew she couldn't admit this yet. "Don't worry about that. I'll come up with them. I'd rather leave after dinner when it's dark, if you don't mind."

He watched her curiously. "I gather there is more to this than wishing to avoid the heat?"

"Well, actually there is, and there's also something I must do first. David, I'd appreciate it tremendously if you didn't mention this to anyone just yet. Not until we get back."

"If you want it that way, why not? I suppose you'll tell me what's going on soon enough."

"Trust me until I can."

"*Trust you?* A noble nurse serving God and country aboard the *Mercy?* Explicitly!"

"Do you really have Woolly's book, or was that to save me from the silence about to swallow me up?"

"I gathered something she had said startled you, so I thought I'd better come to your rescue."

"Then you don't have a copy?"

"No, is it important?"

"No, not that one." She studied his face. "David, are you a British agent?"

He laughed. "What a bizarre question."

"One you're not answering."

"Then I'll answer plainly. No." He sobered. "Not yet."

Not yet? She glanced at him as they hurried toward the door into the lecture hut. She remembered what he had said about the Zionist meetings in London being a place that could be harvested in case war came. Harvested, she assumed, by the British foreign office for the act of spying. But wouldn't that also point to Professor Bret Holden being connected with espionage since he had gone to the meetings to look for possible future spies?

Her mind spun with too many possibilities, and she saw that David was watching her. She quickened her pace. "We're dreadfully late—"

As she and David neared the hut, they could hear the deep, Turkish voice of Jemal Pasha, assistant to the baroness, discussing the latest discovery of a large stairway to a palace at Carchemish. Jemal had always been a curious entity as far as Allison was concerned. He was an expert in ancient Egyptian mummies and, besides working in the summer for the baroness, was a professor at the Cairo Archaeological School. He looked to be in his thirties and was tall and thin with stooping shoulders. He had magnificent eyes, so large that the whites showed oddly against his swarthy face.

Through an open window, from where Jemal's voice floated out, she saw General Blaine's reddish-gray head turn to look out at the sound of their footsteps on the gravel.

"Who's that?" David asked when the general gave her a friendly scowl at being more than twenty minutes late.

She smiled. "General Blaine. He's here as a spectator with his wife, Sarah. They're close friends of my parents. It's Sarah who's the archaeology enthusiast. General Blaine devotes himself to other interests."

David followed her inside, and since only one chair had been saved, he was about to take a seat in the back. General Blaine stood, beckoning for David to take his, and whispered as they came up, "I've had all I can take of old bones and dirt. I'm going back to my hut to rest my back until lunch."

Allison smiled and took her seat, David beside her. She leaned over to Sarah. "Have I missed much?"

"I've taken notes. You can copy them tonight," Sarah hissed and then added, "Where did that husband of mine go?"

"To lie down and rest his back."

"It's just as well. We're all going to Aleppo this afternoon. The bazaar shops there are wonderful!"

The rest of the morning passed without incident. Allison was anxious to return to her hut to report to Leah, but she had to be careful to avoid being seen. As they broke for lunch, she excused herself from David and Sarah and made a quick return to where Leah hid.

Allison entered breathlessly. "I think we may have our answer to the message Reuter left you on his desk."

Leah stood tensely. She bolted the door and drew Allison aside. "What happened?" she whispered anxiously.

Allison explained about Reuter's borrowing the Hittite book from Helga.

Leah's breath came rapidly. "Yes, a book would work. Do you know the title?"

"*The Hittites*. It must be what you're looking for. Because I remembered after Helga mentioned it that I knocked it off a table when Colonel Holman sneaked up behind me."

Leah took hold of Allison's arm so tightly that she winced. "That's it. It must be. I have to get back inside that hut. Is it under guard now?"

"No, there's no one. I was careful to look as I went by. Do hurry; we've little time. The baroness is driving into Aleppo to report you missing along with Neal. By tomorrow they'll surely search all the huts."

Leah nodded. "I'll get in the hut tonight, when everyone is in the dining room having supper."

"Two Turkish security guards are roaming the grounds."

"I'll watch, but I'll need to risk it. That book is crucial. And someone else is alert for possibilities. Did anyone hear Helga mention it?"

"No, just a Jewish friend of mine, David Goldstein."

Leah's gaze came alert. "Yes?"

Allison thought back to the open window in the lecture hut. "We were standing a bit away from the lecture hut, but the door and windows were all open to let in a breeze. Jemal Pasha was lecturing, and the club members were taking notes and listening. Still, we can't be sure of that. Helga didn't seem concerned about lowering her voice."

"Then getting in the hut is urgent. I dare not wait. Where are you going now, to lunch? Good. Everyone else is likely to be there, too." Leah looked at her evenly. "I'm going to try now, during lunch."

"You can't, not in broad daylight."

"It's the chance I must take. You can keep an eye out at the dining room. I'll wait for fifteen minutes after the lunch bell sounds. Everyone will be there, and I'll go to the hut. If the book is where Karl left it, I will find it within a few minutes."

"It's too risky. Anything could go wrong…"

"Sit where you can see both doors. And Allison, if anyone should decide to leave early before the others, it will be up to you to join them. Make a scene outside—scream about seeing a cobra, do anything! But raise your voice so I can hear you."

"All right. I'll try. But you can't stay here much longer. David and I will get you safely out of here before Colonel Holman returns or the Turkish inspector arrives from Aleppo."

Leah sank into the chair. "This Jewish friend of yours, David Goldstein; can he be trusted?"

Allison explained their relationship in London at Oswald Chambers Bible Training School. "We can trust him; I'll stake my life on it."

"You may have to. We both may."

Allison waited until the lunch bell sounded, then walked slowly across the sand toward the dining room where the club members were all drifting in, talking of Jemal's lecture. She waited until the last person had gone in through the door, then followed, her heart thumping. Sarah and David were seated at a table near the front door, and Allison looked about casually as if deciding on a seat. All the seats were taken except for four at the table where Sarah sat, beckoning her.

While scanning the faces present, Allison was convinced no one suspected that Major Karl Reuter was murdered or that Leah was safely hidden in Allison's hut.

David excused himself from the table, and Allison's gaze followed him anxiously. But he was making the rounds of the six different tables, boldly introducing himself as Professor Goldstein from New York. If the situation she was in had not been so serious, Allison would have found his daring amusing.

She guessed that David was making the rounds because he was still on the lookout for Professor Bret Holden. But whether or not

David had found him was uncertain. Her tension grew. Neither Baroness Helga Kruger nor her assistant, Professor Jemal Pasha, had shown up in the dining room. She wondered if this meant they had paid a visit to the Turkish police, or whether they were watching Reuter's hut.

From her chair, Allison could see the outline of her hut and Major Reuter's. Was Leah making her move now? She had said she would wait fifteen minutes after the bell.

Sarah Blaine was in animated conversation with several others at the table about the wonderful bargains they could locate at the bazaar. "I'm going to try my hand at sewing a caftan. How about you, Allison? Say, are you listening? Don't tell me you're still dreaming about Jemal's lecture—Oh! Here he is now—and the baroness herself."

Allison's breath paused with relief as she looked from the window, surprised to see Helga and Jemal stopping at their table. They seemed to have emerged from nowhere. Now everyone was accounted for. She glanced at the clock on the wooden wall—fifteen minutes past twelve.

"Oh, please do join us," she breathed with a welcoming smile, and while Jemal bowed lightly and gestured at the empty seat beside her, Helga declined. Watching David, who was seated by Mr. Blackstone from the Cairo Museum, she walked in that direction.

"The seat—you're saving it for your friend from New York?" inquired Jemal too politely.

"No, please sit down," said Allison, keeping an eye on Helga. "David seems to have pulled up a chair at the other table. I apologize for entering your lecture late, Professor. I was looking forward to hearing you."

His wide mouth beneath the Turkish black mustache seemed to spread reluctantly into a smile that matched his angular form.

Allison didn't think Jemal smiled very often. When he did, it was almost done with apology. His large eyes looked on her kindly, though sadly, like reflective pools.

"Then you will have an opportunity to attend again, Nurse Wescott. Unfortunately, if your cousin Neal does not arrive, I will be obligated to take tomorrow's lecture as well."

"You don't enjoy lecturing, Professor? It's understandable, of course. I'm sure you weren't expecting to fill in like this."

"I don't mind filling in, since Carchemish is providing some interesting finds. As you may know already, I am an Egyptologist."

She did know this and wondered why he was so closely associated with the baroness, whose main interest was archaeology.

"It's Neal we are wondering about," he said. "We sent two men last night to check the road to Aleppo. They found no sign of your cousin. The baroness tells me Miss Leah also is absent. I thought you would like to know that we've notified the authorities in Aleppo. They will arrive by dinner tonight. They will need to search all the huts."

"What's this?" asked Sarah, evidently overhearing and coming to attention. "Something happened to your cousin, Allison?"

"We don't know yet. She wasn't in her hut this morning, and the baroness and Professor Pasha are rather concerned."

"As well they might be Good heavens! A young woman wouldn't simply wander off alone in the desert."

"Leah might," said Jemal with a wan smile. "She is adventurous and intelligent; so if she did, I wouldn't worry too much about her abilities to care for herself."

Allison watched him over her hot *bi 'Inaana*, tea with mint, and wondered how much he knew about Leah.

"I hope this doesn't ruin our jaunt to the bazaar," said Sarah with a thoughtful frown. "I wanted yards of red silk to make a caftan."

"I'm afraid you will be delayed," he said apologetically. "The police will want to question everyone about when they saw Miss Bristow last." Jemal watched Sarah Blaine over his cup.

"I haven't seen her at all," said Sarah with a brisk wave of her hand, when a voice interrupted.

"Forgetful, darling Sarah. We spoke to her when we arrived yesterday afternoon," said General Blaine. He groaned as he pulled out a chair and sat down beside his wife. "It was soon after the Arab boy reported the death of the German officer, Reuter."

"Oh, you're right," said Sarah, looking embarrassed at her omission. "Rex is right. She was coming out of the common room—or was it from the acacia trees? I spoke to her, but she didn't appear to notice. Preoccupied with her duties as club hostess, I suppose."

"Or preoccupied with the death of Major Reuter. Well, the lass is missing now," said Major Blaine, motioning to the servant to pour his coffee. "Add a bit of hot water to it, would you, old boy? Stuff is strong enough to curl my hair on top, if I had any." He looked about, his sleepy pale-gray eyes suddenly curious as they fixed on Professor Jemal Pasha.

"Our sprightly holiday is turning into a regular mystery. Where can she be? What of you, Allison? Any idea?" he asked, as his eyes shifted to her.

"I'm quite sure nothing has happened to her," said Allison. "Professor Pasha is right when it comes to my cousin's adventurous spirit. Most likely she went searching for Neal." ·

"A brave woman. You wouldn't catch me out in the desert by myself. The heat, the scorpions, the Bedouin—not a place for a lone woman, I would say. Well, we'll soon find out," said the general with a sigh. "Here comes the baroness, looking grim and determined. You must lead an unfortunate life of nerves, Jemal, working so closely with Helga."

The look that passed across Jemal's gaunt, dark face gave Allison a shiver. For a moment she'd seen a flicker of hate flash in his usually expressionless face, and there was no mistaking on whom that hatred was fixed—not on general Blaine for his goading remark, but on Baroness Helga Kruger herself.

6

LEAH'S BLUE EYES BURNED INTENSELY and a flush of excitement warmed her face. "We've done it, Allison. We've outsmarted them. There's nothing left now except to turn the information over to Neal."

Leah had carefully hidden the book before Allison ever returned from the dining room, and Allison knew better than to ask her where it was. Leah trusted her, but she couldn't tell Allison everything, nor did Allison expect Leah to. Therefore, Allison was surprised when Leah said, "I've heard from Neal. Everything is going to be all right soon."

"Neal?" Allison nearly choked.

Leah nodded. "I'm to meet him tonight."

Allison watched her, unable to move as the meaning of her cousin's words sank into her mind. She could see that Leah was more relaxed than she remembered seeing her since the club meetings had begun. Leah's eyes almost sparkled with youth.

"Are you sure?" Allison asked. "You're not mistaken? How?"

Leah glanced about, as if deciding. "All right, I'll tell you what I can."

Sitting in the chair by the desk and speaking in a carefully guarded tone so as not to say more than allowed, Leah told Allison how she had first been sent to Jerablus from Bombay to contact and take orders from Professor Neal Bristow, who, since he was her brother, seemed the perfect partner in intelligence gathering. They could trust each other explicitly, and no one would suspect them of working for the British government. Since Leah had always been interested in writing, it was her job to store up the archaeological information for the British Museum. And because Neal was also working privately on a book about the discovery of the Hittites, her presence appeared beneficial to both the family and the museum.

"Between us," she said in a low voice, "we were able to find out what we had been sent to learn about the railway. Only Karl had discovered something even more important. He had hot information for London, and he couldn't get through. He knew he was being watched."

Leah stated all this unemotionally, and Allison leaned forward in excitement.

"As you know, someone knew Karl was British and murdered him before he could meet with Neal as planned. But Neal was alerted ahead of time, almost at the last minute, and his orders were to avoid the meeting. Unfortunately, Karl was trapped. Thank heaven he must have realized a short time before he was murdered that things had gone badly."

Earlier, the espionage situation had progressed to a higher level than either Neal or Leah was equipped to handle, and the lurking menace at the Carchemish Digs, and now here at the huts in Aleppo, had made it necessary for Karl to risk meeting Neal. Neal was to pass on the information to someone in higher authority.

"We were to use the cover of the Cairo Archaeological Club to meet and receive the information from Major Reuter. But everything went wrong, as we both know."

"How did German intelligence in Baghdad learn that Karl was a British agent?"

"The same way we find out things. People who are least suspected are spies. But like with Karl, the role often leads to death."

"And Neal's superior?"

"Neal sent off a call for help, knowing I was probably trapped here and unable to show myself, yet still responsible."

Now Neal had to stay hidden even as Leah did. Visitors were arriving by the score on the railway near the Carchemish Digs, and many came to see the finds. Neal's new contact would come this route, affording himself a cover into Baghdad.

The Berlin-Baghdad Railway. Thinking of it brought Allison a shiver. "Then he came?" she asked in an excited whisper.

"Yes, he's here. Neal will meet him soon. It's the other agent's headache now! But there's something left for me to do tonight. Something important."

The day was drawing to a close outside the window, and the silence and the brooding desert wind seemed to take a step closer to the hut.

"I'm to bring Neal the information Karl left me, and then Neal will meet with his superior."

Allison stirred. "Bring him Woolly's book?"

"Neal doesn't know yet that it's Woolly's book. He thinks Karl left the information in written form. To have done so would be a mistake, of course, and few agents would risk it, but Karl was in a desperate situation so it's conceivable. I'm letting Neal think so as a safeguard on my part."

"You mean you don't trust Neal?" gasped Allison somewhat indignantly.

"Of course I trust him," Leah laughed. "He's my brother. Even among agents we have our orders not to take chances. Don't look so worried. He would want me to be careful. I won't feel I'm out of this until the book is in Neal's hands."

Allison's concerns grew, even though Leah would know better than she what actions were expected of her. "Have you looked at the book? Do you know the message Major Reuter left?"

Leah shook her head. "I wouldn't know what to look for, but Neal does. The less I know, the better it will be for us all. There's less chance of making a mistake, of falling into the hands of the other side. Even if I were so unlucky, I couldn't tell them a thing."

"So...it's the book that's actually all-important. There would be no reason for them to end your life the way they did Major Reuter's?"

She smiled. "I'm counting on that. I feel matters are safer now that Neal has contacted me. He wouldn't have expected me to meet him if there were much chance of my being caught on the way."

Allison glanced about, as though the silent shadows were listening enemies. "You're certain the message was from Neal?"

She smiled. "Quite certain. I'd never risk meeting him if I weren't. Still," she agreed, "I'll need to be on the watch. Don't look so worried. I plan to bring a sheaf of phony documents with me just to make a good cover. I won't produce the book until I'm certain it's Neal and someone isn't hiding with a revolver trained on him."

Then Leah had thought about the possibility. "I don't like it," Allison said. "But it sounds as if you know what you're doing. How did you hear from him?"

"I didn't say anything before, but the Arab boy is on our side," she said simply. "A number of them are friendly with the British. And you might as well know: in the message, Neal told me he was the third man we heard in the hut that night."

"Neal," Allison whispered. "Is it possible? But I called out. Why didn't he answer?"

Leah stood. "He didn't dare. Anyone else may have been listening. It was far wiser to slip away and send the call for help to his superior, which is what he did. Remember, I didn't answer you either. Thank God things have worked out."

Yet Allison's foreboding continued. Despite Leah's explanations and her confidence, something was not quite right. Allison couldn't place her finger on it, but it weighed darkly in the back of her mind. Something she should know, that Leah should have understood but had overlooked.

Leah, however, appeared confident. *If the experts in subversive activities are satisfied,* thought Allison, *who am I to argue their decisions? I'm a nurse, not a spy. And the sooner I get back to Cairo, the better.*

"Then," mused Allison, "Neal knew that Major Reuter was murdered. He was here that night but couldn't show himself. He hid until he could enter the hut to find the message left him in an inconspicuous way." She looked at Leah, frowning. "But you said Neal doesn't know about the book. He expects to receive documents from you. Documents aren't exactly inconspicuous."

Leah shrugged a bit impatiently. "Whatever Neal may have expected to find, I don't know. He didn't say in the message, but he may have thought his contact hadn't the time to take precaution. The matter was urgent, and he would have left what he could, believing Neal would find it before either the Turkish or German authorities stumbled onto its being important."

"The book, left in plain sight. Yes, I suppose you're right... But Neal must have seen the paper on the bureau and recognized the coded word left for him by Major Reuter. Why didn't he respond to it the way you did? Didn't you say that only someone who wasn't on our side would have passed it by as meaningless, the same as Woolly's book? Neal would have gone out of his way to look for it."

"Yes, and he must have done just that and missed it."

"On the desk? Hardly. You didn't miss it. Why would Neal, if he was the third man?"

"It was on the floor when I found it."

Allison leaned toward her in the chair. "But how did it get there? Only the murderer would have brushed it aside while in a hurry, searching—"

Leah frowned. "Remember, the front door was standing open when I arrived. The wind had risen. The curtains were moving. I distinctly recall that much. It would have been easy for it to blow off the desk onto the floor before Neal saw it. I saw it because I lit a match. I don't know what Neal may have done before I entered the hut, or why he didn't find it. It could have been any number of things. He might not have had time to look on the desk but went straight to Karl's luggage."

"The way Colonel Holman did. Yes, but if it were Neal," Allison pressed, "and he did see the coded word 'HITTITEebg,' why didn't he realize the real information was in Woolly's book on the Hittites? Why didn't it ring a bell? Why didn't he guess?"

"Why should he? It took us a day to figure out its meaning. And if he had only been able to begin his search before he was interrupted by our arrival—well, you see. He may not have even gone there yet."

"You're right, I suppose."

"Not 'suppose.' That's the way it was." Utter relief filled Leah's face. "Allison, I'm betting everything is going to be all right. Neal will meet with his contact tomorrow. Between them they'll decipher the message in the book. By tomorrow night we'll both be out of here on our way to Cairo. And, if you let me, I'd like to go home with you for a few months."

"Let you? I'd be delighted, and so would Mother and Father."

Leah's optimism and the change in conversation, with thoughts of home, were enough to offer Allison reason to hope. Even so, a spot in the back of her mind continued to leave its dark blotch of unease.

"Then is Neal coming here? To the hut?"

"No. I'm to meet him. It's safer that way. Someone might be watching for his arrival, but they don't expect to see me since they think I'm gone. They'll be off guard. And I'll wear a scarf to cover my hair when I leave. We won't take chances."

Leah knew more than she was able to tell Allison. It was understandable, but the unknown left Allison struggling against her own frustrations.

"How can you meet him? Is he in Aleppo?"

Leah hesitated, as if debating how much she could tell Allison. "No. There's a small hut out near the digs. We used it as a midway place to store pieces when we couldn't make it all the way into Jerablus. He'll leave a candle burning in the window if it's safe to enter."

"How do you expect to get there unseen? They may be watching the Mercedes."

"I won't be using that, but a vehicle we hid a quarter of a mile from here. Neal took care of that before we ever arrived for the club meeting. Even a mouse has several escape routes. And we, too, leave a second door open for escape, or a third, if we can."

"Can't Neal meet us in Cairo?" Allison pressed as her concerns grew.

She shook her head firmly. "His contact is here."

"You—you mean he doesn't know who his superior is?"

"Not until he meets him. Neither Neal nor I is considered high up. Our job is to collect information on the railway—rumors about what Germany may be up to. It doesn't sound like much, but when it's put together with the information Karl discovered, well—sometimes we strike gold."

Or murder, thought Allison. "And you, Neal, and the British agent found gold at the Baghdad Railway."

"That's about it." She stood, looking about at Allison's books and papers. "Now, all I need to do is gather red-herring information to take with me, just to play it safe. Would you mind terribly if I borrowed your books?"

"Go ahead—take my Bible, too, if you would like. Leah, let me go with you to meet Neal. I'd feel better about this. We both have revolvers."

Leah shook her head, her blond hair swaying. "I've put you in enough danger. And I'd answer to Neal's superior if I involved you too much. If he found out I was confiding in you, I'd be reprimanded, even removed. Remember, as far as they're concerned, there's no reason you should be trusted. For all we know, you may be the enemy."

Although uncalled for, Allison felt insulted. "Me? Why, I'm as loyal and British as his Majesty!"

Leah smiled. "You've proved it to me, but they wouldn't see it that way without thoroughly searching your past, as young as you are. So you see, this is something I must do alone. It was my choice to involve myself. No one twisted my arm. And I accepted this job because I believed in what I was doing." She smiled. "So don't worry. You still have several days left of the holiday; so you might as well stay and try to enjoy it. Now you should be able to. Neal wants it that way, too. He was furious you're involved."

It was like Neal to act like a big brother toward her as well as toward Leah, his blood sister. Allison loved him for it.

"Besides, only I can meet Neal."

"What if something happens, and you can't make it back by tomorrow?"

A faint shadow crossed Leah's face. "If I'm not back by then, if something delays me, I'll be in touch some other way, or Neal will contact you. We'll get you back to Cairo safely somehow."

"It's not my getting back that worries me. I can take care of myself, but you're going off alone."

"If anything looks suspicious, a signal to turn back has been arranged. Don't worry. I know what to do. It's my job." She smiled at Allison's frown. "Look." She opened the flap of her dress, showing a small leather holster with a revolver. "I've got this. I'm never without it. And I assure you, I can use it without hesitation when I must."

Allison remembered her own revolver and who had given it to her. "Have you ever heard of a Bret Holden?" she asked curiously.

"No, why?"

She sighed. "No reason, I guess. I was rather hoping, but..." She stopped. "He was a friend of David's. I guessed from what David said that this Holden could be in espionage work. David was to meet him here, but Bret hasn't shown up either. David seemed to think you and Neal knew him."

Leah considered. "Bret Holden..."

"Almost sounds like Brent Holman," said Allison easily, watching Leah. She wondered if she thought so only because she had found the German officer attractive and hoped he might actually be on their side.

"You don't suppose Colonel Holman was really your contact or Neal's?" Allison speculated. "And he didn't know you were hiding in my hut. So he went to Carchemish looking for you and Neal."

Leah stood staring at her. After what seemed to Allison a long silence, Leah let out a sigh. "I wonder. Good heavens, what if, like Major Reuter, Colonel Holman was one of us? We've crossed purposes! But at least I'll see Neal tonight. The information is safe. And we'll both get a surprise if, when we meet his superior, it turns out to be the colonel."

"It couldn't be," said Allison firmly, rebuking herself for the flicker of hope that arose from the darkness. "He was utterly ruthless.

Once he knew I was British and your cousin, what need was there to badger me? No one else was with us; so who did he need to impress with his harsh questioning?"

"Yes, you're probably right, but I'll keep that name in mind just the same and mention it to Neal tonight."

An hour or two after midnight, the desert winds began to sigh and whistle along the roofs of the darkened huts and stir through the date palms growing in front of the compound. Leah was dressed for survival in the desert heat, and she carried her kitbag, which she had carefully packed with Allison's books, Bible, and a sheaf of misleading papers.

Allison unbolted the back door and stepped out onto the porch, checking to make certain the way was clear. She wished the moon had set, but at least its light on the porch had narrowed as the moon moved up in the sky. The grounds with a fringe of palms appeared deserted. The only movement came from Allison as she looked about her for a moment, listening to the silence. Then, turning, she motioned to Leah that it was safe.

"You've left me no choice," whispered Allison. "I still feel strongly about the need to come with you."

Leah smiled, then unexpectedly reached over and gave Allison an embrace. "Don't worry so. Look for me soon. We'll become the cousins we should have been. For once in my life I feel like going to a grand dinner-ball in Cairo. You can loan me one of your fancy dresses and introduce me to one of your many admirers. I've grown extraordinarily weary of boots and canvas." Then she was gone, slipping away in the shadows with the wind.

Allison stood by the side of her hut looking after Leah, feeling alone and empty. She swallowed. Nothing stirred but the wind and sand.

The Lord bless you and watch, guard, and keep you, she prayed silently.

A minute later Allison turned away with a shiver, though the wind was hot and dry as she made her way back around the side of her hut. She felt unable to cast off the smothering depression that hounded her spirits, despite committing Leah to God.

The white moonlight slanted over Major Reuter's abandoned hut and turned the roof into silver. Below, the wooden walls stood draped in dark shadow. She could hear the distant, muffled mutter of dry lightning on the desert hills. She had not progressed far on the narrow incline between her hut and Major Reuter's when she heard another sound: the creak of a back door closing.

Allison checked, not daring to breathe. She turned and stared toward the abandoned hut. Had someone been in there and just gone out to follow Leah? Someone must have been nearby all this time while she talked with Leah in the darkness, and was now closing the door with extreme care. She heard the click of a door latch falling into place. It was a long time before she dared to move; but she stood in the hot night recalling with a prickling of her neck her cousin's confident words earlier that evening: *I've heard from Neal. Everything is going to be all right soon.*

Was Leah's confidence misplaced after all? Perhaps the murderer of the British agent had been waiting here all the time, as near as Major Reuter's hut, just waiting for Leah to leave.

Allison stood rigid with fear. She waited for footsteps on the porch, but if there were any, the wind covered the sound.

She was still standing there minutes later when the thin path of moonlight moved behind her hut. Her fingers on the gun in her pocket, she moved forward. When she reached the steps to her back porch and looked across at the major's porch, it was empty. Had she imagined that creak? It was possible. The wind did strange things at night in the desert, and she was already tense with fear.

Allison slipped inside her hut and quickly lifted the light switch. Everything was just as they had left it. She bolted her doors for the night and then sank with emotional exhaustion into the chair and tried to still her trembling. She dropped her face into her palms and prayed fervently.

Someone had been out there in the shadows, watching and listening. She was nearly certain of that. Just what did she know about the party of archaeology enthusiasts who had come up for the holiday?

There was the baroness, of course, but she would soon be returning to her social life in Cairo and Alexandria, and Allison couldn't imagine her trailing after Leah. Even though German born with some natural leaning toward the cause of her nation, Helga Kruger had spent most of the last ten years in Egypt. She was well known from one end of the country to the other, and deemed by the British governor-general as strictly loyal to the English cause. It seemed unlikely to Allison that Helga would be employed by the kaiser in subversive activities that would end up in murder.

Then there was her assistant, Professor Jemal Pasha, of Turkish descent. Of Jemal she knew very little except that she had mistakenly believed he was loyal to the baroness and perhaps infatuated with her as well. The look of malice that Allison had seen on his face at lunch had ended that notion. Why would Jemal Pasha have secret malice for the baroness? And why did he persist in serving her in Cairo and outwardly appearing so loyal to her? Perhaps the baroness and her money afforded Jemal the opportunity to pursue archaeology, something he may have been unable to do on his own.

For the remainder of the night, Allison turned restlessly on the bed, her brain traversing the same fearful questions over and over again without any satisfying answers. Then the sunlight warmed the window and announced another hot, suffocating day. Today the German colonel would arrive to corner her with questions she could not answer.

She turned over to go back to sleep, thinking that she wished she had kept her Bible, which saturated her mind with wonderful psalms on the Lord's sustaining presence. The Scriptures would bring her the confidence and strength she needed. It wasn't until the rising sun gave her a feeling of security that she fell asleep at last to dream of being home safe in British Egypt, with the good smells of breakfast cooking in the kitchen and the sound of the boiling teapot. Instead, Allison awoke with a start to a loud, urgent rapping on her door.

7

"ALLISON!" CAME HELGA KRUGER'S VOICE, followed by David's.

"Now look here, she has to be in there. Let's not frighten the poor girl out of her wits."

"Coming," cried Allison, stepping over her luggage and unbolting the lock. In a glare of sunlight, Helga, Sarah, and David stood below the steps looking relieved to see her.

"You had us frightened," cried Sarah. "We had begun to think there was some jinx on the three cousins—all related and all missing. You're all right?"

"Quite. Just overslept. I'm sorry. What time is it?"

"You've missed breakfast," said David wryly, "but not the Turkish inspector. He's arrived." David watched her response as if expecting concern. Allison smiled and pushed open the door wider.

"Of course. I suppose he'll be wanting to search about. I'll only be a few minutes to dress. Has Professor Jemal begun his lecture yet?"

"Yes," said Helga, looking past Allison into the hut. "Looks like you'll be late again."

"Oh, bother, but I won't miss much if you go on ahead and take notes, Sarah. Save me a seat again, will you?"

"Rex is already there waiting. He was more anxious about you than I was. Well, then, we'll see you at the lecture hut."

The baroness lingered. "After lunch we'll all be going on an expedition. Unfortunately the officials have ordered us to stay within ten miles of the grounds until the matters concerning Major Reuter and Miss Bristow are cleared up."

"Which means we can't drive out to the Hittite Digs," said Sarah, disappointed.

"A smaller site isn't far from here, and we'll all go together," said Helga. "I can't promise it to be much, but at least it's something, and everyone is so disappointed about missing the tour to Jerablus. I feel dreadful about it."

Twenty minutes later Allison stepped out into the hot but glorious morning and walked to the lecture where David was waiting outside the hut. He gestured her over to the side, away from the open window.

"The Turks are probing about the huts and asking all kinds of tough questions. I can't afford to stay and take the risk. So far the baroness hasn't mentioned I'm a Zionist, but she will. I'm leaving for Carchemish before the officials detain me. I waited for you last night but you didn't show up—are you still wanting to go?"

"Yes," she whispered quickly. "It's unlikely the officials will detain any of us for questioning until after we get back from the tour." She thought of Leah. By the time they returned in the late afternoon, she would be waiting. There would be no need for questioning David or anyone else, and Leah would have a satisfactory answer regarding Neal's whereabouts that would defuse the Turkish officials. "Can you wait until this afternoon?"

"All right, but it seems a waste of time. It's a long, hot, dusty walk, and there's nothing out at those old digs."

Allison laughed at his frown. "We're not walking; we're taking camels."

Lunch was a hurried meal, and immediately after it, some fifteen members of the club packed their bags with fruit, cheese, and canteens of coffee, tea, and water and strapped them on their backs. They then set off on the four-mile camel ride to the hills near Aleppo. Even General Blaine accompanied them, though he did joke lightly of seeing better hours aboard a ship in a storm than on a camel's back.

The abandoned site was that of a Roman-Syrian town, largely built of earlier materials. As Helga had warned, it was not much to boast of, and most of the club had toured it in the past. But those who hadn't explored the site made the best of it, and the baroness gave a small talk on the Roman period. Afterward they gathered to eat their fruit and cheese and enjoy the hot tea.

As the sun descended, General Blaine said, "By now the Turks have gone through our huts and decided who to arrest for planting the cobra on Major Reuter's lap. Shall we start back before we come across another of the creatures? Who can we blame this time?"

"Rex!" cried Sarah, dismayed.

But Jemal, his large eyes shadowed as he sat beneath a boulder in the shade, said, "He has a point, Mrs. Blaine. The officials are considering murder."

The club members were silent a moment as they looked at each other.

"Absurd," said Helga, breaking the silence. "Major Reuter was a perfect stranger. Who would want to harm him? Or Leah?"

"We're only assuming something unpleasant may have happened to Miss Bristow," said Jemal. "We must not upset Nurse Wescott, as they are cousins." He looked at Allison like a baleful hound. "I am most certain she will arrive before this holiday is over."

Allison was relieved when David stood. "This gloomy discourse has gone far enough. It's time to head back, don't you think, Allison?"

"Yes," she said quickly, replacing her canteen in her bag and standing.

Baroness Kruger was unsmiling, and her eyes cool. "If Miss Bristow does decide to show up after all, she'll have much to explain to me. Her thoughtless delays and Neal's have ruined my expedition. Next year I'll have a difficult time getting people to sign up."

"Now, Baroness," said Professor Blackstone, a Fellow at the Cairo Archaeological School with Jemal, "no one is holding you responsible for the decisions of the Turkish officials. Next season we'll all be lined up only too eager to try again. That's the way it is with archaeology enthusiasts. No amount of rain will dampen our spirits."

"Or sandstorms," quipped General Blaine.

"You're right, General," said Blackstone. "The sky is an ugly color. I saw it like that once on expedition in Khartoum, and it spelt more trouble than a reptile hiding in the rocks. I say we head back as soon as possible."

General Blaine took out his pipe to light as he looked at the distant horizon. "I can think of better things to do with the rest of this holiday than getting caught in a sandstorm. What do you say, Sarah? I'm all for returning to the huts, then loading up and heading back to Cairo."

Sarah looked glum as she finished the last of her tea in the small canteen, tossed the bitter dregs and sighed. "I suppose so. If the baroness is certain we won't be allowed out at Carchemish, I don't see any reason to stay on. But will the officials let us leave?"

"I don't see why not," said Baroness Kruger wearily.

General Blaine leaned toward his wife. "A good thing I'm chums with the British consul in Aleppo. Henry will receive us with British tea instead of these Turkish bitters." He turned and looked at Allison. "What of you, my dear? Coming with us?"

She hoped her alarm didn't show. She couldn't go back yet. Not until she knew about Leah and Neal. "I'm not ready to go home yet, Rex. I'll finish out the holiday and start home on Friday. I'll feel much better about things when I learn more about my cousins. But there's nothing keeping you and Sarah here, if you would like to spoil yourself at the British residency."

"Oh, we wouldn't think of leaving without you," said Sarah. "It wouldn't be fair. If you leave Friday, how will you get back to Cairo?"

"I'll see her to the train," said David.

"Yes, do go on if you wish. I wouldn't want poor General Blaine to suffer too much by roughing it in the huts," she teased.

"My dear Allison," he groaned, "after riding that camel, there's no way I can suffer more than I already have." He picked up Sarah's bag, pausing to look warily in the direction of the horizon. "We had better get going, even though I don't think it will arrive any time soon. What do you think, David?"

"I wouldn't know, sir, since I've never been in a sandstorm. This is my first expedition to Arabia."

"It looks as if something foreboding is on the way," agreed Helga.

"Yes," said General Blaine, "one death in four days is enough, I would think. Coming, Sarah? Allison?"

"He's quite right," said Professor Blackstone. "If we stay here, we'll be buried up to our earlobes in blowing sand."

"They'll be digging us up as a 'find' in a hundred years or so," taunted General Blaine. "I can see the headlines now: 'Missing link found in Arabia.'"

Allison and David laughed, but neither Helga nor Jemal appreciated his wry humor and walked away.

"Keep it up, Rex, and I shall never gain that invitation in Cairo," bemoaned Sarah.

Ten minutes later they were all on the camels and swaying in rhythm as they followed single file across the sand in the direction of the huts. Jemal and Blackstone rode in the lead with two male students from the Cairo Archaeological School. Allison rode with David. They were rounding a small sand dune when Professor Jemal stopped his camel and said something to Blackstone. Allison saw Blackstone climb down from his camel and hurry in the direction of the dune.

"Now what, I wonder?" complained David. "Don't tell me they've spotted another ruin to trudge through? If they have, Allison, I think we should keep going."

Allison made no response and stared ahead, uneasily. Jemal had followed Blackstone, and they both disappeared behind the boulders and dunes.

Helga's voice could be heard. "They've found something."

"A Bedouin keeping goats perhaps," speculated General Blaine, as he lounged against the baggage on the camel's back and puffed his pipe. A curl of gray smoke spiraled upward and was lost in the rising wind.

Blackstone came running back, cupping his hands to his mouth and calling something unintelligble to the others. He pointed toward the dune.

"Something is wrong," whispered Allison.

"Stay here. I'll see." David hastily climbed down from the camel and ran ahead.

The others followed out of curiosity, except for Allison. A premonition of disaster sickened her stomach.

But it's the wrong direction, she kept thinking. *Carchemish is north.*

It was only when she heard Sarah cry out that she forced herself to dismount the kneeling camel and follow them. As she ran, her high-laced boots scuffed in the sand.

Sarah was saying to General Blaine in a nervous voice, "But it can't be—not another accident so soon."

Allison rushed up, stopped, and took one look at the sprawled figure that lay partially covered with white sand beneath the dune. Her heart constricted. It was Leah.

She heard Baroness Kruger warning her not to look, and David caught her arm. But Allison shook herself free, pushing past them. She stumbled forward and dropped to her knees beside the twisted body of her cousin. Leah lay on her stomach, her arms stretched out as though she had been flying, her hands in claws on the hot sand. Allison stared down at her. A little dried bloodstain was on the side of her head where she had fallen, and her soft golden hair was ruffling in the wind as the sand gently covered her.

Allison reached out and touched her. Tears stung Allison's eyes. An overwhelming sense of loss, anger, even guilt at having let her come alone, swallowed her heart. She clenched her teeth. Murdered. Like the other British agent posing as Karl Reuter. No one would ever convince her Leah's death was an accident.

She became aware of David again, his hand on her arm lifting her up. Sarah was whimpering, as she stood with General Blaine, his arm around her. "There, there, my dear, it's over. There's nothing to be done about it."

Baroness Kruger was saying: "Come away, Allison. She's dead."

Allison stood up, dazed. She turned and looked at each one of them and saw blurred faces.

She looked back down at Leah. She had seen all she wanted to see in those first few minutes and had verified her suspicions when she had reached out to lay her hand on a pocket of Leah's dress. The revolver was gone. If it had been an accident, the gun would still be there. And where was the kitbag bearing Allison's books and Bible?

That also meant Woolly's book on the Hittites was gone. Had she expected anything else? She located the bag and saw it was empty.

The wind pulled at it forlornly, as though it had sucked everything away. The wind had also blown away any sign of footprints. As they carried Leah away to the enclosure, Allison looked a little past the dune and saw the motorcar, the one Leah had said was stored nearby.

It wasn't until this moment that Allison understood. This wasn't the location Leah had gone to expecting to meet Neal. The hut, Leah had said, was between Jerablus and the Carchemish Digs. And that was north, toward the Euphrates and Baghdad.

Back at the huts a thorough examination was conducted by the Turkish doctor to eliminate any possibility of foul play. He announced nothing unusual had been found. Miss Bristow had lost her way in the wilderness stretch of ninety miles from Aleppo to Jerablus, had motorcar trouble, had gotten out to walk, and had met with an accident.

"Nonsense," said Helga Kruger when they all met for supper in the dining room that evening. "Leah was no fool. She knew this desert."

Allison noted Helga's response with surprise. Somehow she had expected the baroness to agree with the consensus.

"What else could it have been?" asked Jemal.

Helga stood, unsmiling. "I don't know," she said, turning and walking out. The others were left to muse in uneasy silence.

Allison had to leave and get away from the conversation about Leah and how she might have died.

"Where are you going, Allison?" David caught up with her. They walked toward the huts. One look at her empty room, filled with memories and secrets, brought a tight feeling to her throat.

"I'm going to Jerablus," she stated, "to the expedition hut where Leah and Neal lived. I won't be satisfied until I see things as they are. And maybe a message from Neal will be there."

"You don't believe Leah's death was an accident, do you?" he asked quietly.

She searched his eyes and saw the honest gravity. "No," she breathed, "I think she was murdered."

He frowned. "And I think it's ruddy time I took you back home to Port Said."

She looked at him, searching. "You think she was murdered?"

"Only a fool would see it otherwise," he said roughly, glancing back toward the dining hall. "I disagreed with that Turkish doctor and told him I did. We had quite a row over it until the baroness intervened."

"She's suspicious, too."

"Yes, she's a clever woman, but I wouldn't trust her. I wouldn't trust anyone in this club, Allison. And I don't like your being here. No one's forgetting that Leah and Neal were your cousins."

Were. The past tense of his remark brought a tear to Allison's eyes. Neal could be safe. But how much should she tell David?

"I can't return to Cairo yet," she insisted quietly. "If I did, well, I'd feel as if I'd betrayed Leah."

"Look. When are you going to tell me what you really know?"

"Soon, but not yet. Are you willing to take me to Jerablus? You said you had an interest there yourself. I suppose you haven't found your friend here, like you had hoped?"

"Bret Holden? No." He looked worried. "He may be at the Carchemish Digs or somewhere in the vicinity of the Baghdad Railway. I'm ready to leave when you are, but we had better do it now before they see us. The officials will want to keep us all here to continue their questioning."

"I'll get my things and meet you by the acacia trees. We'll take Leah's Mercedes. She left me the keys."

"Be there in ten minutes," he warned.

8

THE HUT WAS WRAPPED IN SILENCE when Allison entered. Memories reached out to grab her, as Leah seemed to fill the room with her presence.

"No, Leah is dead. She didn't know the Lord. I failed her," Allison castigated herself.

She stood in the grip of loss, but her feelings of spiritual failure went even deeper, to cut across her soul. Whether her sense of guilt was from God or her own emotions at the moment didn't matter, for it hurt too deeply to ignore.

It's my fault. She bit her trembling lip. *I should have tried harder to help her. How many times did I pray for Leah? Not enough, never enough. I should have spoken more plainly about who Jesus is, and why he came. But I didn't—and even when I had the opportunity, when she asked me about my life, I drew back, almost afraid to tell her she needed him for fear she would think I was preaching at her. Oh that I had! I've been willing to work with Aunt Lydia on the Mercy, to give myself to the fellahin, but what have I done for my own family? Now it's too late for Leah. Forever too late.*

Tears streamed down her face. The wind was rising and rattling the window and she heard the familiar sound of sand scattering across the roof. She imagined Leah's body, stiff and cold in the medical hut.

"Oh, Lord, help me!" She buried her face in her hands and sank to the rumpled bed.

After a minute she was able to control herself with considerable effort. Wiping her eyes and finding a handkerchief to blow her nose, she swallowed hard and went to the small bureau. David would be waiting, and it was risky to keep him there by the motorcar. One of the Turkish inspectors might see him and stop him. She must hurry.

Opening the drawers, she began to pack her things haphazardly, then stopped. She stood still, staring down at her drawer. Someone had been searching through her clothing.

At first annoyed, she thought of the officials. It was rather silly of them to scatter her undergarments about so carelessly. They could at least have been gentlemen enough to leave them alone.

Then an unpleasant thought slithered across her mind. Was it the officials, or was there some other, less pleasant, explanation? But who would have searched, and why?

Her heart beat faster. Leah had left last night. And they had found her this afternoon. How long had she been dead? The doctor had suggested the accident had taken place this morning. Then someone had had the opportunity to search Allison's hut before they had ridden the camels to the Roman site. She tried to remember what she had done that morning.

She had overslept and was awakened by Sarah's banging on the door. David had been with her and Helga Kruger. Helga had announced the inspectors were coming. Then what? Allison had gone on to Jemal's lecture, then a brief lunch and the ride to the digs where they had found Leah's body. Who would have had time to search her hut? And why?

A hopeful yet frightening thought came to mind. *What if the murderer hadn't found the book with Leah? What if she had only taken the decoy papers? "The red herring," as Leah had called them?*

Was it possible Leah had been more suspicious than she had let on? Had she taken the book she had found in Major Reuter's hut?

Allison realized she had never seen it, not even when Leah packed the kitbag to leave for her secret meeting with Neal—or the person pretending to be Neal. The enemy had killed her. But he had not found what he was looking for.

Then, thought Allison with a tingle, *someone came back here to look for it.*

The question was, did he find it? She searched the hut thoroughly, thinking Leah may have left her something, but Allison found nothing. It could mean the enemy had found the book or Leah hadn't hidden it in the hut. Since there was little opportunity to place it elsewhere, Allison dismally decided the enemy had found it.

A rap on the outer wall facing the front of the compound made her jump. David's voice sounded through the thin wooden wall, "Allison!"

"Coming!"

The stars gleamed in brilliant silver when, with her bag packed and carrying her kitbag, Allison hurried across the grounds past the wooden buildings that lay scattered like dark mounds to the open-top car. David slid anxiously behind the wheel. "Where are the keys?"

She handed them to him. Not a word more was spoken as the engine started and they made a half-circle, sending up a shower of gritty sand. David turned on to the narrow dirt road built for camels, donkeys, and wagons. Soon they were driving north toward Jerablus, ninety miles ahead.

Despite the earlier warnings about bad weather, the night was awe-inspiring. Relinquishing her grief and fears to the warm Arabian wind, Allison leaned back against the seat beside David, her eyes on the heavenly wash of stars that spilled across the desert sky with holy abandon. She gathered courage from the one who held all in his hand, from a tiny sparrow to the limitless universe. And, yes, even Leah's inopportune death.

This one is my Father, she consoled herself. *What have I to fear? No matter what may happen to me, nothing in all this world or in the spiritual realm can bring me to ruin. While danger and turmoil are all about me, it's also true a heavenly hedge surrounds, and nothing can get through to harm me unless my Father allows it. And if he does, I can still trust him with it; he will in the end see that it all worked for my eternal good.*

David turned his head and glanced at her. "Are you all right? About Leah I mean."

"Not yet. But I'll make it."

"It was a rotten thing to happen. She was with you all the time, wasn't she? In the hut."

She looked at his profile, strong in the starlight. The wind was tossing his chestnut, wavy hair beneath his hat. "Yes. How did you know?"

He shrugged his heavy shoulders. "I figured it out easily enough. I think some of the others knew, too. The baroness for one. And maybe Jemal."

Allison wondered. Sometimes she had suspected Helga knew.

They drove in silence for a few minutes, then David said lightly, "Like Moses in the wilderness, I hope you know the direction we're supposed to be headed. This wilderness all looks the same to me, and in the night it might as well be no man's land. At least we have a full tank. I checked. She had spare petrol tins in the back. I brought some food and canteens of water, too. Just in case."

"I drove this route last year," said Allison. "I have a map if we need it and a torch." Her voice carried on the wind, and she added with more cheerfulness than she felt, "Follow that star."

The star gave way to a dawn sky as the car bumped and jostled along the sandy road. "Ahead, the road gets worse," said Allison. "You'll need to slow down."

"Oh, wonderful," complained David good-naturedly. "Now you tell me. My dear girl, we are already creeping. I should have brought my motorbike."

"We usually use camels and donkeys." She smiled.

Streaks of flaring lavender, gold, red, and green turned the expanse into the breathtaking beauty of a sterile flower garden. It was this that she loved about the Arabian desert. Even though the wilderness had the hostile potential to kill those who were unprepared for its rigors, its beauty overwhelmed her.

Where fog and clouds held London skies to periods of gloom, the desert was wide awake, throbbing with color and glory. Allison removed her scarf and let her long, flame-colored hair ripple like a banner of shining silk. Her green eyes sparkled beneath dark lashes, but the tension of the past days, the death of Leah, and the dreadful thought of what may lie before them, showed in pale smudges of shadow beneath her eyes.

She yawned and reached below to the floorboard for one of several canteens of water. As the yet-cool water came to her tongue, she froze, refusing to swallow. Suddenly the dawn's garden of color and beauty was invaded by the hideous face of the serpent of evil. She leaned over, gripping the door, and managed to spit out the mouthful. The horrid, bitter taste clung to her tongue and smarted her eyes.

"What is it?" cried David as Allison choked. He brought the car to a rattling halt.

"The...water...tastes like it's been poisoned."

"Poisoned!" He grabbed the canteen and whiffed it, wetting his finger and touching it to his tongue. "You're right."

The wind buffeted the car's side and gave a powerful tug, as if to turn it over. The silence and the great expanse of land uninhabited except for bands of Bedouins, vipers, and wind-spiders, imprisoned them.

"I filled them myself," he said with a note of anger. He gathered the others from the floorboard to sample them. Then he frowned a moment later as he looked at her. "They've all been tampered with."

"But who could have done it? And why?" breathed Allison. She was not a known agent. Nor did she have any strategic information.

"The reason seems clear to me," grumbled David. "Someone is trying to frighten you or both of us. There was no chance we would drink this stuff once we tasted it. What I want to know is how it was managed when I filled them myself and brought them to the car. They were never out of my sight."

"Are you certain of it?"

"As certain as I can be. I waited to fill them until after dark. And I made sure no one was around."

"Someone was," said Allison and looked at him.

His brown eyes, sparkling with anger, turned reflective. "All right, I want to know what's going on with you. So far I think I've been pretty patient, sneaking about in the dead of night, helping you slip away unseen. From what? From whom? Leah is dead. Neal is missing. And now this!"

Allison was haunted by her own thoughts and didn't respond. David was right; someone had known Leah was hiding in her hut all along, someone—undoubtedly the one who had murdered Karl Reuter—had out-guessed her plan to drive to the expedition hut at Jerablus. Someone didn't want her to search Neal and Leah's house and had wanted to frighten her to keep her away.

"We'll need to turn back," said David, frowning again. "We can't risk going on without a water supply."

Allison felt the back of her neck prickle. She glanced at David, studying the square jawline.

No, she thought breathlessly, *the enemy could not be David. I'll stake my life on it.*

She realized with an uncomfortable start that she had already done so. They were alone in the Arabian desert. As David had admitted, it would have been impossible for anyone to poison the canteen's water without his awareness. Then how? And who? Or rather, was the question why? Did his political aspirations to establish a Jewish homeland cause him to look to the German Empire for their fulfillment? Was it the kaiser and not England that he felt offered the best hope?

Allison remembered reading something in the Cairo paper recently. It had only been a paragraph, but it had caught her attention because her own sympathies were with Jerusalem. The paper had said that within Russia and Germany, secret overtures were being made to gain Jewish support should war break out. In return, vague promises had been made about some sort of Jewish independence in Palestine. As yet, as far as she knew, no such comments had been forthcoming from either England or America.

She watched David's strong hands on the wheel, the firm grip that spoke of a personality that was determined on its course, wherever it led. In some sense, she couldn't blame him. If she were Jewish, she too would fight any political battle to establish a state of their own in the land that God had promised to Abraham, Isaac, and Jacob.

"I won't go back," she said quietly but evenly. "I owe this to two people I cared about deeply."

"You might end up like Leah." His eyes were masked. "We both might. Say, now! You don't think I did this?" He threw the canteen down angrily.

Allison remained silent and looked at him. He glowered. "A fine thanks I get for befriending you." He vigorously turned the key to start the motor.

"I didn't accuse you. Don't be silly. If you were the enemy, it's too late anyway, isn't it?"

"What do you mean?"

"I mean, you could put a gun to my head this moment, and no one would hear the shot."

He muttered something and leaned back in the seat, shutting his eyes. "To think I'm falling in love with you and you think I'd—"

"Please don't say that," she whispered.

"Don't say what?" he grumbled, starting the motor again.

"What you just said—about falling for me."

He looked at her, frustrated. "Would it be so unthinkable, so terrible? I know I'm Jewish, but—"

"It isn't that, and you know it. You know one of the reasons."

"Ah, yes, you are—shall I say the forbidden word? A Christian. And I'm—"

She swiftly placed a hand on his arm, her eyes pleading. "Not now, David. Please. Let's go on. There's a Bedouin well ahead."

"And there's the missionary Wade Findlay. Yes, I know."

They drove on in silence.

"Do you know where this oasis well is?"

She relaxed when he changed the subject but felt grieved he could be falling for her. *He didn't mean it,* she thought. It was all this death and tension. It made some people behave more emotionally than they would otherwise. The idea of death quickened the soul to grab for a relationship, even if it wasn't real. She must stay clear of involvement and keep a cool head.

In a weak moment she looked at him, saw his hair ruffling under the hat, and felt a tenderness she could not explain and wanted to avoid. "The well's not far ahead. We stopped there last year. We'll be there by noon."

Getting water was not the frightening issue. It was the vulnerability she felt. Someone had poisoned the canteens beneath David's watchful care.

"Well," said David wearily, "I see you're still wishing to keep me in the dark. About what's going on, I mean." He looked over at her. "At least we have the bag of oranges."

Allison watched the sunrise as it lit up the distant hills. By midmorning the heat covered everything, and the sky faded to a monotonous blue.

It was after the sun was center-sky and had begun its descent that they reached the oasis, later than Allison had thought. They gazed on a desert heaven, green, with shade, cool well water, and date palms. The dates could be eaten freely, but the law of the desert forbid any to be carried away. A Bedouin shepherdess in black kept a flock of rangy goats and ignored Allison and David as if they were a mirage. Flies buzzed. The temperature climbed.

While David checked the engine and added the spare tins of petrol, she thought, *There isn't a vicious bone in his body. There had to have been a moment when he wasn't watching those canteens, even if he denies it. It had to be someone in the club.*

She watched as he replaced the fuel tank cap and walked back toward her, wiping his hands on a rag. Then, whistling, he opened his kitbag and produced *aysh* stuffed with meat and olives. "Manna in the desert," he stated with a grin and sniffed it. "As long as it hasn't spoilt. Here, have some. No poison."

"Where in the world did you get these?" asked Allison with a brief smile.

"The kitchen—at the dining room. I bribed the Turkish guard."

"You bribed a guard?" she repeated, surprised it was possible. "How did you do that? They were all ordered to keep everyone under surveillance."

"Yes, so they were." Then he paused. "So that was it. That's how it happened." He looked at her triumphantly. "I left the canteens for a short time. Time enough for someone to tamper with them."

Allison felt a wave of relief as her eyes sought his, but the relief was short lived. Even if it hadn't been David, someone else had anticipated their plans.

Allison helped herself to one of the sandwiches while David tried his hand at climbing the tree to collect dates. He returned, boasting, "If you marry me, you'll never be in want." He handed her a cluster.

She smiled and bit into one. They were sweet and moist, some of the best she had ever tasted.

Soon they were back in the motorcar and on their way again. The afternoon shadows were lengthening as they bumped along the narrow road collecting heat and dust. Allison, tense with uncertainty as she thought of Jerablus and what might wait there, shielded her eyes against the white-hot glare. She scanned the endless stretch of burning desert that filled the world as far as she could see. Having lived for ten years in Cairo, and before that, India, she was well aware of the deadly toll of the heat. The starkness of the desert smothered her from all sides.

She scooped the canteen from the seat beside her and swallowed a trickle of the well water. It eased her dry throat. Holding her sun hat in place with one hand, she turned her head to glance toward the camel-like hills.

Allison's worst fears, like a mirage in the rippling heat waves of the desert, sprang up when David threw on the brakes and brought the motorcar to a halt. The blazing sun relentlessly beat down on them. Flies emerged from nowhere and hummed like the sixth plague of Egypt.

"What is it?" she breathed, tensely. One look at his expression alerted her.

He gestured in the direction of some sand dunes shifting in the wind like slithering reptiles. "We have company."

Allison squinted against the glare, her heart coming to her throat.

"A patrol of Turkish cavalrymen," said David. "Just our luck."

"They've spotted us," whispered Allison. "Shall we try to outrun them?"

"On this road? They're riding Arabians. They would overtake us. It's too late; here they come."

Allison opened her handbag and pulled out Leah's papers. "We have papers granting entry to Jerablus. They shouldn't bother us."

"Unless they know about what happened back at the club."

Allison remembered something the baroness had said the day after they found Major Reuter dead. Colonel Holman had ridden to the German headquarters near Baghdad. Had he alerted them to be on the lookout?

England and the Ottoman Empire, with its throne of power centered in Constantinople, were on friendly terms, she reminded herself. And England was making overtures to strengthen the friendship with the ruling Turks. They appeared to accept the olive branch with confidence.

The Arab tribes in Arabia and the Hejaz were another matter. The English traveled unmolested throughout Arabia ignored by the tribal chieftains—except, as Allison knew, for some of the wilder Bedouin tribes who now and then attacked from the desert like ghostly phantoms. But for the most part the Arabs disliked the Turks even more than they did the British, although they were bound together by the Moslem religion.

Egypt, on the other hand, looked on the British in Cairo as an "occupying force." England, in the face of war, worried about internal rioting, spying for the enemy, and an outright revolt if the Turkish government in Constantinople sided with Germany and called on the Arabs and Egyptians to revolt. A *jehad* was always feared by the British. Friendship with Turkey was critical.

No one in Arabia expected to be shot at by the Turkish cavalry on patrol, but few English, including Allison, underestimated the far-reaching effect of the winds of war blowing across the troubled face of Europe. Now that there was talk of Germany invading Belgium, it was nearly inevitable that tensions should also heat to the boiling point in Arabia where Berlin was building the great railway into Baghdad and down south across the desert.

Allison watched the cavalrymen riding across the blowing white dunes and nearing the parked motorcar. As they approached, their formidable figures in the dark brown military uniforms with cone-shaped cloth hats almost seemed like a mirage because of the rising ripple of heat waves. The sunlight reflecting on their weapons soon dispelled that vain hope. They carried not only German carbines but the traditional curved blade of the Turks called a *scimitar.*

The Turkish captain, hard-faced, browned deeply by the sun, and wearing a short Moslem beard and Turkish mustache, lifted an abrupt hand to halt his half-dozen soldiers behind him. His sharp black eyes, like glowing pieces of coal, searched relentlessly as they fixed first on David, then swerved to scrutinize Allison, whose hair had loosened from the chignon she had put it into several hours ago. She felt a shiver run along her arms despite the broiling heat and the sweat that ran down her rib cage. Her worst anxiety had not imagined the flash of open dislike she saw when he noticed the red emblem on her nurse's uniform.

The medical cross sewn on the front of her now soiled dress also spoke of her dedication to a faith considered a tenet of the enemy since before the time of the Crusades. It had been a mistake to wear her nurse's uniform, she now realized. She had thought it would grant them more leeway should they be stopped for questioning. She had been wrong.

"Your nationality?" he barked at Allison.

"British, sir. We're with the Cairo Archaeological Club on our way to visit the home of my cousins at Jerablus. You'll be acquainted with their expedition house. Here—these papers will explain everything."

A soldier took them from Allison and handed them to the captain. He read them carefully. "Yes, we're acquainted with the people from the British Museum at Carchemish. What are you doing here? Are you an archaeologist?"

"We're staying near Aleppo with the club while we're on holiday."

He handed the papers back and turned to David. "Your papers."

David reached a tanned hand under his tunic.

"Slowly!" warned the captain.

"Why would a doctor who works to save lives shoot the Sultan's trooper?" With a bored smile, David handed him a folder. "You'll find it all in order, Captain."

Doctor? Allison wondered where David had managed to get such papers but didn't dare show her relief. The captain carefully studied the contents. "You're aware, Doctor McGregor, of a German officer's death back at the huts?"

Allison didn't move. She could feel the sweat stand out on her forehead. Then Colonel Holman had alerted the officials.

"My orders are to detain anyone of a suspicious nature," said the Turkish captain. "You will return with me to Jerablus."

"Now wait a minute—" began David.

The Turk jerked a hand for silence and looked abruptly at Allison. "You are a nurse?"

"Yes," she stated quietly.

"What hospital in Cairo?"

"Not a hospital. A ship."

"Ship?"

"The *Mercy*. We travel the Nile, attending the *fellahin*," she said of the Egyptian peasant farmers.

"The *Mercy*."

"It is owned privately."

"By whom?"

She hesitated. It belonged to the British foreign mission in London, a certain death knell to her acceptance by this Moslem Turk. "My aunt is in charge," she said truthfully but cautiously. "Nurse Lydia Wescott. I work as her assistant. She's helped the Egyptian people for thirty years."

The captain shifted his weight, and the leather saddle creaked. The droning flies pestered horse and human without respect for either. The captain's leathery face dotted with sweat showed nothing, and Allison imagined herself shrinking beneath that withering stare. Clearly, he was not impressed with her credentials. Another meddling Christian using medicine to proselytize; so his gaze told her.

"What are you doing here?" he demanded again.

"I've already explained, Captain."

"You are from the Nile, from working with the Egyptian *fellahin*. What are you doing here?"

"Here" was the Arabian desert, perhaps a river of sorts, but one of perpetual sand and, as he said, far from the Nile. He spoke in a tone that attempted to let her know she was not wanted, errands of medical "mercy" or not.

"I'm on leave," she stated. "As I've already informed you, sir, I'm a member of the club near Aleppo that belongs to Baroness Helga Kruger and Professor Jemal Pasha. We've come to the Carchemish Digs to the private home of my cousin Neal Bristow. The digs," said Allison quietly but firmly, "are under British jurisdiction."

Reminding him that the Turks had no jurisdiction there did nothing to make him relent. The heat was nearly unbearable when they were denied the wind of driving. She brushed away the horde of flies. Her cotton dress stuck to her.

"And these other members of the club—where are they?" came his deliberately accusing voice.

"A few kilometers from Aleppo," interjected David, apparently growing irritated with his badgering. "What is this, Captain? Harassment? As Miss Wescott told you, we're a party of private citizens out for a week of holiday, enjoying our interest in archaeology."

"Captain," said Allison calmly, "I see no reason for you to detain us. The papers representing the museum are all in order. The British consul has arranged with local governmental authorities at Baghdad to allow hospitality to the club from Cairo. One of your own, Baroness Kruger, has arranged these matters beforehand."

"You are right, Nurse Wescott. But that was before Major Karl Reuter was murdered."

"Murdered!" scoffed David. "Your own Turkish doctor declared it an accident. And I totally agree. Are you not jumping to conclusions? After all, it was a German officer who got bitten by the cobra, not a soldier of the Ottoman Empire. England and Turkey are allies, are we not?"

Allison held her breath, hoping David's words had won over the captain.

"Word from my superiors at Baghdad supersedes your personal wishes for holiday," he said bluntly. "I am not to allow any strangers into Jerablus. I must detain you for further questioning."

"Whatever for? Our papers are in order!" said Allison.

"I have no question over your papers," he conceded.

"Then why are we being held?" demanded David. "It's not our fault if some ruddy German officer gets himself bitten by a snake.

You heard Miss Wescott. Your sultan has granted permission to the British Museum to access the area around Carchemish. If we're not allowed into Jerablus, we can join T. E. Lawrence and Woolly at the site."

"The English missionary must turn back."

Missionary. So that was how he wished to label her. It was a concern that at the best of times anti-Christian sentiment could lead to violence in the Moslem provinces.

Brushing aside any further protests, he shouted orders to two of his Turkish soldiers, who dismounted and came to either side of the motorcar, opening the doors. They gestured for David and Allison to get out.

David was arguing, refusing to leave the motorcar, as the captain ordered his soldiers to remove him from behind the wheel.

"What do you expect us to do, hitch a camel ride back to Aleppo?" snapped David.

The captain shouted a curt order to the soldier, who swiftly raised the butt of his carbine and viciously struck the side of David's head, knocking him back against the seat.

Allison gave a cry as the soldier grabbed David by the shirt front and removed him from behind the wheel. David, only half conscious, tried to reach for his revolver, but the soldier struck again and threw him into the hot sand. Then the soldier slid in behind the wheel.

Another soldier latched hold of Allison, holding her to the seat. "Stay put. Orders."

She looked frantically behind her and saw David stretched out unconscious on the blistering sand.

"You can't leave him there," cried Allison. "He'll die from the heat! I'm a nurse. Please let me help—"

The soldier who gripped her arm suddenly called out to his captain: "Up on the dunes. Bedouins. They are armed. A German soldier is with them."

Allison looked across the sand to where a group of Arabian horsemen had appeared. She saw the German soldier shake hands with the five Bedouins, their robes blowing in the wind. Then he turned his horse to ride toward them.

She swallowed, her throat dry, and flicked away the flies as the hot, dry wind whipped a strand of her hair across her eyes. The uniform with its Iron Cross was familiar. The German carried a revolver in a shoulder holster, a saber in a sheath, and a rifle. Allison cautiously took in the polished, knee-length black boots, the cool and arrogant manner in which he sat erect on the blooded horse. There was no mistake. Colonel Holman.

His blue-black eyes swept the scene and appeared to miss nothing, centering on David sprawled in the sand. Then he looked at Allison and held her gaze.

She forced herself to look unresponsive, though her heart thudded. Was there any hope he was Bret Holden? She tore her eyes away from his gaze, doing her best to appear outwardly poised and unafraid. In reality, her knees trembled. The Turkish soldier continued to grip her arm so tightly she couldn't help but flinch.

"Your manners, soldier! Are you afraid the lovely English spy will overwhelm you with brute strength and run away? Take your hand from her. I expect the soldiers of the Ottoman Empire to behave as gallantly as the valorous Germans," Colonel Holman stated flatly.

The soldier drew a few steps back from the car door and stood rigid, glancing at his captain.

With relief, Allison looked at the colonel, but he had turned in the saddle to face the Turkish captain. The captain looked furious over having his soldier openly rebuked by a foreign officer.

Colonel Holman appeared utterly cool. "Trouble, Captain?"

"Who asks?" came the too brief reply.

Colonel Holman scanned him with bored dismissal, reaching into his jacket and producing an identity card. He handed it to the captain abruptly, his impatience showing. "Colonel Holman from German intelligence, Constantinople. I've arrived recently to command the Baghdad security police."

The Turkish captain was suddenly uncomfortable and saluted, handing back the papers. "Yes, Colonel, we received your orders to detain all strangers. I am Captain Mustafa from Beersheba, sent to Jerablus to deliver a letter to the commanding officer. I was on my way back to Beersheba when Major Reuter was killed. My new orders were to remain here on patrol duty."

"I assume these are under questioning?"

"Yes, Colonel."

"Good. Is all in order?"

Captain Mustafa shifted nervously in the saddle. "Yes, Colonel. All in order."

Allison's gaze crossed with Colonel Holman's. He was watching her. His eyes drifted to the red cross on her uniform. He took her in, expressionless. Allison again turned away her head, and in calm dignity, or so she hoped, fanned herself.

"I am to meet your commanding officer in Jerablus," said Colonel Holman.

Captain Mustafa gave him a sharp, startled look. "Jerablus? You will meet Major Kameel in Baghdad!"

"I have not come to meet your major. I do not have time to waste on meetings with low rank! The news I bring is for a private audience with your general."

"The general, sir, is in Gaza. He will not arrive until next week."

"Next week? Is that any way to treat the chief intelligence agent of General Kress von Kressenstein? I have arrived from

Constantinople with crucial information."

"I am sorry, Colonel. I can do nothing until the general arrives next week."

"Such ineptitude, Captain, is deemed unacceptable to the German military."

The Turkish captain swallowed, but his black eyes were hard and bitter. "Yes, Colonel. Will you have us escort you into Aleppo?"

"It is not necessary. I know this desert, Captain, as well as any Turk—or Bedouin. I will not return to Aleppo tonight but Jerablus. The food and wind are more to my liking."

"Yes, Colonel," he said through gritted teeth and saluted energetically.

Colonel Holman halfheartedly returned the salute, as though it were a waste, and then gestured with a smartly gloved hand toward Allison.

She had been watching the display with cautious curiosity. He was full of conceit, or was it an act? She stiffened when she heard him say in a lower voice, "The English *Fräulein,* see she is sent to my quarters at Jerablus tonight."

Captain Mustafa's face flinched with disgust. "She is British. A missionary. She claims to come from Cairo."

"Yes," he said, "I am aware."

"What of him?" Mustafa gestured toward David.

"Arrest him," said Colonel Holman.

Arrest David. She couldn't allow them to take him away. In desperation, Allison opened the car door and stepped out, the sand burning beneath the soles of her shoes. The soldier guarding her glanced at her sharply but made no move.

"Please, Colonel Holman, can't you see he is hurt? Are you all beasts that you allow him to lie there on the burning sand? What harm can he do you? You, who have soldiers and weapons everywhere. Do you fear an unarmed, injured man?"

"The woman is insolent," said Captain Mustafa.

"You are quick to bestow your skills of mercy, *Fräulein.* Is it because your poor, unarmed, injured Zionist is of special concern to you?" Colonel Holman said derisively.

Her eyes swerved to his dark gaze. Zionist. He knew. And it meant the end for David. At once she saw a glitter of hate spring into the Turk's eyes.

"Zionist?" breathed Captain Mustafa. "He told me he was a doctor! McGregor is his name. I saw his papers."

"His papers are forged," said Colonel Holman tonelessly. "You have much to learn from German intelligence, Captain."

Allison's energy drained from her, leaving her fraught with disappointment. If he would alert the Turkish officer that David was Jewish, betraying him, then he was not Bret Holden. Her gaze turned icy as she looked at him.

"It is my medical duty to help him, Colonel Holman. I am sure you know little of mercy in your perfunctory duties." Risking herself, she gathered up a canteen and turned to walk to David. Her back was rigid with the anticipation of hearing his curt order to stop. But it didn't come. Nor did the soldier stop her.

She stooped, gathered David's bloodied head onto her lap, swishing away the biting insects that had already located the open wound. Then she heard Captain Mustafa say to the Colonel, "I must bring the Zionist to headquarters in Aleppo for questioning, Colonel. I am under orders from my commander to detain and question all political troublemakers."

"I suggest, Captain, you pay more attention to scouting and leave intelligence gathering and questioning to the Germans. It so happens this man is a spy from Jerusalem, and I am under orders to bring him to Constantinople."

Allison stared down at David with dismay. A spy for England!

And she and Leah had doubted him! If only they had confided in him back at the huts, they might have escaped. She held him gently now, touching the bloodied side of his head. David, David. Her heart wrenched. The Germans would kill him. Or the Turks would.

"Any further move on your part to thwart my orders will be dealt with by your own General Kismet Bey," said Colonel Holman.

The Captain looked uncertain. The German continued his rebuke with provocative disdain. "The British and their Zionist friends are nosing about like fleas. Any stupid action will only cast more suspicion on the German presence in Aleppo. This man was to be arrested quietly. General Kress von Kressenstein will not look lightly on this blunder! Now I must deal with the *Fräulein* to keep her silent. She is the daughter of the governor-general of Egypt."

Deal with her? As Allison knelt beside David, the insects droned noisily. Or was it an insect?

Allison raised her eyes to the cluster of smaller rocks and glittering sand beside the road. She froze. The noisy insects she had heard was a warning coming from a reddish-gray viper with an X on its head. Evidently its resting place away from the daytime heat had been disturbed by the movement of horses and soldiers. Nocturnal in habit, this one sat coiled, sending off its warning by rubbing its scales together. Its aggression and highly toxic venom made it one of the more dangerous reptiles in the area. It attacked indiscriminately, often leaping several feet from its coil.

Allison's heart beat in her throat, and a prayer was on her lips as David took that moment to begin to stir from the whack on his head. She stared, transfixed, waiting.

A bullet smashed into the viper's head, splattering bits and pieces across the sand and wetting her hand. She gave a sob of revulsion and pulled back, staring at the dead viper.

She turned her head toward the soldiers to see who had come to her aid. Startled, she saw it was Colonel Holman.

He spoke to the Turkish commander, "He will prove useful for information. Put him in the motorcar."

David would prove useful alive, but what of her? Had he not implied he must "deal with her" to keep her silent over this incident? Then why hadn't he allowed the viper to silence her once and for all? How easy it would have been. She was careful not to look his way for fear the renewed hope she felt might betray her.

Captain Mustafa apparently did not see the contradictory message in the Colonel's action. He gave a brief, curt command to one of the soldiers to bring David.

"As for you, Captain Mustafa, see the Zionist and the British nurse to Jerablus and bring them to my quarters. I want you there when we make the Zionist talk. Or are you more squeamish than you boast?"

A satisfied gleam warmed the captain's eyes. His smile turned friendly as he understood the meaning behind the colonel's orders. He would get the pleasure of interrogating the Zionist.

"No, Colonel, no objection."

"Good." The colonel pulled down his hat. "See there are no further delays." He saluted.

The Turk returned the salute and looked with diabolical pleasure at David Goldstein.

Allison, confused, angry, and frightened, struggled to her feet and looked up at Colonel Holman. He met her gaze evenly, and she knew he must read her disgust, her revulsion. His jaw set. He scanned her, whipped his horse about, and rode ahead.

Captain Mustafa dismounted and came to take the wheel of the motorcar. A soldier led her to the front seat and ushered her inside. She slid in reluctantly and watched as David was hauled to stand on his feet and then shoved toward the back seat, where the soldier got in with him.

This is what Colonel Holman wanted, she thought bitterly. Without another word he had ridden ahead in the direction of Jerablus. At that moment she loathed him and everything he stood for. He was turning David over to the commander, who obviously hated Jews. He had openly invited the Captain's brutality. If she had mistaken the colonel's killing the viper for a moment of unguarded valor, she had been wrong.

Her emotions numb, she sat there while Captain Mustafa turned the key in the ignition and pressed the starter button. The motorcar stirred up dust and sand as he drove forward.

Allison felt herself give way to her despair. *Oh God,* she prayed, *what hope?*

9

ON A DESOLATE STRETCH OF WILDERNESS ROAD near the small village of Jerablus, a band of Kurds in turbans was waiting in the road on camels. They numbered more than a dozen, each one carrying a rifle, and Captain Mustafa was forced to stop. He shouted an order to his small troop to prepare to shoot, but one of the Kurds waved a white rag on a pole above his camel's head.

"Ride to meet him," commanded Mustafa.

Allison watched nervously. A rivalry between the Kurdish, Arab, and Armenian peoples existed against the ruling national oppressor—Turkey—since the Seljuk Turks had conquered the territory before the Crusades. The Moslem Turks had eventually invaded Christian Constantinople and sections of Greece, ruthlessly persecuting both Greeks and Armenians, and they had little use for the Kurds, whom they had driven into the isolated mountains to live in poverty.

The armed Kurds on the road outnumbered Captain Mustafa, and Allison wondered if she were to become trapped in an exchange of bullets. Several minutes later the Turkish soldier rode back to the motorcar and handed Mustafa a sheet of paper.

"Orders have been changed, Captain. The British nurse is to be handed over to the Kurds. They are friendly and serve the German headquarters at the railway north of here. Colonel Holman says to bring the Zionist spy to his headquarters on the Euphrates."

Allison tensed, and David, who was conscious and in pain, scowled murderously. "You're insane if you think I'll let you turn Allison over to this band of renegades," he told Mustafa. "Where she goes, I go."

"You have nothing to say in the matter!" shouted Captain Mustafa over his shoulder, the official message in hand. "I have my orders from the colonel, and they will be carried out."

"Duty before decency, is that it?" demanded David. "You are all the same!"

"Silence, Zionist! Your hour to talk will come."

"My hour will come all right—the hour I see you ruddy Turks kicked out of Palestine!"

The captain turned with a rage, gripping his revolver as though he would enjoy using it on David, but Allison cried, "Please! I'll go as ordered. David, just do as they say. We're both innocent, and they have to release us eventually."

"You're dreaming," scoffed David bitterly. "You're measuring the Turks by British standards."

Mustafa leaned over and threw open the door. His black eyes were cold as he looked from David to Allison. "Good day, Nurse Wescott."

Her eyes pleaded with his. "My friend is innocent. You'll give him opportunity to explain, won't you?"

A smirk showed beneath his square mustache. "We will give him much opportunity." He waved the paper containing his new orders. "You are to be brought to the British expedition house at Jerablus. Colonel Holman will be in touch with you, as soon as he has finished with Dr. McGregor."

Expedition house! Neal and Leah's home?

Allison got out of the car, her eyes anxiously meeting David's. He offered a half-smile. *Don't worry,* he seemed to say. *They won't get a word out of me. You can count on it.*

She did believe in him, and her heart wrung with anguish as the car drove away leaving a trail of dust. David would face torture and death before he ever betrayed the Jewish cause or told them anything about Leah and Neal.

Allison stood there alone, watching the dusty motorcar disappear down the road.

Her uneasy gaze turned toward the Kurdish riflemen. One of them rode toward her, a friendly smile on his face, and nodded his head in deference. "Do not be afraid. We mean you no harm."

Allison soon found herself seated on the camel and swaying in motion as they rode across the barren terrain in the direction of Jerablus.

How could this have happened? she wondered. Except for David, who would undergo interrogation by Mustafa, she couldn't have asked for a better alteration of plans. While she waited for the dreaded arrival of Colonel Holman, she could search the house. She doubted she would find anything important, but the search needed to be done anyway. Maybe Neal, like Major Reuter, had left some sort of coded message, though she had no idea how to recognize it, even if she found one.

The village life at Jerablus was grim. Glancing about as she rode on the camel behind the friendly Kurd, she could see little in the way of shops, not even a bazaar where shopkeepers could barter fruit and bread. The people were downtrodden and poor. Despite her own problems, Allison's compassion soared at the sight. She imagined herself one of the women, downcast, clothed in Moslem black, with no opportunity to better her life on earth or in heaven. Words from various parts of the apostle Paul's letter to the church at

Ephesus came to mind, "Separate from Christ…, alienated…, strangers from the promises…, having no hope and without God in the world."

I wish I could give them the Bible in their own language, she thought. Without his love and comfort they were orphans, alone. Without his words, they and their children were prisoners of darkness, blind to the gifts offered them freely by God through the Lord Jesus.

Unless the light and truth of his word reaches them, thought Allison, *the darkness will multiply with the succeeding generations.*

Neal and Leah's stone expedition hut had several rooms. Spreading tree branches formed a roof over the front courtyard and showered the stones with mottled shade. The green branches were noisy with birds that fed on the black olives. The olives, in turn, dropped to the ground, staining the area with oil and drawing ants.

Neal, of course, was not there, and the house greeted her with ominous silence. Allison had been informed by the Kurd that he would remain on guard in the courtyard, that she was to stay here until notified, and that she may yet be called to the German headquarters farther north toward Baghdad. Food was in the cook room, he told her, along with a small container of dried tea leaves. He then left, and Allison stood by the window musing over her circumstances and watching the Kurd water his camel and unload his bundle.

Why would she be brought here? Surely the German colonel knew that she would not sit idle waiting for his next move. She would search Neal's work room to find any bit of information that might prove useful, and if she found a way to escape, she would, though the possibility was a slim one. Even if she could slip out of the house, without transportation she would never be able to cover the ninety miles to Aleppo.

Warily, she turned away from the window and stood gazing about the unfamiliar room with its frazzled pieces of furniture: several simple wooden chairs with bright orange cushions—probably Leah's work as a seamstress; a black-upholstered divan that had seen better days; a rough wood table; and one extraordinary looking lamp. The base seemed to be blue marble and was magnificently carved into the shape of a robed woman with a basket on her head, apparently carrying bread. The lamp appeared to Allison to be worth a good deal of money. She was rather surprised that it was still here, unmolested by thieves eager to sell to dealers.

The area was known by the British Museum to be rich in Hittite seal stones, and all kinds of ancient objects had been bought readily from villagers, who supplemented their meager incomes by robbing graves and selling their finds to *"antika"* dealers based in Aleppo. Many such poor villages were located near the Euphrates, and private dealers toured them in search of Hittite seals to sell to the museums.

As she stood there, she was struck by a knowing sensation that she was not alone in the house, and that she was being watched. A cautious survey of the other rooms, however, disclosed little more than her frayed nerves. *I must stop imagining evils at every sound,* she rebuked herself.

The Kurdish guard had brought her bags into Leah's small room, and after tossing aside her hat and kitbag, Allison went to work, dedicating herself to a thorough search. With the lamps lit, the curtains closed, and every window and door bolted from the inside, she began by looking in the obvious places.

As nightfall settled in, she had found nothing except some old letters from the archaeology school in Cairo. She was about to replace them in the little olivewood box when she saw that one of the envelopes postmarked from Cairo had come from Jemal Pasha.

Now what would the gaunt-faced Jemal have written Leah about? Archaeology, of course, except that he had never mentioned knowing Leah. Were they business acquaintances? Friends? Yet, when the discussion in the archaeology club's dining room had turned to Leah and Neal, Jemal had made no mention of knowing them. Had he preferred to keep it quiet? If he did, the obvious question was why? What did he have to hide?

Now that Leah was beyond caring about protecting her privacy, Allison kept the letter. There might be something worth noting in the words. She slipped it inside her dress pocket and went on searching, but the task proved far from easy since the Kurd on guard was apt to check on her at any time. Tomorrow the colonel might arrive and end any possibility of further searching, so even though she found it wearisome and disheartening work, she continued on doggedly.

It was well after nine that night when she came to the room that had belonged to Neal, and lighting the lamp, she began to rummage his desk and drawers. The room was also his office and contained samples of pottery, books galore stacked here and there on the floor, and mounds of paperwork written in pencil.

After a long and tedious search, she produced nothing of considered value. Then again, how would she know? What was she even looking for? The name of Karl Reuter? A message from Neal or Leah? It was frustrating. She had little to go on—only the bits and pieces Leah had given her. When everything else had been searched, Allison turned with resignation to the stack of books on the floor beside Neal's worn chair.

It was late, probably sometime after midnight. She had no way of knowing the exact time since the clock on the table beside his bed had stopped, perhaps days ago. Tired and hungry, she decided to take a break from the thankless task and sample the fruit and tea the Kurd had left. She lit the oil lantern that waited on a table beside the cook room door and entered the stone room cautiously. In the dimness she saw a small stove and imagined the luxury item had been Leah's pride and joy. It probably had been brought up with pieces of furniture from Cairo or Aleppo. She struck the match and filled the kettle with water to boil for tea. While it simmered, she gathered the fruit she preferred from the wooden bowl—lush purple grapes and several figs—and cut a chunk of bread. She would take these with the tea to Neal's room and spend the late night hours searching his books.

Some twenty minutes later, she was seated in Neal's big chair beside the lamp, a table drawn up in front of her and the stack of books at her feet. After munching grapes and sipping good British tea, she continued her search. It proved to be a disappointing endeavor, though occasionally she did come across a book that dealt primarily with the Hittites. These she examined methodically for anything curious: underlined words, or Leah or Neal's handwriting, which she knew well enough to recognize. She examined them page by page. In one she found a half sheet of scribbled notes by Neal, but his remarks proved to be mere professional calculations and deductions that had nothing at all to do with German espionage.

Exhausted and unsuccessful, yet too tense to sleep, she leaned her head back in the chair and stared across the small room at the Hittite sculptures and inscriptions on the small library shelf. She must finish searching the remainder of the books before dawn in case her time here was cut short.

For the moment she lounged in the chair, listening to every creak and gust of wind about the house. She committed herself, Neal, and David, to the faithful God she knew was always there. Yet life was full of tragedy, she reminded herself, and she must not ever think that the proof of God's presence and blessing meant that circumstances would end well. The winds of tragedy and the floods of unexpected and unexplained hardship ending in earthly disappointment swept through the lives of even the most trusting of his saints.

What if all this espionage turned tragic in the end? Leah had not been a Christian, and the unthinkable had happened. Somehow Allison had lulled herself into thinking that eventually Leah would turn to the Lord and that God would allow her to live until that day. Instead, her life had come to a brutal end.

Opportunities were like moving shadows, Allison decided. They ended just as surely as the sun ran its circuit through the heavens and then set. Night always came, no matter how bright the noon. Time ran out. Her gaze moved to the clock on Neal's desk, the silent clock.

Outside, the black night was full of noises: the murmur and mutter of the wind-driven leaves and branches on the trees in the courtyard, and the creaks that sounded on the roof as though a cat puttered across. The curtains on Neal's window fluttered faintly from the draft sneaking in through the tiny cracks in the stone walls. Could anyone peer in as she sat beside the lamp searching the books?

Again the unsteadying sensation that someone watched her tickled the back of her neck. She kept her eyes on the book in her lap afraid to look up, afraid she would see a face. The Kurdish guard perhaps? He had not appeared evil, but rather a disciplined warrior-type with comfortable gray in his mustache. Somehow when looking into his eyes she had thought she'd seen kindness, even sympathy. Consoling herself with this conclusion, she stood, and with determination decided to get several hours sleep in Leah's room.

She picked up the clock, wound it, and set it to her approximation of the time. Then leaving the lamp in Neal's room burning, she passed through the watchful house into Leah's bedroom. She still had the gun and placed it beneath her pillow. Lying down on Leah's bed, she remained fully dressed except for her shoes. She awoke some time later, sitting up with a start, every sense tense and alert. What had awakened her?

The wind was blowing in savage gusts, and in the brief lull between them, Allison could hear a rapping sound. It was several minutes later before it was silent again. She carefully moved from the bed and went to the window, drawing aside the curtains. There was no moon, and the surroundings were black.

Several minutes passed before she realized the light in Neal's room was out. She reached for the lamp and found the switch, but the light did not come on. *The storm,* she thought. A draft of wind rattled the window in Neal's room. Apparently the flimsy hook and eye latch had come undone. She wasn't about to venture into the room to close it. She felt under her pillow for the revolver and stood beside the bed, listening. After several tense moments, she heard nothing but the shutter moving to and fro in the wind.

I'm being too suspicious, she thought. *After all, the guard is on duty right outside in the courtyard. If someone were trying to get inside, he would need to pass through the court to get to Neal's window, unless he came over the back wall. No one is there. It's just my nerves. I'll shut the window or the room will be full of sand in the morning*

She moved across Leah's room into the doorway of the sitting room and passed into it. No gleam of light penetrated through the curtained windows, but to her left in Neal's room she felt the wind coming through. She listened, but the roaring wind was too noisy, smothering any other sound. In the lulls, the warped shutter creaked.

Enough of this!

She walked toward the room and in the doorway could make out the moving shutter but little else except the darker outline of the furniture. Allison stiffened, not daring to move. Her alarm turned to stark fear when she sensed movement behind the desk. She turned, unable to silence the catch of her breath.

She opened her mouth to scream for the guard but froze. What if it were he? Her hand tightened on the gun.

Oh, God, what am I going to do? she prayed.

Whomever it was must have heard her. A hard breath drew in. "Allison?"

"Who's there?" she gasped shakily.

"A friend. Bret Holden."

A hand torch flashed on, scanning her face, and she turned her head away from the painful light. He set it on the desk and a match flared up and steadied into a flame. He lit the oil lamp, and Allison, pale and frightened, stared at Colonel Holman. He was altogether familiar, yet a total stranger.

"You," came her dazed, dry whisper.

"I'll explain eventually," came his smooth voice, void of the curtness she'd come to expect.

In place of the German uniform, he wore a cool white cotton shirt like the locals wore. A leather shoulder holster with a revolver was secured in place. The dark blue eyes were softer, less ruthless; yet they retained a distant callousness that suggested familiarity with danger. His good looks were even more apparent now that he had removed the Iron Cross and everything hinting of Kaiser Wilhelm. Allison felt her face flush for no reason except that she feared he could read her thoughts.

His brow shot up. "Put away that revolver, will you?" he quietly suggested. "You'll end up shooting your transportation home to Cairo."

Her spiraling fears came crashing down with such relief that her strength poured from her like water escaping the bottom of a rusty bucket. She felt her knees wouldn't hold her up. Down she went to the floor in a heap.

The next thing she knew his arms were around her gathering her up. "I'm sorry, Allison." Bret sounded genuinely apologetic. "I rapped on the door, and you didn't answer. The guard was dead. I didn't think you were here. I came in through the window. It was half pried open. It's all right now," he soothed her, his voice strong and resonant. "I'll get you safely back to Egypt."

Already partially pried open? She shivered. The terrors, confusions, and doubts that had haunted her since the night she followed Leah into Major Reuter's hut were over. The arms holding her close did not belong to a ruthless member of the German secret police but to Bret Holden, a British professor—and she found them far too comforting.

Her eyes rushed to his, and she noted again that while his appearance was the same bounty of good looks, the cobalt blue eyes were no longer ruthless or mocking, but warm, sympathetic, and much too captivating. She pulled away from his embrace, her lashes lowering.

"You won't need that now." He reached for her limp hand, taking the revolver and shoving it in his belt. "Here, better sit down." He drew her away from the doorway to the small divan facing the desk. "Are you all right?"

She nodded and said in a shaky whisper, "The Kurdish guard you left is...dead?"

He gave her a level look, revealing none of the painful emotion he must have felt. "Yes. At first I thought I had misjudged you, until I saw that window. Someone tried to break in here after eliminating the guard."

She froze, "You thought I did—"

He frowned. "But I see you're as innocent and trapped in this event as I first suspected."

"He's dead," she gasped, shivering. "Then someone did come here. I thought I heard something earlier. Was that you rapping a while ago?"

"Yes. When you didn't answer, I became worried. Then I went around to the back and saw the window. I may have frightened off the intruder. The Kurd hasn't been dead long."

"Then, if you hadn't come, someone else would have come through that window," she reasoned, and tensed to keep from shaking as she sat on the divan watching him. "You thought I killed the guard?" Her strength returned with a flash, and she sat up straight, looking up at him accusingly.

"Yes," he admitted frankly, and his mouth twitched with restrained amusement. "And I wondered if I'd been a fool to give you that gun."

For some reason she felt indignant, as though he should have known she was the kind of a woman who didn't go about shooting people. Then she realized it was unfair on her part to think this of him. He knew as little about her as she did about him.

She watched him, musing. "Do you really think I could do it? That I'm working as a spy for—for—I don't even know which side!"

Bret tapped his chin. "No," he said with calm consideration. "I don't. Not now. But it was possible. A demure face, among other noticeable charms, always makes a potent nemesis. And, I might add, the qualities of a brave and noble nurse out to conquer the dragons of evil add to your dangerous mystique. Especially one hardly out of her teens. How did you get mixed up in this?"

"I'm far from a babe in the woods, if you mean to imply as much. I graduated nursing school in London all of two years ago."

"A very long time, I gather." A smile formed on his lips, which were a trifle more vulnerable than she had remembered. "Of course I was cautious of you, even if Neal and Leah are your cousins. You were snooping about Karl's hut that night, and Leah would have been desperate enough to need a confidante." He gave her a level look. "How much do you know?"

"More than I know about this 'alias' Colonel Holman. Why should I trust you?"

"I'm afraid you've little choice in the matter. Without me you won't get a foot out of Jerablus. And sporting that red cross on your uniform the way you did when you came riding boldly into Turkish territory was naive and reckless."

"Now that you've made your opinion of me clear," said Allison breathlessly, "would you mind, if it's not too much to ask, telling me what you're doing here?"

He smiled. "I arrested you, remember? Lucky for you I did, and David, too. It took a great deal of wit to save you both from Captain Mustafa."

"You mean—" she began, confused, "you did it purposely, about unmasking David, I mean?"

"It was the only way to deceive the Turk. Don't worry about David. He's a good friend of mine. Turning him over to the Turk was a necessity. If I hadn't lured Mustafa away with the diabolical prospect of taking out his venom on a Zionist, he would have beaten a path back to his headquarters and blown the whole thing wide open. I couldn't let anyone know I wasn't Colonel Holman until I had completed what I came here for."

"You mean David isn't on his way to Baghdad?"

"He's on his way here."

Relief eased some of the momentary concern, and she smiled for the first time. Under his gaze, she quickly grew serious. "How did you manage? What about Captain Mustafa?"

"Mustafa is cooling his heels under Kurdish guard until we're safely out of here."

"The Kurds are your friends, I gather."

"They hate the Turks. They want their freedom, their own land again; as do the Arab factions and the Jews. But let's not get into that now."

"No, let's not, Professor Holden."

He smiled. "Major Holden. But Bret will do nicely."

"Is it for real—the Major part of your new role? Maybe you're not German or British, but American. Just who are you? Would you mind dreadfully telling me the truth?" she said with a touch of impatience.

He regarded her meditatively, appearing to turn over something in his mind. After a moment or two, he apparently came to some decision, for he moved away from the desk and went to the window to latch it. He turned and came back, sitting in the chair opposite her. "All right. My rank is genuine. I have indeed been demoted from colonel to major, but that's quite all right because I'm definitely British and suspicious of the German Empire. I also shed the uniform with relief, finding no pleasure in the role of a devotee to the Kaiser. I happen to work for the military and soon will be assigned to Cairo intelligence."

"And your name? Is it really Bret Holden?"

"It is. Satisfied?"

"Not entirely. Well, this is a pleasant surprise, Major Holden."

"Bret. I apologize for my rather rude behavior. I hope I didn't intimidate you too much."

She smiled ruefully. "You make a convincing colonel in the secret police."

"You understand it was necessary, I hope."

"Actually, you saved my life," she said too casually, and reminded him about the crackshot which eliminated the desert viper. "I didn't think it wise to thank you then."

"Quite understandable," he said gravely, but his eyes smiled.

"Please accept my gratitude now. For tonight as well. I'm sorry about the Kurd, your friend." She thought of Leah. He must know. David would have told him. Suddenly she realized the matter of Leah's death was a perfect test. If he was who he claimed, if David was safe and waiting, then this Major Holden would know about Leah's death.

"You've been in the Middle East for long?"

"A few months," was all he said, and she gathered he didn't want to say much more about it.

"Where were you stationed before that?"

"Constantinople."

"You came to Baghdad as Colonel Holman?"

"Yes."

"You knew Neal—and Leah?"

"Maybe," he said noncommittally. "Now it's my turn to ask questions."

"Not yet. I'm not satisfied you are who you say."

"And you think it's important I satisfy your curiosity?"

"Personally? No, but if you wish to ask questions, you won't get the answers until I'm certain you're telling me all the truth."

He smiled. "All? You'll have me in trouble with my superior."

"And whose superior are you?"

"For a naive rosebud, you speak boldly. Don't you know you're playing a very dangerous game?"

"I may be naive, as you put it, but I know what I'm about. And I intend to see it through to the end. Because—" Allison checked herself suddenly. "No. Tell me first why you were masquerading as a German officer that night in Major Reuter's hut."

Bret hesitated, then staring at her a moment, he said firmly, "You won't be staying. I'm seeing you straight back to Cairo to the watchful eye of your family."

"Maybe," she said.

He laughed shortly. "Not 'maybe.' Yes. You're going back."

She smiled wryly, scanning him. "I think you are telling the truth—at least about being a British major. You know how to give orders, don't you? And you expect me to follow them."

He smiled. "For your safety, of course."

"Or for your own?"

"I admit your presence does put a certain damper on my activities. Getting you back without being noticed by the Turks isn't going to be easy."

"I didn't mean that."

"What did you mean?"

"I meant that you would naturally wish me back at Cairo tucked away somewhere to safeguard your identity—if you really are Colonel Brent Holman. Maybe it's the British Bret Holden you're pretending to be."

"Now we are getting complicated."

"Maybe you killed him tonight—and his friendly Kurdish guard out in the courtyard." She shivered.

"Then you are in grave danger. We are alone."

She drew back a little, but somehow she didn't really believe there was any threat.

"You're safe," he said. "At least from my German ambitions to silence any spy carrying crucial information back to Cairo."

He didn't say what she wasn't safe from, and she looked away when his gaze briefly scanned her face. "How well do you know David?" he asked.

"Didn't he tell you?"

"No. We didn't have time to discuss cozy strolls in London Park. I assume you and he had several of those."

"No, more like discussions." Her eyes met his evenly. "We discussed whether Jesus is the Jewish Messiah or not."

A dark brow lifted. She added firmly, "Any cozy strolls through London Park were done with the man I'm going to marry, Wade Findlay."

His expression remained impassive. "A fine gentleman, I'm sure.

Nurse Wescott wouldn't look at him twice if he didn't meet all her expectations. Very wise of you."

She turned away. "He's coming to Cairo as soon as he graduates from Oswald Chambers Bible Training College."

"I commend him. And you. And now that you have warned me to stay away from you, shall we pursue the matters of life and death?"

She looked at him, his bluntness taking her by surprise. A faint glimmer of cynicism showed in his smile. He hadn't been far from the truth when he suggested she wished to keep him at an emotional distance. It was a warning to herself as well.

"Are you going to tell me what you were doing that night in the German major's hut?" she asked. *Does he know Karl Reuter was a British agent?*

He leaned back, his relaxed posture contradicting his earlier suggestion of a life and death discussion, and placed his arm across the back of the divan. "I knew the man who was killed. He was a friend of mine. You knew him, too, didn't you? You were there in his hut looking for something. How about it, Nurse?"

Allison held back, her eyes meeting his level stare as the minutes ticked by.

"What were you looking for?" he demanded too quietly.

The wind blew against the side of the house, and the light from the oil lamp flickered in the draft, throwing leaping shadows on the low ceiling.

Allison spoke at last, uncertainly, "I didn't go there to search for anything. I told you why I went there when you interrogated me. I saw someone enter the hut. I suspected a burglar. I didn't know the dead German officer."

Bret stood and walked over to Neal's desk where the stack of books sat. He looked down at them thoughtfully, and then at

Allison. She knew he suspected her of having gone through them.

"Find anything?" he asked flatly. When she said nothing, he walked back and stood over her, frowning. "You're involved in something much more dangerous than you imagine."

"You're wrong. I do know. Major Reuter was murdered; so was your Kurdish friend tonight, and—" she stopped, her eyes searching his in the lamplight. They were penetrating beneath black lashes, almost moody, she decided.

"And so was Leah Bristow," he filled in for her quietly. "Yes, I know. David told me. They came across her body out at the Roman-Syrian Digs. He also told me something else, something not even you knew he understood. Her kitbag was empty, and her revolver was missing. Both were taken by the enemy." He looked at the stack of books belonging to Neal. "Did you think you would find what was taken?"

For a long moment she stared into his calm unwavering eyes and seemed to draw strength from them.

"You can trust me," he said.

She saw no reason to keep anything from him now, and she nodded, clutching the chair's arm. Allison believed him. Perhaps it was his gravity or the care in his quiet voice when he spoke of Leah's body, but whatever it was caused her to lower her head into her hands and blink hard to keep back the emotional release of tears.

"No, I didn't think I'd find what they took here."

He sat down beside her and said softly: "I'm sorry, Allison."

"She told me she received a message from Neal. She had been waiting to hear from him for two days; since before the agent was murdered at the huts."

Alert, he attended her every facial expression. "Yes?"

Allison shivered suddenly, as though the air had become cold. "After she left, I heard a noise at Major Reuter's hut, like a door moving on a hinge. I felt as though someone had been out there listening to us. I was afraid, but I couldn't turn to anyone. She made me promise to say nothing, no matter what might happen. The Turkish authorities must not be brought into this, she kept telling me. And if anything were to happen to her, I was to—to—" Her voice faded, and she swallowed back the emotion that wanted to break out.

His eyes flickered over her face. "Yes? Carry on her work?"

She nodded. He was silent for a time, then: "You know who Karl Reuter was?"

She nodded. "A British agent."

He let out a breath, his displeasure growing.

"Leah needed my help, and she believed she could trust me," Allison whispered defensively.

He didn't look pleased but asked firmly, "How much do you know?"

She lifted her face and looked at him now, this time with open curiosity. "Enough to know we're all in danger. She had no choice. Without me she wouldn't have made it as far as she did."

"I don't know how much she told you," he said, "but I'm afraid she told you more than she should have. She may have needed your help, but by involving you she's also placed you in the same dilemma she was in. Someone tried to break in through that window tonight. If I hadn't come when I did…Well, you get the picture, I'm sure."

She remained outwardly composed.

"I think you had better tell me the truth, Allison. All of it."

"Are you one of them? A British agent?"

"You'll need to take my word for it. I don't go around carrying papers. And I'm obligating you to silence."

Her relief provoked a half smile. "Instead of papers saying 'Major Holden,' you go around snapping orders in German. I shall miss being called 'Fräulein.'"

"Maybe I can do something about that in Cairo."

A small flush warmed her face, and to conceal it, she said too firmly, "I don't think so."

Amusement flickered in his eyes. "Wade Findlay. Yes, I quite get the message, but again, we're getting ahead of ourselves, aren't we?"

"Yes. Quite ahead," she said quickly. "If you are, as you say, on our side, what is all this about?"

"First, how much does the noble Nurse Wescott know? Everything please, from the beginning."

Allison told him, starting with her arrival at the huts for her holiday. She spoke quietly, this time keeping her emotions under firm control, for something in his level gaze restrained her. She explained again how she had been awakened to hear someone entering the officer's hut, and her surprise at seeing it was her cousin Leah. She had followed her, only to have someone come up behind her, pushing the cold barrel of a gun against her neck.

"I didn't know who you were in the dark," apologized Bret. "You might have been looking for the information. I admit you gave me quite a shock when I came back and switched on the light."

Once again she could almost hear the stealthy footsteps of the third man after Bret had gone out the front door after Leah. Allison went on to explain how Leah had been waiting for her when she returned to her own cabin after his interrogation. How she had kept Leah hidden there for two days while they waited for Neal and avoided the ominous Colonel Holman. She admitted that Leah had found the coded word.

"You know about that?" he scowled.

"She didn't explain what was in the information, only that it would hold an important clue as to where to find it. I'm not even sure what 'it' is we're looking for."

"Not 'we'; you're not going to get further involved. No wonder I was foiled when I searched Karl's hut. Leah had already taken it."

"Only the code word."

"Say that again?" he said sharply.

Allison leaned toward him. "We only guessed what the word meant after a day. It was Woolly's book, *The Hittites*. Major Reuter had left it on the table."

"Ruddy luck! I saw it when I searched."

"You didn't have the code word. So you wouldn't know."

"Thanks for making excuses for me, but I beg to disagree. I should have suspected. Anyway, go on."

"While I watched the club members in the dining room during lunch, Leah went back into the cabin and retrieved the book."

He took hold of her arm. "Are you saying that you have it?"

"No. Leah had it. She took it to Neal."

He stood, pulling her to her feet, his eyes holding hers. "That's impossible. Neal isn't anywhere around this part of Arabia."

"She told me she had received a message from Neal. She was to meet him. She believed it."

As Allison talked, it was as though she were reliving the incident. She saw Leah's face again in the oncoming evening shadows, heard that stealthy sound on the back porch after Leah had left to meet Neal.

"Someone followed her."

Once again she seemed to hear Leah's relieved voice, see the almost happy face, as if a heavy load had been lifted from her heart when she grew certain the message was from Neal and that their superior had arrived to take up the burden.

Allison explained in a quiet voice about their disagreement. How she had believed something was odd about the message coming from Neal. "We discussed the very thing that happened to her, but it was as if she wanted to believe it because she had grown hopeless," said Allison. "I couldn't understand why, if the third man had been Neal, he hadn't been able to understand the coded word at once when he saw it, the way Leah had."

Allison saw Bret frown and understood he wasn't happy about her knowing so much. It was too late to worry about what he thought, she told herself. She did know, whether it had been wise of Leah or not, and she went on with a determined voice, using more calmness now to try to convince Bret Holden that she was capable and trustworthy.

"She was the happiest I'd seen her since I arrived—" Her voice broke in a dry whisper. "But I didn't want her to go. We debated the possibility of it being the murderer waiting for her instead of Neal, and I wanted to go with her, but she refused."

"She was right," said Bret.

Allison couldn't resist. "Yet without my being there with Leah, you wouldn't know about the supposed message from Neal or where she went or about a number of other important things I haven't been able to explain yet."

"Then it may be too late," he said more to himself than to her. "If the book passed to the other side, they can locate the information first. I've no notion where Karl stored it for safekeeping."

She raised her head. "Maybe they don't have it. There's more. Leah was careful. It was expected of her, she said. Even with Neal she had her orders to play it safe. So she took a sheaf of papers in her bag, as though it were the information. It was a red herring, she called it."

"Good! Smart woman!"

"And my books, even my Bible. She took those as well, for a diversion. Whoever killed her for the information has the wrong thing."

"Your books and Bible—and you let her, I suppose? What were you thinking of?"

She didn't understand his objection. "Of course I let her. They made the perfect red herring."

"Exactly. And made you the new bait instead."

She shuddered. "What do you mean?"

"Leah wouldn't have done it deliberately. It sounds as if she were desperate. But by taking your books and papers, she unwittingly convinced the other side you are involved. Don't you see? They'll think she may have told you the information. They may even think you have it." He looked toward the window thoughtfully. "No wonder someone tried to break in here tonight. That's why the guard is dead."

Allison shivered. "I don't understand."

"It's simple. After Karl was eliminated, it left two people who knew about the book: Neal and Leah. Neal sent a Mayday to me, but—"

"Then you were his superior?"

"Yes, but that's between you and me."

"Of course." She scanned him. "But they know about you. So that makes four people who knew about the book."

"Three," he repeated. "They don't know about me. The arrival of Colonel Holman took care of my identity. With Karl dead and Neal delayed, that left only Leah. We know what happened to Leah," he said gently. "Because of the 'brilliant' red herring, they now have someone else to worry about: Nurse Allison Wescott. They aren't certain how much you know, but they don't take chances."

She shuddered. "I hadn't thought of that."

"No," he agreed, "I didn't think you had. Now do you see why you're going straight back to Cairo?"

"But I promised Leah—"

"Whatever you promised Leah you can turn over to me, where it belongs. You're a nurse serving on a medical mission ship, if I recall, and that's where you belong. After I get you home, you're out of this."

She lifted her head, and her mouth set. "You're so sure of that, Major Holden? Because I'm not. And you haven't explained yet what it's all about."

"Look, Allison, three people are dead—all friends of mine. All dedicated to a patriotic, noble cause, if you don't mind my putting it that way. This is not your fight. I don't want to see you end up like Leah."

She stood with dignity. "You're wrong, Major. It is my fight. Patriotism is not enough. I owe England and the cause of freedom my full support, and I'll do what I can, what I must, to see whatever it was Leah died for come to a successful end."

He frowned. "Yes, I'm afraid you mean that. All very noble and charming but unwise, if you wish to live long on the good earth and see your grandchildren."

"*Afraid* I mean it? You who risk your life every day to serve your country? You are disturbed that I feel patriotic? That I care? After finding Leah in the sand, what else could I feel?"

He watched her. "You are too curious, too brave for your own good. Save your valor for the *Mercy*. Wasn't that the name of the ship? Then show your mercy on the *fellahin* and await the arrival of your true love from Chambers Bible school. If you don't…Well, you get the message, I hope."

"How like your type, Major, to send me to the stands while you risk your life every day among the lions. Well, I won't go sit in the stands. If you won't let me help you, then I'll do so alone. For Leah."

He gave her a narrowed side glance. "Pardon me, but you'll do nothing of the sort. If I must resort to certain influences I can apply in Cairo, I'll do so to have you kept out of this."

"You forget who my father is," she said with a victorious smile.

"He's quite patriotic and would be proud to see me involved."

He gave a short laugh. "So you think. It may be that I know him better than you realize. By the way, what did you mean I'm behaving like my 'type'?" he inquired dryly. "You have me all figured into a nice, neat little package, do you, Miss Wescott? And just how do you see my 'type'?"

She walked away from him to the divan and sank into it. She wouldn't tell him what she thought of him, because it wasn't what he expected. She found him valiant and bold—and too memorable. She changed the subject back to Leah.

"I'm beginning to think that Leah might not have taken the book with her after all but hid it before she went to meet Neal."

"A gold mine, if it were true. It would leave the door wide open. It means I'm still in the fight."

"I think she didn't take it because my hut was searched, not before her death but afterward, just before David and I left to come here."

"Ah."

"Then you see what I mean?"

"Of course. If they had what they wanted, they wouldn't still be looking. You're certain it wasn't the Turkish officials? David said they arrived to search all the huts."

"I thought so at first, but I'm not convinced now. They were late in arriving and only had been there a short time before David and I left. But my drawers were searched before that. Yet I don't know how because we were all out at the digs when Leah was found."

"It could have been someone who's not in the club, and we don't know when she was murdered. It could have been the night before, which gave the morning free to search before you went to the digs. I don't suppose you remember if anyone was missing from the dining room at breakfast?"

She looked guilty. "I overslept and missed it. So I wouldn't know. But obviously, if I were still sleeping, no one could have gotten in."

He smiled. "And what did you do after breakfast?"

"I attended a lecture."

"It could have happened then. You went out to the digs afterward?"

"Yes, after lunch. But, Major, if Leah didn't take the book, where could she have hidden it? And wouldn't she have been careful enough to leave some sort of message in case it wasn't Neal after all?"

"Yes, and I wish I knew."

She told him of her own suspicions of Baroness Helga Kruger and of Professor Jemal Pasha.

"We've been watching Jemal for months."

"You have? And there's something else. Leah wasn't supposed to have gone to the abandoned digs to meet Neal. I know, because she told me about a hut halfway between here and the Carchemish Digs. They sometimes stored pieces there. Neal was to have a candle glowing in the window when she arrived, if all was safe for her to enter."

"If she got that far, I'm certain the candle would have been burning brightly, " he said bitterly. "She would have walked straight into a trap. But the trap was much closer at hand—only a mile or so from the huts. The motorcar, for instance. You said she told you it was concealed a half-mile away?"

"She said Neal put it there for a safeguard."

"Most likely whoever it was knew about it and was waiting there. Disposing of her at the abandoned digs would have been easier than driving the ninety miles here to Jerablus—and much closer, if it were someone in the club or in Aleppo. I'm not ruling that out, either. A German consul there works closely with the Turks."

"You mean the enemy may not be someone from the club after all?" She felt relief.

"Nothing can be ruled out. I'll need to search the hut where Neal was said to be waiting for Leah."

"But she didn't go there. It was too far."

"I don't think she did, but I may find something else there. Anything. How well did you search your hut before you left with David?"

"Meticulously. There was nothing—certainly not something the size of a book."

"Nevertheless, I'll check it again myself, just to make sure."

"How can you? If you return, they'll know you're not Colonel Holman."

"My dear, I rarely am as open as I had to be when portraying Colonel Holman. I prefer to work in secret. I am a skilled but honorable burglar. What I need to do, I'll do without getting caught."

"If only Leah and I had known who you were," said Allison.

"Yes, we crossed purposes, didn't we? A rotten bit of luck. But you're still alive, and I intend to keep you that way."

"Believe me, I didn't come on holiday to run into espionage but to learn more about archaeology. My interest was purely biblical, and I just sort of…well, bumped into this."

"Yes," he said smoothly, "I recall the memorable moment in Major Reuter's hut when we did 'bump' into each other. However, I'd give anything if it had been the third man, instead of you. One thing is certain, it wasn't Neal." He stood. "Whatever happens, we'll need to get out of here as soon as David arrives." He frowned. "He's late. Anytime anyone is late, I have sound reason to worry." He walked over to the desk. "The Turkish officials will soon know that Colonel Holman is due to arrive this afternoon from Baghdad. When they do, they'll be scouring all Jerablus for his counterfeit."

He looked at her. "Have your things ready and packed, will you?"

"They are. I never unpacked them. Will David come with a motorcar?"

"If he's successful. Otherwise we'll use my horse. He'll need to make it on his own. I can't take chances and wait, not with you here."

In the little silence that followed, the lantern flickered. He stood looking down at the books, deep in thought.

Allison walked up. "Then no one else knows the information Major Reuter discovered? Not even you?"

"No, although—" he stopped.

"Although what?" she pressed.

He looked at her, his blue eyes intense with musings all their own. "I have an idea. I've seen and heard enough to understand what the Germans are planning. Even so, the documents our agent confiscated in Constantinople were crucial because they contained the official proof needed by the British government."

Her excitement grew. "Official proof of what?"

He didn't answer, and Allison said: "With Reuter's death, and now Leah's, what hope is there? How will we ever know the truth? You've no idea where he might have hidden the documents?"

"No. The answer is likely to be found in the book."

The wind whined along the side of the house, and once again, as earlier that night, Allison became aware of the sensation of being watched. Yes, the book, but where had Leah hidden it?

In the lull of the wind, and the silence following, footsteps sounded outside in the courtyard.

PART 2

On the Road from Jerablus

10

ALLISON'S EYES DARTED TOWARD THE WINDOW on which someone tapped, and a startled gasp came to her lips as she took a step backward against the desk. Bret threw an arm about her shoulders, drawing her toward him, his face inscrutable as he held her to him.

"Don't be afraid; it's only David."

Allison managed to calm herself and nodded, unsure whether his presence made her feel more secure or not. The last few days of peril leading up to Leah's death and culminating tonight with Bret coming in through the window had left her jittery.

Bret released her, and she drew away, feeling somewhat foolish after insisting she was capable of carrying on Leah's work. To divert Bret's attention from her reaction, she asked, "What happens now?"

"First, let's hope he was able to obtain a vehicle." Bret walked to the window, giving an answering rap.

Her eyes followed him across the room, noting his muscular build and how he looked every inch a well-trained soldier, even in the white shirt and trousers. The floor vibrated beneath his calf-length military boots. She must not notice. She felt a sense of guilt when she remembered Wade Findlay.

"What happened to the Mercedes?" she asked.

His dark head turned, his level gaze noncommittal, and his tone casual. "Oh, the Kurds had a bit of trouble convincing Mustafa to release David to their care. It was damaged a little."

She dared not contemplate what that meant. "I see."

Bret nodded toward the pistol on the desk. "I'm going out to talk with David. We'll be gone a short time. If anyone you don't know comes in, use it."

Her heart quavered. "Where are you and David going?"

"To look about," he stated evasively. Giving Allison no time to protest, he passed through the darkness of the sitting room. A moment later she heard the front door close behind him and his footsteps crunching on the scattered sand of the courtyard.

Allison stood still, straining to catch every sound in the night, her heart thumping. She had the wild notion to run after him but clamped a restraint on her emotions and moved over to the desk where she reclaimed the gun he had first given her in Major Reuter's hut.

Taking a moment to remember, it hardly seemed possible Major Bret Holden could be the same man who had so intimidated her with accusations on the night of the agent's death. Bret was now risking his security to salvage her own. Had he wished to do so, he could have escaped alone with a far better chance to make it back to Cairo undetected by either Turkish or German authorities. She was aware that for the three of them to escape Jerablus and drive the ninety miles back to Aleppo would be harrowing indeed. As Bret had said earlier, the German headquarters near the railway would soon discover he had been an impostor of the real Colonel Holman.

She wondered about Bret. He had purposely left much undisclosed for security reasons, and much he hadn't mentioned because of the brevity of time. If they returned safely to Cairo, she decided, she would inquire about him from her father, Sir Marshall Wescott. As retiring consul-general, he would have access to certain information about what was happening in the Cairo intelligence department. Suddenly, she longed to see her father again. During the last several years, she had seen little of him. His work and dedication to King Edward had long been a source of friction between him and her mother. Her mother, Eleanor Bristow Wescott, believed Sir Wescott had for too long neglected his family and marriage for the good of the British Empire.

Her father was soon to arrive home from India, where he had been for the last three months in meetings with the British viceroy of India. Now Allison longed to be home, too, in Port Said. *Perhaps I'm not made for espionage after all,* she thought.

She was still thinking of all this when Bret returned alone some twenty minutes later. He stood in the doorway with the lamplight flickering against his silhouette. Without expression, he looked at her. When she walked up to him, however, she could see the deliberate restraint of an underlying concern in his narrowed gaze. While he may have been looking at her, his thoughts were elsewhere.

She tried to match his calm. "Well? Where is he?"

"David?"

"Yes, David! You said it was him. You mean it wasn't?"

"No, it was Hamid, but David is on his way. We have a vehicle, and we'll need to leave in a hurry as soon as he arrives."

"Who's Hamid?"

"My assistant and a friend." He walked quickly to the stack of books Allison hadn't searched and grabbed a satchel from the floor beneath the desk. He tossed in the books, along with the contents of the drawers, as Allison walked up.

"Your insinuation that matters are under control is only meant to quiet me, isn't it? Something happened to David," she said.

He looked at her, keeping that same, imperturbable manner that unnerved her. "No, he should make it."

She struggled to emulate his unearthly calm. "Should? You mean he might not?"

"In this business there's always that chance, but David is capable and steady. I noticed that about him in London. So I'm counting on him." He looked at his watch. "He has ten minutes."

She swallowed, brushing a curl back from her face. "Ten minutes? What happens in ten minutes? Why not fifteen. Why not twenty?"

He threw open a drawer and took out several folders, stuffing them into the satchel. "In ten minutes we leave, with or without him."

She stared at him, unbelieving. "Leave without David?"

"Yes. We've no choice in the matter."

"I won't," she stated with incredulity. "He's a friend of mine. You said he was yours as well."

"He is," he admitted briefly, ignoring her gaze.

He was behaving badly, and she didn't understand it. Earlier he seemed to go out of his way to try to shield her from her fears. "If the authorities catch him, they'll transport him to Baghdad," she warned, knowing he already knew this. Frustrated, she clipped, "A fine way to deal with your friend, Major Holden."

He stopped and looked up from the drawer. "What do you prefer, Nurse Wescott, your death? Mine? Hamid's?"

Her eyes questioned his as her hands turned cold with anxiety. "The Turkish officials know we're here, is that it?"

His eyes held her's evenly, glimmering with warning. "Germans."

She swallowed.

"They know who I am, and who Hamid is," he said. "That much in itself wouldn't convince me to abandon a friend like David, but you're here. I don't doubt for a moment you would end up the victim of an 'accidental' death reported to the Turkish officials, who would in turn notify the British consul in Aleppo—with apologies."

She stepped back, wishing to let out a gasp of fear but determined to show herself calm and courageous. She turned away, biting her lip. He firmly closed the desk drawer.

"I'm sorry, Major. I shouldn't have intimated you were abandoning a friend."

"Think nothing of it, Miss Wescott."

She watched him. "I suspect you're quite valorous when it comes to friend and country."

The shadow of a cynical smile showed as he briefly scanned her. "You may find that estimation also exaggerated. I'm neither coward nor hero, but caught up in something I can't turn loose of until I see it through to the end. I stumbled into it quite by accident. So you see, your English Bible student—what was his name?—Wade Findlay?—is quite more the valorous gentleman."

Allison flushed. She feared Bret saw through her avowed disinterest and had deliberately mentioned Wade to watch her response.

"That isn't true about you either, is it?"

He regarded her. "What isn't true?"

"Your 'stumbling' quite by accident into this espionage situation," she stated. "You're not caught up in something you don't care a rap about. You care about it deeply; it's written all over you."

"Caring strongly has something to do with my 'type' again, I suppose? You'll need to explain it to me sometime when the Germans aren't breathing down my neck. As for my being transparent, I didn't think I was." He added with faint dismay, "I hope not."

She didn't find him transparent and suspected he knew she didn't. Except for a deliberate, militaristic deportment, he was utterly unfamiliar. She could only make a guess at what he was actually like. That she was faintly curious brought as much concern to her as the idea of transparency apparently did to him.

He buckled shut the satchel and turned toward the doorway into the sitting room as footsteps announced Hamid. Allison saw a Kurdish warrior, but he looked nothing like she had expected. Except for a faded black scarf wound about his head, he was dressed much like Bret, in a canvas tunic and trousers with heavy boots. He seemed to be in his forties, well conditioned to the Arabian desert and apt to defeat any who dared to come at him. He had a collection of fierce looking weapons, most of them Western in origin, and he looked as if he was well versed in their use. His walnut-colored face was rugged and quietly determined; he had thick, dark brows above eagle-sharp, black eyes that were not so hard that they didn't pause to look kindly at Allison before addressing Bret. "There is little time left, Major. If you delay longer, they'll be upon you. Go; take Miss Wescott with you. I will stay, and perhaps David and I will meet you at the oasis."

The friendship and respect that passed between the two was not lost on Allison. Bret had been right; Hamid was his loyal assistant.

If Bret was displeased over the risk this brought to his friends, he didn't show his emotions. Life and death already had been decided on between these two friends—she could tell by the cool, unemotional response displayed by both of them—but there was also no mistaking their bond.

Bret handed the oil lamp to Allison to take with her into Leah's room. As she rushed for her bags, she overheard Bret ask Hamid in a low voice, "Any success?"

"Guns and ammunition in the back of the vehicle."

"How many?"

"Enough for him to take to the others."

"Good work. Spare petrol?"

"Not enough. They heard me."

"Then we'll need to find it on the way. You know where to locate me? You know what to tell David?"

"I will tell him. Go, Major. We will make it."

Surprised and wondering, Allison hesitated in the doorway where she could just make out their silhouettes. Guns?

180

Ammunition? For whom? Where had they gotten them, and why?

Bret must have seen her standing there, for he said something indistinguishable to Hamid, then with less secrecy added, "See you don't become a martyr with your heroics. We'll need you for a more desperate time."

"Maybe it won't come. We have good plans, you and I."

Allison came out, dressed modestly in a plain, high-necked and long-sleeved blue cotton frock that reached to her ankles. Actually, it was an older uniform she had used during her nurse's training, but she had removed the cross from the bodice. She hadn't bothered to roll her hair into a chignon, for there was no time, but had tied it back with a ribbon and carried a canvas hat with a wide brim. With the rising of the sun, the day would be long and miserably hot. Her shoes were heeled leather boots, comfortable and practical for desert wear. She held her kitbag and looked at Bret, her eyes still pleading for David.

Either he didn't notice or chose not to, for he retained an inscrutable expression. "Ready?"

She nodded, not trusting herself to speak.

Hamid led the way, a hand resting on his rifle. Bret took hold of her arm and propelled her out the back door and swiftly across the dark courtyard. The wind met them head on, hot and dry, throwing sand at them and scattering brown, brittle leaves.

"Where are we going?" she asked in a half whisper.

He gave a brief laugh.

A car waited, and Hamid ran to the passenger door while Bret went to the driver's side and threw it open. Allison scrambled in beside him, wondering what manner of vehicle it was. Hamid slammed the door as the engine raced to life.

The vehicle backed out of the courtyard, the lights still out. Allison's heart was in her throat. Then she heard Hamid call, "He's coming!"

"David," cried Allison joyfully, looking over her shoulder. "He's running."

The vehicle swept back in a tight arc and paused. Bret reached back, flicking open the back door lock. David scrambled in, Hamid just behind him.

Before Hamid shut the door, the vehicle swept around and was shooting for the narrow back exit. Bret flipped the headlights on for a moment, then off again, and Allison held her breath. The engine ran smoothly as the narrow road flew past, the headlights still out.

"A ruddy mess!" said David, his voice breathless from running. "They're not far behind."

"How many?" asked Bret stepping on the throttle.

"Five, six, maybe eight. Sorry. I didn't mean to lead them to the rest of you."

"We're glad you made it. You had me worried," said Bret. "I was wondering if you had what it takes." The goad was tinged with just a flicker of humor, and David mumbled, looking behind his shoulder through the rear window. "I was beginning to wonder, too. I still am."

Hamid gave a chuckle and hit him on the shoulder. "Is this the first time a Jew and a Kurd teamed up against one enemy?"

"If it is, old man, it won't be the last," said David.

"Where are they now?" Bret looked through the rearview mirror while adjusting it.

"I don't see them following," said Hamid.

"Don't count on it," warned David. "I thought I was five minutes ahead, then from out of nowhere this ruddy German vehicle bore down on me and opened fire. They blew out the back tire, and I swerved off into some peasant's front yard, nearly killing them a chicken for supper. I was able to outrun the Germans on foot through a yard. Some grandma with a basket of eggs was yelling at me, shaking her fist."

Hamid laughed.

Bret smiled. "Lucky for you she didn't have a basket of rocks instead. She would have landed you for the Germans."

"I saw their car head toward the expedition hut. By now they're there," warned David.

Both he and Hamid looked through the rear window.

"I don't see them," David said.

"I don't suppose they're using lights either," noted Bret.

His voice, Allison thought with chattering teeth, was as unexcited as though discoursing on the weather.

"Keep watching," said Bret. "If they follow, they'll need to flash them on when they near the back drive."

Allison, too, turned in her seat to stare out the small rear window.

Bret swung the vehicle onto the main road where they were soon speeding toward the desolate wilderness.

Allison saw a brief flash and exclaimed, "They're coming."

"They're onto us," said Hamid.

Allison looked at Bret and saw him glance at the speedometer.

"What are they driving, David?"

She knew why he asked. They would need to run for it, and if the Germans had a faster vehicle, they were in trouble.

"Looks like a Hun machine," said David. "Probably a Mercedes."

She glanced at Bret, but either he was used to concealing his thoughts or he knew she watched him, for David might as well have suggested they themselves were on mules.

"There is always hope," said Hamid pleasantly, and ambled off on a story about a lame-footed camel and a Turkish armored car.

"I suppose the camel prevailed in the end," said David.

Hamid smiled. "Why not? The camel can go without water for long distances, and the armored car needs petrol."

"I don't see that the tale applies. We both have petrol, but they have the Mercedes," David observed.

"Ah, but the Mercedes depends on tires and a radiator."

"So that's what Bret has in mind—"

Bret glanced over his shoulder at Hamid. The exchange must have told the Kurd something, for he reached to the floorboard. Allison heard him opening a case. Several seconds later he lifted out two guns. Allison suspected they were German-made, but other than that they were unfamiliar. Hamid also produced several carbines and boxes of ammunition, placing them within easy reach.

She tensed, gripping the seat, and looked again at Bret. He swerved suddenly and drove the vehicle off the road and toward some dunes.

"For speed we're no Mercedes, but we're built for traction. Hold on!"

Allison clung to the seat as they slowed sharply to a bumping, swaying crawl down what looked to her to be a caravan road made for camels and horses. On either side of them were mounds of sand and rocks.

Bret didn't wait long before he gestured to Hamid and David, who flung open their doors and clambered out, carrying the weapons. Allison reached for her door to do the same, but Bret's hand caught her wrist, and their eyes met in the moonlight reflecting off the white sand. "Stay here. We'll be back when it's over. Understood?"

She tried to swallow the fear that came to her throat. She guessed they were going to ambush the German vehicle, and her heart was thudding so hard she was breathless.

"Don't worry," he whispered, adding casually, "Hamid and I have done this before. I was hoping we could avoid it, but…" He opened the door and was out. "Stay down," was all he said. "There are scorpions, so don't wander."

The door shut, leaving her enclosed in hot stillness. She felt the wind buffet the car's side with grains of sand. Looking through the side window, she saw they already had vanished into the desert night.

She huddled on the seat, her heart crying out to God for the horror they were experiencing. She could only imagine what they were doing with the guns near the side of the road. To reject the evil hour, to avoid the reality of violence and death, she closed her eyes and placed her sweating palms over her ears.

How long—four minutes, five? Then rapid gunfire crackled through the scorching darkness. She waited for what might have been ten minutes. David came running toward the vehicle, flinging open the door to the back seat, while Bret arrived supporting Hamid. They hauled him into the back. Hamid had been struck during the gunfire exchange. David tore aside the front of Hamid's shirt.

Allison scrambled from the front seat, but Bret caught her arm and turned her around to face him. "There's no time. We've got to get out of here."

Startled, her eyes rushed to his, but he refused to allow her to search, to understand his action. There was no outward apology for his apparent indifference to Hamid. He propelled her back toward her seat.

She could feel the thick tension that came between them as vividly as a descending wall. In the starlight, his restrained tension showed in the handsome, rugged cut of his jaw, in his burning, uncooperative eyes.

Allison was appalled. "He's your friend," she gritted in a whisper.

"I need no reminder. Get inside. Please." Allison glanced back toward Hamid's silhouette, sweating and gritting against pain, then to Bret. Her indignation slowly stirred to life. He had been willing to leave Jerablus without David, and though she understood her own life may have been safeguarded by his doing so, she believed Major Bret Holden to be so coolly proficient that he was callous.

"I won't leave him like that. Do you care if he dies?"

For only a brief moment his vulnerability showed, and Allison felt the sting of her remark. She wished she hadn't said it, but his eyes held hers steadily. She tried to soften her response, as if he didn't understand. "This environment is no friend to a wound. You know that, Major. Even a blister can lead to blood poisoning within less than an hour. I'll need a light."

"German soldiers are still out there," he said flatly. "Any light will draw them to us."

She understood now, but he turned toward David and said in a toneless voice, "Assist Miss Wescott. There's a torch in the back. I'll keep watch."

Alarmed, she wanted to cry, "No!" but he took his weapon with him and disappeared back into the darkness.

Allison looked after him, then scrambled into the back beside Hamid while David rummaged in the trunk until he located her small medical kit and brought it to her.

"I'll need ten minutes," she whispered.

David took up one of the guns and went after Bret.

She worked with surprisingly steady fingers, trying to remain calm and concentrate on what she was doing. But her mind and heart were divided between Hamid, and Bret and David on guard in the darkness between them and any German soldiers concealing themselves near the road.

Gunfire crackled again, and her eyes shut briefly as sweat broke out on her forehead. *Please God, no.*

The men returned in a run. Not a word was spoken as Bret backed swiftly toward the narrow main road, swerved onto the hard track, and with the headlights out and the vehicle pointing in the direction of Aleppo, pressed on the accelerator, and they sped away.

Allison looked toward what she knew was the darkened German car ambushed on the road toward Aleppo.

"How is he?" asked Bret a minute later.

"The wound was too high for the lung," she said, surprised her voice was calm. "It may have shattered his collar bone. I can't be sure. There's nothing more I can do now except try to prevent poisoning. I don't have the instruments needed to remove a bullet. He'll need a bed and a doctor. Major," she added, "I didn't understand about soldiers still being out there. I wouldn't have—"

"They're all dead now," he said briefly.

Hamid's black eyes focused on her, and he tried to say something, but he was too weak. She nodded, soothing his frustration. "It's all right," she whispered. "We're on our way to Aleppo."

David produced a canteen of water, handing it to Allison who unstopped it and lifted Hamid's head to drink, letting the water dribble drop by drop to his tongue, making certain he could swallow. David then handed it to Bret, who drank thirstily, wiping the sweat from his face onto the back of his now soiled shirt.

He was speeding as fast as the vehicle would travel, and no one spoke. Allison, feeling numb, rested Hamid's head on her shoulder and looked ahead where the headlight beams picked up miles of wilderness.

David talked in low tones to Bret, but Allison picked up Bret's reply. "The sooner we abandon this vehicle the safer we'll be. And we'll need to separate. We're less likely to draw attention. A car is waiting at the house. You'll take it and go on with Miss Wescott."

"With the supplies?" asked David.

"No. Not now. It's too risky. She'll be with you."

"Your bringing the supplies like that wasn't part of the plan.

They'll be breathing down your neck. I was to risk it alone. I didn't mind because I believed in it with my soul, but you—" David was interrupted by Bret.

"It's a choice I've decided to make. Let's just say I believe in more than you think."

"What of Hamid? He'll stand out like a black eye for any on alert."

"We've been through worse tight spots. I'll take him with me. Once we reach Aleppo, we split up. We'll meet in Jerusalem."

"All right. We won't forget this, Major."

"Nor will I. We expect a harvest, remember?"

"We'll be there. Her name is Rose Lyman. Her brother works under another name for the Turkish officer. It's a perfect setup, Major, and I don't see anything going wrong."

"Never trust plans to go as well as they look on paper. If anything can go wrong, it will. But if we know that, we won't let it stop us."

David leaned back in the seat, and they drove on in silence again.

Jerusalem. Despite Bret's words that plans usually went awry, she believed he made them with extreme care, that he was a military major who rarely made mistakes. And when he did, she believed they ate at his insides even while he pretended they did not.

She wanted to ask him about the guns and ammunition, but she checked herself, believing she had misinterpreted his judgments enough for one night. She wasn't supposed to know that Hamid had mentioned them to Bret back at the expedition hut. It was wiser to keep silent.

Had it been part of some plan for David to smuggle them through to Jerusalem beneath the Turks' noses? A dangerous proposition, but if it were so, what did he expect to do with weapons in

Jerusalem? It wasn't lost on Allison that Bret was quite in charge, both willing to change plans and to take the greater personal risk when it appeared necessary. It hadn't been his first plan to deliver the guns himself.

Bret appeared callous; perhaps he was cynical. But how was she to really know? The real Major Bret Holden lived and moved behind a barricade of callous indifference. Unless he chose to cooperate, there was no way to break through.

Perhaps she shouldn't be curious, she warned herself. Trying to understand what lay behind that cool and brash exterior could place her at risk emotionally.

Aleppo was quiet and dark when they arrived, but soon the dawn would break in the east. Had either the Turkish or German authorities near Jerablus wired the officials at Aleppo to be on the lookout? Did the British consul know about one of their own masquerading as Colonel Brent Holman? The British official would be fast asleep this time of night and was perhaps as innocent as a lamb, or so he could inform the Turkish authorities tomorrow when word arrived of what had happened on the road outside Jerablus.

Bret had informed David that he had silenced the communication line when they attacked the Germans on the road. She wondered what it all meant, yet she wasn't sure she really wanted to know. Involvement with Leah and her death had been tragic and life-changing enough.

As they entered Aleppo, Allison considered her situation. It certainly was not without risk now that she had involved herself with Bret, David, and Hamid in whatever they were trying to accomplish with the guns. She wondered if it had any connection with Leah and Neal's work or the death of the British agent posing as Major Reuter.

Perhaps there was no direct connection.

She debated her plans, wondering what they were except for returning safely to Port Said to wait with her mother for her father's arrival. Sir Marshall would soon be home from his government business with the British viceroy in India. Allison had her work with Aunt Lydia aboard the *Mercy*, of course, and it was there, involved in medicine and sharing the message of Christianity, that her heart found its final and true calling. But how could she ever be the same again now that Leah had been murdered? If Major Holden was right and war was inevitable with Germany, what was to be her response? Did she not owe it to Leah to become involved? And what of cousin Neal? As yet no one seemed to know where he was. If Bret knew, he wasn't in the mood to tell her. Then there was David and his passion for a homeland in Jerusalem. She had so much to think about, to decide, that she longed for the restful atmosphere of home in the safety and solitude of the Port Said residence.

Bret maneuvered the motorcar down a rather dirty, narrow stone street that Allison believed to be no wider than seven or eight feet. At any moment she expected to hear the sides of the car scrape against the clutter of small square houses built on top of each other amid crowded shops. Then the street began to widen into a *suk*, a square or bazaar crowded with stalls. Bret pulled to a stop beside a fruit stand.

It was still dark and relatively quiet, though already some businesses were preparing for the day. The fragrant smell of baking bread filled the air. Several donkeys carrying loads of fruits and vegetables three times as wide as their backs trotted down toward the end of the *suk* where it narrowed again into jutting stalls. Beggars were there, reserving their favored positions for the new day by sleeping on the spot. She saw a cat prowling and looking up toward roosting pigeons who, in turn, looked down with condescension from their vantage points. A dog barked with a monotonous yapping as though it dreaded the prospect of another long day of insufferable heat and flies.

Hamid was asleep, and David stirred as Bret turned toward him. "This is where we part," said Bret. He gestured ahead. "Turn left up the street. An Arab will be sleeping in a lift. Tell him I sent you. He speaks English. He'll take you to where the car is kept. You'll find the keys in the courtyard by a door where poppies grow. Don't wait. Drive straight through. Spare petrol is in the trunk."

David, in a moment of emotion, clasped Bret's shoulder, and his eyes flashed warm and brown. Without a word, he got out and waited for Allison. She hesitated, her eyes meeting Bret's. They looked at each other, but while she was in the starlight and feared her eyes were luminous and revealing, he was in the shadows of a roofed stall, and she couldn't see his face.

"You may need me to help with Hamid. Perhaps I should—"

"I've a friend here in Aleppo," he interrupted. "A Kurd. I'll leave Hamid with him. He'll see to Hamid's care until I can get back."

"Then, I suppose this is good-bye," she said.

"So it appears. Good-bye."

If she expected Major Holden to turn suddenly warm and sentimental, portraying the camaraderie of two friends who had been through much together, she was forgetting his emotional detachment. He leaned over and opened the door where she sat.

He's so arrogant, she thought.

"I'll see you in Jerusalem," he added when she got out.

If there was more to that suggestion than casual inference, she refused it.

"I'm not going to Jerusalem, Major," she stated. Whether he knew it or not, she had just made up her mind. She didn't want to lay eyes on him again. "I'm going to the British consul here in

Aleppo. I just happen to have some friends there who drove up from the archaeology huts. Good-bye," she added with deliberate indifference. She closed the door, feeling a stain of emotional anger on her face.

But she had only taken a few steps in the direction of the shop doorway where David waited in the shadow of the stalls, when she heard Bret open his door and get out. In a brief stride, he caught up and intercepted her.

"You can't go there," he said in a low voice.

"I certainly can and will."

He laughed. "You'll need to go home to Cairo by way of Jerusalem, unless I can arrange a boat trip by way of Haifa to Port Said."

Her eyes rushed to his, and she was confronted by warm flecks of cobalt blue. "You needn't arrange anything. I'm perfectly capable of arranging my own passage."

"I don't see what you're in such a huff about."

"I am not in a 'huff'!"

"Let's not argue," he said with a smile. "I don't have the time. You'll simply do as I ask. Please."

She paused, calming her pounding heart. "Why? Why must I go by way of Jerusalem?"

His tone was evasive. "For your safety."

"But I don't have the book—"

"Don't mention that," he cut in quietly. "You're not to mention it to anyone ever. Understood?"

She looked about as though he had alerted her to ghostly shadows hiding behind the stalls listening. "You don't think—" she began, but he drew her toward the bonnet of the motorcar.

"Your safety may count on amnesia. And yes, I'm thinking of your safety as well David's, Hamid's, mine, and others—many others."

192

"I don't understand," she whispered, searching his deliberately neutral gaze.

"I know. I'm asking you to trust me, Allison."

It was one of the few times he had spoken her name. The stillness, the hot, smothering smell of animals and dust and old stone seemed to squeeze off her breath.

"I do trust you. Would I have told you about Leah if I didn't? But I don't see why I can't avail myself of a comfortable feather bed and a bath at the British consul. I came up with the Blaines. Why shouldn't I go back with them?"

"For a simple reason I can't explain now. It's not General Blaine and his wife I'm worried about, but you mustn't be there tomorrow when the Turkish or German officials show up. They'll be swarming all over the place demanding answers. If they find you there, even if you pretend you know nothing of what happened, they'll learn you were with Leah, if they don't already know."

She hadn't thought about that. "But if I don't show up or send some explanation to the Blaines, they'll be desperately worried about me. They are family friends, quite trustworthy."

"I've no reason to argue that." His dark lashes lowered a little. "Just do as I say, will you? We're wasting precious time. Every moment we stand here gives an advantage to those who would stop us."

Suddenly she felt exhausted and emotionally spent. She was troubled that her presence was putting him at extra risk. He saw it and took hold of her arm. "I don't want to sound rude, Allison. It's not my intention to harass you, if that's what you think. Seeing you like this is ruddy hard on me."

"All right. I'll go with David to Jerusalem," she stated. "I'll need my bags. They're in the back of your car."

A faint flicker showed in his gaze, then he went to the trunk, opened it, removed her bags, piled them by the stall, and walked to the car door. As their gaze met briefly, his mouth showed a shadow of smile. Without another word exchanged between them, he got behind the wheel and closed the door quietly. The next moment the car pulled away down the narrow stone street and, turning a corner, disappeared.

Allison looked after the dusty vehicle, knowing too well it was a marked car as far as German and Turkish intelligence were concerned. Yet he had insisted on David driving the second car toward Jerusalem. She felt a pall of uncertainty tighten her heart as she contemplated Bret. She had never met anyone like him before and didn't know whether she wanted to know him better or completely avoid him.

She was still standing there, perspiring and miserable, longing for a bath and contemplating the long, arduous journey to Jerusalem, when David gathered up her bags and said in a hurried, low voice, "Come along, Allison. Let's get out of here."

It was still dark, but dawn was fast on the heels of the fading night. They hurried along the edge of the stalls, aware that life was beginning to stir. With the ascending, rosy dawn, the *suk* was coming alive with an influx of local Arabs. Several camels came down the street under their loads and headed toward the end of the sharply narrowing street between jutting rows of food stalls. Ragged children played and ate their breakfast of bread while the adults opened their stalls for the long trading day.

"We're to turn left just ahead," said David, and she hurried along beside him, glancing about the bazaar. She was more tired than she had realized, for her kitbag was already getting heavy. David, who carried the rest of the bags, shifted them in his hands.

They threaded their way out of the packed square and turned down a narrow, rutted street where the sunlight now brazenly struck the dust.

"There must be a dozen Arabs with lifts," she said. "How do we know which one?"

They hadn't walked far when they neared a section of small houses partially made of mud.

"That must be him. He's the only one dozing on a lift. We'll soon find out."

"Or get trapped trying." Allison hesitated while David approached the Arab and in English offered the name of Bret Holden.

The man was wide awake. Perhaps he had been all along. He climbed down from the wooden, wagon-like contraption, calling to her "Allo" and "Good morning."

David tossed the bags onto the back, and the Arab went around to the front to drive the donkeys. Allison stepped up to sit on the edge of the lift, and David jumped onto the back as the donkeys trotted away, their hoofs raising powdery tan dust.

They arrived where the car was located more quickly than she had expected, and she looked about curiously, uncertain where they were. An outer courtyard showed little life at the back gate where they had stopped. At first glance the gate didn't seem to lead any-where. She wondered at the stifling heat, which was already trapped within the high, whitewashed walls. An odor of chickens and goats permeated the air. Then she saw it, parked in some morning indigo shade—a small motorcar. The Arab left them, and David went quickly to the hiding place, retrieving the keys near the wall where poppies grew in profusion. It was a stylish little car, British, she sup-posed. She wondered to whom it might belong. Bret? Did he have a house in Aleppo? In the next minute, they were in the car with the engine running smoothly. David looked at her with a grin.

"This week in Jerusalem," he said.

11

WHEN ALLISON HEARD THE BIRDS taking their morning bath in the garden's fountain and saw the sunlight glinting through the rattan blind in the little bedroom, she remembered where she was. She raised her head, fully awake now, smelling freshly brewed coffee and eggs. A smile softened her face as she sat up , tossing aside the thin coverlet and snatching her wrapper from the foot of the bed.

She was a guest in the home of Mrs. Rose Lyman, a middle-aged Jewish woman with dark brown hair and friendly eyes. Her warmth of hospitality almost made Allison feel as if she, too, had Jewish blood and had come home to visit relatives.

Then it occurred to her, *I'm in Jerusalem, city of the great King, the land where my Lord became my Savior.*

She didn't move, for her heart was pounding as she let the full meaning of her location sweep across her soul. A host of biblical heroes marched across her heart: Abraham and Sarah, Isaac, Jacob, Samuel, David, Isaiah, Peter, James, John, the apostle Paul, the persecuted Church.

Now war loomed on Palestine's horizon. What waited in the whirlwind of dust and sand and in God's purposes for history?

She turned her head toward the open window where the birds' song cheered her. It had been night when she and David had arrived. The city had seemed old, dusty, and not very different from Aleppo. But it was different. This was the chosen city, chosen by God in the past, chosen by him for the future. To this beloved city Jesus Christ would one day return and reign. One glorious day.

She recalled how tired she had been last night, but even then weariness hadn't dampened her growing enthusiasm for being here. She was pleased now that Major Holden had insisted she come. She remembered how Mrs. Lyman had welcomed her to stay as long as she needed, and David, too. Of course, Rose Lyman had expected him. He had written to her from London, and she had corresponded with him as a mother writes her absent son, telling him of the political climate in Jerusalem, of the band of Jews who worked for some manner of independence and rule of their own in the city. David Ben-Gurion was their spokesman, and Mr. Ben-Gurion knew important people in the British government—Lord Balfor, Chaim Weizman, and others who were friendly toward Zionism.

Last night she had told them they would meet Mr. Ben-Gurion. Perhaps in a day or two, just as soon as it seemed safe for a gathering in her home. The Turkish officials were fiercely against any independence movements of Jews or Arabs, she had said. They treated both groups as outcasts, imprisoning many Arabs from Turkey who had also come to organize for freedom from the Ottoman Empire.

Allison glanced about the sparkling room with its little white cotton curtains, handmade furniture, and vase of yellow roses from Mrs. Lyman's garden. A plate of figs, dates, and sesame candy stood on an olivewood table.

Allison drew in a deep breath and hurried to the door. Last night Mrs. Lyman had told her the door opened to a flight of stone steps that would take Allison up to the flat roof, which was used much like a terrace. There, she could look out on Old Jerusalem. She might even be able to see the temple site.

Allison didn't know what she expected as she climbed the steps, feeling the bright Jerusalem sunshine sprinkling her head and back like a warm blessing. She smiled to herself. Did she think she might be transported back in time to see the Lord riding into the city on a donkey? "Hosanna," she whispered. "Hosanna to the Son of David, to the Son of God."

But when she reached the rooftop where some tables and chairs were pleasantly arranged, the smile vanished from her face. The Dome of the Rock, the Moslem shrine, glinted brazenly from the site where the temple had once stood. Minarets dotted the skyline, and to her ears came the unwanted cry of the muezzin, as the Moslem call to prayer echoed in the city.

She was still standing there when a child's voice interrupted her thoughts. "Happy morning, Miss Allison. My mother says come. It's time for breakfast. And she has a surprise for you. I know what it is, but she told me to say nothing."

Allison turned from the rail with a smile tinged with sadness. Mrs. Lyman's little boy, Benjamin watched her with stark curiosity in his soft brown eyes. He was a comely child, though small for his twelve years. He was now a son of the law, he had told her last night, since he had undergone his bar mitzvah last week and could rattle off portions from the Torah. Proudly he had announced to her that he had been born in Jerusalem. "But Mother was born in New York. We came here to live with Uncle Samuel. He used to be a rabbi, but he isn't anymore. They won't let him. Even my bar mitzvah had to be done in secret. But Mr. Ben-Gurion says all that will change. Do you think it will, Allison?"

She had smiled. "May God grant it, Benjamin. But what happened to your father in New York?"

"He died in an accident in the warehouse where they made shirts. I don't know how exactly, but he got caught in a machine."

Mrs. Lyman called up from below in the small, stone courtyard behind the house. "Benjamin? Did you find Miss Allison?"

He ran to the rail and peered over. "Yes, we're coming now. I told her you had a surprise for her."

He looked at Allison and smiled. "Better hurry."

"I will!" Caught up in his excitement, she quickly descended the steps to her room to change.

Ten minutes later, Allison opened the door into the main section of the house and was greeted by the homey fragrance of biscuits.

"The Sabbath is over," said Benjamin, meeting her, "so we can have biscuits with honey. It's my favorite."

She followed the boy through a small sitting room and into a dining room that opened onto the courtyard. The citrus trees that grew in tubs were green, with waxy leaves, and the oval shapes of oranges and limes were nestled within, ready for picking. A garden of herbs grew in a neat wooden square, showing varied colors of greens, grays, and reddish textures. Then she stopped short, astounded.

"Neal?" came her breathless question, as if seeing a mirage. The man who stood there was no mirage. His thick, sandy hair that scuffed the collar of his cotton shirt was in need of a trim. Beneath heavy golden-brown lashes, his brittle blue eyes were like Leah's. His desert-tanned face reflected the outdoorsy good looks that had originated with his deceased father.

"I thought the smell of my cooking would rouse you. Good morning, you lazy creature."

She let out a cry, a smile appearing as she exclaimed, "Neal!"

He laughed, opening his arms to give her a brotherly hug as she rushed to him. "Welcome to our home away from home. I see Rose has made you comfortable."

"Oh, how good it is to see you, Neal. How dare you frighten us so with your disappearance at Aleppo!"

"Ah, yes, I can explain about that sometime."

"I assume this isn't the moment," she said. "More secrets I suppose. Ah, well, I'm learning to live with them, but it isn't at all easy. You might have let us know you were safe."

"Yes, I'm sorry about that. But David tells me you've met Major Holden."

She looked at him, wondering if this was his way to ask how much she knew. "Yes, a man of all trades," she said meaningfully, thinking about his roles as a colonel, a professor, and now a British major with Cairo intelligence. "Any word of his arrival yet?"

"Then you do know," he said quietly. "I wasn't at all sure. He told you? And Leah?"

Leah. Surely David had told him. Yet his outward appearance contradicted any grief for his sister, and she tensed, believing he didn't know. Apparently David had been unable to bring himself to tell Neal, deciding to leave it to her.

"Leah explained what she felt was safe to disclose. Major Holden helped David and me escape Jerablus, but he's rather uncooperative about cluing me in."

"We're expecting him tonight, if all goes well," Neal said.

If all goes well. Please, Lord, it has to. Please protect him.

She was thankful for the diversion of the cup of hot tea Neal handed her. He watched her thoughtfully, as though he guessed she had troubling news but wasn't ready to share it just yet.

"Bret will be stationed in Cairo," he went on. "So I suspect we'll be seeing a lot more of him, especially if war breaks out. You'll have plenty of opportunity to learn what's going on. Unfortunately, neither Leah nor I are at liberty to go into detail. Bret could, if he wished. Perhaps he doesn't want you involved. Those in intelligence can be brutal when it comes to clamping down on wagging tongues. I can explain some things, and I think that goes both ways. But this isn't the time. We'll talk later, if we can get away."

She nodded that she understood and fingered the hot cup, keeping her gaze averted.

David came in from the courtyard with Mrs. Lyman and Benjamin.

"I hope Neal is making you feel at home," said the smiling woman to Allison. "David and I wanted to give you time alone together, but Benjamin here couldn't wait to see your response to our surprise. One would think he had arranged it just for you."

"I'm delighted," said Allison with a laugh. "Seeing Neal safe and indulging his favorite pastime has restored some joy."

"My favorite pastime is eating, not cooking," said Neal lightly, using the spatula to flip the cake with expertise. Benjamin clapped, and Neal said for Allison's benefit, "And these, cousin, are delectable indeed. If you haven't tried potato latkes with a smidgen of Rose's preserves, you haven't lived."

"We usually have them on Chanukah," said Benjamin, and he quoted, "'The temple was under siege, and there was oil enough for only one day to light it. But by a miracle it lasted for eight days.'" He smiled. "The fat used to fry them is a symbol of the oil."

"I'm starved," Allison said with a laugh. "When do we try them?"

Neal glanced toward the door. "Just as soon as that sister of mine rolls out of bed. Or has Leah decided to sleep until noon?" He turned to Benjamin. "Benny, why don't you run up and see what's keeping Leah?"

With a pang, Allison's eyes swerved to David.

David's gaze faltered. Allison's face must have altered perceptibly, for even Mrs. Lyman winced. Looking down at Benjamin, she said, "I need to gather a few oranges. Come help me, will you?"

"But there's a whole bagful on the—"

"Benjamin," she stated quietly but evenly, "I need your help. Come along, son."

"Yes, Mother, but—"

She drew him away, and they walked out into the courtyard where the sparrows were chirping loudly and flitting from tree to tree. David walked to the open doorway with his back toward them and stood staring out.

Neal, picking up the tension, watched Allison. "What is it?" he demanded in a low voice.

"Oh, Neal!" Her voice broke.

Almost at once, Neal tossed down the spatula and ran into the sitting room, on his way to the bedroom, as if he must see for himself that Leah was not there.

Allison turned and ran after him, but he had already stopped in the sitting room, as if putting a brake on his emotions. "She's not here?" she heard him say in a breath of dismay.

"No," she whispered. "I thought you knew. I thought David had explained."

"Explained what? I thought she was doubling up with you."

Allison looked at him hopelessly. What could she say? What comfort was there to offer? "Leah's dead."

He didn't move, and for a second she didn't think he had heard her. She nearly repeated herself, but then she saw the pain breaking in his blue eyes.

"God," he whispered reverently in prayer, hoarsely, "why?" He sank into the chair, head in hands.

She went to him and knelt beside him, her hands on his arm. Tears streamed down her face, more for Neal's pain now than for what could not be changed for Leah.

After a few minutes he said in a cracked voice: "How did it happen? Or am I being a fool to ask when I know already how it must have been."

"They—we found her at the Roman-Syrian Digs, the abandoned

site near the vacation huts," she explained. "They said it was an accident..."

His eyes came to hers. She knew he understood. It was no accident. Pale and tense, Allison waited for him to recover.

"Does Bret know?"

"Yes, he thinks as we do. Neal, she was murdered by the enemy. The same enemy who killed the man you were to meet at the huts that night, Karl Reuter."

"How much do you know of all this, Allison?"

She glanced about the silent room. "Is it safe to talk here?"

"Rose is one of us."

"I thought she might be when David said he had been corresponding with her about the Zionist movement. The guns and ammunition, are they for friends here in Palestine?" she whispered.

His hand closed about hers. "Not now. Tell me about Leah, about how much you know of this."

As much as she trusted him, she felt constrained not to mention the book. She remembered what Leah had said about safeguards being necessary even when dealing with her own brother. It would be left to Bret, as Neal's superior, to explain if he chose. Bret, too, had told her to keep silent.

"I know as much as Leah. She had no one to turn to. I had to help her. I hid her in my hut for two days, until—" She stopped when he groaned.

"She shouldn't have involved you in this. It's dangerous, as you know by now."

"So Bret has told me. Well, I am involved, and there's no changing the facts. We'll need to carry on as best we can." She stood and paced as she told him everything that had happened, ending with the attack of the Germans who were following them on the road from Jerablus.

"They were on Bret's trail," he said. "The real Colonel Holman must have arrived from Constantinople. The four of you were lucky to get out as you did. David told me about Hamid, but he thinks he'll survive." He stood and walked about the room. "But I won't be satisfied until Bret arrives. That motorcar is a marked vehicle. The Germans would have wired ahead to every telegraph to have it stopped at all costs. And now he has the guns and ammunition."

She swallowed, thinking of the long trek across the wilderness.

"Tell me more about Leah," he said. "What was she doing alone out at the abandoned digs?"

"She left that last night we were together to go meet you."

"To meet me?" he asked incredulously. "My orders were to leave the area at once. As soon as our agent was killed, the plans shifted. Bret was to take over. Leah should have know that. We had made plans earlier. If any one of us was trapped, the others were to get out quickly. I thought she had escaped to Damascus."

"Damascus? She never mentioned it. Are you sure?"

"Of course."

"We had been waiting to hear from you. Odd, but she seemed to think she had a reason to expect you to contact her."

"Did she? Odd, indeed. I can't understand it. We had our orders. What did Major Holden tell you?"

"Nothing. Does he know? About Damascus, I mean?"

"I would think so. He's higher up than either Leah or me."

She shook her head, bewildered. "I don't know. She expected you. It was one of the reasons she didn't leave."

"One of the reasons? There were more?"

She looked at him. "She had this notion the agent had left behind some message for her."

"Reuter? Yes. It was meant for me. I see now. Leah would naturally be obligated to pick up where I had left off. If something happened to me, it was in her lap. But I knew Bret was arriving to take my place. I'd heard how qualified he was. He had worked in Constantinople before this, then Baghdad. And I thought Leah would have escaped at once to Damascus."

Allison sank wearily into the chair. "It seems we all crossed purposes, doesn't it? Bret didn't know Leah was there, either. If he had, she might be alive today." She looked at Neal across the room, his face drawn and grief in his eyes. "Until the very end she expected you might show up."

He groaned. "She was ripe for a trap. I don't know a thing about this message, Allison. I'd never have lured her away from the hut, least of all ask her to meet me alone somewhere with the information."

"She believed it. She was relaxed and hopeful for the first time since I had arrived. She kept saying your contact had arrived, that soon the terrible burden would be gone from her. She expected to return with me to Cairo."

"The contact arrived, all right," said Neal wearily. "But not in the way she assumed. Bret came as Colonel Holman. Poor kid, I let her down."

"No, Neal, how were you to know she was there? Bret, too, only acted on the knowledge he had at the time. No one is to blame. Not Leah, either. She was brave and dedicated, and she gave her life willingly for the good of England. It's left to us to see she didn't die in vain."

He looked at her. "I don't like the way you say that. Does Bret approve of your being involved in this?"

"You ought to know better than to ask that question."

He smiled wanly. "You're right. He wouldn't. Well, good! The sooner you're home safe on Aunt's boat, the happier I'll be. You're all I have left now, you know, now that Leah—" He stopped. "Ruddy development! Why did it have to be Leah? It should have been me. She was filling in for me!"

Allison went to him. "You mustn't blame yourself. You were following orders. From what I've learned, following orders from your superior is absolutely crucial. There's little room to branch out on your own, especially risking information out of personal feelings. Oh, Neal, you thought she was safe. And if she died in your place, well, she did it willingly, didn't she?"

"Maybe. But she thought she was meeting me. She trusted me, and I wasn't there!"

Allison held her cousin, and his body convulsed as he sobbed. "Oh, Leah, my poor little sister, left alone out there in that wilderness to face the murderer."

Allison led him to the chair and held his sandy head against her until his weeping had ebbed into silence.

Minutes passed before either spoke again. When they did, Neal's voice was once again steady, his emotions under control. "So that's how they lured her there. They made her think I had arrived. Clever of them. What else did she tell you?"

Allison looked at him. "She was to bring you the information Karl Reuter left for you in his hut."

Neal breathed something inaudible. "Did she?"

Allison wavered. How much should she tell him? How much should she leave out? This was her beloved cousin. She trusted him with her life. Yet she was to say nothing of the book.

"She brought a satchel with her."

"Do you know what was in it?"

"No," she said truthfully. "She was careful."

"Then they have it," he said wearily. He sank into the chair and lapsed into silence.

Maybe not, she wanted to say.

"That night," said Neal thoughtfully, "when she left you at the hut to meet me, what time did she leave?"

"Around eight, I think, when it was very dark. They must have pulled a gun on her and forced her to drive out to the abandoned digs. They took the information and killed her." Allison swallowed, imagining it all. "After she left, I heard a noise, like someone had been in Reuter's old hut listening to our good-byes."

Neal walked to the window and, without moving the blind, stared out into the courtyard.

"It's over now," he said grimly. "There's little left to hope for except the safe arrival of Bret Holden."

In the grim silence that followed, Allison's concerns strayed back to the safety of Bret. Then David walked in and joined them.

"I'm sorry," he said, throwing up his hands. "I didn't have it in me to tell him about Leah. Anyway," he half-grumbled, "it seemed best to come from a family member. I hardly knew her."

Neal looked over at him. "Hardly knew her? I didn't think you knew my sister at all."

"I didn't say anything, but I met her when she first arrived at the huts, before the club members came. She had driven down early, she said. She was hostess or something like that. We talked for a while, that's all; then I left."

Allison frowned. "But you didn't arrive until the next day, after Major Reuter's death. Remember? I met you coming out of the hut."

He smiled crookedly. "I rather misled you, Allison. I'm sorry. I didn't want you to know the real reason I'd come. I didn't know if I could trust you or not."

"Well, thank you very much," she said, folding her arms.

"You know what I mean," he hastened. "I'd come to meet Major Holden, and it was to be a secret. Lives were involved, and I didn't want you at risk. So I said he was a professor of archaeology. It seemed fitting considering the club and all. Little did I know you were already into something even more dangerous than arranging a delivery of guns and ammunition. I began to suspect Leah might be in your hut, and I felt it had something to do with the death of the German officer, but I didn't know what. I had no idea Bret was masquerading as Colonel Holman until he and some Kurdish soldiers rescued me from that droopy mustached Mustafa! I'd like to meet up with that guy again. I'd knock his block off." He touched the side of his head where he had been clobbered.

Allison didn't know how much David knew, but it appeared as if he were more involved with Bret Holden than she had thought.

Neal seemed to know what she was thinking and said quietly, "Our involvement with David is a fork in the road from what's going on at the Berlin-Baghdad Railway. The only thing that's the same is our singular interest in defeating Germany and Austria, if war breaks out and spreads to Arabia."

"The guns and ammunition," she asked, "who are they for? A resistance army?"

"Not exactly." He looked at David.

"She might as well know," said David. "I don't think Major Holden will mind. We're linked with the Zionist movement, with loyalties to Ben-Gurion and others here in Jerusalem and elsewhere."

"You mean Major Holden?" she asked, surprised.

"Privately, he shares our dreams. But militarily? No, he's not linked except by friendship. He has his own orders." David's brown eyes became serious and intense as he leaned forward in his chair. "You know our passion for a homeland. Jews like myself, like Rose, like the others, are willing to fight and die to make a home here in the land God gave us. We want some independence from the Turks, just like the Arabs here do. Rose says a few of the leaders have been arrested by the Turks already. Any public demonstration on our part, and the Turks will immediately arrest and imprison us.

"Rose, Mrs. Lyman, is one of us, a friend of Bret's. It was Bret who told me about her in London when we met at the Zionist meeting that night. Mrs. Lyman has offered to serve the British government as a spy here in Palestine, should war break out. The guns and ammunition are for our personal protection from the Turks or the Germans, if it comes to that. That little matter we have to thank Major Holden for. He arranged it. Just how, you'll need to ask him." David smiled his enthusiasm.

"A spy? Mrs. Lyman?" said Allison. It was hard to imagine the warm, middle-aged Jewish mother as a spy for England.

"She's not the only one. We've formed a spy ring. Rose is one of the leaders. What better spy than a grandmotherly sort who makes good chicken soup, I ask?"

"I think it's wonderful," whispered Allison, moved as always by sacrifice and courage in others. Yes, who would suspect a middle-aged woman? And, of course, Leah had done her part, giving her life.

"Rose is also offering her services in geography," said David. "She's an expert on Palestine. She'll aid the British troops, mapping out water wells for their use, if war comes. The British hope Turkey won't enter on the side of Germany, but they want to be prepared."

"And you?" she asked. "You're staying on?"

"I've come as a relative from London, with ties to her family in New York. I'll live here, help in every way I can. I expect to involve myself with Ben-Gurion and the movement."

"A movement," said Neal quietly, "that will end in tragedy for every Jew if the Turks learn of the political meetings. I've had word this morning that General Pasha has arrived from Constantinople to look into them. Arrests are imminent."

"The ruddy Turks," said David bitterly. "I'll live to see them kicked out of Jerusalem. They are the new, cruel taskmasters. They would have us all out making bricks without straw, if they could. I'll admit the truth: I hope Turkey enters the war on Germany's side. And then we'll be at liberty to fight them until we boot them all the way back across the Bosphorus."

"You'll forgive me if I don't agree," said Neal. "At least about Turkey entering the war. If they side with Germany, we've one long and miserable war ahead of us, here in Palestine, Arabia, and Europe."

"Let it come," insisted David. "I'm ready."

Allison moved uneasily, thinking of the death and terror that would engulf the world if it came. Yet, looking at David and seeing his passion for a Jewish land, she knew she would support the cause if she could. Little Benjamin walked in, and David stood and drew him in his arms with sudden enthusiasm.

"For his sake, for the children's sake, we must have our own land. We must have a place to live, to be Jews, to worship the Lord God of Israel, and one day, yes, to build our temple like Solomon's temple. It will happen. As sure as there is a sun and a moon in the heavens. God has promised! If the Turks, the Germans, or the Moslems wish to wipe us from the face of the earth, they must first do what, Benjamin?"

Benjamin looked up at him, his brown eyes gleaming. "I can quote it, David. I know it by heart, it is from the Book of Psalms. 'If his sons forsake My law, and do not walk in My judgments, if they break My statutes and do not keep My commandments, then I will visit their transgression with the rod, and their iniquity with stripes. Nevertheless My lovingkindness I will not utterly take from him, nor allow My faithfulness to fail. My covenant I will not break, nor alter the word that has gone out of my lips. Once I have sworn by

My holiness; I will not lie to David: His seed shall endure forever, and his throne as the sun before Me; it shall be established forever like the moon, even like the faithful witness in the sky.'"

"Psalm 89," said Allison, recognizing the passage. "To get rid of Israel, the enemy must first remove the sun and moon from the heavens."

"They'll never do that," said Benjamin gravely.

Allison smiled at him. "Not so long as there is a God in heaven. You're right." *A faithful God,* she thought, touched deeply. *And if the Lord is faithful to unfaithful Israel, then he will also be faithful to me, who at times is unfaithful. What a loving Savior, what a God of grace.*

"You're crying, Allison," said Benjamin. "How come?"

David threw his arm about the boy and walked him back toward the dining room. "You ask too many questions. C'mon, Benny boy, let's try those latkes with your mama's preserves. Coming Allison? Neal? If you don't, I won't promise to save you any."

By evening, Bret had not arrived, and their tension grew. Had he escaped from Aleppo? What if the Germans had overtaken him? Anything could have gone wrong.

When the morning dawned, the mood in the little house was sober.

"I still haven't given up," said Neal to the grave faces around the table. "Major Holden is no novice. He's survived dangerous times in the past. He's a pro, better than any of us here. If it's possible to get through, he will. It's too soon to give up hope."

David stood, restless. "I'm going out for a while. There's talk of more arrests. I want to see Ben-Gurion."

"Be careful," said Rose. "If there are arrests, the slightest trouble will give them more excuse."

David laughed shortly. "Do you think I aim to take on the Turks single-handedly? I just want to see what I can find out."

"Be careful," she said again.

When David had gone, Rose went to her tiny office to work on her map while Benjamin went out to play with his friends. Allison was alone with Neal. She turned the conversation away from the dark prospects at hand. She could see he hadn't slept well the night before, probably remembering Leah and blaming himself by mulling over all the things he might have done differently.

"I guess you know dear Aunt Lydia misses you tremendously," Allison began. "She would be singing like an English robin if you would come back with me for a visit. Mother and Father have missed you, too. A good rest would do you so much good."

"How is the old dear?" he asked of Lydia. "Still rising at the first light of dawn to minister to the sick?"

"Always."

"She's quite a woman. I suppose you'll join her on a new voyage down the Nile?"

"It's my intention, but I'm not certain yet. I'll spend time at home with my parents first. They'll be disappointed if I don't. This will be the first time in ages we'll all be together. Mum's dying to speed away back to London with Father. She's weary to death of Cairo."

"She'll be a bit disappointed, I'm afraid."

"What do you mean? He's coming home, you know. He should be back from India when I get there. I hope you'll think about it and come with me."

"I wish I could, but I can't. There's too much left undone here. And Bret will have my new orders. I don't know if I'll be sent back to the Carchemish Digs now or not. They won't have anything against me since I wasn't on the Jerablus road. Besides, T. E. Lawrence is still there with Woolly for the British Museum. It will seem quite logical for me to return. I can say I've been away, grieving for my sister. They won't suspect a thing."

"Maybe not the Germans at the railway, but whoever murdered Reuter and Leah must know you're working as a spy of some sort."

"You forget, he won't want to hang about either. If they have the information Reuter brought, they've accomplished half their purpose."

Perhaps they don't have the book, she thought. But she couldn't tell him. "Maybe," she said. "But even if they do, they won't be satisfied until anyone who may have known something is permanently silenced. That includes you."

"And Nurse Wescott," he said gravely. "Don't forget that."

"I haven't. But I don't know very much. And I'm going home."

As soon as Bret arrives, she wanted to say, but thinking of him only brought concern for his absence.

She changed the subject. "Why did you say Mum would be disappointed about whisking my father off to England? You know how she's been planning for his retirement from foreign service for the last year. She's even saved money to buy a pleasant cottage in the English countryside—with a white picket fence and climbing roses. If anything goes wrong, I don't think she'll stay on," she said quietly. "Their marriage is suffering."

"Then I don't envy her." Neal looked at her, his face tired. "Nor you for that matter."

Surprised, she lifted a brow. "Why me?"

He reached over and patted her hand. "Because, dear, I've information I've been saving. It's not pleasant where Uncle Marshall is concerned."

She became uneasy. "You've heard from him?"

"Yes. A wire came just before I left Aleppo, before all this nasty business broke. It's not going to be pleasant telling your mother he isn't going to retire from government service after all."

Allison felt the blow as a physical impact. "Not retiring? But he was so certain. He promised her. It was a gift for their marriage. I know, because he told me."

He shrugged. "Well, you know how things are in the world. The foreign secretary asked him pointedly if he would stay on for a time because of the uncertainties in Europe, Egypt, and the Suez Canal. Someone steady who knows the Egyptian mindset and the Turks will need to keep a hand on the helm of the state here."

"She's been packing for the past year, anticipating quitting Egypt," Allison said. "I don't know how she'll take this news. You're certain?"

"The telegram is with my things. I'll give it to you later. But by now, I'm sure Marshall has wired her, or even gone home to tell her himself."

Allison considered. "Even if he does, I don't think she'll accept his decision. There's been so much misunderstanding between them recently I don't think she's in the mood to forgive him about this." She moved uncomfortably. "It's no secret she hates the British life in Egypt."

Neil settled back. "I'm glad I'm not going to be there when she finds out." His smile faded as he turned thoughtful, and she had the suspicion he was keeping something more from her.

"I can't go home yet, Allison. I've some work of my own to do here in Jerusalem. Then Carchemish."

"You're very considerate," she said wryly. "I can't wait to be the one to tell Mum her dreams of going home to England have once again been interrupted by the viceroy of India."

"It wasn't the viceroy; it was Kitchener," he said of the British prime minister.

"Oh, dear."

By lunchtime David had not returned, and Bret hadn't arrived in Jerusalem. Both Neal and Mrs. Lyman were concerned. Neal suggested he could at least find out what was keeping David.

"I'm going with you," said Allison. "I could use a good walk. And I haven't seen much of Jerusalem in the daylight."

The old city was a maze of narrow stone alleys running amid dusky purple shadows. The smell of sun-baked stone permeated the still air of the afternoon.

Allison walked beside Neal toward a square where the ancient Tower of David cast oblong splotches of shade across the worn rock. Allison looked around, taking in the spiked Muslim minarets, the small crooked houses, Jewish shops, and—Turkish soldiers!

A crowd of angry Orthodox Jews—all of whom were dressed in black coats, hats, and shoes—were converging on the square, hurling words of rage at the soldiers galloping by on horseback. Allison's eyes widened when she saw the soldiers' sheathed scimitars slung over their left shoulders.

"There's David," cried Allison.

Neal left her by the square as he ran ahead. When Allison caught up, she saw David was scowling.

"David, are you all right?"

"I am," he said bitterly, "but they are not. It's inhumane! It's a transgression against God!"

"David—"

"Don't worry, the Turks aren't here because I stirred up a riot. They have raided Jewish leaders' homes and arrested the men."

"You mean David Ben-Gurion?" cried Allison.

"Among others."

"But why? What have they done?"

"Done?" he shouted above the crowd's noise and the soldiers' shouts. "They have done nothing! The newly appointed Turkish military commander of Palestine has arrived in Jerusalem. General

Pasha has rounded up five hundred Russian immigrant Jews and ordered them to be deported by sea from Jaffa to Egypt. At the harbor, it's reported whole families with their hurriedly collected belongings—old people, mothers and babies—are being driven onto the boat in wretched disorder."

Allison shared his anger. "What did they do to deserve such treatment?"

"They're Jews," he snapped, his eyes flashing.

Word spread quickly in the crowd of more atrocities by the Turkish general, and the people were shouting, "Murderers!"

On General Pasha's way from Constantinople he had passed through Beirut, where he had hanged a number of Jews for being Zionists, and Arabs for being leaders of a national movement.

"This looks bad," warned Neal, looking about. "If the Turkish general is here, you can be sure more arrests are coming. Someone had better get back to Rose and warn her and Benjamin. Tell her to hide that map and anything else she may have in the house that links us with Ben-Gurion's movement."

"I'll go," said David. "But what about you?"

"I'm going to warn Ben-Zvi. Allison, go with David, will you?"

"Be careful, Neal."

He smiled and touched her shoulder, then disappeared into the throng.

At the house, the news had already spread to Mrs. Lyman through anxious neighbors. A rabbi had come through the wall into the back courtyard with the warning. His eyes watered and his gray beard shook as he spoke rapidly in Hebrew, gesturing in all directions. David, who spoke Hebrew fluently, now and then filled Allison in on what had happened.

During the night many arrests had been made. Ben-Zvi had already been arrested. He and Ben-Gurion were members in the local Ottomanisation Committee. They had obtained permission to recruit a Jewish militia to help defend Palestine against Germany and her allies should war come.

"But that means they're willing to fight on the side of the Ottoman Empire," said Allison. "Why arrest them?"

"It doesn't matter," said David impatiently. "General Pasha disbanded the militia. He's announced that anyone found with Zionist documents will be put to death."

Allison tensed and took hold of his arm. "David, we have to hide you; we have to get you out of here! And Rose and Benjamin—"

"I'm not leaving," came Rose's calm but tight voice. "I've run too much and I'm tired." She sank into the chair, and Benjamin drew near, his eyes wide with fear, but his mouth tight as if he was determined not to cry, no matter what.

"I vowed when I set foot in Jerusalem that I'd never leave," she said. "This is our home, and we're not leaving."

The rabbi wiped his tears as she answered him quietly in Hebrew.

David looked at Allison, his expression determined. "I'm not leaving, either."

"But you must," she argued. "If you stay, it's certain death. What good to die for a cause that is sure to be defeated for the moment? Return with me to Cairo. You can work for a homeland from there—"

"No, it's no good," said Mrs. Lyman, shaking her head. "We will take our chances here. They can't prove me a Zionist, nor my son, Benjamin. We have papers saying we are British subjects. Major Holden got them for us. But as for you, David, she is right; you must go and come again another day. I will be in touch with you in Cairo."

The rabbi was raising his voice, and they turned their full attention on him. After a minute, Mrs. Lyman said, "Ben-Gurion and Ben-Zvi were manacled and put on board a ship at Jaffa with a note from the governor of the port."

"What did the note say?" Allison asked.

Rose's dark eyes were haunted. "'To be banished forever from the Turkish Empire.'"

The rabbi's face twitched. David threw down his hat in disgust. But it was Benjamin's face that sent a pang through Allison's heart. Bewildered, afraid, haunted. His large brown eyes met hers and stared at her. Allison felt their pain as her own.

"'Banished forever,'" repeated David. "We shall see if the ruddy Turks have the guts to enforce their own edict. May the war come," he breathed. "And I pray to God that the Ottoman Empire sides with Germany. I know the men, Ben-Gurion and Ben-Zvi. They will not crawl away like dogs. We'll rally the Zionists to the side of England and France to help raise troops for a Jewish Legion. We'll fight; and if God wills, we will live to see Jerusalem taken from the Turks!"

The hours dragged by, and Neal did not return. But neither had Turkish soldiers shown up at the house demanding to search or making arrests. As twilight over Jerusalem turned lavender, with streaks of silvery-blue, they sat in the unlit room, waiting.

The ominous rumble of an approaching vehicle neared the house outside, followed by orders shouted in Turkish and Arabic.

Allison stood, as did the others in the room. "Quick! Hide," she told Benjamin, and David pushed his way to the front door.

"Allison, get out of here and take Benny with you!"

She reacted at the command of his voice, grabbing Benjamin and running with him out of the dining room into the cobbled courtyard.

"I can't leave her," the boy protested, with his first show of tears. "I must stay, Allison. I must! I am a Jew!"

She grabbed his small shoulders and gave him a desperate shake. "Your mum will be all right. David will help her. She wouldn't want you taken away. We'll hide and come back later. Do you know of a secret place? All boys do, don't they? We'll go there now, but we'll come back at midnight. Come, Benjamin, do it for me. Will you? Please? I'm afraid." In some ways she said this to win over his boyish pride, but in another way, it was the truth. She was terribly afraid, and her stomach felt nauseous.

He rallied like a little soldier, his shoulders straightening. "It's all right, Allison. I'll protect you. Come on. Hurry! I know a place they'll never find us!"

They ran through the darkening courtyard and a side gate that brought them to a narrow, cobbled street that was ancient before the time of Rome. With Benjamin leading the way, they darted down the street, keeping close to stone houses and donkey carts. Now and then he would pull her behind one, and they hid when they heard voices.

"Now what?" she whispered when he hesitated, new anxiety over his mother and David coming to his face. "Where do we go from here?"

"This way," he whispered, and they ran on again, until Allison could hardly keep up.

They ducked and darted through yards and trees to emerge at last in an Arab bazaar, closing up for the night. The shopkeepers were removing their fruits and vegetables from the stands to bring them indoors. Like the *suk* at Aleppo, camels, donkeys, and people were everywhere, apparently oblivious to the Turkish arrests of both Jewish and Arab activists.

Benjamin must have understood her interest in Jerusalem, for he said proudly, "I'm taking you where King David fled when his son Absalom led a rebellion against him."

She guessed where they were going and was deeply moved by the thought. However, it wasn't King David that she thought of as he guided her on the way to their hide-out. It was another rejected King she remembered and worshiped in her heart, as the night deepened and the stars came out white and brilliant above the darkening city.

They crossed Brook Kidron and climbed the hill outside the city to the Mount of Olives. Benjamin collapsed under a gnarled olive tree and sat staring toward the city, his mind and heart clearly with his mother and his friends. "They took Ben-Gurion away in chains," he said into the starlit darkness.

Allison half listened, her hands touching the trunks of ancient olive trees as she walked silently through the grove. Had these gnarled trees been silent witnesses on that late night after the Passover meal when Jesus had prayed to the Father? Was this the ground that had received his tears, his drops of sweat like blood, as he had prepared to become the offering to pay for the sins of the world?

My sin, she thought, overwhelmed with gratitude. *Oh, Lord Jesus, thank you!*

"They took him away—" Benjamin was saying. "He was the only one who could save us from the Turks."

Allison looked over at the boy and through her dimmed vision saw that he had finally broken down, weeping unashamedly. She went to him and knelt, her arms going around him. "Oh, Benjamin, the battle for Jerusalem's freedom isn't over. It hasn't truly begun." She soothed his damp hair. "Benjamin? Tell me about King David, tell me the story of how he came here rejected by his people even though he was their anointed ruler."

"His own flesh and blood turned against him," he wept. "They didn't want him to be their king. They chose Absalom instead."

When he had finished, she said softly: "There's a story of another King I want to tell you about. He was rejected, too. He was from the royal lineage of David. Will you let me?"

He looked at her, tears on his cheeks, his soft brown eyes sparkling in the starlight.

"Don't interrupt me until I've finished," she said. "Even if you won't like it at first, let me tell the story."

He nodded. "I'm listening."

There, beneath the old olive trees on the mount, as the stars glinted high in the heavens and the full, pale moon came up behind the Judean hills, Allison told him about that other King and his rejection, of his visit to the mount on the night before his crucifixion. "And on the third day he arose from the dead. Now he sits, King of kings at God's right hand. His name is Yeshua. One day he'll return. His feet will stand again on this very mount."

Benjamin was silent, and she said no more. For the next few hours, they remained in the olive grove, at times talking amiably and then sitting in silence. The moon began to wane and dip behind the trees. A breeze rustled through the hill grass and nodded the bright heads of the summer poppies.

When she believed it safe and the hour late, she stood, dusting off her skirts. "I want you to wait here for me."

"Where are you going?"

"Back to the house. If it isn't safe, I won't go in. I'll need to find out what happened. Maybe everything will be all right after all."

"Maybe—maybe Neal's back now, and Major Bret, too. Maybe the Turks left."

"I'll find out. Rest here under the tree. Try to sleep. I'll be back by dawn."

"All right, Allison, but if you don't come back—"

"I'll be back," she promised.

12

ALLISON DEPARTED FOR THE LONG WALK back to Jerusalem, but she hadn't gotten far when the approach of rushing footsteps in the darkness startled her. Turkish soldiers must be searching for the Jews who had fled. She stopped, cringing backwards, heart pounding, debating whether she should turn and flee. But she didn't want to lead them to Benjamin.

Then she heard, "It's Allison!" The voice belonged to Rose Lyman.

"Rose? Oh, thank God it's you! You're all right. I have Benjamin. He's safe in the olive grove. Are David and Neal with you?"

At the sound of their voices, footsteps came running toward them from another direction. Evidently David had embarked on a secondary trail that led into the mount by way of a cemetery. Allison rushed toward him, her fright ebbing as she realized he was safe.

"Oh, David, David, I was so worried about you."

She embraced him beneath the starlit darkness, but no sooner did she hold him than, like a jolt, she knew it wasn't David. Bret's warm, strong hands enclosed her. She pulled back quickly.

"Sorry to disappoint you," came Bret's soft, low voice.

A warm flush enveloped her as her palms tingled with the feel of the muscle beneath his damp shirt and his returning grasp, holding her if only briefly.

With a show of outward poise contrary to her emotions, she turned her head in the direction of Rose, who was hurrying toward them. "Benjamin is up there," said Allison, pointing.

"I'll get him," said Bret, and he climbed the slope.

Allison embraced Rose, and for a moment they clung in an unspoken bond.

"How did you know where to find us?" asked Allison a moment later.

"Major Holden remembered. Benjamin had told him about his favorite place when Major Bret visited us a month ago. It was then the major gave me the papers. Thank God!" She lifted her eyes toward the heavens. "These papers saved us tonight, Benjamin and me."

"What papers?" asked Allison, interested at once.

"Papers saying we are Turkish citizens. Imagine! They look so official not even the Turkish colonel could tell the difference. Me, Turkish—" she laughed, but it bordered on hysteria. Allison swiftly grabbed her shoulders and gave her a little shake. "It's all right now. We're safe. It worked."

"Yes, yes, it worked, and I've the major to thank. Here they come. Benny! Thank God!" She rushed toward the boy and clasped him in a bear hug to her heart. "My boy, my poor brave boy! You're all right?"

Bret walked up to Allison, and in the starlight she could see no trace of a smile. "You can't do anything more here. We need to get out while we can. The Turks are still rounding up suspected Zionists."

"I can't leave now, Major. What of Rose, of Benjamin?"

His gaze flickered. "Involved emotionally already? First espionage, now a Jewish homeland. You'll soon find the world's sorrows enough to break any heart. Better stick with delivering babies. At least you have something to show for all your sweat and tears. Come, we're taking the railway this time."

Allison pulled away, and Bret stopped. As he briefly looked at her face, he smiled. "Go ahead and say it. 'Your arrogance, sir! How dare you tell me what to do, how to feel? It's my heart!' And so it is. But if you wish to invest your ideals in anything in the future, you would be wise to cooperate with me now. Unless you want to stay and answer General Pasha's questions. He has no qualms about arresting women spies and torturing them into telling all."

"You're frightening me on purpose."

"Ah, yes. I am a heartless cynic."

"Are you, Major?" she asked suddenly, and met his eyes evenly, searching his face. As she did, Rose came up with Benjamin and reached a hand to grasp hers.

"Thank you, Allison. The major is right. You can do nothing more here. We'll be all right now. We have a way of surviving the worst."

"Won't you come with me to Cairo? It's so dangerous here for you."

"Yes, but we have a cause, one that will not die no matter what they do to us. If something happens to us, then others will grow like new plants from where we fall. Israel must live. And the struggle, the pain, the tears will be worth it, if not for us now, then for another generation. We lay the foundation, and others will build. I cannot leave. With the Turkish papers, Benjamin and I at least have a chance. That is more than many others have."

Allison looked at Benjamin, and his gaze dropped. She smiled. "Good-bye, Benny. I'll see you again one day. Take care of your mother. And thanks for showing me your secret hide-out."

Bret had walked ahead, and Allison turned from Rose and Benjamin to follow him. She had gone a few feet when Benjamin called quietly, "Allison?"

She stopped and looked back, seeing two darkened figures holding each other below the Mount of Olives.

"Yes?"

"I liked the story you told me. I liked it a lot."

Her eyes moistened, and she smiled faintly, then lifted her hand in a good-bye gesture.

Bret was far ahead, waiting, as though he knew she would come. Pain from a blister on her foot had set in, a consequence of the ill-fitting shoes she had worn in the flight from the city. She tried not to limp, not wishing him to notice. She was dusty and bedraggled, too, with several strands of hair loose and her dress soiled and stained with perspiration. She didn't think he noticed, but she was wrong.

He paused. "I'll carry you. You've been through enough."

She didn't know why, but the idea alarmed her. She wanted to stay as far removed from Bret Holden as she possibly could. Had David or Neal made the offer, she would have accepted gratefully, but Bret was an emotional risk.

"That isn't necessary, Major," she said distantly. "I'm quite all right. Thank you just the same."

"Very self-sufficient and all that," he said. "Very commendable of you, Nurse."

She tossed him a glare.

Bret smiled and slowed his stride so she could keep up. "You don't belong out here, you know. You're like a water lily in a rock garden."

She shrugged, looking ahead. "I don't think so."

"No? It's my imagination then."

She limped along, furious with herself. Why wouldn't she simply allow him to carry her without making an issue of it? It was too late now. She had already alerted him that she was too aware of Major Bret Holden.

"You're afraid to have me carry you."

"Absurd. Why should I be?"

"Good question."

"I simply wish to walk on my own, that's all." Her face felt hot.

"I admire your unfaltering courage, the spirit of the dedicated young nurse shining through with all its attractive nobility!"

She gave a laugh. "You don't think that. You think I'm a nuisance, and the sooner you get me off your hands, the more relieved you'll be."

"Relieved, yes; but happier, debatable. I rather like lilies, especially when my parched soul is sick to death of the desert. But your noble spirit can prove a problem."

"Do you have something against women with, as you say, 'a noble spirit'?" she asked defensively.

"I haven't found many."

Allison laughed. It was, despite herself, a rueful laugh. "I suspect there is a reason for your being such a cynic. I suspect you have known one too many women."

Bret's smile was brief. "Guilty without a shred of evidence? I'm disappointed in you after all. Admit it, you know absolutely nothing about me. And yet you rush to assume the worst. Now why, dear lily, would you do that?"

"You're right, Major. I don't know your past, but I assure you, any rush to judgment isn't because I'm—I'm attracted to you and avoiding the unpleasant discovery—"

"Perish the thought," he said smoothly. "It would never do, would it? Rest assured, Nurse, that it never entered my mind." He looked at her with curious intent. "So you do have faults beneath that demeanor. I'm curious. You have your protective armor all in place, and you've drawn your sword against me before I've even thrown down the gauntlet."

"Gauntlet?"

He smiled faintly. "When a knight wishes to duel an opponent for a lady, he throws down his gauntlet. You're a bit over-protective, aren't you? You're emotions are very safe, since I haven't said yet that I wished to take on Wade Findlay."

She looked at him but fell off in confusion when his disarming smile called a truce. Was he serious?

Despite herself, she smiled in return. "Major, I am sorry. You're right, I'm being rather silly and defensive, aren't I?"

"I'll forgive you, considering what you've been through recently."

"Thank you for your charity, Major. Somehow I didn't think it was one of your characteristics."

"Back to that again. Of course, you're probably wondering why I've told you I've avowed no intention of awakening the emotions of such a noble-spirited young woman."

She drew in a breath but kept her eyes ahead. *Of all the nerve...* "I do not wonder. It never entered my mind."

"I'm sure it has, even if you won't admit it. A proper girl wouldn't admit it, of course. So I'll tell you."

"I assure you, Major Holden, I am not in the least interested in your reasonings."

"One reason is that, when I do find an obvious charmer such as yourself, with a noble tilt to her chin and a gleam of sacrifice and duty in her eye, it's rather disturbing to what you so bluntly call my cynical outlook."

"I gather I should be flattered that I'm one of the few you have classified as noble."

"You're anything but typical. But then, the others never held much interest for me."

"Maybe it's just as well you haven't thrown down the gauntlet since neither Wade nor I would accept the challenge."

"A disappointment. But if I ever decide to challenge that too-glib refusal, I'll play fair and warn you first."

"Warn me!"

"Yes, that I intend to win, regardless. Until then, you can relax in my presence. Romance is the last thing on my mind with Germans and Turks on my trail."

"Oh, I'm so glad you've told me. For a dreadful moment I'd thought otherwise. I feared that I might end up breaking your hard and conceited heart, and I should hate to have it on my conscience."

He looked at her, his eyes narrowing faintly, and laughed, but it was unpleasant. "Ah, the lily has thorns. Then again," he went on, "you are rather young. I would say eighteen or nineteen?"

Impossible, infuriating. "A woman never tells her age."

"I can find out easily enough when I'm ready. You could use some growing up before I would seriously entertain any notion of barging into your idealistic world."

She was too angry to answer.

"And," he said softly, "I haven't the heart to shatter your noble spirit. It becomes you. Unfortunately, there are other dangers besides romance; it's reckless of you, not to mention dangerous, to intrude into espionage and the struggle for Zionism."

Her heart felt as if a rock had fallen into its cavern. "Thank you," she said stiffly. "I shall keep your words in mind, Major. If we are each to be on guard with our emotions, we shall fare well enough. But you needn't concern yourself with my losing the idealism you seem to think I have. I have no intention of doing so since what I believe has a firm foundation far removed from any human loftiness. Christianity is quite up to equipping me to face the ugliness of life and the dangers of getting my angelic wings singed."

He stopped, hands on hips, and tilted his head. A slight smirk showed in the moonlight. With determination he swung her up into his arms and strode onward. Allison settled into meek silence, trying to think of everything but his arms about her.

He walked in silence until they came to where he had parked the vehicle, hidden behind a myrtle tree. He set her down, and she leaned against the dusty car, removing her shoe.

"Be careful," he said. "There are scorpions."

"I know all about it, Major." She tossed her shoes into the back of the car. "Where are David and Neal?" She looked about, her throat dry. "I thought they were waiting for us—"

She stopped, her eyes swerving to his.

The wind came against them, and she looked into his inscrutable face. For a moment she couldn't speak. A new uncertainty was rising painfully in her heart and squeezing out her ability to breathe.

Bret sighed and sank back against the tree. Her suspicions settled into a dread certainty.

"Neither you nor Rose mentioned them," she said in a low voice. "But I was sure—"

He straightened, took her arm, and opened the door. There was a gentleness both in his touch and voice, quiet and deliberately calm. "You've had a trying day, haven't you? Are you up to a bit more?"

"Where are they?" she asked, desperation creeping into her voice. "Are they waiting somewhere else for us?"

"No."

She clasped her arms about herself and fought the tears that wanted to erupt. "Why not?" she half accused, as though he were to blame. "What have you done with them?"

"My dear, I haven't done anything with them. Why should I want to?" He let out a breath. "They've been arrested. I haven't been able to do anything about it yet. I can try when we get to Cairo, but there's nothing I can do here now. If I try, they'll be on me like a hornet's nest.

I once met General Pasha in Constantinople. He knows who I am, and by now he knows I walked in the German boots of Colonel Holman."

Allison wanted to vent her anguish, but his sudden grip on her hands, squeezing his sympathy and understanding, shot a bolt of strength through her. She swallowed hard.

"That-a-girl, Allison. You've got what it takes."

"No," she half sobbed, "I don't, I don't—you don't think I do—"

He held her tightly. "You're wrong!"

She pushed away.

The wind rippled the leaves of the myrtle tree, and the branches creaked. The moon had gone down, and the darkness held them alone in a desolate wilderness.

"I'll do what I can in Cairo," he whispered firmly. "The best thing I can do now for us all is to avoid getting caught."

She hardly heard him above the painful cry of her heart. She wouldn't envision what Neal and David might be going through at the hands of the Turks. If she did, she might scream. Despite her good intentions, she choked on a sob.

"I didn't want to tell you," he said. "Try not to think about it. There's nothing you can do to change things; nor can I, not now."

"That's easy for you to say—"

"That's where you're wrong. It's miserably difficult for me! They are both friends of mine. And I don't ever find it easy. Especially now, with you—" he stopped.

Allison looked at him.

"I'm getting you back to Egypt," he said gruffly.

Allison got in, and he drove without speaking. She felt mercifully dull.

Reaching under the seat, he handed her a canteen and a bag. "Life goes on," he said rather irritably. "And I'm hungry and thirsty. There's bread and meat in the bag. Fix me a sandwich, will you?"

She did so, her hands feeling heavy and slow.

He ate, but she could not. Instead, she unstopped the canteen and drank, expecting water. The delicious hot coffee was welcome.

Bret watched the road ahead. "We'll board a steamer to Port Said at Jaffa. Should the Turks ask about us, we need to get our story straight. We're married."

Allison looked at her soiled dress and her bare feet with a blister. She thought of her wind-blown hair. *A fine marriage,* she thought ironically, and then she laughed harshly.

Bret smiled dryly, but his eyes reflected sympathetic patience. "Hand me the coffee, Mrs. Holden."

They had left behind Neal and David, Rose Lyman, and Benjamin in the thick of a political and religious storm. Bret had promised her he would do all he could at Cairo intelligence to get Neal and David out of Turkish imprisonment. As for Rose and the movement for the Jewish homeland, those involved would always risk the threat of death. Rose would never abandon the cause for safety. What of David?

The Arabian desert, Aleppo, the Hittite archaeological site near Jerablus were also left behind, along with the lonely grave of cousin Leah. And the book, the book that held the key to the information so important to Bret and Cairo intelligence. Where was it? In the hands of the enemy? Bret didn't think so, and she probably agreed. Had Leah hidden it? Where?

It all waited for a future hour of discovery.

The motorcar rolled toward Jaffa, where David Ben-Gurion had been expelled from Jerusalem in chains. In a few days, she would arrive in Port Said to the safety of her family in the comfortable white house, and her spacious blue and white bedroom. A sweet bath, her wardrobe, and days of sleep in a soft feather bed would be waiting. She nearly sighed aloud thinking of it.

She looked over at Bret when he didn't notice and studied the handsome, masculine lines of his face as he rested his head in one hand, his elbow propped against the car door, the other strong hand on the steering wheel. As she studied him, she wondered if she really was sorry the British major was going to be stationed in Cairo.

She shut her eyes with determination and found herself thinking it would be better—she was not sure for whom—if Bret were transferred to some other post. Her father, she thought, could possibly arrange it. Thinking of her father brought the disturbing news to mind that had been shared with her by her cousin Neal at Mrs. Lyman's house. Her father would not be retiring from his post as her mother had expected. There would be more family discord, more trouble between them. She was helpless to know what to do about it. And if matters came to the worst and her mother bought passage home to England, she would naturally wish Allison to go with her. With Leah's death, Allison's mother would be even more adamant that the dangers of Arabia and Cairo posed too great a threat for her daughter. And now, Neal was imprisoned.

Allison thought that Bret would likely be the military official who would inform her parents of Neal's captivity, and she, of course, would need to be there. If the threat of war with Germany loomed as dark as Bret seemed to think, her mother would make plans to voyage to England before the danger of torpedoes threatened civilian ships. How could she tell her mother that she was considering staying behind to serve the British and Australian soldiers as a military hospital nurse?

Suddenly that thought seemed quite possible and even compelling. How could she leave when Leah had given her life? When women like Rose Lyman stayed on in the threat of imprisonment and torture? And David. Even now he was under the ruthless hand of the Turkish general.

But her mother would never understand all this. She would insist her daughter return to civilized England. Allison had much to explain when she returned home. She looked again at Bret.

He could help her explain if he decided to, but would he want her to stay or journey to England and out of his life?

PART 3

13

THE SINAI, THAT GREAT AND TERRIBLE WILDERNESS, home of the Israelites for forty years after the Exodus from Egypt, lay inland like a triangular thumb from the northern coastline of the Mediterranean. The inland plain of Sinai was marked by shifting dunes that became the forbidding gravel and limestone plateau marking the beginning of the *al-Tih*, "The Wandering."

But as Allison arrived with Bret from Jaffa at El-Arish, on the coast between Turkish controlled Gaza and Egypt's Port Said, the beaches at El-Arish were blue and warm. The tiny waves washed over the white sand. Farther inland the Bedouins were gathering on this particular Wednesday for their *suk*, the open-air market.

Allison was accosted by the familiar smells of camels and goats, and bartered goods ranged from animals to rugs. Cheese, cloth, jewelry, flour, tea, and rifles were spread out in the bazaar. She noticed Bret speaking to one of the leaders who had several carbines, and she remembered the ammunition and guns brought into Jerusalem. What had Bret done with them? Were they to have been delivered to David Ben-Gurion and the Zionists?

The Bedouins were a familiar sight to Allison. Dressed to withstand the burning rays of the desert heat, the men wore flowing robes that allowed a cooling breeze. As a nurse, she knew the robes lessened moisture loss in the hot dry wind, thus helping them avoid heat stroke. A cloth wound about their heads shielded their faces from sun and blowing sand.

The women were dressed in black. At first she had thought the color forced on them by their Moslem religion was unfair, since black heats up faster than white, but the outer clothes were worn over dresslike garments of flowing material that was surprisingly cool. Their head coverings were embroidered with a tiny cross-stitch design in blue for unmarried or red for married. A veil was worn with the same colored stitches, and she saw many that were decorated with coins or sea shells. The coins reminded her of the woman in the Lord's parable who had lit a lamp and swept her house as she searched diligently until she found her lost coins.

Am I as diligent in seeking the spiritual welfare of the lost? she asked herself. *Do I care for these Bedouin tribes, or am I content to leave them lost within their Moslem beliefs, telling myself I have no right to disturb their culture? What lie of Satan is this that entire peoples should be left to the fatalistic helplessness of Islam? The gospel is not cultural,* she thought. *Nor does truth destroy what is good in any culture. Why couldn't the Scriptures be translated into their languages so they could know the truth, yet retain their culture undisturbed by British influence?*

The Bedouins were lovers of hospitality, and their tents were always open to receive visitors. Bret insisted they accept the hospitality of a certain Bedouin leader, but Allison was skeptical.

"Why are you so interested?" she whispered as they followed him.

"What makes you think I am?"

"Because we didn't need to stop at El-Arish. We might have gone straight on to Port Said. Since there's little here except lovely beaches and the Bedouins, I gather you have a particular reason for coming, especially when we are both anxious to arrive in Cairo."

"Very observant. Remind me never to underestimate your powers of deduction."

"Thank you, Major," she said airily. "I suppose that's as close as I'll come to receiving a true compliment from you."

"I suspect, Miss Wescott, men pay you too many compliments, and so you've come to expect them."

He had avoided answering her question about his interest in El-Arish, and she looked at him. His dark blue eyes hinted at amused tolerance.

Rankled, she breathed, "No need to bother, Major. I doubt if you know how to pay the kind of compliments a woman would find flattering."

"Not so. But I first have to consider the consequences."

Allison pretended indifference and marched along beside him toward the Bedouin tent. It was constructed of goat and camel hair panels that the women had woven and then stitched together.

"I've heard that Bedouin women put English women to shame when it comes to submission and hard work," he said.

She ignored his deliberately baiting tone.

"Men are their masters," he said.

"Necessarily so, of course." Allison walked along, refusing to look at him.

"When the Bedouin moves," he went on, "it's the wife who's in charge of taking down the tent. She secures it on the family camel and reassembles it at the new site. She can roll up its side to let in pleasant desert breezes or stake it down to secure it in the sand. If there's a divorce, she's permitted to keep the tent while hubby takes all the domestic animals and leaves."

"In search of a new woman able to work a trifle harder no doubt," she said. "Maybe she didn't have the muscles to grind his flour fine, and so he had to endure lumps in his bread."

"Interesting observation. I always did think muscles should be fairly high on the list of priorities when a man shops for a bride."

She glanced at him. He smiled and gestured to the tent. "As for my reason in coming here, maybe it's as simple as wanting what the man offered. To the Bedouin, hospitality is mandatory. Guests are welcome to stay for three days and three nights."

"I hope you don't intend to accept all that is mandatory, Major."

He smiled. "In exchange for tea or coffee, the male host expects long and friendly conversation. He keeps informed of news in the population centers that way."

"Is that why you've come, to give or acquire news?"

"Always suspicious."

"I'm beginning to think everything you do is for British espionage, even sharing a cup of coffee with a friendly Bedouin."

"Not everything."

Outside the tent they paused, as the Bedouin spoke to his wife and daughter.

"Maybe you wish to gather information for your own interests?" she whispered. "Won't you be bothered by my presence? I too shall hear everything since I know a little Arabic."

Bret smiled. "No, I've arranged for you to have tea behind that veiled partition in the company of women."

"You have it all figured out, don't you? You don't want me to hear."

"I could have left you wandering the *suk,* but you know the Moslem mind. A woman alone wearing Western clothing and with her hair unbound would be misunderstood."

Allison suspected Bret was interested in El-Arish because of its desert location near Gaza and Beersheba. Should war break out, it was a likely spot for British troops, but what the Bedouin might know or could offer remained guarded by Bret.

The orange sun was low in the blue sky when they left the Bedouin tents and boarded the El-Arish steamer for Port Said. Standing on deck with Bret, she rested against the rail while enjoying the Mediterranean breeze. "Are you interested in El-Arish for a military camp?" she asked.

"Don't you think you know enough to keep you in trouble for a while?"

"A polite way of reminding me to mind my own business."

"For a good cause. I wouldn't want Wade Findlay to arrive from Oswald Chambers Bible Training College and find I've consigned his fiancée to the same fate as Leah."

Mention of Leah ended her brighter mood at being on the blue water with the warm wind. She grew sober as the glowing globe of the Egyptian sun set in an orange and crimson splash over the desert horizon.

She admired his profile as they stood in the warm twilight, and he turned and caught her gaze. She flushed, afraid he had noticed.

"Did anyone ever tell you your eyes are as pale green as warm sea water?"

She laughed to cover her fluster. "So you do compliment women after all, Major Holden."

"And with the breeze in your auburn hair, you're breathtakingly lovely."

She looked away, the heat coming up her neck to her cheeks.

"You didn't comment when I said you were Wade Findlay's fiancée."

She wrapped her palms about the rail, watching the Mediterranean. "I didn't consider it a question."

"My statement was meant to give you an opportunity to set the record straight."

"Yes, I gathered it was."

"You haven't satisfied my curiosity." He reached over and unloosed her left hand from the rail, holding it up for inspection. A brow lifted curiously. "I don't see an engagement ring."

She pulled away her hand. "Bible students aren't known for having an income." Her voice was steady.

"Does your evasive answer mean you're not actually engaged to him?"

Allison pushed her hair from her eyes and avoided his gaze, enjoying the cooling breeze against her warm skin. "I suppose you could say we're engaged. Perhaps we assume more than we've openly agreed to."

"You don't sound very excited about the prospect."

She looked at him, a little startled. Then, as a mild rebuke, she said, "I don't think a sound and good relationship needs to be based on breathless infatuations, Major Holden. There is so much more in a marriage to contemplate besides romance."

"Granted. Much more, including shared spiritual values, which I assume you have with him, and friendship. You could be left in isolation by the strong silent type. You strike me as a woman who would want long conversations to pour out your heart while he listens, understands, and offers more than quick answers to resolve what's bothering you."

His insight was disturbing. Allison looked away. She thought of the long discourse she had had with him that night in the expedition hut while they waited for David's arrival. Safeguarding her vulnerability, she said easily, "Oh, Wade Findlay and I are quite close in our interests. I've missed him terribly."

Bret smiled wryly and folded his arms. "Is that why you've been carrying his unopened letter for days?"

Confronted by his challenge, she hastened to explain, "You may assume too much by that."

"I could, but do I?"

"The right moment to open and read it hasn't arrived because it demands my full attention. Anyway, how did you know about the letter?"

"It was in your kitbag," he said evenly.

She turned to face him, growing indignant. "You looked in my kitbag?"

"Yes. All on the up and up, of course. Strictly business. You didn't expect an agent not to at least suspect Leah of planting Woolly's book in your bag, did you?"

"The book—" she stopped. She hadn't even considered that possibility. Her eyes narrowed. "And were you satisfied, Major, that I haven't carried it away in secret beneath your very nose?"

"Come, Allison, don't look so indignant. I apologize, but I couldn't take any chances."

"You might have simply asked me to open it so we could both find out," she countered stiffly.

"I could have, but that would permit you to know as well. And I wasn't sure if you were keeping it from me deliberately."

"You still think I could be a spy for the other side?"

"With limpid green eyes and auburn air? You'd make a potent opponent. I'm glad to discover you're as innocent of espionage as you are of romance with Wade Findlay."

"That's not what I said."

Bret leaned against the rail, watching her. "Well, you will soon have all the proper time to indulge in his love letter. You can lock your bedroom door and swoon all over the page."

"I don't swoon," she corrected. "Anyway, Wade isn't that sort of a letter writer. He would have better things to say than that he is love sick. He would tell me about what is happening at the college and about his plans to come to Cairo as a chaplain with the military."

"All commendable. But why is it, Miss Wescott," he mused, "that I think you too easily scorn the idea of knowing or appreciating the depth of love?"

"That isn't true," she choked. "I do know. There was someone—" She stopped abruptly, catching herself. He became alert, but she quickly turned away her head, holding the rail too tightly.

He was quiet for a long minute, and she bit her lip, angry with herself for allowing Nevile's memory to surface.

"I see I was wrong," he said and turned away to look out to the darkening sea.

She remained silent, allowing the wind to blow against her, easing the pain in her heart.

"I gather it wasn't Wade Findlay," he said.

"No. But I don't wish to discuss the past, Major. It is Wade now, and there's nothing more to be said."

"I think there is a great deal more to be said, but you're right. This is not the time, and I understand why."

She gave him a side glance, expecting to see the pain of some past love relationship reflected on his face. She might have known a man of his qualities would have had a number of women interested in him, but had he cared about any of them? In studying him, she found his expression inscrutable. He too took emotional solace behind a facade of armor, and she wondered what it might be like to lure him out.

No. Bret Holden, above all men, must be the one to stay away from romantically.

The next day, just after five o'clock, the steamer docked in Port Said, a curious city of both ancient and modern Egypt that was the northern gateway to the Suez Canal. Many streets were lined with buildings dating back to the previous century, and people who had traveled in America said the structures' pillared-porch facades resembled the French *Vieux Carré* quarter of New Orleans. Allison's family had a home here as well as in Cairo, but Lady Wescott preferred Port Said with its British influence, although she spent half the year in residency in Cairo.

The Mediterranean beaches facing the houses with their wrought iron and terraces offered pleasant breezes and a view of the passing ships that was quite unlike Cairo's Moslem-Egyptian atmosphere. Port Said's main street ran along the beach, and a second ran along the canal docks where Allison and Bret disembarked from the steamer. Bret hailed a small lift to carry them to the Wescott house.

The sun was low in the sky, and its fading rays turned Port Said's waters to rose-pink and amber. The Mediterranean swelled with waves. Pomegranate and sycamore trees grew along the street near the house. In the front yard were several lush banana trees, which were first believed to have entered Egypt during the time of the Crusades. These particular trees flourished under the devoted care of Lady Wescott's gardener, Ayub.

Allison's steps quickened along the walk toward the front terrace porch, past green ornamentals of Persian lilacs and jacaranda, coral, and flame trees. While Bret lingered just inside the door, Allison entered the front hall and called cheerfully, "Mother? I'm home. We've a guest."

Lady Eleanor Bristow Wescott was thirty-seven but could easily pass for much younger. According to the standards of her day her life was all but lived, and in her own troubled mind she had wasted what little there was of it as the wife of the consul-general of British

Egypt. She made no apology for disliking the culture, nor did she feel it welcomed her, a true daughter of England. For that matter, she believed the man she had married neither loved her nor cared a whit about her needs.

Sir Marshall Wescott was married to the British government. She was merely the mother of his two living children, Allison, who was the eldest, and Beth, who at fifteen had long been in need of schooling and a social life in England.

Eleanor opted to live in Port Said for as much of the year as she could. There her view of the Mediterranean and the ships coming and going fed her imaginings of escape from Egypt. In Cairo she rarely ventured out to shop in the bazaar for, as she explained to Sir Wescott, "I'm ruthlessly pummeled by noise, dirt, and the chaos of the street. Dreariness is everywhere—and flies."

Cairo's foreign flavor made Eleanor feel dislocated and alone. "I regret I ever came here. Why can't people speak in conversational tones rather than shout everything as though people are deaf?"

Eleanor felt vulnerable. She didn't belong to the British foreign service and she never would, despite having endured Marshall's "calling" for ten years. Before Egypt it had been Bombay. She hadn't felt at home in India either, but she had managed to cope much better with the British of the East India Company than she had managed in Cairo. There were the wives of the other British officials, of course, and General Rex Blaine and dear Sarah—what would she have done without Sarah?—but there were few others, and none of them was an intimate friend in whom she could share her marital frustrations when Sir Wescott was away, sometimes for months.

Lady Wescott had shared all these thoughts with her daughter Allison, but it hadn't seemed to assuage Lady Wescott's pain. She had expressed immense relief when her husband had agreed to resign at Christmas or as soon as his replacement arrived. He said he was willing to spend the rest of his years in the English country cottage she had put money down on, and he had promised to do some of the things she seemed to think were important. Now, the coming war was about to change all that. Allison wondered how her mother would respond to the disturbing news from her husband.

14

THE RICH MAHOGANY OF THE POLISHED HARDWOOD FLOOR sounded under Allison's steps as she walked through the entrance hall, kept cool and shaded by the drawn inner wooden shutters on the windows. Light streamed through the double French doors leading into the large sitting room that faced the garden. She crossed the hall floor to the doorway and stood there glancing about for her mother, who was usually out in the garden this time of evening.

Her senses were embraced by the comfort that came to her in seeing the familiar sofas, chairs, and ottomans, which were upholstered in ivory brocade and embroidered with small, blue-gray leaves. The fabric matched the thick drapes that had been drawn back to allow the coolness from the garden to drift in along with the familiar fragrance of her mother's Persian lilacs.

Allison saw her then, walking up the garden path. For a moment Allison was transported back to England, to a time of great ladies, of elegance, of graciousness. Lady Eleanor Bristow Wescott was carrying lilacs, and her soft gray satin dress set off her reddish-gold hair to perfection. A few lines were on the supple skin, and her delicate brows arched with womanly grace above eyes a lighter green than her daughter Allison's.

Eleanor saw her and paused with brief surprise, then smiled.

Setting the lilacs down on a wrought-iron table, she came up the terrace steps into the sitting room. "Allison, darling, I was so afraid!"

Allison rushed toward her across the room. "Mother, I'm dreadfully sorry. I should have sent a wire saying I was all right. Have the Blaines been here?"

Eleanor embraced her tightly. "They were here last night for a small dinner party. Sarah said you had simply vanished in Aleppo. Imagine my horror when, at the same time you disappeared, Sarah informs me Leah died and Neal disappeared. I feared something quite dreadful had happened to you as well. Where on earth have you—" Her words were left hanging in midair when her eyes went past Allison to Major Bret Holden.

Bret stood in silence near the sitting room doorway. Allison saw her mother study him cautiously.

"Um—this is Major Bret Holden," said Allison in a rushed voice, hastening to add when her mother's brow arched with delicate suspicion, "He's been transferred from Constantinople to the Cairo intelligence office."

"Oh, indeed? Intelligence, you say?"

Allison relaxed a little as she read the swift approval stealing into the place of suspicion. She could understand her mother's concerns. Allison had disappeared and then shown up in the company of an exceptionally good-looking British major.

"I can explain everything," began Allison. Then she heard Bret's polite voice saying, "I've escorted your daughter home from the Archaeological Club, Lady Wescott. There was a bit of trouble, as you must already know if General Blaine informed you about your niece, Leah Bristow."

"Yes, he explained about her death," she said quietly. "A dreadful accident. I understand the Turkish authorities are still looking into matters, and the British consul as well. Please, won't you come and sit down, Major? I'll have Zalika bring some refreshment."

With concealed amusement Allison watched Bret suavely step in and take over explaining all that had happened. She noticed that he avoided any mention that his service in Cairo intelligence stemmed from his previous activities in espionage. His work in Cairo, he explained, would involve "various military aspects," some of which would take him back to Baghdad and perhaps Constantinople as well. Since he had "some family" in Cairo, he was satisfied to have been transferred to Egypt.

Allison wondered why he hadn't told her earlier that he had family in Cairo. But that thought was swiftly eclipsed by another startling remark made by her mother. "Ah, so that is where I heard your name. Lady Walsh mentioned it only last Sunday after church service. She said her niece Cynthia had arrived from England. Lady Walsh's niece is your fiancée, I gather?"

Allison didn't move. Bret's composure had not cracked as he said, "Then Cynthia is here. I had begun to be concerned. She was to have arrived last month."

Allison was careful to keep her expression bland and reached for her tea cup. But, much to her dismay, she upset it on the saucer. "I'm sorry. What a mess I'm making."

"Zalika?" her mother called calmly for the serving woman, and Allison stood, for she had splashed some on her skirt. Bret Holden mopped off the tea with a napkin. She hoped he wouldn't mistake the spilled tea for a reaction to mention of Cynthia.

"It's quite all right, Major," she said tonelessly, plucking the napkin from his hand. "My dress was rather soiled anyway after travel."

As he straightened, their eyes met, and Allison's irritation grew when she felt warmth flare up in her cheeks and saw a touch of a smile on his mouth. Zalika came unobtrusively to replace Allison's cup with a fresh one.

Bret steered the conversation back to Carchemish, and while not coming out and agreeing with the Blaines that Leah's death had been an accident, he made no effort to contradict that report. By the time he had finished, Allison was quite certain her mother was convinced Major Bret Holden was a fine and gallant British officer intent on little more than honorably filling out his military term in Egypt, marrying Cynthia Walsh, and returning to a quiet and civilized life in England.

Allison was not as certain, at least about his future. He had made no earlier mention of wishing to return to England anytime soon, not that his silence on the matter proved anything. She realized she knew little about his ambitions and that they had shared little except the danger they had experienced together. Why she would be disturbed by the mention of some young woman named Cynthia was a matter deserving more thought later, when Allison was alone and free to contemplate the meaning.

She realized her mother was looking at her and speaking. Allison quickly turned her attention to what Lady Wescott was saying, aware that Bret was watching both mother and daughter with restrained thoughtfulness.

"General Blaine informed me you had left the archaeology huts at Aleppo at the same time the young Jewish activist, David Goldstein, also disappeared. You mentioned David to me several times, but I must say I was surprised to hear he had left England to come here. Does he have an interest in archaeology as well? Is that what brought him to the club meeting?"

It was time to tell her mother the dark news of his arrest, and of her nephew's, since the Blaines had not known what happened after Leah's death and Allison's own disappearance with David.

"David is a Zionist," said Allison. "I told you about their desire to establish a Jewish homeland. He came to Aleppo to bring me a letter from Wade Findlay and..." She hesitated, wondering if she should mention Bret and how he and David were friends. Again, Bret came easily and smoothly to her aid, informing her mother of David's arrest by the Turks.

"Unfortunately, Lady Wescott, I've some more unpleasant news for you. Your nephew Neal Bristow was with David and is also being held for questioning. Once in Cairo I expect to do all I can to see both men released. I've no doubt Neal will leave Jerusalem, and he will probably come here to see you. I'm not as certain about David. His heart is in Jerusalem, and he'll likely stay there, if he's not expelled."

"Expelled? That's rather despicable of the Turks, but likely," said Eleanor. "I read just this morning in the Cairo paper of the arrival of more than five hundred Jews whom General Pasha expelled from Palestine. Something ought to be done about it by the European governments. It seems to me the Jews have as much right to live in Jerusalem as the Arabs and Turks. Perhaps more, since God gave that land to the Jewish patriarchs. And this is troubling news about my nephew." She looked at Bret curiously. "What was Neal doing in Jerusalem instead of the Carchemish Digs?"

"I wasn't able to see Neal. He was arrested along with David before I arrived."

Allison wasn't sure if her mother noticed Bret avoided her question. "It might have had something to do with the British Museum," her mother offered. "Neal's work has taken him to various ancient cities and archaeological sites. But the Turks will need to release him," she said firmly. "I'll speak to Marshall when he arrives. As consul-general of Egypt his influence may help." She looked alert and showed more interest in national affairs than Allison remembered.

"Don't you think, Major, that the Ottoman Empire is behaving more insolently toward the English government than in the past? I'd almost think they were more sympathetic toward the kaiser's ambitions in Europe than with being our ally."

"You're very insightful," he said noncommittally.

"Speaking of the Ottomans and their treatment of the Jews," she said, looking at Allison, "the paper was asking for volunteers to help with food, clothing, medical care, and shelter."

Pleased that her mother cared so deeply, a surge of pride filled Allison's heart. There was so little her mother seemed concerned about when it came to either Egypt or Arabia.

"I thought I might try to stir up the English ladies to do something to help," said Eleanor. "It seems we ought to use our time more constructively than gossiping at bridge parties or watching our men battle it out on the polo field. By the way, Major Holden, do you play polo? The officers are in need of a good man since General Blaine hurt his back at Aleppo. From the looks of you, I would think the brigadier's team would benefit tremendously from your participation. I'll mention you to the brigadier's wife at the charity ball Saturday next." Giving no chance for Bret to respond, Eleanor turned again to her daughter.

"Beth wants to attend the ball with you this time. I haven't decided. Fifteen is rather young."

Thinking of her sister, Allison smiled. "I've the perfect dress for her; it's white and charming."

"Then perhaps I'll relent. It will do for a going away party before we sail next month."

The mention of the voyage to England brought Allison an uneasy moment as she remembered what Neal had told her in Mrs. Lyman's house. Her father would not be leaving his post as soon as her mother expected. Knowing how much it meant to her mother to return to England and settle down in the countryside, Allison wondered how she could rally the courage to disappoint her mother so soon after

Leah's death and Neal's detention in Jerusalem.

"I'll tell Beth she can attend the ball tonight at dinner." Eleanor looked at Bret with a friendly smile. "Won't you stay and dine with us, Major Holden?"

Bret had stood when the conversation between Allison and her mother turned social. Allison noted that he looked as if he were eager to depart.

"Thank you, but I can't stay. It's urgent I return to Cairo as soon as possible."

"Yes, the Jerusalem matter. I quite understand. I shouldn't have detained you. Thank you for escorting my daughter to Port Said, Major. Perhaps we'll see you at the charity ball or the polo field."

Bret's brief smile convinced Allison he had no interest in either at present. He would have his free time taken up by Lady Walsh and her niece, Cynthia.

"If I can make it," he said and looked at her mother thoughtfully. He removed a sealed envelope and handed it to her. Allison thought she noticed restrained sympathy.

"Sir Wescott asked me to deliver this to you."

"Oh? A letter from Marshall?"

"Yes."

"Strange, I expect him home this Thursday. I wonder that he didn't wait or at least send me a wire."

Allison, too, was surprised. Not over a letter coming from her father, for she suspected he had preferred to send it in place of a wire to explain more fully and apologetically to Eleanor about the unwelcome change in their plans to leave Egypt. Allison was bewildered that Bret would have the letter. Had he carried it all the time they were in Arabia?

Allison leaned over to her mother to catch a glimpse of the familiar handwriting belonging to Sir Wescott, as though she expected Bret to have made a mistake. When had her father given him the letter? Had Bret been in Bombay? She cast him a curious glance, but he was watching her mother as if he knew she would be handed a disappointment.

Allison concluded that if Bret hadn't deemed it of any interest to mention a girl named Cynthia, then it should not surprise her that he had not felt obliged to tell her of the letter he had received from her father. That he hadn't told her of either reinforced her conclusions that Bret was mysterious and careful. It was her mother's reaction to the letter that troubled Allison now. Bret told her mother good-bye and then turned to Allison. She was confronted by a polite but distant military demeanor, his eyes unreadable.

"I'll send word about Neal and David when I have something worthy to pass on. Good-bye, Miss Wescott."

While her mother moved to the other side of the room with Marshall's letter, Bret walked from the sitting room to the entrance hall. The door opened and shut while Allison, glancing toward her mother to see her deep preoccupation with the letter, slipped away and ran after him.

He was already crossing the front garden walkway. "Major, wait!"

The sun had completely set, leaving traces of sapphire touching the sky. Sounds from the shipping canal weighed on the Mediterranean water as Allison brushed past the heavy stems of fragrant lilacs and came to where he had stopped. Bret appeared to know what she would ask and was in no mood to explain more than he had inside the house. Instead of cooperation, she detected a lightly sardonic smile as he stood in the shadows of an overhanging jacaranda tree.

"This isn't a final good-bye. I wouldn't miss an opportunity to have a waltz with you at the charity ball."

Momentarily off guard, she was speechless. "Your conceit is

detestable. That isn't why I came running after you. You can save your waltz for Cynthia, as I've no intention of being there. I've more important work to do with Aunt Lydia."

Her words didn't seem to faze him. "I need to catch one of the boats down the Nile."

"Boats run every hour," she stated tonelessly. "And don't think I'm trying to keep you here for any reason except—"

"I would never presume. The proper demeanor of Miss Allison Wescott is beyond reproach and quite settled in my mind. You want to interrogate me about how I met your father." He smiled. "And I'm determined to avoid that discussion, at least for now."

If she weren't so concerned about matters, his polite but cool manner would have derailed her from proceeding. "When did he give you the letter?"

He folded his arms. "I don't remember. Maybe two months ago."

"That isn't true, is it, Major? Two months ago you were in Constantinople."

"I was?"

"You told me so at Carchemish."

"You only think I did. I told you I had previously been stationed in Constantinople. That might have been any time in the past."

Her eyes narrowed as she studied his face in the starlight. He didn't intend to explain a thing. She could only assume he had his reasons and that she must be content to wait until he decided to tell her more on his own initiative. She felt a rise of frustration but restrained herself.

He stood looking at her, the wind touching his dark hair and shirt. For a moment she felt as though something important could be slipping through her fingers as he disappeared out of her life, for even though he intimated he would see her at the charity ball, she was quite certain he had no intention of doing so. Allison knew if she tried to grasp him, she would lose. Bret appeared just challenging enough to convince her that one too many women had tried to grasp and hold him before, and they had failed. She wondered about Cynthia. Had she come to lay her claim to his heart because he was expected to respond? Or was she desperate to try to lay claim on him? Suddenly Allison believed she might feel sorry for the girl named Cynthia.

Allison casually turned away. "Very well, Major, I shall respect your wish for secrecy."

If her change in attitude took him by surprise, he didn't let on. With dignity she moved toward the house. Zalika was turning on the lights a room at a time, and the golden glow flooded the front terrace.

Allison half hoped she would hear him call out for her to wait. He did not, and it wasn't until she climbed the steps to the terrace and opened the latch on the front door that she glanced back. Bret stood watching her. She could only guess what stirred in the tough mind of a man who wouldn't be easily ensnared by enemy or friend, especially by any woman who allowed the dreamy starlight to shine in her eyes when she looked at him.

Allison entered the house and shut the door. She stood there in the shadows looking toward the brightly lit sitting room where her mother would have read the letter by now.

She heard Beth's voice exclaim with disappointment, "Not going to England! But what of my schooling? I'm sick to death of Egypt! Oh, Mother, can't we go anyway? Can't Father join us in a few months? And—and we could surprise him by going out to the house in the country on weekends and getting it all ready. There's bound to be so much to do—you said I could decorate my own bedroom."

Allison swiftly walked into the room and in one glance saw her mother's look of disappointment, which she was trying to mask from Beth. Allison's understanding glance met her mother's and then swerved to Beth.

Her sister took after their father's side of the family, with dark hair and earthy brown eyes. She was taller than Allison, a matter that always upset Beth, for she bemoaned that she couldn't wear heeled slippers at a ball because it would make her too tall. Neither did she appreciate her sultry appearance but felt cheated that her eyes were brown instead of sea green and that her hair was plain brown instead of shimmering with golds and auburn.

"I don't know why I have to be plain old Miss Shoe," she had murmured more than once, and when assured she was anything but plain, she refused to accept the compliment.

"I look like an Egyptian," she would snap. "If I were too long in the sun, I'd tan too easily. Life isn't fair."

Now Beth, on seeing her sister in the doorway, must have read the mild rebuke in Allison's gaze that told her she should have more concern for their mother's disappointments. "I'll never attend a fashionable school like Geraldine and Francis," Beth said. "And I've scrimped my allowance these past months to add to my wardrobe."

"You can attend music school here," said Eleanor vaguely. "I was talking to Herr Frederick Ridder just yesterday. He informs me he is opening a second school in Cairo, close to the museum. Baroness Helga Kruger highly recommends him as a Vienna instructor."

"Oh, Mother, why can't we sail as planned? It's unfair of Father—"

"Beth, do not speak so about your father."

"Mother is right," said Allison, quickly going to Beth and sitting beside her on the sofa. She caught up Beth's hands. "Anyway, the delay isn't going to be permanent. Only a few more months. After that it will be England as planned."

"That's easy for you to say. You've already gone home and attended nursing school."

"Beth," warned Eleanor, "you're being rude to your sister and behaving badly. What's more, with the news of your cousin Leah's death and now Neal's detention in Jerusalem, this is no time to bemoan our own disappointments. We'll be having a memorial service for Leah tomorrow, and I expect some respect for the next few weeks. When your father arrives, well, we shall discuss the matter of England then."

Beth's eyes welled with sudden tears. "I'm sorry. I didn't know about cousin Neal. But I hardly knew Leah."

"It doesn't matter," said Eleanor. "She was your cousin. You'll show proper respect for her death."

"Yes, Mother. Did—did Father say exactly when he would arrive from Bombay?" she asked hopefully.

Eleanor sighed and turned toward the table where the crystal lamp gleamed down on the sheet of paper. "Christmas," she said. "He'll be home for the holidays. He'll be moving to Cairo."

Allison caught the usage of "he" instead of "we."

"Cairo?" she asked. "Then he's decided to stay on as consul-general?"

"Unfortunately. He promised to explain in more detail when he arrives, but I'm not so dense that I don't know what he plans. It seems Prime Minister Kitchener has asked him to remain in place indefinitely. Having been consul-general of Egypt himself, Kitchener believes it's important to have men in position who understand the Egyptian mind and the problems the nation faces while under Turkish suzerainty with British control of the Suez Canal. If war comes, protection of the canal's shipping lanes will be crucial for England. He feels your father is the most qualified of the men whom he could appoint to take the position."

It grew uncomfortably still, and Allison saw something in her mother's usually quiet eyes that brought alarm. It was a flare of impatient anger. Her mother was far more frustrated with this decision than she was letting on in front of Beth. If Lady Wescott vented her frustrations now, Beth would have even more reason to join in and show disrespect for her father. Allison had always appreciated her mother when she was growing up because, despite the problems she faced in her marriage to Sir Wescott, she never spoke disparagingly of their father. Now that she was a woman, Allison could look back and remember times when her mother had gone to her room, informing them she was ill, or had taken the carriage to visit the reverend and his wife. At the time, Allison hadn't understood what was behind those visits to the reverend, or the long talks with his wife. Now she believed she knew they were an outpouring of her mother's unhappiness and an attempt to avoid separation or divorce.

Allison shivered a little and tensed as she thought of her own future. Having seen so much unhappiness in her parents' marriage, she was reluctant to become seriously attached to any man. She felt she had already made one serious mistake by falling for Nevile when she was only sixteen. She had thought she loved him desperately and had gone away to nursing school in England with a promise made between them that, upon graduation four years later, they would marry. In the second year of her training at Florence Nightingale's Nursing School, the news arrived that Nevile had married the daughter of a British colonel and had been transferred to Australia.

The painful news had been the most disappointment she had yet experienced. Two years later, after graduating and while attending Oswald Chambers Bible Training College in London, she had met Wade Findlay, a godly and dedicated young man. They had become friends, and then slowly she had come to believe Wade was the man the Lord intended her to marry to serve him here in Egypt—Allison in medicine with Aunt Lydia, Wade as a military chaplain stationed at Zeitoun.

Beth stood morosely. "I suppose there'll be no charity ball now that we're in mourning."

Allison glanced across the room at her mother. She had been standing in the light of the lamp simply staring at the letter as though transfixed in thoughts of her own. Her mother looked over at Beth, and seeing the downcast expression, she smiled. "No, we won't cancel the ball. Leah was the kind of young woman who would have wished us to go. And the mores of British Egypt are not Victorian England. We'll attend the memorial service I've arranged, then go on with our lives. I do think we ought to show some concern for Neal. I'd hoped your father would be home this weekend to send a protest to the Turkish ambassador, but now I think I'll write the letter myself."

"An excellent idea, Mother," agreed Allison. "And Major Holden will be reporting to his superiors in Cairo, too. Together, perhaps something can be done quickly."

"All we can do is try, and pray. I'll go to Marshall's office and write it tonight. I'll have it posted officially in the morning on our way to the memorial service. And Beth, I've decided to permit you to attend the ball on Saturday. I expect a quiet demeanor, considering the family tragedy."

Beth's brown eyes gleamed with excitement, but she struggled to look subdued. "Yes, Mother. I won't wear any rouge, so I shall look pale."

Allison smothered a smile, and Eleanor arched a brow. "Rouge? You will not wear it on any occasion. You've enough youthful color in your cheeks already. And the white gown Allison is lending you will do much for your brunette hair."

When Eleanor disappeared into her husband's office to write the dispatch to the Turkish officials, Beth turned to Allison and smiled happily. "I can hardly wait to tell Geraldine and Francis. They'll be green with envy. And Allison, may I use the little satin purse that goes with the dress? The one that snaps to the waist so prettily. Don't tell Mum, but I bought a lipstick. I want to carry it in the purse. Who knows? A handsome officer may prefer brunettes to redheads!"

Allison laughed despite herself. "Yes, you may wear the beaded purse. But if you use lipstick, Mum will see it at once. Better stick to bringing a comb."

Beth hurried up the stairs to the bedrooms. "I'll get the dress and bag from your wardrobe now. If it doesn't fit, we may need to lengthen the hem."

After the memorial service the next morning Allison had her first opportunity to speak with her mother alone. Beth had gone to spend the day with the Hollingsworth girls, Geraldine and Francis, and Allison was with her mother driving back from the church in a hired *calishe,* a horse-drawn carriage. This one was small with an open top, a torn leather seat, and faded carpet.

"I know you're disappointed about Father's decision," she said softly.

Eleanor drew in a breath and looked out on the narrow, winding streets lined with tall houses with *mashribiyya,* wooden-lattice coverings for windows.

"I'm keeping it from Beth, but you might as well know. I'm taking your sister and leaving Egypt for England before Christmas."

Allison swallowed, for her throat felt dry and aching. The decision hadn't been easy for her mother. Allison knew by the dark circles under her mother's eyes that she must have been up all night.

"Perhaps, if you wrote him in Bombay, he would come here before Christmas."

Eleanor turned and looked at Allison, her eyes hard with determination. "I don't intend to write Marshall. I'm going to Bombay with Beth. We'll catch a vessel sailing to England from there. He'll either be on that ship with us, or it's over between us. I'll not come back here, ever."

Allison stared at her, dumbfounded. "You're going to India?"

"Yes. I spoke with Reverend Radbourne this morning. That's why I was late. What I want to say to your father won't wait until he decides to arrive for the holidays. It must be decided between us as soon as possible. I can be in Bombay in a few weeks. I'll have two weeks or so to spend with him before the sailing season becomes difficult. I think he should know where matters stand between us."

Allison had told herself she wouldn't intervene, she wouldn't argue with her mother for fear she would alienate her. But she hadn't expected the decision to come so soon or with such determination.

"Mother, is it wise to offer such an ultimatum? I mean, you know Father, he's bullheaded and—"

"Bullheaded indeed. No, dear, I know quite what I'm doing. It's been coming to this hour for years, and I'm afraid I've reached the point at which it's rather late to turn back. It's our marriage or his career. He'll need to choose now what he wants because I've had quite as much as I can endure of this life. I was rather hard on Beth last night, but I agree with her longings. She dislikes Egypt as much as I, and I want her to have the kind of life I didn't have. I won't have her marrying some soldier and being forced into foreign service in the Sudan, India, or Egypt."

Her mother was serious. She had made up her mind. Allison lapsed into painful silence, torn between understanding and sympathy for her mother and love and compassion for her father. She loved both of them and understood both of their wishes and differences. She knew she must somehow avoid siding with one against the other. The emotional dilemma was almost too much to endure. She was glad her mother wouldn't tell Beth yet.

"How will you explain to Beth? Won't she guess why the two of you are sailing to Bombay?"

"No, she'll be told it was planned; that your father will go with us to England from India."

Allison searched her eyes. "And when he doesn't?"

Eleanor smiled wearily. "So you, too, assume he'll settle for Egypt instead of his wife?"

"Mother, I didn't mean that. I only meant that if Prime Minister Kitchener has personally ordered him to stay on as consul-general that he'll find himself between the devil and a stone wall. An ultimatum is likely to drive a further wedge between the two of you even if he sails with you and Beth for London. He isn't likely to forget you twisted his arm. Deep in his heart he'll resent you for forcing him to make such a decision when he wasn't ready."

Eleanor's eyes flashed and unexpected tears came. "I've endured for the last ten years, and does he care? I've always taken the last place in his agenda, in his duties, in the honorable demands placed upon him. I live in emotional isolation, and I'm weary of pretending. I have sacrificed enough!" Her voice rose to a pitch that Allison had never heard before, and she threw her arms around her mother.

"Mother, I'm sorry—I'm not lecturing, I'm not being critical. I love you dearly. I wish—I wish I could have helped you more, but I didn't know how."

Her mother stiffened to hold back any sob that might escape and squeezed Allison's arm. After a moment she said too calmly, "There's no reason for you to have any guilt, darling. It wasn't your burden any more than it's Beth's now. But you must understand, I've sorted through this years ago. It's only Beth's schooling that has brought the final decision now."

They lapsed into silence. The sounds of Port Said filled the air.

"I'm tired," said Eleanor in a dull, flat voice. "I've shared him with everyone else all our married life. I wanted these last years to be for us alone. I was planning on it. Now he's been taken from us again—and Marshall permitted it. He knew I'd leased the house in the country. I even sent for the fruit trees to surprise him, and now he's allowed Kitchener to talk him into staying in Arabia. I've lived my life giving to others. We all came last, and—" Her voice snapped, and she dropped her head into her hands, her shoulders shaking.

"Mother," whispered Allison, her throat tense and hurting, "I'm so sorry."

15

ALLISON DIDN'T WANT TO DISAPPOINT HER MOTHER, especially in light of Lady Wescott's recent decision, Leah's death, and Neal's incarceration. Yet Allison felt she couldn't voyage with her mother and Beth to Bombay and then to England, even though her mother seemed to think she would. "You'll have much more opportunity to advance in nursing in England."

How could Allison explain that advancement wasn't what she wanted, but that it was her desire to fulfill a mission she felt called by God to pursue? The day of the polo match and the charity ball she learned from Beth that their mother had bought a passage for the three of them.

"What are you going to do?" asked Beth, watching her intently. "How can you stay here alone? Think of the gossip. It's just not fitting for an unmarried woman to be on her own in Egypt."

Allison knew all this well enough and had struggled to come up with an answer for the last two days. "I'm not leaving," she said quietly, removing her dress for the day from the armoire. "I've trained hard for my career in medicine, and this is where I belong. Besides, I won't be alone. You've forgotten Aunt Lydia. I'll be with her most of the time. When I'm not, well, I can come home to Port Said to the house. Zalika will be here, and maybe Aunt will come as well. She's getting old, despite her insistence she feels as strong as ever."

"After Leah and now cousin Neal, Mother will be upset if you stay."

"I know she will," said Allison quietly, frowning to herself. "But honestly, Beth, it isn't fair to expect me to drop everything I've worked so hard for to leave now."

"You sound like Father."

Allison looked at her, surprised at the comparison. She hadn't thought of it before. Maybe she was a little like her father.

"Lydia needs me on the Nile. There's concern of a typhoid outbreak near Thebes."

"Ugh—you can have ancient Thebes," she said. "All those huge images of pharaohs. Zalika says the Valley of the Kings is haunted by evil spirits."

"If it's haunted by anything, it's archaeologists," said Allison dryly. "Anyway, I'll need to do my best to make Mother understand. I'll promise to come home once a year for a visit."

Beth sadly shook her head, her dark curls swaying. She was working to pin them up, as she copied Allison's sophisticated hairdo. "You know Mum; she'll be scandalized if you stay on without her."

Allison fumbled with her zipper and pinched her skin. "Ouch—oh bother! I don't know why I'm going to such a fuss. I don't even want to go to the polo match or the ball."

Beth smiled mischievously as she helped Allison with the zipper. "You're not fooling me. I got a glimpse of him. Actually, it was more than a glimpse. I watched him from the stairs, and I know why you want to go." She sighed. "He's almost too good looking—except for that little scar on his chin—but it looks so masculine."

Allison met Beth's eyes in the mirror. "I am not going because of Bret Holden. He won't even be there."

"Yes he will," said Beth confidently. "There Zipper's in place, and you look stunning. Oh, sometimes I hate you," her eyes skimming over the folds of pale blue silk with gleaming threads of silver.

"Beth!"

"You know what I mean, silly. Not really 'hate,' but you're so pretty. And I feel so tall and gangly—"

"You're fifteen. You'll fill out plenty. Next time I see you in London you'll be all grown up. Hand me that wrap. Why did you say the Major would be there? He won't. He's in Cairo."

"I know he'll be there because I heard General Blaine telling everyone Major Holden agreed to fill in for him, at least for today. It's the last game, and the brigadier was up in arms about the loss. So General Blaine went to Major Holden and talked him into it."

"What? Bret joined the brigadier's team? I don't believe it."

"Why?"

Allison shrugged. "Because he's easily bored by such things. I don't think he cares much about anything except—" She had wanted to say working in British intelligence, but then realized that Beth didn't know, nor did anyone else, except her mother and father.

"Except what?" asked Beth curiously.

Allison was at a loss. "I'm surprised he has agreed is all."

"Well, he did. And the brigadier says he plays well and rides aggressively, whatever that means."

"It means he can ride a horse and hit the ball with the best of them."

Beth flounced toward the door, looking back at Allison over her shoulder. "Cynthia is coming, too. I saw her. She's even prettier than you." Looking sympathetic, she sighed. "Dreadful bit of luck." She opened the door and went out, leaving it ajar as usual. Allison's unsettled emotions held her in a vise of unease.

✂◦◦✄

Beth was right. Cynthia Walsh could grace the cover of *Vogue* fashion magazine. Allison calmly told herself she had no reason or right for fear and jealously.

"But she's dreadfully uppity," said Sarah Blaine to Allison later that day, smoothing back a strand of gray-tinged hair from her temples. "If she holds her chin much higher, I fear she will have neck strain."

General Blaine leaned toward his wife and stroked his mustache. "My dear, you're being terribly catty tonight."

"Meow indeed," said Sarah, leaning back in her lawn chair. The three of them were sitting at the edge of the polo grounds watching the game. "I'm not the only 'cat' who thinks so. I wonder how she could bear to leave London for Egypt."

"The answer to that is no mystery at all," interjected Allison with a little smile, her eyes following Major Bret Holden on the racing polo pony.

"Ah, yes…," said Sarah, watching the game over the rim of her lemon slush. "So I've heard from Mrs. Walsh. She's suggesting a fat diamond will soon weigh down the delicate hand of our vogue miss."

"Came all the way to the land of the pharaohs to get it, I suppose?" said General Blaine, adjusting his sunglasses lower on his nose. "Well, well, I don't blame her. But you girls don't know everything."

"And they say men don't gossip," taunted Sarah to Allison with a wink. "Out with it, Rex," she said, nudging his arm with her elbow. "You mustn't make us suffer so. What have you learned?"

"About Miss Vogue or him?"

"Him, of course. Allison's interested, naturally."

"Sarah!"

"Uh-oh," said the general, lowering his glasses to peer at Allison.

"Uh-oh what?" Allison said with a laugh.

"He may be staked and claimed by dear Cynthia, but she's only one of a long line who think they've discovered gold—or should I say the latest archaeological treasure?"

Allison bit the rim of her glass, watching Bret Holden, but Sarah turned her petite head toward her husband. "What are you saying, Rex?"

"My dear, don't you know anything?" he mimicked in the tone of a dowager. "The man is a cad and has left many a broken heart along the Romantic Trail as he proceeds undaunted toward new conquests."

"I hadn't heard that," said Sarah. "But I have heard he speaks Arabic and a bit of Turkish rather well, a commodity of interest in London. Maybe a smidgen of German, too."

Allison took a sip of her lemon slush and tried to change the subject. "He plays polo well."

"Where did you hear about his speaking other languages?" asked General Blaine.

Sarah wrinkled her nose at him. "My dear, don't you know anything?"

"Not nearly enough. Must we worry about our Allison?"

"No," said Allison, setting down her glass. "You've both overlooked the fact that I'm practically engaged to Wade Findlay, who will be arriving next year. And it appears Major Holden has already proceeded on his way undaunted where I'm concerned. He's not glanced my way since Cynthia arrived with Lady Walsh."

"You see?" said General Blaine. "He's an impossible prospect. Allison's much too sensible and dedicated to higher causes to waste her time."

"Thank you, Rex," said Allison with a smile. "I didn't think you had noticed—about the higher cause, I mean."

"Ouch."

"She's right, dear, we haven't been to church in months."

"Not so. What did we do the other night if it wasn't adorn the cathedral with our good taste in clothing and jewels—and I saw Reverend Radbourne giving your blue bead the 'evil eye,'" he said, looking pointedly at the turquoise stone she wore around her neck. "They usually wear crosses," he said. "You're heathen, Sarah sweet."

"Oh posh, and that wasn't exactly attending a worship service but a memorial for poor Leah Bristow. I still shudder when I think of that afternoon out at the abandoned digs. It was dreadful to find her that way—"

"Now, now, you'll cast clouds of doom and gloom over Allison's pretty head. Let's not embark on the accident at Aleppo—except, I'm still smarting from my own accident. That sprain in my back hasn't healed, Allison," he said, looking toward her over his glasses. "Haven't you a smidgen more of something to help besides sugar pills?"

"Aunt Lydia has on the boat."

"Dear, dear Lydia. I haven't seen the saint in three years now. How's she doing?"

"As spry as ever. I'll be seeing her soon. She is on the boat down the Nile at Thebes."

"Thebes!"

"You know, Luxor, as it's called today. I'm used to hearing the archaeologists call it by its ancient name. I've plans to go there soon. Come along, you and Sarah both. She would be delighted to see you."

"And try out her new voodoo techniques on my back?"

"Rex," scolded Sarah.

"I'll consider," said General Blaine. "We ought to drop her a line first to let her know we're coming. I suppose she receives mail on that medical boat?"

"All the conveniences," said Allison with a smile. "Anyway, you know the British consuls along the route—you can write the *Mercy* from anywhere and the mail will be held for Lydia at the residencies. Do come! You haven't seen the latest finds—the Valley of the Kings is the richest spot for pyramids and tombs."

"Don't mention tombs," said Sarah, lifting her shoulders with a little chill. "Two accidents at Aleppo are quite enough for me. If I come, I'll view the sights from the *Mercy*. A Nile voyage sounds pleasant enough."

"And if you come," said Allison, "you'll both be saving me an unwanted voyage to Bombay."

"Bombay! Whatever for? Don't tell me Marshall isn't coming home yet?" asked Sarah with a frown. "Eleanor will be up in arms."

"I'm afraid she is," said Allison. "She's sailing with Beth to see him about it. She wants me to go, too, but if I travel to Luxor with you and Rex, she'll be more apt to accept my not wanting to quit my work to go home to England."

"The Blaines to the rescue," said Rex, patting his rounded belly. "I do hope Lydia knows how to cook."

Since Allison had returned from Arabia, everything that had occurred during the meeting of the Cairo Archaeological Club had seemed to fade from reality. Even Jerusalem seemed distant, another world; and while she was concerned about Neal and David, she was sure the British government would soon be on their case arranging for a release. She wondered if Bret Holden had brought any news from Cairo, but with the arrival of Lady Walsh and her niece, Cynthia, Allison was reluctant to make any move in his direction. She was also, if she would admit it, a little put out because he appeared to be avoiding her. She was determined to maintain an affected disinterest, especially after learning from General Blaine and Sarah that Bret was the adoring object of so many feminine traps.

The afternoon ended and was followed by a garden supper at the club given by the brigadier's wife, followed by the club charity ball.

"I hear the baroness will be there," said Sarah. "And Professor Jemal."

"Oh, no, not another lecture on the Hittites," groaned General Blaine. "I've had all I can swallow of the tedious fellow. Looks as if he's recently emerged from one of the ancient tombs himself, sallow-cheeked and deep-eyed like a mummy."

"Don't be silly, darling, one doesn't lecture about archaeology at a charity dance. We waltz about in tune to simply lovely strains, while the Egyptian moon shines like a fiery globe."

"Sounds like a fine spot to take a nap under the violins. And with my back, I won't feel like promenading about the waxed floor. I can see it now—you and the Turkish professor doing the Spanish tango. It's enough to begin the war."

"Jemal doesn't dance, tango or waltz. That reminds me, Allison, I still haven't wooed that invitation to the Christmas extravaganza Baroness Kruger is giving at her house in Alexandria. Eleanor promised to put in a word for me, but I've heard nothing from Helga. Do remind Eleanor before she sails for Bombay, will you? I may not be here to see her off. Rex needs to go into Cairo next week."

"But hopefully we'll be back before the voyage to Luxor," said Rex. "When do you plan to leave?"

"Soon after Mum and Beth leave."

"Oh, hullo. Speaking of the grave-faced sultan, here he comes," said General Blaine.

Allison looked up to see Professor Jemal amble toward their lawn chairs, his lean face shadowed beneath his smoke-blue turban. Otherwise he was all in black with a western-style, knee-length frock coat.

"Never trust a man who wears a winter coat in late July," whispered General Blaine behind his cupped hand, sending Sarah and Allison into smothered giggles.

"Hullo, Jemal, playing polo are you?" asked General Blaine, while raising his hefty frame with its protruding belly from his chair. "I didn't know you all-brain archaeologists had the other kind of outdoor stuff in you—only spades and shovels and mummy graves."

Sarah rolled her eyes in despair and reached for a fan, but Allison laughed. "They don't use such crude tools, Rex, Professor Jemal especially."

"Sorry."

"Don't be, General Blaine," said Jemal with a wan, forgiving smile, as he nodded his turbaned head. "I wouldn't expect a retired military man to know much about digging."

"A benign rebuke, graciously taken. Who won the game, do you know?"

"The brigadier's team, I think. I wasn't watching, but they seem to be celebrating. Although I did think I heard the brigadier toast your sprained back."

"Ho!" said Rex with a laugh. "I've underestimated your sense of humor. I thought it was as lacking in the sultan's palace as it is in Berlin."

"Oh dear! I seem to have splashed my lemon slush," said Sarah.

"Yes, on me," said General Blaine. "You might be a little more subtle in your rebukes, Sarah dear. I think she just gave me my cue to take a stroll," he remarked jovially to Jemal, as he snatched up his empty glass. "I'll meander into the club for a refill and leave you three to chat old bones."

Allison stood as well. "I'm afraid I must leave, too. That's Beth coming now."

"Ready, Allison?" Beth called from the edge of the dusty polo ground.

The supper was held in the gardens of the British Club while the large communal ballroom extending off the court was being readied by locals for the dance. The sky behind the feathery date palms at the far end of the garden was turning from blue-gold to warm shades of rose and orange, and the breathless air hung with the fragrance of roses oddly mixed with outdoor cooking.

Allison was hardly in a festive mood. Unlike the days and nights following her arrival home, which had wrapped her in a comfortable complacency of the familiar, she had come to feel as though something were not quite right. She had no idea what disturbed her ease. But as she sat in the garden having supper and hearing the lull between the rise and fall of voices and laughter, a certain foreboding came to her on the first stir of breeze that rustled the leaves on the tall oleander bush she sat beside. The night was growing darker, the light from the lanterns that hung in the trees was surrounded by bugs, and the lanterns cast swaying shadows on the stone courtyard.

She left her half-eaten food on the plate for the servants to carry away later, and looking toward the ballroom, she noticed that no one had arrived there yet. It stood in shadows, too, except under the lights hung from the high ceiling above the orchestra stand.

Someone was waiting in the unlighted ballroom, she realized. Was it Beth?

She walked into the room, drawn there like a moth beating its wings against a bulb. Looking across the polished floor toward the stage where the light flooded down, she saw the musical instruments were all there. The curtain behind the stage stirred as if a wind had rustled its soiled hem. Had Beth gone back there?

Allison walked through the shadows toward the lighted stage and stopped. "Beth?" she called.

Had her senses deceived her? Beth did not step out from behind the curtain, nor did she answer.

Allison had been so sure it was Beth that she walked toward the steps at the side of the stage and started to go behind the curtain when an odd sensation gripped her. In a moment she was reliving the terror of entering Major Karl Reuter's hut following Leah.

Leah was dead. The British agent was dead, and—

A step behind her made her turn swiftly, expectantly. It was only an Egyptian in a long white *galabiyas* and cloth wrapped about his head, his tanned face and dark eyes as emotionless as the death mask of an ancient pharaoh.

"Oh," she whispered, "you frightened me."

He bowed his head. "Very sorry, madame." He walked past to the other side of the large room, his feet silent, and switched on a blaze of lights. The ball was to begin momentarily, and the musicians were drifting in from a side door, but not from behind the curtain. Had she seen someone go back there? If not Beth, who? And why?

I'm being silly, she thought. *It's the tragedy of Mum and Father, of so much about Neal and David being unsettled, and because I'm not enjoying today. I shouldn't have come. It was a mistake.*

She felt foolish standing on the side steps of the stage in the limelight and swiftly retraced her steps, aware that several heads had turned in her direction. She went out the side door the musicians had used and found herself on the other side of the garden where some low recreational buildings in the form of bungalows were located. They were dark, and she assumed locked. She wondered if she might not just go home, when she nearly bumped into a tall, gaunt figure that emerged from a side door from the back stage.

Jemal bowed his head in greeting. "You are lost, Miss Wescott?"

"Um—well, yes, I suppose I am. Terribly embarrassing of me, I thought—" She stopped, for he stood looking down at her with large, impassive eyes that showed neither humor nor friendliness. He looked like quite a different person from the archaeology professor who held lectures and tours at the Aleppo huts or the friendly guest who had stopped to chat at the Blaine's table near the polo grounds earlier in the afternoon.

His expression changed, and his mouth moved into a wide smile. "The door is this way, behind you. The music has begun. May I have the first waltz?"

She swallowed, nearly choking. Oh bother! Sarah had been wrong about his dancing. The last thing Allison wanted was to return, to waltz, especially with this rather frightening, somber man, but how could she possibly refuse him without appearing to be a British snob?

"Why, yes."

As they entered the ballroom, walking to the center of the floor, Allison felt conspicuous, for only a few couples were there for the first song, and the chairs along the sides of the pale blue walls were filled. People were still arriving and standing in the doorway chatting as they did.

"So you are going to Thebes?" he said congenially.

"Yes, how did you know?"

"Mrs. Blaine mentioned it. I envy you. The Valley of the Kings lures me there as often as I can get away from the university.... Have you heard from your other cousin, Neal Bristow? When you ran off the way you did, we thought you had gone to meet him at Carchemish."

"Yes, we heard from him. Business had taken him to Jerusalem, and he ran into a bit of trouble there with your Turkish General Pasha. He's being held now. You couldn't intervene in any way, could you?"

"My general, Miss Wescott? He is not my general. I have no heart for war. I am a professor and as such stay out of politics."

"Yes, I didn't mean—"

"I am sorry about your cousin. I hope the matter isn't as serious as one might think. However, since I do not know the Turkish officials at Jerusalem, there is little I can do for Neal. Nevertheless, I will certainly call upon Ismet Bey in Cairo," he said of the Turkish official. "Perhaps he will look into the matter."

"Anything you could do would be appreciated. By the way, Professor, I've been concerned about the lamp at the Jerablus expedition house. Shouldn't the museum safeguard it until Neal can return to the digs there?"

"A lamp? Unfortunately I've not seen it. Is it valuable?"

"Oh, but you must have seen it at Neal and Leah's house. It can't be missed. It's right in the sitting room."

His shadowed eyes were blank. "I have not been to the Bristow house in Jerablus, only out to the digs last year. So I would not know of the piece you speak about. I will mention it to Baroness Kruger."

"But the letter—" she began, then wisely stopped.

"The letter?"

"Oh, I do beg your pardon, Professor Jemal! There—I've gone and stepped on your polished shoe. How clumsy of me."

"It is nothing," he said stiffly.

"Oh, but it is very beastly of me."

"Please. It is nothing."

"I feel like such a bore—"

Just then someone jostled her, pushing her to the side. She turned, grateful for the interruption. Bret, with Cynthia Walsh, said, "Excuse me, rather clumsy of us. Oh, hello, Professor, I see you've decided to stay after all. Can't blame you." He looked at Allison with a disarming smile that told her the interruption hadn't been an accident. "Pleasant evening, isn't it?"

She scanned him briefly, noting how well he wore the British uniform—a far cry from Colonel Holman with the Iron Cross. It was the first time she had seen him looking so British, and the uniform fit his personality as well as it did his masculine build.

"Rather warm I was thinking," said Jemal, and his sad eyes ran over Bret's military rating. "I didn't know you were in Cairo intelligence, Major."

"Unfortunate bit of luck. My commanding officer had me transferred with him. I speak some Arabic, and he doesn't. I'd rather have stayed in Constantinople." Bret turned casually to the raven-haired woman on his arm, who was eyeing Allison.

"Cynthia, have you met the most brilliant Egyptologist about? This is Professor Jemal. Professor, Miss Cynthia Walsh. She's here for a visit from England."

Jemal bowed with stately charm, no doubt warmed by Bret's exaggerated compliment. *It isn't like the major to be so warm and generous with his choice of words,* thought Allison.

Cynthia merely smiled and ignored Allison. Snapping open a small lace fan and swishing it, Cynthia glanced about. "It is dreadfully warm in here, Bret."

"Since you were commenting on the heat as well, Professor, perhaps you wouldn't mind being the envy of every gentleman here and attending to Miss Walsh for the next few minutes?"

Bret turned to look at Allison, smiling briefly. "Nurse Wescott, I'd like to discuss a matter with you during the next dance. Would you mind if I tore you away from the brilliant professor? I promise not to keep you long."

Not waiting for an answer, Bret smoothly deposited the surprised Cynthia on Professor Jemal's arm and took hold of Allison's at the same moment. He drew her away onto the ballroom floor.

Allison smiled sweetly. "By your pragmatic form of address, Major Holden, I assume you need to discuss my recommendation for the alleviation of some new form of disease?"

He smiled, unperturbed. "Yes, I find that I'm often seriously misunderstood, Nurse Wescott. Do you think you can help me?"

Her contradictory smile continued. "No."

"Another hope crushed."

"But I imagine Cynthia would be quite obliging."

At that moment, the band struck up a noisy quickstep with a clash of cymbals and drums. Allison smiled victoriously. "Somehow I can't imagine Colonel Holman doing a Spanish fandango with *Fräulein.*" She laughed softly. "Of course, if you're willing to try…"

His sardonic smile flickered, and he drew her away toward the side door, which opened onto the back side of the garden. Allison, realizing he was leading her to the place where she had nearly bumped into Professor Jemal earlier, held back.

"Don't worry. Our little stroll is strictly business."

"Why should I think it otherwise?"

"You're not disappointed?" he asked with polite innocence.

She looked up at him, resisting the dark blue intensity of his gaze.

"Let's not debate now," he said. "My little exchange with Jemal and Miss Walsh worked like a charm, didn't it?"

"Miss Walsh? How formal of you, considering she's expecting a solitaire on her engagement finger."

"Very well, then, 'Cynthia.' I see my private concerns are fast making the rounds of female gossip."

"As a matter of fact, I learned it from a man. General Blaine."

"Charming. That makes all the difference."

"It makes absolutely no difference to me."

"I didn't come to discuss Cynthia. And, if you don't mind, I'd like to leave that for what it is, a personal matter."

Stung, she lapsed into silence, more angry with herself than Bret. Whatever had gotten into her? She would never have permitted herself to behave this way before. What had she expected from him? Did she think he would try to convince her there was nothing between Miss Walsh and him? What right did she have to expect him to explain, or to assume he wouldn't care for someone?

"I'm sorry. I deserved that—" she began.

"No," he interrupted softly. "You didn't. You deserve much better than I can offer, but this isn't the time for sentimentality."

"Sentimentality is not one of your weaknesses."

"Another personal matter. Now, about Professor Jemal. I could see you were trapped and got you out of it, but for a reason. I want to know what he wanted of you. He's not a dancer."

"You're the second person who's told me that. Then I guess I should be flattered he broke his own rule and asked me for the first waltz. What makes you suspect I was trapped?"

"Well, weren't you?"

"Yes, but how did you know?"

"I followed you inside the ballroom, when it was still empty. I saw you start up the steps to go behind the curtain. I was about to stop you when you took a swift exit out the side door only to meet Jemal coming from the stage."

"But it wasn't the professor who went behind the curtain."

"What makes you so sure?"

"Because…" Just why was she certain? "Because he was coming from the outer garden when I met him."

"He made it look that way, then deliberately startled you by asking you to dance. His action took your mind off seeing him go behind the curtain. Am I right?"

She realized it had. "I used the same tactic on him when I startled him by stepping on his polished shoe, then behaving like a ninny by repeatedly apologizing. It worked. He forgot my mistake."

His alert gaze sought and searched hers. "Your mistake? What mistake? What was it you wanted him to forget?"

She didn't explain at first. "But why would he slip away behind the stage curtain? And why did he pretend he hadn't been there? After all, he could have made some simple excuse and let the matter go. I had thought it was my sister, Beth. Why did he go there?"

"I was going to ask you that. I thought you knew and had decided to play detective again and follow him. A reckless decision."

"Follow him? Why would I want to? And how do you know all this?"

He took her arm and walked her across the court. "Because I've been keeping an eye on you, whether you think so or not."

She concealed her pleasure. "Have you really been watching me? Then maybe that was what I sensed earlier."

He looked at her curiously. "What do you mean?"

She remembered the odd sensation she had felt earlier in the garden during the outdoor supper. It seemed silly to try to explain. Somehow she thought Bret would attribute it to feminine instincts. Not wishing to appear foolish, she tried to avoid the subject. "I guess I was just feeling nervous."

"I think it's more than that," came his sober reply. "Don't forget, the information Leah and Reuter were killed for is still missing, and someone may think you have it. You haven't forgotten, have you? Has Port Said changed your thinking so much?"

He wasn't playing games with her, and she realized she should have known he wouldn't. Bret didn't play games. His expression was grave.

"No, I haven't forgotten. How could I?"

His hand on her arm tightened. "This isn't the place to talk." He led her farther into the back garden.

"Do you think it's proper to escort Nurse Wescott into the Egyptian night?" she asked in a breezy attempt at indifference.

"I gather, from the withering looks you throw my way, you don't like to be called by your professional title." He smiled a light invitation. "What else do I dare call you?"

"Never mind. Was it really true what you told Professor Jemal about your commanding officer arranging your transfer to Cairo because he needed you?"

"Something like that," he responded evasively.

"I take it it's not quite that simple. You do, however, speak Arabic, because Sarah said so."

"Who is Sarah?"

"General Blaine's wife. I told you about them in Jerablus."

"I see you've been discussing the curious Major Holden. What else did she have to say?"

"That you speak some Turkish."

"Language was a major study for me. It's crucial in my work."

"You mean espionage."

"I wish you wouldn't say it aloud. Anyone else bring it up?"

"By now everyone knows you work at Cairo intelligence, even Professor Jemal. He mentioned it tonight."

"Yes, pretending surprise. He already knew. You're right, everyone does know, but working in intelligence is not the same as being a foreign agent. So remember to play coy when I become the topic of conversation. What did the Blaines tell you about me?" he persisted.

As they walked onto the lawn, she looked at him sideways. "I was warned," she said bluntly.

His mouth turned in wry amusement. "I see. Suppose I told you all the talk is part of my cover."

"You mean, Major, you don't have a dozen fair beauties like Cynthia out to lure you into a matrimonial trap?" she asked with false innocence.

He laughed and escorted her across the lawn, but she noticed he didn't answer the question.

He helped her to sit in a lawn chair made of wicker and stood looking down at her for a moment. The smile was gone and so was the casual, conversational style. A frown showed on his handsomely chiseled face.

"Let's get serious, Allison. I want to know what made you think you needed to be careful with Jemal."

"I need to be careful with everyone. You told me that in Jerablus. And so I have."

His eyes narrowed, and he folded his arms, obviously unimpressed with her explanation. "Yes, but what did he ask you?"

"Nothing important. Let's see—oh yes, he asked about whether or not I'd heard from Neal."

"You told him?" he asked with interest.

"I didn't see any reason not to. Shouldn't I have?"

For a moment he considered her query. "I suppose it doesn't matter. The news of his detention in Jerusalem is out."

"Which reminds me, you haven't heard anything yet?"

"No, unfortunately. We're working on it in Cairo. So far, the Turks have been typically uncooperative." He grew thoughtful, as though something bothered him.

"What is it?" she asked quietly.

"They're insisting they don't have Neal."

"Is that unusual?" she asked tensely.

"No, but it strikes me as odd since they admit to holding David. I wonder…" She wasn't to know what he wondered, for an Egyptian serving man came softly across the lawn carrying a tray of cool refreshments for those who had opted to leave the ballroom. Bret gestured, and the man came over offering the tray. Handing her a cool lemonade, Bret took a frosted glass for himself and sat opposite her. After the man had gone, he asked quietly, "What else did Jemal ask?"

"Let's see...he asked if I was going to Thebes soon."

He watched her over the glass rim. "Luxor? Are you?"

"Yes. My work with Aunt Lydia." She wondered what he thought about her missionary work.

He frowned lightly, fingering the frosted glass. "I wish you wouldn't go yet. It makes it much more difficult for me to keep an eye on you. If you must leave, why not go with your mother and sister to Bombay?"

"How did you know about Bombay?" she smiled. "Is that bit of work also part of your espionage?"

If it was, he preferred to ignore her half-hearted question. "Your mother asked me to arrange passage."

"Odd...that she would ask you. You're going as escort?"

"Not a chance! I was stationed in India for the first five years of my service. How do you expect to convince your mother to let you stay on here alone? My impression of her is that of a great lady with precise beliefs."

Allison smiled wistfully. "She is all of that. And I hope you're not implying that I lack propriety by not sailing with her."

"My dear, you're the paradigm of culture and innocence. Complimenting Lady Wescott wasn't intended to throw a shadow across your path. I was merely hoping she would exert influence over you where I cannot. I wish you would either stay in Port Said or go with your mother."

"Thank you, Major," she said too gravely, sipping her lemon slush.

His mouth turned. "Not for any reason except your safety. You would be better off returning to England with your family and forgetting all that's happened in Arabia."

"Do you really think I can?" she asked gravely, remembering Leah.

"No, but for your sake, you would be wise to try."

She hastened to say, "I'm of age for one thing; so my mother won't insist. She respects my interest in nursing with Aunt Lydia. I hate to disappoint my mother, though. Anyway, I won't be alone. The Blaines are coming to Luxor, too, for a few weeks' stay. I'll be with my aunt on the boat and with friends."

He frowned. "Can't Luxor wait? Its a good distance from Cairo, and I'll be tied up there for a time. I can't keep tabs on you."

The idea of Bret keeping watch was more comforting than she wanted to admit, even if the reason was for quite another purpose than romantic interest.

"I'll be perfectly safe in Luxor. Busy, as a matter of fact, with a myriad of inoculations against typhoid. Aunt Lydia is expecting the medicine to arrive soon. She'll have things ready when I get there."

He watched her with an unexpected intensity that made her skin tingle. "Saving the children, I gather, is the reason you're willing to risk journeying up and down the Nile. I admit it fits you well."

"If that's a compliment, Major, thank you. I'm surprised."

"You shouldn't be. So Jemal asked about Luxor. What exactly did he want to know?"

"Only if I were going. Sarah had mentioned it earlier. He's interested because of the pyramids and monuments, of course."

He seemed satisfied. "All right. Now, why did you find it necessary to make him forget by stepping on his shoe?"

Allison set down her glass, wiping the dripping moisture onto the napkin. "It was a letter I found in Leah's bedroom at Jerablus—"

She stopped, looking past Bret. Her expression must have shown how startled she was, for he stood and turned.

"Major Holden," said Baroness Helga Kruger, coming from the lawn's shadows. "The brigadier said I might find you here. Ah, Allison. It is timely to see you again safe and in congenial company. I will not lecture, but you did give us all a dreadful moment when you disappeared at the huts so soon after Miss Bristow was found dead. Eleanor explained to me what happened, however."

Allison stood. "I regret I couldn't leave a message for you, Baroness."

"Couldn't?"

"David was in such a hurry to get to Jerusalem—"

"He knew Neal Bristow was there on archaeology business," interjected Bret, taking control of the conversation. "You'll be interested to see his pieces for the museum when General Pasha agrees to release him. We were hoping you would put in a good word for him."

"I do not know General Pasha."

"No. Of course you wouldn't."

He said it honestly enough, but somehow Allison wondered if he meant it. The baroness seemed to hesitate as well.

"I had your friends at the museum in Constantinople in mind," said Bret. "Sometimes civilians in responsible places can have a quiet impact on government officials."

"Yes, yes, that is a possibility. I will send a wire in the morning. Anything to be of help."

Bret gave a brief bow of his head. "You are a woman of rare insight, Baroness. That fact has not gone unnoticed by the British officials. You wished to see me about a matter?"

"Yes, but I would not want to interrupt…" She looked pointedly at Allison.

Allison recognized the hint. A glance at Bret showed he wasn't pleased with Helga's interruption, but his bland gaze told Allison it might be better to cooperate.

"I must be going anyway," said Allison. "It's time I looked up Beth to see how she's faring. This is her first ball."

Bret drew back a chair to clear a path. "Good night. I'll do what I can about your cousin," he repeated as though she had been meeting with him about Neal. "I'll be in touch from Cairo by letter or wire."

"Thank you, Major. Good night." She turned to Helga who watched her, a subdued hint of the curious in her dark eyes. "So good to see you again, Baroness."

"Yes, and I hope to see you at some of my dinner parties this year. You must come and bring Sarah Blaine with you."

"Sarah would be delighted."

The Baroness smiled as though the matter were settled and turned to sit in the chair that Allison had vacated.

Allison walked across the velvety lawn back toward the clubhouse where the bright lights in the ballroom glittered like diamonds in the hot night. Had Helga overheard her mention the letter she had found in Leah's bedroom in Jerablus?

She was reminded that she had been so busy since her arrival that she hadn't gone through the stack of papers and letters from Leah's dresser drawer.

I'll do it tonight, she thought. *Bret will want to know what was in the letter. I suppose he'll be in touch before he leaves Port Said for Cairo.*

Obviously, Helga hadn't seen Bret at Aleppo in the disguise of Colonel Brent Holman, nor had Professor Jemal. Had anyone else? she wondered. She didn't think so. How could they? Someone would have mentioned it. Nor would Bret be so casual about showing himself for who he was.

Allison was interested in what Helga had wanted of him and wondered if he would explain.

16

ALLISON FOUND HER MOTHER WITH SARAH in deep conversation at one corner of the ballroom and casually announced she was more exhausted from the Arabian trip than she had thought. Since she wasn't in the mood for an Egyptian band playing cymbals and drums, she was going home for a sound night's sleep. Her mother offered to leave with her, but Beth would have been tremendously disappointed, and since neither of them wished to lower the curtain on Beth's first charity ball after only the first four dances, Allison insisted she would just as soon go without them.

"I'm not up to this dreadful music myself," said Sarah, wincing toward the band. "Knowing Rex, he'll be only too glad to slip away. We'll give you a ride home. Now where did he go?" She looked about. "Probably smoking one of the brigadier's dreadful cigars and discussing the polo game. That Major Holden was classy today, I'm told. I don't see him anywhere, either. Oh, dear, isn't that Cynthia Walsh? Doesn't she look as if someone put hot vinegar in her lemon slush?"

"Don't bother with me; I'll just hire a driver," said Allison quickly, wanting to avoid Cynthia. "Enjoy yourself, Mother. Good night." Leaning to give her mother a quick kiss, Allison gathered up her silk wrap and handbag from the chair. "Good night, Sarah. I'll be in touch about Luxor."

"You do look wan," said Eleanor. "Take a sleeping draught and don't get up for breakfast. I'll have Zalika bring you a tray."

"You're spoiling me. Aunt Lydia expects me up with the egrets!"

Allison left through a side door where a number of *calishe* waited, hoping for business.

When she arrived in front of the house, she paid the driver and walked past the Persian lilacs and banana trees to the front door as the sound of the horse and wheels faded into the night. Using her key, she entered the lighted entryway, half expecting to be greeted by Zalika, who usually waited up for them until they retired.

But Zalika must have gone to bed, for stillness hung in the rooms, though several dim lights were on. Then she remembered that Zalika didn't expect them home until after midnight. She had asked permission to visit her sister, whose husband worked at the docks.

Allison shut the door behind her, locking it. She could use a cup of tea but would forgo it since she was eager to sort through Leah's papers and read the letter from Professor Jemal. Odd how he had said he had never been to the Jerablus expedition house.

She removed her long silk wrap as she walked to the stairs, her slippers clicking on the polished wood like an intruder. Zalika had left the light burning at the top of the stairway, and Allison started to climb the steps when she noticed the hall table contained mail. The post must have been delivered late since Allison had checked earlier that afternoon. Zalika probably left it there before going to visit her sister.

Allison hastily skimmed through a few circulars, some bills belonging to her mother, and a letter for Beth from a friend in Cairo. Just as Allison was about to lay them aside and hurry up to her room to the small box that held Leah's papers, a letter posted from Luxor winked up at her. It was a letter from Aunt Lydia. Allison rushed up the steps and down the dim hall to her room, opening the door and switching on the light as she entered. Tossing off her slippers and pulling off her earrings, she went to the chair beside the table with the crystal lamp. Turning it on, she sank down to indulge in Lydia's latest news from the *Mercy*.

But the message was brief, which was unlike Lydia. Allison held it beneath the lamp to read the light-colored ink.

Dear Allison,

I'm in a hurry to post this before the boat leaves; so excuse my haste. The medical supplies haven't arrived, and after rechecking with Arlington, the consul down the Nile, he insists I left him orders to send the goods to the residency at Cairo. I don't recall doing this. Do you? When the crates arrived a week ago, Arlington took extra pains to have them sent at once to Lower Egypt. He was so offended that I should question what he had done that I didn't have the heart to argue with him. He suffers from the jitters and a weak stomach, which I've been treating, and I didn't want to pro-voke an attack. The supplies are waiting in Cairo. Can you come and bring them at once? The threat of an epidemic grows with the passing days. You will need to rent a falukka and leave from Cairo. Do come as quickly as you can.

Tell sister Eleanor I shall make up to her for stealing you away so soon after your vacation in Carchemish. You can tell me about it when you arrive.

We have some new archaeologists from France, the most hideous in manner we've come up against. They informed me I had to move the Mercy farther down the Nile because I was attracting too many fellahin, who were interrupting their work. Imagine!

When you get here, you have a package waiting. I would have sent it on, but Arlington, who delivered it personally, told me a message came with it that asked him to leave it with me on the Mercy.

I close with the words of Paul, "Do your best to come before winter."

Lydia.

Allison frowned. It would be dreadfully difficult to collect the medical supplies in Cairo and deliver them herself by boat. Whatever gave Mr. Arlington the notion that Aunt Lydia had told him to send them down river? Now she must leave Port Said as soon as possible. But perhaps this provided a solution to her dilemma of how to convince her mother to let her stay in Egypt. All things did work together for good to those who loved God, she thought, turning bright instead of gloomy. Her mother shared the compassion Allison and Aunt Lydia had for the poor and sick, and if the epidemic of typhoid was expected, her mother would wish her to aid Lydia in administering the innoculations.

A draft blew the letter in her hand, and Allison tensed. She slowly turned toward the terrace with its wrought-iron rail. The door was ajar. She didn't recall leaving it open when she left around three that afternoon, but Zalika must have opened it to cool the room.

Not that it mattered. She would have opened it herself anyway when she entered her room, if she hadn't been so eager to read Aunt Lydia's letter and go through Leah's papers and letters.

Allison went at once to the small dresser where she kept the box of Leah's papers. She took a small key from beneath a crocheted doily to open the dresser. Lifting out the box, she carried it to the bed where she emptied the contents onto the satin spread.

A sound like a creak in the hall floor outside her door brought her up with a start. She stood staring, her eyes fixed on the open latch. She listened; there the noise was again.

Her heart pounded. Swiftly she stuffed the papers back into the box, her fingers trembling, and as quietly as possible, slipped the box under her bed. Then noiselessly she crossed the floor, switched off the light, and hurried barefoot to the terrace, pulling open the door and stepping out.

The night wrapped about her with suffocating stillness, starlight spilling from the blackness above. She went to the rail, bending over to look down into the garden. Zalika had left the lanterns glowing, and golden light fell across the paving stones. A flight of outer steps led down, and she took them now, quickly, careful not to trip on the hem of her ball gown. She was prepared to run through the garden and out the gate into the street when someone walked through, jacket slung over his shoulder.

She froze, then said breathlessly, "Bret..."

He did not appear to hear her, but then she remembered his training had taught him not to give anything away by his actions. He walked forward into the garden and out of the lantern light. When he was concealed, he said quietly, "Allison?"

The next moment she grasped him so tightly she might have been strangling him, but he took it patiently enough. She half expected a light remark about her ardent greeting, but he must have sensed something was wrong. His voice was quiet and calm. She could feel the unhurried beat of his heart. "Someone in the house?"

She nodded.

"See who it was?"

She shook her head, still unashamedly holding him.

"He—he may have a gun."

"So do I."

She realized, to her own comfort, that he could be dangerous. Unlike her, he could afford to be confident and unafraid.

"Where is he now, do you know?"

"In the hall outside my bedroom—there was no lock and so I came out through the terrace. There are steps—"

"Then he's still there. I don't think he heard me since I got off the *calishe* a block back." He gently disentangled himself. "Wait here."

Without a watch to tell the time, Allison had no idea how long he was gone. She waited tensely, breathlessly, where she had withdrawn to the edge of the fence. If someone came scrambling across the yard trying to escape, she didn't want to get caught between the intruder and Bret.

It might have been three minutes, five, or ten, but as she stood in the garden shadows staring up past the terrace to her room, the light came on. She half expected to hear tables and chairs crashing, then someone climbing over the terrace. Lights began to flash on throughout the house as though Bret were quickly searching from room to room.

The intruder must have escaped. Leaving the fence, she walked across the garden to the steps. She stood below, debating whether or not to go up when Bret appeared, carrying something in his arms.

"Yours?" he asked.

Allison sighed and went up the steps. Bret leaned against the rail calmly scratching the sides of the black kitten's face. She looked from the kitten's luminous green eyes into Bret's dark blue ones and would have been shamefully furious with herself if there had been any amusement in his face, but there wasn't.

"Thutmose III," she said with sober dignity. "Belongs to Beth. Don't tell me that's what I heard, because I know the difference between a kitten's meow and a floorboard creaking under a man's weight."

"I gather there was a Thutmose II?"

"And a Thutmose I," she added stiffly.

"Father and grandfather cat have been very productive. Here." He leaned over and deposited the warm kitten in her arms. Allison followed Bret into the room, placing the kitten on the chair. She walked quickly to her door and stood looking into the hall. The light was on now, and everything appeared as it always did.

"There's no one here," he said. "I searched every room."

"Bret, I heard someone out there!"

He came up behind her, catching her arm and turning her around. "Steady, Allison. I don't doubt you for a moment. But he isn't here now."

His level gaze and slight frown brought the steadying influence she needed. "Now tell me what happened," he said quietly.

"I was in here, when I heard the floor squeak as if someone had walked up quietly and stopped." She shivered.

His hand moved to the side of her hair. "Before that. What happened at the club? Did anyone see you leave?"

"No, I don't think so. Only my mother and Sarah Blaine. They were going to come as well, but—" She looked at him, suddenly alert.

His brow lifted. "Yes?"

"How did you know I was home? I left you with Baroness Kruger," she half accused.

"We had our meeting, and she left. I suspected you had come home early, and when I didn't see you in the ballroom, I asked Lady Wescott. She told me you had left a few minutes earlier. I intended to finish our discussion that Helga interrupted. Satisfied?" he asked with a smile.

"I wasn't accusing you of being a second burglar, if that's what you think."

"Maybe I was. The steps to your terrace, 'Juliet,' are tempting."

"Do be serious. There was someone here tonight."

"Yes, and it's time you came clean and told me what it was he was after."

She looked at him. "What makes you think he was after something?"

He watched her soberly. "If it was the same thing that Leah had, and he thought you knew where it was, I'd pack your bag myself and put you on the first boat to England."

She smiled for the first time. "What makes you think I would go?"

"Because you'll do as you're told," he said firmly. "If you don't, I'll go straight to Lady Wescott and inform her that her daughter is playing spy and likely to have a funeral sooner rather than later."

"Thutmose, what are you telling me?" she said as the kitten rubbed against her ankles twitching his tail. "You spoiled creature. I suppose Beth didn't give you that horrid smelling fish food. Well, you'll need to wait."

"My guess is," said Bret, "that whoever was here didn't know you had left early and thought he had enough time to accomplish his task."

"But what could he have wanted? You don't think—" Her voice lowered uneasily, "Do they suspect I have the book?"

Bret glanced about the bedroom, musing. "Maybe. It might have been something else on his mind. I wish I knew." His eyes came to hers. "What did you tell Professor Jemal tonight?"

She stared up at him, for only now did it begin to dawn on her. She picked up the kitten and handed it to him, then rushed to the edge of her bed and knelt, reaching under to draw out the box. But no matter how far she extended her hand, there was no box.

"No," she whispered, "impossible—no one knew—"

Bret placed the kitten in the hall and closed the door. "What?"

She looked at him. Her face was pale and her eyes wide. "The box full of papers and letters I took from Leah's bedroom at Jerablus."

Bret walked up, took her hand, and pulled her to her feet. "You what? You had them and didn't tell me?"

"I didn't think there was anything important. I meant to read them at once, but so much has happened since then, first at Jerusalem, then here."

"You told Jemal about this box?"

"No, I'd never be so foolish. I didn't tell anyone. That's why it's impossible for anyone to have known, to have come here tonight searching for it."

"When did you put the box under the bed of all obvious places? The first spot anyone would ever look."

She stiffened under his exasperated gaze. "When I heard the noise in the hall. Before I left by way of the terrace."

He let out a breath and dropped her arm, standing with hands on hips. "Then he found it and left before I came in."

"Whoever it was couldn't have known," she protested feebly, feeling guilty.

"Someone knows a good deal more than either of us seems to think," he said. "I suggest he came for that purpose, while you waltzed away the night in blue silk," he said, gesturing to her ball gown.

"It isn't silk," she said dully. "It's taffeta."

His eyes narrowed, and she looked away, then brushed past to the terrace. "All right, Major, I made a dreadful mistake."

"Yes," he said, "you did."

"I should have told you sooner about Leah's papers and letters. I've no excuse except that I thought them unimportant."

"Did you look at them all? Do you remember anything?"

"No, I gathered them the night you came creeping in the window at the house, the night the wind howled and Leah had only been murdered for a day."

"Enough said. I've been a little impatient. My humble apology."

She gave him a glance that dismissed his apology, and he walked up and leaned in the doorway. "Back to Professor Jemal, whom we seem to have a difficult time discussing. If I didn't know you better I might think you were trying to protect him."

"There was a letter from Jemal to Leah," she said quietly, wincing when she heard him suck in a breath. "Yes, I know. I should have read it. And tonight, when I told you I'd startled him into forgetting something the way he did me by the stage—it was the letter that I'd made a mistake about." She turned quickly, her eyes pleading with his. "I'm sorry."

He remained silent. Then he said, "Do you think he guessed?"

"No. Because I didn't mention the letter. I told him I hadn't realized he and Leah knew each other in Jerablus. He said he didn't know her well. That was the second time he told me so."

"The first time being at the Aleppo huts?"

"Yes. But I think he's lying. Because Leah mentioned he had visited. And then there was this letter. Leah had kept it for a reason."

"And now it's gone. Did you tell him you knew he had visited the expedition house?"

"No. But I now think he must know. Because I mentioned a certain lamp that's in the house. It's a rather rare piece. Even I could tell that."

"The one with the woman carrying a basket on her head?"

"You saw it?"

"I couldn't miss it. Looks valuable."

"So I thought. And I told Professor Jemal someone from the Cairo Museum should go there to retrieve it, or put up a Kurdish guard until Neal is released from Jerusalem."

"And what did he say?"

"He pretended he didn't know about it. I thought it odd because anyone with his background would have seen it immediately."

"And this mistake you said you mentioned? If not the letter, what?"

"I told him he must have seen it since he had visited Leah there. But he said he had never been there. I remembered the letter and was about to mention it as well when I thought better of it."

"Then you squashed his foot?" he asked with a brief smile.

"Yes," said Allison defensively. "And he forgot all about our conversation. Then you added to the grand moment by arriving with Cynthia and depositing her on his arm. He's probably still waltzing with her. No, I take that back. Before I left, I saw Miss Walsh alone and quite nettled. You'll have a good deal of explaining to do tomorrow, Major."

"Hmm, so he said he hadn't been at the Jerablus house."

"He's lying."

"Apparently, but why? The question is, did he know you had the letter and was it he who came here tonight looking for it?"

"I don't think so."

"If not Jemal, then who?"

Wearily, Allison lowered herself onto a pink satin stool.

Bret looked toward the terrace, alert to a noise before she heard it.

Allison stood. "Oh, no, you mustn't be caught in my bedroom. I shall never hear the end of it from Beth. That's she and my mother arriving now. They must have decided to come home after all. Please! They mustn't see you!"

He offered a bow as chivalrous as an English cavalier. "I shall escape by way of the terrace, Lady Allison. Anything, beloved, to save your reputation and my neck."

Allison rushed to lower the lights, then followed him to the terrace. They waited in the starlight until the voices of her mother and Beth disappeared behind the front door.

"It's safe now," she said.

"Remember, be careful. Don't say anything about the intruder tonight. The more this gets around, the more difficult it will be to keep a lid on it. Whoever it was got what he wanted, so he won't be back." Then he took hold of her forearms, holding her gaze. In the starlight Allison felt a compelling tug on her heart and wanted to pull away.

"Go with your mother to Bombay," he said evenly. "Leave all this mess to me, will you?"

"No, Major, I can't. I don't want to leave. Even if I could, I wouldn't do so. Not now."

"What do you mean, 'not now'? After everything that's happened, especially tonight, haven't you risked enough?"

"I received a letter from Aunt Lydia tonight." She explained to him about the medical supplies. "I have to go to Luxor. She needs those supplies."

"If I promised to have the supplies delivered, would you be on that ship with your mother and sister?"

She smiled softly. "No. I'm leaving for Cairo as soon as I explain matters to my family."

His mouth turned down, and his grip relaxed. "Without any doubt you are the most frustrating young woman I've ever encountered. But also the most interesting."

She was still hesitating and had not yet pulled her arms away. Standing with him on the terrace in the warm Egyptian starlit night was enough to awaken her to other dangers.

"Considering that I am a calloused creature who is not easily given to sentimentality, I am impressed that your charms have not gone unnoticed." He leaned toward her, and Allison caught the fragrance coming from his clean white shirt opened at the neck. "For the sake of pure romance, you wouldn't ease the frustration of my day and offer the kind generosity of a good night kiss? Very chaste, of course. We'll keep it a secret from Cynthia and dear Wade Findlay."

Allison struggled with the drawing desire that reached out to spin a warm web around her emotions. It would be so easy to say yes; her heart had already said yes.

Too easy, she thought. *I'd be just like the rest of them. One more young woman melting in his arms, falling in love with the cool British intelligence agent who has no intention of becoming a permanent fixture. He even implied so. Just a simple kiss—it would mean nothing—forever to remain a secret from Cynthia.*

As he leaned toward her, she forced herself to turn her face away. His lips brushed her cheek. He seemed to lose his balance as she leaned away, and he tried to follow, steadying himself on the terrace rail with one hand as she retreated to the safety of the terrace door.

She didn't think he would pursue. He wasn't the type. He was as suave as any man she had seen. She half smiled, satisfied with herself for resisting. That would draw a distinctive line between her and all the others. He was more likely to think about it, to remember her.

"Good night, Major," she said softly but confidently and shut the door, clicking the bolt.

Weakly she drew the drapes shut as well, and stood there, heart thumping in her eardrums. She reached a hand and touched her cheek. She was likely to remember, too.

The Tigris set sail for Bombay on the morning of July 15, and Allison bid her mother and Beth good-bye amid embraces and the hope of a reconciliation between her mother and father.

"He's bound to understand, Mother. I'm convinced of it. He does love you. I'll be coming to England next Christmas to spend it with the three of you."

Her mother smiled, but her eyes were sad as she leaned to kiss Allison good-bye. "I feel as if I'm making a mistake going off like this and leaving you, Allison. I know you're of age, and I understand your commitment to your work with Lydia, but I don't feel at peace."

"You worry too much, Mum. Aunt Lydia and I are two of a kind. We'll hold each other up. Maybe I'll even convince her to return to England for the holidays."

"That's as likely as my convincing your father to retire to an orchard of fruit trees and buzzing bees. Maybe I should—"

"Mother," cried Beth, exasperated, the warm Mediterranean wind tossing the green feather in her hat. "We'll miss the ship. Allison knows what she's doing, don't you?"

"Good-bye," cried Allison, blinking back the tears that sprinkled her lashes and smiling bravely as she waved. "Good-bye! I love you, Mum, Beth. Good-bye! Bon voyage!"

Eleanor's face was strained as she smiled and waved along with Beth. "Take care of yourself, darling. Be careful on the Nile voyage. And don't wear yourself out taking care of others!"

"I won't."

"Don't forget to write!" cried Beth. "And take care of Thutmose III."

"I will. He's coming with me to Luxor. Good-bye!"

The loud blast of the ship's whistle drowned out the words her mother continued to call out, and Allison waved and stood on the dock watching until they had disappeared.

Lord, I did make the right decision to stay, didn't I? Take care of them.

Help Mum and Father come to a blessed understanding. Grant a safe voyage to Bombay and home to England.

"The Lord bless you and keep you," she prayed from Numbers 6:24. "*The Lord lift up His countenance upon you and give you peace.*"

Alone, she felt the wind. The permanence of her decision settled into her heart like an anchor.

"Good-bye," she murmured again.

PART 4

Back to Arabia

17

THE NILE

GENERAL BLAINE AND SARAH had left Port Said for Cairo several days earlier. Allison, who was still at the family residence arranging for her stay with Aunt Lydia in Luxor, received a message by post from Sarah. Everything was scheduled for their voyage along the Nile into Upper Egypt, which on the map appeared to be "Lower" Egypt.

Sarah had written that General Blaine had arranged to rent a "good, clean" *falukka* with a trusted captain and crew of eight since Allison knew little about such things. He had found the boat at the port of Boulak in north Cairo. Their own supplies were being seen to now, wrote Sarah. "You know how Rex enjoys his food, tea, and coffee." They also had plenty of pots and pans, linen, bedding, a portable bath, and several guns plus ammunition. Rex wanted to set sail on July 20.

"His fatherly concerns have blossomed," wrote Sarah brightly. "He even made the arrangements to load Lydia's medical supplies for you." But, she added, Allison would first need to go to the dealer in Old Cairo to sign the authorization slip releasing the medicine from England for the *Mercy*.

"Be careful when you get there. Rex thinks the Turkish shop owner is not to be trusted and that he deals behind the up-and-up in opium. Rex and I both wonder why Lydia would arrange to have the cholera medicine brought to Old Cairo, of all places."

Allison had no answer, for Lydia had wondered as well. The entire episode had turned into a debacle. If only Mr. Arlington had not sent the supplies to Cairo. But there was no time to worry about it now. If the Blaines wanted to set sail on the twentieth, she had no time to waste in Port Said.

She scooped up Thutmose III and called downstairs for Zalika to send the boy to carry her trunks to the waiting *calishe*. At the last hour Zalika had surprisingly requested she come with Allison to Luxor. Since Allison could use a friend who spoke Arabic, she was only too pleased to have the older woman with her, and she wondered what had prompted Zalika to go with her when the woman's sister was in Port Said. On closer inquiry, the smiling older woman admitted that she had been paid handsomely to do so by the "nice Major Holden." So, after closing up the family house for an expected three-month absence, Allison, Thutmose, and Zalika boarded the dirty train for the slow and tortuous journey into Cairo. The trip was supposed to take two hours, but because of the crowded passenger list and inevitable delays, it arrived three hours and twenty minutes late.

A day after their arrival in Cairo, Allison and Zalika were mounted on rented donkeys, astride a type of saddle called *à l' Arabe*. Soon they were out of the Western section of Cairo and being led through the narrow, crowded streets of Old Cairo by a young Arab boy.

They traveled in the midst of dim-alleyed streets thronging with men wearing *galabiyas,* and Moslem women swathed in black gowns and veils. Allison and Zalika merged into the noise and confusion of bawling merchants in the Khan el-Khalili, a fourteenth-century bazaar in the heart of the district.

Old Cairo bustled with rich merchants, poor peasants, and beggars; with camels, goats, and donkeys; with bazaars offering fancy silk and cheap cotton; and with open-air coffee houses and street vendors selling water from a bronze communal cup. Far beyond Cairo the vastness of the golden desert stretched toward an endless horizon.

Allison heard the high, twanging voice of the muezzin echoing with what she believed to be a forlorn cry to Mohammed's god, Allah. In her mind the cry was little different than the priests of Baal contesting Elijah's Yahweh. The muezzin's echoing cry had much the same effect. The myriad Moslems following the self-proclaimed prophet Mohammed went down on their foreheads—which were flattened from years of dedicated religious contact with the floors of ancient mosques. No one could accuse a Moslem of not being dedicated, more dedicated to prayer than many Christians, but was it enough? Allison thought of what the apostle Paul had said of the Jews, "They have a zeal for God, but not according to knowledge."

Man's religion, ever since Cain and Abel's time, has been unacceptable to God, mused Allison. Sinful men could never be cleansed by bringing him their own good works. We must come to God in the one way that Abel's offering foreshadowed and John the Baptist introduced, through the Lamb of God that taketh away the sin of the world. God himself has provided the way for cleansing. All other ways, however sincere, are like the work of thieves and robbers trying to enter the sheepfold over the walls instead of by the door. "Verily, verily, I say unto you, I am the door of the sheep," said Jesus.

It was midday by the time they reached the small shop, dim and crowded with bronze pots and pans, bolts of cloth, and Turkish rugs. Allison entered with Zalika at one elbow and the Arab donkey-boy at the other. She was at once overwhelmed by vases, bowls, lamps, and dinnerware in every size, shape, and color, from pomegranate purple to Nile blue, all painted with birds.

Allison was surprised by General Blaine, who emerged from a

dusty, heavily embroidered curtain, hailing her, while holding a small vase in his big hand. "Ho, my dear Allison! I was afraid you had gotten lost. Wouldn't blame you if you had. A perfectly wretched place to meander." He held up the vase in gold leaf for her critical eye. "What do you think? Will Sarah go for it or not? It's our anniversary, twenty-five years tomorrow."

"It's perfectly lovely, Rex. Knowing Sarah, she'll be more delighted that you remembered than with anything you buy her."

"Hmm, then maybe I should save my money and visit the tinsel shop across the street."

Allison laughed. "Don't you dare."

"Who's this?" he said, looking at Zalika. ·

"Mother's maid. She's coming with me to Lydia's. You don't mind one more on the boat, do you?"

"Mind? My dear, I'm delighted. You forget—sweet Sarah is terrible when it comes to cooking. She's not only all thumbs, but also when she does decide to favor me with a baked trifle, it's so hideous I wonder if she hasn't got arsenic on her mind instead."

Allison smiled. "If she heard you say that—"

"Ah-ha, but she didn't, and you, my demure little godchild, aren't telling on Uncle Rex. We could use a good cook. What's this?" His bushy brows shot up. "Good grief! We're being invaded! One would think this out-of-the-way opium den had become the good British Shepheard's Hotel in the Ezbekiah Gardens. Hullo, Bret, Helga, Cynthia. As they say, fancy meeting you here. Come to buy a vase, too? Or looking for a spot of tea?"

Allison turned, surprised, to see Baroness Helga Kruger enter, accompanied by Major Bret Holden and Cynthia Walsh. Bret, who casually included Allison in his greeting, did not look the least uncomfortable in the setting, nor troubled by the cramped room or stifling, stale heat. His rugged uniform was spotless, and he looked as if he had slept soundly—or was it the company he kept that refreshed him? Baroness Helga, dressed in stunning black, fanned her elegant powdered face, her brows and lashes painted and sultry. She looked around as though she owned the shop, didn't even notice Allison, and made straight for a beaded divider into the next room, calling out something in German as she did so. Immediately the shopkeeper—or was he the owner?—emerged in a flurry of robes, bowing as if she were the archduchess. "Ah, Baroness! Baroness!"

Rex leaned toward Allison and said in a goading voice, "Always did say the dame was overly warm and friendly. It's the German way, you know."

Cynthia smiled at Allison with sweet confidence while she rested her hand on Bret's arm. She asked the shopkeeper to see a certain Moslem glass piece in the window.

Allison remembered that the Baroness had also sought Bret out on the lawn during the charity ball. Turning her back as if interested in a bolt of red silk, Allison calculated the age difference between the Baroness and Bret. Perhaps it wasn't as great as she had first thought. The Baroness could also be said to be startlingly attractive as well as very rich. Maybe Cynthia had more to worry her than a young, naive Christian nurse she wished to snub.

General Blaine had left Allison to discuss the vase with a white-robed Egyptian proprietor, and as Bret had disappeared behind the beaded curtain to where the Baroness had gone a minute earlier, Allison found herself temporarily alone.

A little perturbed, over finding Bret in the company of two women and eager to sign for Aunt Lydia's crates and leave, she saw another archway that went down a step into an even larger store-room. There a handful of workers were busy unloading boxes and crates. She went in search of a proprietor.

It seemed everyone had disappeared, even Zalika. The storeroom, dim and stifling, was empty. "Hello? Anyone in here?"

She walked ahead. The wood shutters were barred so no fresh air or light could enter, except what came through some high, narrow windows. Suddenly, she was uneasy, as though unfriendly eyes watched her from the shadows of stacked crates.

Allison stopped. She could hear muffled voices coming from the main rooms of the shop, then she heard a step behind her. She whirled, tense, but it was Bret. He glanced back over his shoulder and, evidently seeing the others occupied, he walked swiftly toward her, taking hold of her arm. "What are you doing here alone?" he asked in an exasperated whisper.

"I came for Aunt's supplies, if you must know." And she added, because she was a trifle irritated when thinking of the two attractive females accompanying him, "I don't see that it necessarily concerns you. I'm quite able to take care of myself."

"I'll remind you of that the next time Thutmose sneaks about the house creaking the floorboards."

"It wasn't the kitten I heard that night, and you know it."

"My point exactly. I'd feel a lot happier about it if you didn't wander about Cairo behind darkened crates and dusty curtains. I suppose Lady Wescott and Beth have sailed, and that's why you're free?"

"I don't see what puts you in such a concerned mood this afternoon. After all, Major," she said meaningfully, "isn't escorting *two* women about Cairo enough for one day?"

His eyes narrowed with a hard flicker of impatience, and he glanced back toward the archway. "I knew you were coming here. Is your aunt a bit batty sending medicine to a place like this?"

"Aunt Lydia is as sharp as a thorn, and she doesn't make mistakes."

"Then suppose you explain this."

"I can't—I mean, I don't have the answer myself."

"Do you know what this place is?"

"I have an idea," she said, her mood changing to unease and meekness. "But I had to come to sign for the medicine. General Blaine tried to handle it for me, but the proprietor wouldn't permit it. What about you? If you knew what this place was, why are you escorting the baroness? She behaves as if she owns it."

"She does," he said bluntly.

"What!"

"Hush," said Bret. "I'll explain later—" He stopped abruptly. Casually turning to face the archway, he placed his hand firmly on Allison's arm and led her forward toward the main storeroom. "As I was saying, Miss Wescott, the baroness and Miss Walsh would like a Nile voyage to Luxor to see the Valley of the Kings. So if you're certain your aunt won't mind, we'll be coming down in a week or so."

"There you are, Allison," said General Blaine, standing in the archway. "Don't wander off, my dear. Hullo, Bret. Coming to Luxor are you?"

"What's a trip from England without seeing the pyramids? This is Miss Walsh's first visit to Egypt."

Allison stood, trying to appear at ease, as though Bret had actually been discussing a trip to Luxor with her.

"The crates are loaded. All you need do is sign," said Rex. "The sooner we escape this den of ill odors and suffocation the sooner we can lunch at Ezbekiah Gardens before we set sail. Sarah's waiting there now."

"Yes, I'm coming, Rex."

As she went up the steps to enter the shop, Bret held her back a moment. "Stay close to Sarah, will you? When you get to Luxor, don't leave the boat until I arrive."

"Then you're actually coming?"

"Yes, but not with the women. I'll have some excuse when I arrive."

"Do you expect to volunteer to help inoculate the children?" she asked with a smile.

"Maybe. Just be careful. I need to have a good look through those medical crates before you leave."

"Here? Now? But why?"

"Think of something to convince the proprietor to open them—anything, even if you accuse someone of thievery."

She looked at him, confused. But his gravity convinced her.

"Tell him anything—a crate is missing."

"But why? What are you looking for?"

He glanced toward the main shop to make certain no one was listening. "A certain book."

She was startled. Her eyes searched his. "You mean Woo—"

But Bret's hand went swiftly to her mouth. "There's too much sudden interest in Lydia's supplies." As Allison stared at him, amazed he could even think that Woolly's book could be here, he raised his voice in casual conversation, "—and the Frenchman's house is there too, I think. What was his name? Napoleon's man who found the Rosetta stone and unlocked the mystery of the Egyptian hieroglyphics?"

"Jean-Francois Champollion," said General Blaine. "But it's at the British Museum now. We wisely wouldn't let Napoleon leave Egypt until he surrendered it. Allison, what do you think? I've exchanged the vase for this Egyptian doll. Do you think Sarah will like it?"

"Oh, it's positively darling. You've more expertise in antique pieces than I, though."

"Tell that to Sarah." He winked. "She insults me by insisting I wouldn't know the difference between a rare archaeological piece and something from London's East End."

"Oh, dear," said Allison, feigning dismay.

"Something wrong?" asked Bret.

Allison frowned as she went to the open doorway facing the street and stared out at the crates being loaded onto the wagon driven by two donkeys. "I'm sure there's one crate missing. Aunt Lydia insisted there would be six. There are only five."

"Looks like enough medicine to inoculate pharaoh's army. Or did they all drown in the Red Sea?" said General Blaine.

The proprietor walked up, agitated. "Something wrong, Miss Wescott?"

"A crate is missing," Allison told him, feeling guilty over the disturbance.

"Impossible!" he cried, and fussed and fumed and insisted otherwise. Allison, embarrassed, nevertheless insisted until Baroness Kruger came from the other room and spoke to him in German.

"He says they are all here," said Helga.

"Perhaps we had better check the contents to make certain," suggested Bret.

"Yes, could we?" asked Allison. "Perhaps six crates weren't needed."

"Where's your list?" asked Bret.

Allison dug into her bag and handed it to him. Bret studied the list of contents.

"While you check the crates, I'm going across the street for a cup of coffee and a water pipe," said General Blaine. "Anyone care to join me?"

"I will," said Helga. "But not for the pipe. How about you, Cynthia? Allison?"

"Yes, go ahead," said Bret. "I have your list. It won't take us long."

The four of them walked across the crowded street. Where an Arab brought chairs outside and arranged them around the table.

Turkish coffee was served with small dark chocolates that were rather strong and bitter. As they discussed archaeology and Luxor, Allison glanced across the crowded street to where the proprietor was ordering his workers to load Aunt Lydia's supplies onto a wagon. She saw Bret come out to check the load, then cross the street toward their table, dodging camels.

"All in order," he said as he came up and handed Allison the slip. Their eyes met. "Your aunt must have gotten her figures mixed up."

"Typical of the dear old girl," said Rex. "She ought to retire to the countryside of London. Maybe she will if Eleanor convinces Marshall." He stood, groaning. "Hope it's cooler down the river. My back is worse in this heat. Glad I don't need to load and unload those crates. Coming, Allison?"

"Yes, quite ready. Thank you for the coffee, Baroness. Thank you, Major. Good-bye, Miss Walsh. See you all at Luxor."

As Allison's gaze swerved to Bret, she could see by his level, bored gaze he hadn't found what he was looking for. He reached over and lifted Cynthia's untouched coffee cup and finished it. Allison felt a dart of irritation.

Later that afternoon when she boarded the *falukka* with Zalika and the Blaines, Allison watched the setting sun like a pool of fiery orange and crimson bleeding into the cloudless blue sky above the White Nile. The ancient river had not changed much in thousands of years, she thought as the *falukka* made its winding trek south into what was called Upper Egypt, or *Saeed* by the Egyptians. The banks of the great river where pharaoh's daughter had found baby Moses were still lined with papyrus and tall reeds. Beyond the banks of the river, in the green, fertile fields, the *fellahin* grew their crops of cotton, beans, corn, and wheat. Allison watched as the peasants followed hand plows pulled by brown oxen. Water buffalo trudged round and round, turning the wheels that carried the Nile's water to the fields. Women walked to the river with huge clay water jars balanced on their heads while stately white egrets swooped over the still waters to stand gracefully poised amid the water reeds.

The Nile had been worshiped as a life-giver by the ancient Egyptians, and as Allison sat in the boat beneath the shade of a reed shelter, the book of Exodus came naturally to mind. She considered how God smote the river, turning it into blood, showing pharaoh that "by this you shall know that I am the Lord," the only life-giver. She imagined the millions of frogs that had come up out of the Nile to cover the land of Egypt and to enter the pharaoh's palace. When they had died, they were stacked in heaps upon the banks. The Egyptians, who had worshipped the frog-headed goddess Heka, must have become sick of a god who had died and made the land foul.

Each day the *falukka* was anchored on the bank by a village, and Allison and Sarah, using parasols to protect themselves from the blazing sun, walked to the shops filled with butter, eggs, dates, fruits, and vegetables. The houses were mud structures with a charm all their own, surrounded by clusters of tall date palms and offering shadows of purple shade to the pigeon roosts. Almost always, so it seemed to Allison, a Moslem tomb of some great man, covered with a dome, was part of the village.

The miles along the Nile drifted by slowly. It took nearly a week before Allison and the Blaines arrived at Luxor. The deep blue Nile reflected the same coral-pink hue of the Theban hills beyond it, and the ominous shade of the mammoth Karnak Temple. The massive statues, pillars, and walls of all the temples, carved with hieroglyphic tales, scenes of war, and ancient pageantry, looked down on their boat with the same mute silence as the ancient statues of the pharaohs.

The sight of the *Mercy*, painted white, brought a smile of sheer pleasure to Allison. Aunt Lydia, a woman who was anything but soft, gray, and delicate, was standing on its deck. She was tall, with a waist as wide as her shoulders, and she wore a faded brown pair of canvas trousers, boots, a knee-length white tunic of Egyptian style, and a wide reed hat. Her wrinkled, tanned face creased into a smile when she saw Allison. Her long gray hair hung in a braid wound in a loop at the back of her neck, and she leaned on a cane because of a fall she had taken years earlier when exploring the pyramids. Her twisted knee had never recovered fully, but what alarmed Allison was a white bandage on the side of her aunt's head, near her temple.

"Bless God, you've come, Allison. What? Is that you, Sarah, General Rex? Glory be! Hassan! Hassan!" she shouted to her silent cook and companion. "Put an English kettle on. We've guests."

In the shadow of the environs of the forbidding Karnak Temple, mysterious with the ancient past of the great pharaohs, including Rameses II and Queen Nefertiti, Allison basked in the company of the one woman she loved more dearly than any other, Aunt Lydia Bristow, missionary nurse for forty years. She referred to God as "my hope, my true Shepherd, he who has never failed me all these hard and difficult years, but who supported me in both heat and cold, in the lonely night on my bunk, and amid suspicious villagers, crocodiles, and water vipers."

Allison embraced her aunt. "You've taken another fall. Auntie, how many times have I begged you to be more careful when getting up at night? Always light the lantern first. You promised me you would."

"And I did, Allison, dear. Can I help it if a burglar was aboard?"

Allison stared at her, terror freezing her bones. No...they wouldn't dare hurt her aunt...

"I heard a noise in your cubbyhole and went to look, thinking I'd left the window open and one of the cats had gotten in. It had been a dreadfully hot day, and I'd forgotten to close it. I lit the lamp and found your things in shambles, your books spread all over the bed. I realized it couldn't be one of the cats, but I didn't have a chance to see who it was because just then I was struck on the head."

"How positively beastly," cried Sarah indignantly, when Allison didn't move.

"You notified the British consul of course?" asked General Blaine. "Arlington, isn't it?"

"Hassan took care of things for me. I confess, at my age, the blow put me quite out of commission for several days. I nursed myself well enough."

"Are you sure you can trust this Hassan?" asked Rex crossly, his tone doubting.

"Hassan? Explicitly! We're of the consensus it was some local, thinking I'd gone with Hassan into Luxor to shop and spend the night. The ship is vulnerable. It's never mattered before, but I may need to hire a guard."

"What were they after, medicine?" he asked.

"They couldn't have been because they didn't touch it. Money or items to sell to the antique dealers is probably more like it. They were disappointed, though."

"Why do you say that?" asked Allison, finding her voice for the first time.

"Because they didn't take a thing."

No one seemed to notice that Allison had become silent. Nothing was taken, and yet her room had been searched, especially her books. Why the books? She was sure the intruder had not been a local thief, but someone hoping to find the book Leah had not taken with her to meet Neal.

But what would make them think the book might be on the *Mercy*? Leah had never been on the ship, nor had Allison been aboard since before the archaeology club met at Aleppo.

She was deeply troubled. It was one thing to place her own life in danger but quite another to involve someone like Aunt Lydia. *The severe blow might have killed a woman of her age,* she thought angrily. She shivered. If she had any doubt about the kind of individuals they were up against, she had her answer now, and it was frightening indeed. It was one thing for the enemy to kill the British agent acting as Major Reuter and though a woman, Leah had been working for the British cause and knew the risks involved. Aunt Lydia was another matter. The enemy, determined to locate the information that Leah had failed to provide for them, had no qualms about eliminating Allison's aunt if she got in the way.

Which meant Bret was right. Allison's own life was in danger.

Evidently it was assumed she either knew where the book was hidden or could unwittingly lead them to its discovery. *Something I must not do,* she determined. *No matter the cost to myself.*

They hadn't found what they wanted in her things, but could she be certain they wouldn't be back? Or would her arrival bring more danger to Aunt Lydia?

Perhaps she shouldn't have come after all. She could return at once to Cairo, but how could she explain her strange action to her aunt and the Blaines?

She thought of Bret, more anxious than ever for his arrival, yet he wouldn't be in Luxor for at least a week. She could go to the consul and wire Bret at Cairo intelligence, telling him about the suspicious attack on her aunt and the search of her own cabin. Bret was wise enough to guess at once what it was about, and the risk of unveiling his identity to the enemy was too great. It was common knowledge that little remained private over the wires in this part of the territory, with Europe on the brink of war and Arabia a hotbed of spies and intrigue. Her father had commented that wires sent from India to Egypt might as well be printed in the daily newspaper since the wires were open to scrutiny by many eyes. Received messages were passed from hand to hand, easily read by anyone of unfriendly loyalties.

No, thought Allison, *I can do nothing now.* Informing Bret about what had happened could alert the other side that he was the agent who had been sent to Aleppo in response to Neal's Mayday.

The enemy would be pleased to know who had been Reuter and Neal's superior. To kill someone higher up would be deemed a far greater accomplishment than removing Leah. Allison must wait.

Later that warm evening they dined on the deck of the *Mercy.* General Blaine was not disappointed by the supper beneath the stars with the background of the mammoth stone kings. Aunt Lydia's serving man, Hassan, prepared a feast fit for Rameses: roasted leg of lamb stuffed with green pistachio nuts and dates; sweetmeats sticky with honey; fresh warm bread; bowls of black olives; chunks of feta cheese; cucumbers; slices of peeled melons; and dates with chopped almonds. It was followed by coffee, tea, and goat's milk, which General Blaine shuddered to drink warm. He later emerged from the *falukka* with a bottle of wine. Everyone else refused to partake, but he settled back in his wicker deck chair and groaned with satisfaction. "My back feels better already, Lydia. I can see Sarah and I are going to be delightfully happy here until Major Holden arrives with that beastly German wench, Helga."

"Rex!" gasped Sarah, embarrassed. "And in front of Lydia."

"Nonsense," he said. "Dear Lydia has already met the baroness and quite knows how dreadful the woman is. Hand me another sweet cake, Allison. That's a good girl. Any ghosts at night, Lydia dear? From Rameses or Thutmose IV, or V?"

"Don't be obtuse, Rex, my boy," said Lydia. "The only ghosts prowling Karnak Temple are a few wild beasts and birds. They do make an awful howling sometimes. Ask Allison. It's enough to give even me a fright."

"I was hoping for a good night's sleep," said Sarah. "Let's not talk of it. Where do you plan to sleep, Allison?"

"Aboard the *Mercy*. I'm home at last. I've my little cubbyhole again, don't I, Aunt Lydia, darling?"

"Assuredly. And I have it all ready for you. I'll put Zalika aboard, too."

"And be sure to confiscate that yowling kitten," said General Blaine to Allison. "He jumped on my face last night, and I awoke fearing the Egyptian curse after all."

"Yes, of course I will. I'll get him now. And my bags. When do you want to load the medicine crates, Lydia?"

"In the morning, dear. We're all tired now. And Hassan always goes into Luxor village at night and comes early in the morning on his own smaller boat. We'll need his help. He cooks on his boat and has it all done when he arrives. Hear that, Rex?" she teased. "We'll have breakfast sent to your boat by seven o'clock." She went to the rail and called after Allison, "We began inoculations in the village on Sunday. Thank God you've come in time. So far no outbreak this far south, but cases are reported farther toward Aswan."

The next morning the Egyptian sun cast a path of fire across the Nile. Allison stretched, Thutmose III, curled up near her pillow, reached out a paw and touched her face. Rising and dressing, she looked out her window at the date palms growing along the bank and at the feeding egrets. Her secret concerns cast shadows on the satisfaction of being back on the *Mercy*.

Just then Aunt Lydia ducked in with a breakfast tray, setting it on the small bureau of drawers. "Good morning. Sleep well?"

"As sound as a winter bear. Breakfast looks wonderful, but you mustn't wait on me."

"Your first morning home. Oh, did you find your package?"

Tense, Allison looked at her.

"I must be forgetting things," said Lydia with self-scorn. "That rap on the head did more damage than I thought."

"Package?" repeated Allison quietly.

"I thought I mentioned it to you in my letter."

Allison stood still, remembering, *"...you've a package waiting. I would have sent it on, but Arlington, who delivered it personally, told me a message came with it asking him to leave it with me on the* Mercy."

Allison stood perfectly still, her heart thumping.

Lydia went to the bureau and opened the drawer. "It should be here...Mr. Arlington is the cause of the blunder over the medicine crates. Whatever got into him, I wonder, sending them to Old Cairo like that? It doesn't make a bit of sense, and I wanted to tell him so. Unfortunately, he had already left for a month at Suez, something about the canal's vulnerability. Of course, if the war comes, the Suez Canal will be of strategic importance. I must say, I didn't mind seeing the man depart. But it does leave us with no British consul. Only a Turkish fellow, rather rude, I thought. He's been trying to force the *Mercy* out of this region for weeks now; since before Mr. Arlington left. I rather think the Turkish consul was a bit more than Arlington could handle, and that's the reason he left. Odd. I was sure I'd put the package here."

Allison rushed to her side. "When did you see it last?"

"Weeks ago. After I'd sent you the letter to Port Said. The burglar, you don't suppose he took it? What was it, do you know?"

Allison's heart grew deathly still.

"There was no return address on it," said Lydia. "And Arlington didn't say who had sent the message to him asking that it remain on the boat until you arrived." She looked at Allison, and seeing her distraught expression, frowned apologetically. "I hope it wasn't valuable."

Her eyes brightened. "Oh, I didn't put it in the bureau. I remember now. I was going to, but I was interrupted by Hassan. He arrived below the window in a boat. His little boy had fallen and badly cut himself. I remember putting the package in my medicine trunk and—"

Allison sped through the small living room, dining room, and into the pantry that Lydia had turned into a dispensary. Quickly Allison threw up the reed blinds. The morning sunshine reflecting off the Nile spilled into the room. She turned to the trunk containing Lydia's supplies. Sarah and Rex Blaines' voices on the *falukka* moored close beside the *Mercy* filtered in through the open window. Sarah's voice sounded alarmed. "Are you sure? It will be such a disappointment to Allison."

Allison wasn't paying attention but called to Aunt Lydia to bring the key to the trunk. Lydia, carrying the key on a chain at her waist, unlocked the trunk. Allison's anxious gaze skimmed the bandages, bottles, and boxes until her aunt lifted a small wrapped package and handed it to her victoriously.

"There. We foiled the burglar after all. Looks to be the size of a piece of jewelry. Perhaps it's from Wade Findlay." Her eyes twinkled. "A ring perhaps?"

Allison's hopes crashed. She didn't hear the footsteps in the dining room and stood holding the package, staring at it.

Sarah's voice called, "Allison? Lydia?"

Allison and Lydia walked into the dining room where Sarah stood by the table, a piece of paper in her hand. "It seems the burglar wasn't trouble enough. It's for you, Allison. You've received a wire from Cairo—unpleasant news."

"What is it?" asked Allison uneasily.

Sarah handed her the paper. "Major Bret Holden has met with a terrible accident in Cairo."

18

BRET INJURED AND IN THE MILITARY HOSPITAL? The news caused the breath to go out of Allison, and she lowered herself into a chair at the table. *No, not Bret. Please, Lord, not Bret.* Her hand shook as she stared at the wire from Cairo.

"Who is Bret Holden?" asked Lydia, noting Allison's concern and frowning her own response.

Allison couldn't answer but sat clutching the wire.

"A British major," said Sarah quietly. "He had become rather friendly with Allison, though Lady Walsh seemed to take it for granted that her niece, Cynthia, would marry him."

"What happened?" asked Lydia, frowning and touching her bruised head, as though her accident was soomehow linked with the Major's.

Allison read the wire first to herself then aloud for Lydia: "'Allison, I won't make it to Luxor after all. I've met with a small accident. Nothing serious, but it will lay me up for a few weeks. Maj. B. Holden, Cairo Office.'"

Sarah sighed. "Too bad, indeed. The major is an interesting man. I don't blame you if you're attracted to him, Allison. But play it safe. You know about Cynthia, and a more determined young woman I've yet to meet. Well," she said as her thoughts moved on, "there goes our holiday expedition out to Karnak Temple and the Valley of the Kings. Looks like we'll need to be satisfied with Professor Jemal and the baroness for company. I doubt now if Cynthia and Lady Walsh come to Luxor. They'll want to be near Bret in the hospital. There's nothing like sweet sympathy to woo a hurting man, you know."

"What's that?" asked General Blaine from behind them in the living room doorway. He was dressed in expedition canvas and looking pleased with himself. "Are you interested in giving me a back massage, Sarah?" He groaned with exaggeration.

"Good morning, Rex," said Lydia jovially. "Have you had enough breakfast? There's more in the kitchen, and I'll put on another pot of tea."

Allison was still holding the wire and sitting thoughtfully at the table. "Did you say Professor Jemal was coming up?" she asked, keeping her voice non-commital, even while her heart sank at the prospect.... And now, Bret wouldn't be here to protect her.

"Rex, isn't that what you said?" asked Sarah.

"He's already here," said General Blaine dourly. "The owl-eyed mummy-digger must have followed us within a day after we left. Says he's come to meet with some archaeological expedition near Karnak. If it wasn't for his murky mood, I'd think he was moon-smitten over Allison. But the man's so morbid I can't see him falling even for her."

Allison was unable to smile. Jemal was here, and Bret was injured and in the hospital. He must be seriously wounded, for she couldn't see Major Holden succumbing to a hospital bed for anything but a serious injury.

What had happened? Why hadn't he explained in the wire? Perhaps he couldn't explain.

"Oh, what's this?" asked Sarah, lifting the small package from the table. "Feels awfully light. A present, Allison? From whom?"

Allison froze, not wishing to snatch it away. Aunt Lydia's teasing voice smoothed over the moment. "An engagement ring from Wade Findlay. You know about the young man she's going to marry, don't you, Sarah?"

"An engagement ring? How tremendously exciting. But rather odd. Why didn't he bring it himself?"

"He won't be coming out until after his graduation from the Bible Training College," said Allison, her voice calm.

"Listen to her, would you?" teased Rex. "One would think she's discussing fish and chips. The man sends a ring after emptying his bank account, and Allison refuses to open the package."

Allison managed a laugh and took it from Sarah. "With all of you looking on? I feel like a member of a circus. I'll do so at my leisure. Major Holden...I wonder how he met with an accident?"

"Probably running away from Cynthia," said General Blaine wickedly. "Serves him right. Now he'll be at her mercy in the hospital. Oh, hullo, speak of the dead—here comes our mummy-digger now."

Allison stood quickly, snatching up the wire and putting the package in her skirt pocket. "If you don't mind, I'll use this moment to make my exit. I'm not up to your 'mummy-digger' this morning."

"Do hurry, dear," said Sarah. "You're coming with us to tour Luxor Temple today, aren't you? We'll be gone all day."

"Um—I don't think so, Sarah," she called over her shoulder, hastening to escape. "I've just gotten home, and there's so much to do today with settling in. That odious burglar tore my room apart. I want to organize my things, then help Lydia unload those medical crates and put them away in the dispensary."

Sarah's brows tucked together. "That's right, I'd forgotten you had come here to work and not play. Then we'll go with Jemal."

"No need to abandon Allison," said Rex. "We'll stay and help;

then we'll all go together. How does that sound, Allison?"

"A grand idea," said Aunt Lydia. "Those crates are heavy."

"Then it's settled," said Rex amiably. "Now, where's that tea, Lydia? Here comes Jemal. Well, if we can't avoid the man let's put him to work."

Later that day, as they had planned, the group visited Karnak Temple. As they disembarked, Sarah noted, "The Nile is as smooth and unwrinkled as gray-blue glass."

"Odd description," said Rex. "Doesn't look like glass at all."

"You're too logical, Rex. Be a dear, will you, and get the picnic basket. I left it on the boat."

Allison had wandered away into the temple ruins, awed as always at the sight of things ancient, mysterious, and rich with history. The Karnak Temple complex had been built on a mammoth scale with giant stone idol-gods, and it sprawled across much of northern Thebes. Her eyes swept the massive pylons and pillars of the Temple of Amun. At the Great Hypostyle Hall, she studied the battle reliefs carved on the outside of the northern door. Here, Seti had inscribed the chronicles of his great battles conquering Palestine to the banks of the Orintes. The doorways were flanked with depictions of the ritualistic massacre before the idol Amun; Seti defeating the Hittite king and conquering Yenoam and Bethshael; and Seti returning with the Hittites and offering them to Amun as slaves to his temple.

Outside the wall, Rameses II also had battled the Hittites and launched his chariot against them, chasing them to a place mentioned in the Bible: Kadesh Barnea.

The Hittites, thought Allison. *Yet more references to the code word the British agent had left for Leah.* Allison's hand touched the small package in her pocket, and she glanced about the ruins uneasily. She might open it now, but did she dare? Bret would be furious with her. She could see him now, confronting her over why she was wandering about alone, when in her pocket, she might have the secret to where Leah had hidden the book.

The sun was low in the sky and threw long, gold-violet shadows across the mammoth pillars and walls. The wind, coming up with sundown, danced and whined its way through stone arches and along the deserted palace walk. The wind's groans covered the sound of footsteps but not completely. Allison whirled, startled, a cry dying in her throat as she saw a formidable figure slip behind a pillar.

She ran in his direction, determined to see if it was Jemal, but when she reached the pillar, he had vanished. She walked forward through the stone archway with its huge statues of the pharaohs mutely staring. The wind whistled and whipped about her. She saw him again; he had slipped behind Rameses. She hesitated.

Suddenly a stone crashed some feet ahead of her, and she halted, taking the warning seriously. Maybe it wasn't Jemal. She backed away, turned, and fled.

That night, back on board the Mercy, Allison closed herself in her cabin. Until now, she had never had a reason to bolt the door, but she wished she had a bolt now to lock out any intruders. All was quiet as Rex's hearty voice faded away on the makeshift gangway, calling to Jemal. The ship rocked gently and creaked in the silence.

Allison tore open the package. She hadn't expected it to be from Wade, but when a sealed and folded envelope fell out onto the bed, she stared expectantly. The envelope was addressed to Nurse Allison Wescott. The handwriting was Leah's.

Allison held the envelope, her hand turning damp with excitement. She glanced toward her door, then the small open window behind her shoulder facing the eerie towering pillars of Karnak Temple. As she held the envelope, she felt as if a hot breath from the

Arabian desert and the mysterious shadows of the Aleppo archaeological huts crept closer to the small ship. Allison could almost see cousin Leah standing there looking as she had the night she left to meet the murderer masquerading as Neal.

The glue under the seal tore as her cold fingers opened the envelope. This was what the burglar must have been searching for in this very cabin when Aunt Lydia surprised him—or was it "her"? Leah had outsmarted them a second time; she hadn't sent the book, but a tiny package, a mere message.

Allison removed the sheet of paper and eagerly read the note.

Allison,

By the time you receive this, I'll either be with you, and this message won't be necessary, or I will have been stopped here in Aleppo. Destroy this letter once you've read it. Tell no one the information I now give you. If Neal is there, go to him, or the agent who responded to Neal's Mayday, if you've learned who he is. Otherwise, trust no one. I'm afraid the book's safety is in your hands. I left it under the porch of Major Reuter's hut. It's the same place I hid the other night undetected. The spot saved me then, and I'm counting on it as a safe place to store the book now. Go there as soon as possible and look for it if anything has happened to me. Trust no one but God. May he be with you.

The message was unsigned. Allison read it several times. Then she took it to the small basin, struck a match with a surprisingly steady hand, and held the flame to the paper, watching it shrivel and darken into powdery ash. She took the pitcher of water and rinsed the ashes down the basin drain where they would be carried away on the Nile. She had just ended any possibility of the enemy learning where Woolly's book was hidden, but she trembled suddenly, as she realized the knowledge now rested with her alone. She could not even wire Bret to tell him. Nor would he arrive for weeks, if at all.

If something happened to her, if she met with some unexplained "accident" while in Luxor before Bret arrived, the enemy would have succeeded. Leah had died to protect that information. So had the British agent. And cousin Neal remained in a Jerusalem prison unable to fulfill his mission. Perhaps even now he and David were being tortured to learn what they knew. How could she fail them? How could she let Bret down?

The ship creaked, and Allison became aware of the silence surrounding her. Bret had not met with an accident; she was quite certain of that. An attempt must have been made on his life after someone found out who he was. Or had it been a successful ploy to keep him from coming to Luxor?

A shadow appeared in the window, and she whirled, startled. But it was only Thutmose, who had leaped to the sill.

Without Bret, she was alone, vulnerable, and staring danger in the face. Professor Jemal was here. And the baroness would arrive soon. Mr. Arlington of the British consul was away. Who was the Turkish official that Aunt Lydia had said was so unfriendly? Could he be involved? Who was the man she had seen at the Karnak ruins?

Allison argued with her own fears until she knew she couldn't simply hide away and pretend it all hadn't happened. If she remained on the *Mercy,* she would endanger Aunt Lydia, perhaps Sarah and General Blaine, too. If she sent a wire to Bret, would it even get through to him?

If she did nothing and hid her head in the sand, the enemy would eventually come to her. She must take the initiative before they expected her to act, and perhaps she would catch them off guard. She must go at once back to Aleppo, to the huts, to Major

Reuter's porch and find the book Leah had so carefully hidden. If she didn't, her own "accident" would be carefully arranged, and then it would be too late.

But how could she leave so soon without drawing everyone's attention? She wouldn't make the mistake of hiring a *falukka*. The railway could take her from Luxor to the Red Sea. She would cross by steamer, then reboard the Hejaz Railway in the vicinity of Medina. The Hejaz would take her to Damascus and Aleppo.

She must be on that train tonight. And she must not let anyone except Aunt Lydia know she was leaving.

The book waited under the porch. She could salvage the plans gone awry—perhaps thousands of lives depended on the book reaching the British government, keeping it out of the hands of German agents. If she didn't risk her life to get that book to Bret, who would?

She thought of Leah's simple grave in Aleppo with the Arabian winds blowing across it in a lonely, desolate sigh. It seemed the memory of a young woman with blond hair and a revolver beckoned her to come.

"Will you help me?" she had asked that night in the hut.

Allison had promised she would. "What are families for?"

And what is patriotism, if not for this? she thought. Some things were worth fighting for, even dying for, David had told her. So had Rose Lyman, a spy for the British, if war came. The face of young Benjamin also seemed to watch her from the shadows of her mind. Neal was held in Jerusalem, David faced the Turks who had ejected David Ben-Gurion from Palestine "forever." Major Reuter had thought the information important enough to die for, and Bret had risked his life on several occasions.

Now it's my turn, she thought.

She had just enough time to arrange for the rail. So here she was, back where she had first begun, heading toward the archaeology digs near Carchemish. Only this time she was alone. No, not alone. The Lord was with her. Perhaps she was called, like Esther, for such a time as this.

"I don't understand this," said Aunt Lydia when Allison explained she needed to take a trip. "But I know you well enough. Whatever is prompting you to do this must be very important. If you must go, you can trust Hassan to take you upriver to the nearest rail connection. Passage on a steamer can be bought easily to take you to the Gulf of Akaba. I assume from there you'll take the Hejaz Railway?"

"Yes. And Lydia, it's crucial you don't give my destination away to anyone except Major Bret Holden. And since it's not likely he'll arrive..." Her voice fell off.

Lydia frowned. "Does all this have anything to do with the burglary and that package?"

"I'd be betraying friends if I said more, and the less you know, the better. You mustn't worry about me."

"After what's happened to Leah, I'd be a fool if I didn't. But I see you're bent on your decision to leave. Very well, Allison, your secret is mine; you can depend on my utter silence. When will you leave?"

"As soon as possible. Before the others return from Luxor Temple."

"What of Zalika?"

Allison hesitated, for she hadn't made up her mind. She trusted the woman, who had proven her loyalty these past ten days, but she didn't dare take her. Was there another way to reach Bret other than sending a wire? If anyone could get back to Cairo undetected with a brief message to Bret, it would be Zalika.

"I'm sending her to Cairo," she said simply.

"Then I'll call Hassan to ready his boat. Let me know you're safe as soon as you can. Send me a wire."

Allison embraced her aunt tightly, almost as if she would never see Lydia again. "I will. When I can, I'll be back to serve on the *Mercy*."

19

SOMEONE WAS WATCHING ALLISON, someone unfriendly. The sensation crept up her spine with certainty during the stopover in Damascus while waiting for new passengers to board. But no one could have followed her. She had been too careful.

The Hejaz Railway ran south from Mecca and Medina into Arabia and northeast to Baghdad. Allison had first boarded four days ago at Tell Shahm. Now the train traveled through Hejaz, which consisted of mostly little-known Arab villages, under jurisdiction of the *sharif* of Syria. This particular *sharif* was a chief Moslem religious ruler from a family who claimed lineage from Mohammed. The Turkish sultan in Constantinople ruled over the Hejaz but treated the *sharif* with caution, afraid the masses of Moslems he held sway over might rise up in rebellion. Little did the sultan know that the *sharif* was already in secret meetings with the British, negotiating for independence should war break out.

The entire Hejaz was a sensitive area to travel in, and Allison was aware of her precarious situation as she avoided public scrutiny on the train to Aleppo. They had already passed through villages she knew nothing about, places with exotic and mysterious names: Ghadir el Haj, Faraifra, Sultani, Ammon, and Derra. Then the more familiar-sounding Old Damascus, where the apostle Paul had received his sight after actually talking with Jesus on the Damascus road. She was a little comforted when remembering that these real geographic localities were Bible lands long before the Moslem religion had taken hold of the Arabs and converted them by drawn sword, much as the Crusaders had tried to do. True faith, she knew, must be based upon truth, not coercion.

But, as the train rocked and swayed to the clattering of the iron wheels beneath a warm desert sky brilliant with stars, Allison's own assurance of safety seemed to loosen from its moorings. The train had pulled out of Damascus before noon and by late that night was whistling across the empty Hejaz toward Aleppo, Carchemish, and Baghdad. The rhythmic clacking of the wheels echoed through the lonely Arabian night.

Sleep had descended like a drugging daze upon the passengers in their compartments or seated in the lower-class sections, but Allison remained restless. For the second time since midnight, she sat up from the lower berth and flashed her torch toward the door that connected her small, dirty compartment with the next compartment, which was empty. Fixing the beam of light on the bolt, she could see it was securely in place.

The train rumbled along the track, and the wind moaned around her small window. Strange, she thought, how strongly she felt that someone unfriendly had boarded at Damascus, someone she must avoid, who was there to stop her. Or did that person expect her to lead him to where Leah had hidden the book? He would keep in the shadows undetected until she unearthed it, then silence her as they had her cousin. Perhaps her own body would be discovered in the blowing sands.

Stop it! You need no secret enemy; you're frightening yourself!

But her fears were not without foundation. Three people had been murdered since this had all begun, and Aunt Lydia had been struck.

Even Bret had warned her how dangerous her meddling was.

Bret. If only he were here, she thought with sudden fierce longing, remembering his strength and resolve. He had handled matters efficiently and firmly at the expedition house in Jerablus that night when they had all escaped. With a pang she visualized him injured in the Cairo military hospital. Someone must have tried to kill him. They must have known he was an agent.

Allison felt so strongly about being watched that she hadn't left her compartment since having lunch in Damascus. She had asked the grave-faced Turkish conductor to have her dinner sent to her compartment instead of joining the other passengers in the crowded dining hall on the train. The tray of cold food sat untouched on the table, the dishes rattling.

But I couldn't have been followed, she told herself again, firmly. To strengthen her resolve she went over the facts as she knew them. To begin with, no one had witnessed her departure from the *Mercy*. She had left before Professor Jemal had returned with Sarah and Rex from a second trip out to Luxor Temple, and no one knew she had received the note from Leah. They thought the package contained an engagement ring.

By now they knew she was gone, of course, and Helga would have arrived, perhaps with Cynthia and Lady Walsh. Allison, however, was a week ahead of anyone who might decide to follow. Unless someone had suspected she might leave and had followed closely behind undetected.

She shivered. Now she began to think that someone other than Mr. Arlington of the British consul had deliberately sent the medical crates to Cairo. Because, like Bret, someone thought the book might be concealed within. When it wasn't found there, that person had decided to search Aunt Lydia's boat, but her aunt had unwittingly placed the package in the medicine trunk.

Then, thought Allison, *if they did suspect a message would be sent to me while I was on the* Mercy, *someone had to be waiting for me. Who, besides Lydia, had known?*

Only Bret. Could it be...? No, she trusted Bret.

Who had seen her leave the *Mercy?* Aunt Lydia, Hassan, and Zalika. Her aunt had vowed her serving man was reliable, insisting Hassan was a secret Christian and utterly trustworthy. Allison must take her aunt's word for it. And Allison was just as confident about the loyalty of her mother's Egyptian serving woman, Zalika. While Hassan had brought Allison down the Nile to board the steamer at the Red Sea for Akaba, Zalika had been safely deposited on a Nile boat back to Cairo. Even Aunt Lydia didn't know precisely where Allison had gone.

How, then, could anyone have followed? Someone could have been watching, waiting, prepared to trail at a distance until Damascus. At Damascus the trail narrowed because she was on the last length of her journey to the huts. They could afford to be a little bolder but still keep to the shadows of the train. She must not lead them to the book.

She had already seen most of the passengers, and they were strangers. There wasn't a familiar face among the Turks, Arabs, a few Germans, and one or two British.

A strong wind buffeted the train's side, and she envisioned the wide expanse of hot, arid desert sweeping past outside her small, soiled window. Since leaving Damascus they had journeyed past Ras Baalbeck, ancient Hohms, and Kalaat el Hosn—the old French Crusader castle, Crac des Chevaliers. Next came Hama, and sometime tomorrow she would step off the train at Aleppo.

If she couldn't rent a car, she would hire an Arab to take her to the huts. Suddenly she remembered something—the Arab Bret had told her and David to meet in the alleyway behind the *suk*. He had been a friend and responded to the name of Bret Holden. Could she contact him again? Would he be anywhere nearby with his lift in that crowded little alleyway? She believed the chances were slim.

She thought of Hamid, Bret's assistant. If only she knew where to find him in Aleppo. By now he would have recovered from his bullet wound. Getting out to the huts would be left to her, but she would go only if convinced she wasn't being followed.

The compartment was close and stuffy, and she stood in her wrapper, walking about the tiny floor. Then she sat on the edge of the lower berth staring into the close darkness.

She thought she heard a faint sound coming from the compartment adjoining her own, but as far as she knew, no one had claimed it. Then something clicked inside that supposedly empty compartment, followed by a faint ribbon of light showing beneath the adjoining door. She held her breath. The train rumbled and groaned. The wind tore at the outside window. Her heart thudded in her ears. Maybe someone expected to silence her before she ever arrived in Aleppo.

She stood in the hot darkness as someone quietly tested the latch from the other side to see if it was bolted. Allison stood in cold fear, her fingers closing about the revolver in her robe pocket, but she knew that in the end it was only the Lord who shielded her with his protection. And yet—and yet—people who believed and trusted in God sometimes met with violent and unjust endings.

My life is in your hands, she prayed. *Nothing can come at me except you allow it for some purpose I do not understand. Please, Lord, help me, protect me! If I was rash to come like this, forgive me and defend me now.*

She waited, listening, but heard nothing except the train's movement. Minutes crept by, and then she heard someone pass by in the outer corridor—or had they passed? Were they now standing outside her door?

Allison waited, not daring to move. As time elapsed with no further disturbance, she tiptoed to the door and placed her ear against it but could hear nothing except the train's vibration on the track.

Whoever it was had left as quietly as he had come. Allison stumbled to her berth and sank to the edge, shaking. *Look at me! I'm a nervous wreck—and am I the girl who thinks she can go alone to the huts and prowl beneath that darkened porch of Major Reuter's hut to find the book? I'll go screaming with the first footstep I hear!*

Angry with herself, she stood again and paced. She stopped—the light flickered again from beneath the adjoining compartment door, and she heard the sound of metal scraping against metal. Someone was trying to file through her bolt.

Her hand went to her mouth. She stepped back. Then a light knock sounded on the door to the outer corridor. At the same moment, the filing stopped, and the light went out in the adjoining compartment. Whoever it was couldn't be in two places at once.

A deadly calm stole over her, and she drew the revolver from her pocket while reaching to unlock the outer door. She held the gun steady and stood back while she opened it just a crack…then slowly more. Bret Holden stood in the light of the swaying lamp, garbed in black. Her strength crashed to her feet.

A more handsome and formidable depiction of masculine security could not have emerged had she been able to conjure him up from the fabled genie's lamp. He was here—not weak and injured. But how?

With relief she threw herself into his arms, clutching him, starting to whisper, "Oh, Bret—"

But he clasped a hand over her mouth and backed her into the compartment, silently bolting the door behind him. He gestured with his head toward the adjoining compartment, now dark, and she knew he understood. He released her and moved toward the door.

"Open it," he whispered, his voice barely audible. She looked at him as though he were mad, but she moved to do as he said. She slid back the bolt. Bret gestured for her to speak.

"Who's there?" she asked, her voice shaking.

A faint noise sounded in the other compartment, then a terrifying sound reached out to grasp her. "Allison?" the muffled voice asked.

"Yes—who is it?"

Bret had taken his position beside the door against the wall, his revolver drawn. He reached over, pulled Allison aside to safety and opened the door. It swung open, and Allison stared as a strong figure appeared.

"Neal," she gasped.

"Yes, it's me. Hello, cousin."

She stared at him, unable to see his face, her heart pounding. *No...please, no...*she kept thinking, confused and tormented by her thoughts. Then Bret turned up the lanterns, and they were illuminated with weaving golden light as the train jostled its way down the track.

Neal looked at Allison, nothing in his face. Then he said, "What are you doing here? It was supposed to be Jemal." He looked at Bret. "Didn't expect you here either. Well, things look rather badly for me, don't they?" Bret watched him, unsmiling.

The cool, hard look he gave Neal made Allison tremble. She looked from one to the other, holding her breath, waiting for some clue of what to believe, what to expect in the rigid moment.

"Look, you don't think I was after my cousin—?" began Neal, his gaze questioning Bret.

In the lapse of silence, no one moved. Bret gestured to the other compartment. "Inside, Neal. Back up nice and slow."

Neal made no argument, but his face tensed. He seemed to

know that any argument now might end in tragedy.

"I can explain, Major," he said in a low, firm voice.

"You will. You and me, alone. Move."

Neal lifted both hands and backed inside.

"Turn the lanterns up first," came Bret's quiet command.

A moment later the compartment was flooded with wavering yellow light.

Allison couldn't see inside, but Bret could. Satisfied, he walked in. "Bolt it behind me, Allison," he told her and closed the door.

She moved numbly to slide the bolt in place.

No, it can't be Neal. Not him. Please, anyone but him ...The words continued to repeat themselves in her heart.

Cold and trembling, aching with disappointment and emotional pain, she sank slowly to the lower berth and clasped her knees, unable to think, to even want to. She buried her face against her lap.

When the sun climbed hot in the eastern sky, Allison was still sitting there. She awoke with her neck cramped. The train had stopped, and sunlight filtered into the compartment around the edges of the window hanging.

For a moment, between sleeping and waking, she thought she was in her cabin aboard the *Mercy* and wondered why she felt so depressed. Then, almost instantly, she remembered the horrible incident. It was like awakening the morning after someone you dearly love has died and a pang of lonely desperation settles in. *But, God!*

Yes, he remained the one source of steadfast strength and hope, however dark the night had been. Despite the heavy, smothering sense of depression, remembering Jesus illuminated her soul with a warm light of hope. *All is not lost. Hope lives on because he lives and is always here with me.*

She remembered again—on the other side of the thin wall Neal was under arrest by Major Holden. Allison's mind jerked away desperately. She did not want to think of it or to believe it of Neal.

What had happened last night in that compartment, so quiet, so secretive? For a time she had heard their voices, Bret asking brief questions, no emotion in his tone, and Neal's long, quiet explanations. It had seemed to drag on for hours.

She rushed to the compartment door and tapped. No one answered her urgent request to open. She hesitated, then unbolted the door and tried the latch. It was unlocked. She opened the door and looked inside.

Empty. Both Bret and Neal had disappeared. She looked about the compartment and saw that the berths were untouched, the window covering was up, and there was not the slightest evidence anyone had been there. She turned at once to the latch and examined it. The file marks proved she hadn't imagined the whole thing.

She stood there, thinking. Bret couldn't have arrested Neal. They were working together. Yet what had her cousin been doing filing the lock to her compartment? She shivered, remembering that ominous sound. Had he thought Professor Jemal had her compartment, as he had said?

How had Neal escaped from Jerusalem? Did his release mean David was also safe? And Bret—how was it that he was on the train? How had he known she was here? Had he sent the wire from Cairo saying he was injured? If not, then who? Why?

The enemy couldn't be Neal. He would never harm Leah. There must be some explanation to all of this, but what should her response be now?

She must proceed with her plans, and Bret would somehow be in touch with her, she decided. He must know by now that her trip here meant she had the information he was looking for. He must have followed her, along with Neal. But then, she thought, confused, it hadn't appeared last night as though Bret believed Neal had a valid reason for trying to enter her compartment. She remembered the way he had held that revolver, as though he would use it in an instant, if necessary.

Dazed, she thought again, *Neal wouldn't hurt me; I know he wouldn't.*

But Bret thought she was in real danger when he came to her compartment last night. If he hadn't thought so, he wouldn't have revealed his presence on the train. Other than herself, from whom had he been concealing himself? Neal?

But Bret had appeared as surprised to find Neal behind that door as she had been. *No,* she thought, her stomach queasy, *there must be someone else.*

Where had they disappeared to? Why had they left her without explanation? Were the German police on Bret's trail? Perhaps he had had to escape. Returning to Aleppo and Jerablus would place him in danger after impersonating Colonel Holman. Then there was Captain Mustafa. He would have reported the incident involving David on the road. And what of the German vehicle Bret had attacked?

She pulled aside the window covering. The train had stopped at a station in Aleppo. Several men were standing on the platform who appeared to be Turkish and German soldiers. One, who stood with his back toward her window, wore a German military hat. What if they knew Bret was aboard? What if they had come to arrest him? How could he escape?

She stood there frowning, then let the blind fall back into place and turned to dress quickly, packing her nightclothes into the bag. Bret and Neal must be waiting outside, she decided. But they couldn't loiter, waiting for her, with German soldiers and Turkish officials in the depot. Why hadn't Bret left a message in her compartment?

Allison turned to the small cracked mirror to wash her face and arrange her hair, troubled that her hand shook in the process and that her face was unnaturally pale in the morning light. The sea-green eyes with their tilting black lashes looked at her with restrained fright. She pulled her auburn hair back and tied it with a ribbon. Her shaking fingers struggled to loop the myriad of tiny pearl buttons that went down the bodice of her cool white cotton dress. Absently she tied the narrow sash about her waist, the flaring skirt reaching to just above her ankles. Her leather shoes were styled for desert wear, a safeguard against vipers and scorpions.

The attendant was rapping on her door and calling in Arabic and English, "Aleppo!"

Allison opened the door to look in the corridor. The blinds were no longer drawn over the windows, and a bright morning sun glared down onto the railway tracks and Turkish buildings.

She didn't dare alert the attendant or risk describing Bret and Neal. If they had made their quiet escape, no one would have seen them.

"Wait, please," she called. "Is there a message for Miss Wescott?"

"No message, miss."

Allison shut her door and stood there. Now what? Should she proceed with her plans to go to the huts? The men couldn't simply disappear, nor would Bret go without leaving her some message.

Her gaze swerved to the doorway of the other compartment. Bret stood there. As she looked into his handsome, tanned face, she noticed the small scar on his chin that reminded her of some past danger, perhaps as serious as the one they faced now.

She took a step toward him. "You have an exasperating way of vanishing."

He closed the door and bolted it.

"Where's Neal?" she whispered. "You didn't turn him over to the officials?"

His gaze was level, his face deliberately bland. "One of our own? Hardly. He's with Hamid."

She searched the depths of his blue eyes, but they defied analysis. "He must have explained everything to you," she questioned hopefully, watching his response. "I know he isn't involved in any of this."

"Do you?"

"You mean, you aren't sure?" she asked uncomfortably. "Neal would never harm Leah or me."

"He insisted he escaped Jerusalem and was trying to contact me again through Hamid."

"You don't believe him?"

He walked to the window, drew the blind, and glanced out thoughtfully. "I don't know what to think. There are too many loose ends. Too many variables. I don't like what's happened. Things have gone wrong that weren't supposed to. There's a traitor among the agents."

She shuddered. A traitor among those who worked with him?

"Not Neal," she whispered desperately. "He wouldn't. No more than Leah would betray us."

"Neal may be involved. As it is, I'm not in a position to trust him. Not now. That makes it ruddy hard for me. I'm short two men since Hamid will need to keep him under guard at the house. And you're here. It wasn't supposed to be this way."

Her mind was in turmoil, darting from one unanswered question to the next. But she was sure the answers would all come eventually.

"I think you should believe Neal. He's innocent."

"You would think so, of course. He's your cousin."

"And Leah was his sister. He couldn't possibly have killed her!"

"Maybe not Leah, but Karl Reuter," he mused.

"Do you believe he did?" she asked, her heart hanging on to his every word.

"Maybe," he said smoothly, leaning against the wall.

She looked at him exasperated. "I can't imagine you don't have opinions."

"I have many. I could take a chance and release him."

"Did he say he boarded the train at Damascus?"

"No, at Amman." He caught the tension in her voice. "Why?"

She couldn't explain her feelings but felt relief.

"What about Damascus?" he urged. "You're relieved he didn't board the train there. Why?"

She shrugged, deciding the whole matter was rather foolish after all. "No reason, I suppose."

His eyes narrowed with quiet determination. "Suppose you tell me anyway."

"I just had a notion of something dangerously unpleasant when we stopped at Damascus and new passengers boarded." She glanced at him. "I'm sure it was my nerves."

"I'm sorry I allowed you to come—" He broke off suddenly and frowned.

She caught the slip in his suggestion at once. *"Allowed* me to come? I don't see that you have," she said bewildered. "I came on my own initiative."

"Yes, because you thought I was languishing in a hospital. The noble and self-sacrificing young Christian nurse would feel it her patriotic duty to carry on where Leah and I had left off," he said with a trace of self-incrimination in his voice.

Allison asked suddenly, accusingly, "The wire—the one saying you were injured; then it was you who sent it to me?"

He frowned. "The department did. It was part of the safeguards. We wanted certain individuals to think I was out of the game." He watched her response.

"So I would be placed in a precarious position," she stated too quietly.

Their eyes held. "That was the idea, yes. But you weren't in as much risk as you are now. I knew I would be following you on the train to Aleppo. Hamid was here, too. And I expected someone to make his move."

"But matters have changed," she said flatly, "is that it?"

"Yes," he said with a hint of callousness, but she knew he was worried.

"Then," she said haltingly, "you knew I would come to Aleppo? You even wanted me to come?"

Bret watched her with the same self-irritated moodiness that she had observed before. "Yes," he admitted evenly. But she knew he was having second thoughts when he added, "I've blundered."

"I don't understand," she said unsteadily. "Because of Neal last night? You mean you expected someone in that compartment," and she turned to glance toward the bolted door, "but not Neal. Is that it?"

"Yes. Hamid was watching and assured me—" he stopped suddenly.

Her eyes swerved to his, and she wondered at the expression on his face. "Yes," she whispered, "what about Hamid?"

He didn't answer but walked to the window again. He rubbed his chin; his mind elsewhere. "Hamid," he repeated to himself. "It couldn't be—it couldn't…"

She followed him. "What do you mean you've been watching me since I left Cairo? That isn't possible. I would have seen you."

He turned, regarding her. "I was determined you wouldn't. I couldn't let you leave Cairo alone. It wasn't safe."

She drew in a shaky breath that matched her weakening knees. "You mean you expected Leah to send a message to me?"

"When I didn't find the information, and it became apparent the enemy hadn't either, I was almost certain she had. At first I thought it was in the medical crates."

"Then it was you who arranged for them to be sent to Cairo?"

"No. I don't know who did. But in Port Said, when you told me about the supplies, I began to suspect the crates. Someone else did, too, and had them sent to Helga's shop."

"Perhaps Helga herself," she half-accused.

"No." His determination didn't waiver.

"What makes you so sure?"

"You'll need to take my word on that now. I followed you to Luxor. You're a precious commodity, you know, one we can't afford to let slip through our fingers."

She noted his choice of words. "We," he had said, not himself. He was speaking of the British government.

"I've been watching you since you left with your aunt's medical supplies. I expected you to encounter some risk, but this thing with Neal last night took me off guard. I never suspected him. And I'm not sure I do now."

She set aside her feelings and looked at him. "You were in Luxor?"

"Remember Karnak Temple?"

Her narrowing eyes met his. She shivered slightly. "That was you?" she whispered.

He watched her with a curious intensity, and seeing she remembered, said gently, "I couldn't give myself away, but I'm sorry I frightened you. You were getting too close, and I couldn't be discovered."

So he had followed her to Luxor to watch her without informing her. He had deliberately kept her in the dark as to his intentions and his motives. She wasn't convinced he had watched her just to protect her, but for reasons of his own. She thought she began to understand why now, and why he was secretly on the train.

Bret noticed her reaction and frowned. "It was necessary that you didn't know. Unfortunately, it hasn't turned out quite as we expected."

"By 'we' I gather you speak of British intelligence. You mean," she began, "you knew I was coming to Aleppo to find the information?"

He held her gaze without apology. "Yes," he admitted gravely.

"And you didn't tell me. You kept me in the dark." She stood looking at him, feeling unduly betrayed. "I see," she said a little coolly.

"I doubt if you really do," he said with an edge to his voice.

"Oh, but I do—now," she half accused. "You knew I'd find the message from Leah."

"Yes."

"And after the wire arrived telling me you had met with an accident, you guessed I would set off on my own to come here."

He smiled faintly. "Something like that."

"Then," said Allison, "you deliberately allowed the trap to be set—on this train. You expected the enemy to make his move here—last night."

Bret said nothing. He shoved his hands into his pockets.

"So I was the bait to lure the murderer into following me. And at the right moment of discovery, you would have him, the way you thought you had him last night."

"You needn't make it sound so cold and methodical."

Allison felt unreasonably perturbed. She looked at him accusingly, remembering how frightened she had been when Neal had filed away at the lock. True, Bret had been there the moment she needed him, and if it had been the real enemy, matters would have come to a satisfactory end. But if the enemy weren't Neal—and she believed it wasn't—then the trap was still empty, and the murderer was still following her.

"I was confident I'd be here when you needed me," he said. "If not, I would have stopped you from coming. But after last night…"

His countenance turned vague.

"After last night," she concluded, "you realized something had gone wrong?"

"I've trusted people I shouldn't have; I don't blame anyone but myself." Bret walked restlessly across the compartment, moving the blind to look out, then letting it fall again. He came back to Allison and stood watching her thoughtfully, frowning.

"I can't afford to make mistakes. That's why you're going straight to the British consul. I've changed my mind about your involvement. You'll stay at the consul until the matter is settled here. If anything goes wrong and I don't return, wire your father in Baghdad."

"Baghdad? But he's in Bombay."

"No," he said evenly, "he isn't. He's been in Baghdad for a month. That's how I got the letter to deliver to your mother. I've been taking orders from him."

She could only stare at him. Her father was in intelligence? But what of her mother and Beth? By now they would have docked in India, only to learn that Sir Wescott wasn't there.

"What are you going to do?" she asked, worried.

"You're going to tell me where Leah put the book. I'm going there alone."

"And if Hamid must guard Neal, that means you'll be on your own, without anyone on watch," she said nervously.

"I can handle it," he said tonelessly. "It's my work. Something I've chosen to do, whatever the cost. You, however, are another matter."

"Without Neal and Hamid as guard, you'll need me."

"No," he insisted, his eyes turning a brittle blue.

"I don't blame the agency for wanting to use me to lure the enemy here. It makes sense. And it's necessary. Now, more than ever. I promised Leah I'd help her, and I intend to keep my promise. Instead of stopping him on the train, you'll stop him at the archaeology huts.

I'll—I'll lure whomever it is there. And when he shows up for the information, you'll be there."

His eyes narrowed. "No. It will be more dangerous at the huts than on the train. Someone could be there even now, waiting for you. You would need to arrive before me, as though alone. I won't risk you like this. The plan has so many holes in it, it leaks like a sieve! Anything could go wrong. I was confident I could protect you here on the train; so I went along with using you, but even then I didn't approve. Now things have worsened."

He walked up to her, taking hold of her arms and turning her toward him. "Now let's get to business. Where did Leah put it?"

"If I tell you—"

His hands tightened, and his mouth curved. "*If* you tell me?"

"I've come too far to retire to some locked room at the consul, while you face everything alone," she said in a rush.

"Your concerns are noted," he said softly, "but I can take care of myself. I've done it often enough. Things are in a state of high risk now, and I have to settle them."

Allison's gaze clung to his. "Matters may not have turned out as you first expected, but there's no reason we can't proceed."

"Yes, there is," he said shortly. "In fact, plenty of reasons."

"You didn't catch the enemy last night. At least we're not sure if you did. Certainly not the principal people involved, and we agree the enemy is still about." She tried not to shiver. "If they don't know about Neal being detained, then perhaps they don't know you're here either. They think I'm still alone. They'll expect to follow me to where Leah hid the information."

"That's exactly the point! I meant to stop them here. It was never to go further. You're not going out there."

"It makes more sense for me to go. And—and you'll be right behind me, won't you?"

"Allison," he said softly, "I admire your willingness tremendously, and I think you're brave for wanting to do this, but—"

"The only thing that's changed in your plans is that you have to find someone at the huts instead of here in this compartment. Why not?"

He frowned, his eyes searching hers. His hands were fists. "You're not a trained agent. It's unfair to ask so much of you."

"No, it isn't asking too much. At first I was bothered that you were willing to use me without my knowing. But it was only—I suppose I wanted you to care too much about what would happen to me—" She stopped; she had revealed too much.

"Did you want me to care?" he asked softly. "Then you can forget your concerns because I do—more than you think. I'd give anything if you were safe in Cairo instead of here."

"But I don't feel the least troubled about it now, and I do want to see this to the end. I want to be with you when you unearth the information. And Hamid can't be with you. I can be trusted. And I've got a revolver. I can use it, too. If the war comes, I plan to enlist."

"Out of the question. I won't let you."

"I beg your pardon, Major Holden, but suppose I don't listen?"

"You'll do as you're told," he said roughly.

She smiled. "My father has always been patriotic and devoted to the military. So was my grandfather and his father. And so am I."

"I'll remember that if we get out of here. I commend your father, grandfather, and great-grandfather, but duty ends there."

"No, I expect to do my duty as a nurse on the front lines, if it comes to that."

"I think you mean that," he said with exasperation.

"I do. And I've had some training with a weapon. Which means you can use me now."

"No," he said firmly, dropping his hands. "I've not changed my mind. You're going to the consul to wait. I want you in one piece in Cairo."

"Bret, listen. Everything that's happened—Major Reuter, the Kurdish guard, Leah—the information you're after is important, isn't it?"

"You know it is. Very important. But I can retrieve it on my own."

"And become a marked man? They'll be waiting. If I go, it will be different. As soon as I have it in hand, they'll come out. And then—" She swallowed.

He frowned.

"—you'll be there."

"If it came to it, yes, I promise. But can you do it? This isn't going to be easy."

"If Leah could manage that lone trip to meet one she thought to be Neal, then I can do this. And I'll have one thing she didn't—you."

He watched her for a long moment. He walked to the window and looked out again. He turned his head and looked at her gravely. "All right. But you'll need to promise you'll do everything exactly as I say. We can't afford anything to go wrong. Not with you under the gun."

She pretended undaunted courage, and said brightly, "Anything you say, Major."

"Now, I need to know what you've learned from Leah." He walked back to her, and Allison whispered: "It's under the porch of Major Reuter's hut. The same place she hid the night she slipped away from you. She was hiding there when the murderer ran out. She heard his steps above her head on the porch." She shuddered.

"Ah. The one place no one thought to look. Leah was a smart woman." He looked at her, alert. "What did you do with the message?"

"I burned it at once, as soon as I'd read it several times."

"Good. And you've said nothing to anyone?"

"No one—only you."

Their eyes met. *What if he really is a German agent?* A warm shiver prickled the back of her neck.

Bret saw it, and his mouth curved wryly. "You'll need to trust me implicitly."

"Oh, I do," she hastened. "About as much as I could trust any man."

He lifted a brow. "That remark would turn Wade Findlay into my enemy."

She busied herself with gathering her bag and hat. "I didn't mean it that way. Anyway, Wade doesn't see others as enemies. You've yet to meet a more warm and generous man. He's going to serve as a chaplain to our forces at Zeitoun."

"I'm sure his competition will be keen. But when I make up my mind, I'm not easy to get rid of."

She looked at him, faintly surprised.

He held her gaze. "I told you in Jerusalem I'd warn you if the time came for me to throw down the gauntlet of challenge. I intend to take you away from Wade."

Allison's heart fluttered feebly. A warm flush came to her face, and she was furious with herself because it did. She went to tie on her hat, her hands shaking. The words to hold him off would not come.

"We'll need to make our plans," he said.

She turned, stunned at his boldness, and then realized he had changed the subject.

He lifted a brow and smiled. "Plans to get to the huts. Our personal concerns must wait. Unless," and his eyes glinted with a hint of amusement, "you've already made up your mind."

"Of all the—I mean, no! No, Major. You may be certain that I haven't—"

"I see you're going to be difficult. The first time I've found a woman I really want, and she's reluctant."

Was he serious? "The others were too agreeable?" she asked.

He smiled wryly but didn't deny it. "We'll need to plan this trek to the huts carefully. I want to make certain you know exactly what to do—nothing must happen to you."

She glanced at him, as he drew up a chair to the tiny table and removed a piece of paper and a pencil.

She wondered about the status of his Christian beliefs. He appeared to have some, but she needed to be absolutely sure before she could put her emotions at further risk. There could be no compromise here, Allison reminded herself again. God, not man, was the creator of marriage, and he was also its greatest foundation—the foundation of any true, growing, and lasting relationship between a man and a woman. She wanted to ask Bret about his relationship with the Lord. She would pray and ask the Lord to arrange the right moment.

With the plans made and carefully instilled in her mind, Allison picked up her bag and turned to leave the train alone. Bret was leaning against the door, frowning slightly.

"I'll be all right," she whispered.

He watched her but didn't let her pass, his blue eyes turning a warm, riveting blue. Then, surprisingly, he drew her into his arms.

Allison clutched her bag and didn't think to drop it. "Major," she whispered shakily, "you don't know what you're doing."

He smiled. "Oh, but I do. I've thought about this often enough. I suspect you have as well."

"Let go," she breathed, her emotions in a riotous jumble.

"I must refuse. Danger and uncertainty provoke me to bold endeavors."

"No—"

"You'll forgive me if I don't take no for an answer? I intend to kiss you good-bye. I've decided anything could happen to me, and I may not get another opportunity."

"Don't say that! You must not—!"

"Life is precarious. And too many soldiers are buried with fair visions of what might have been if tomorrow hadn't ended too soon."

He lowered his head and kissed her, as warm and comfortably as though he had all the time in the world. Allison's mind halted as she stood locked in his embrace. Then she dropped her bag and pushed against his chest, her mind and heart spinning out of control.

Bret's lips drew away, but he continued to hold her tightly.

The train whistle blared loudly, and the warning sounded that it was receiving final passengers. He released her, and Allison, flushing warmly, stepped back angry because her heart was pounding like a rabbit's.

A dark brow lifted at her expression, and he smiled faintly. "All right, I apologize."

"You're not very convincing," she accused breathlessly.

"I've behaved abominably," he said too gravely, his eyes warm and glinting.

He caught up her bag, handing it to her. "If it helps, know that I will cherish our moment, stolen as it was from Wade Findlay."

"Oh!" Allison snatched the bag from his hand and, tearing her eyes from his, rushed past him out the door, her heart still thudding, not sure how she felt about the fact that her very first kiss had come from the oh-so-arrogant Major Bret Holden.

20

ALONE, ALLISON LEFT THE TRAIN, careful not to look disturbed as she glanced casually about the depot. Tension gripped her, along with a sudden premonition of danger. Bret was nearby but concealed while he kept her under watch. He was convinced of her ability to go through with this, trusting her calm nerves.

She walked past the train cars, looking to either side, careful to avoid the officials who patrolled the depot. Was the enemy watching her, too?

Running feet gained on her from behind, and she stopped, turning abruptly. An Arab boy grinned. "Allo, miss! Good morning, miss! I carry bag, miss! This way, yes?"

His brown eyes twinkled with what appeared secret amusement. Had Bret sent him? He hadn't mentioned it.

The boy trotted ahead and turned down a narrow stone street with indigo shadows. She hesitated. His small bare feet padded along the stones worn smooth by centuries of other feet and hoofs of camels, horses, and donkeys. He paused and urged her to follow.

Allison stood still, and as the boy reached a narrow archway, Neal stepped from the shadows. She glanced behind her down the narrow street toward the train, half expecting to see Bret standing there. Instead, she saw an Arab who moved into the shadows.

Neal tipped the boy and beckoned her to come. She walked

toward him, carrying her bag. Neal smiled as she came up, and taking her arm, tried to lead her off into the shadows of ancient stone walls and latticed windows. Allison pulled back, staring at him.

"You didn't think I was really under arrest by Hamid?"

"Bret certainly gave me reason to think so."

"You don't think I'm a traitor to England, do you?"

"No, I can't think that of you."

"Good. Because I'm not. I don't know what Major Holden told you, but Hamid insisted my arrest was only a pretense."

"Hamid told you that? Because that isn't what Bret told me."

"Hamid let me go."

"He did?" she said, surprised.

"Yes, he said the entire thing was a ploy. Bret wanted Jemal and the baroness to think I'd been taken away. They're here. They were on the train. You and I are to go to the huts, though I prefer to leave you here. Bret insisted. Rather odd."

"Neal, there's something wrong with what Hamid told you. I just left Bret, and he believes Hamid is holding you in detention at his apartment. He isn't certain he can trust you."

His face tensed. "He didn't tell Hamid to release me?"

"No. Hamid must have done that on his own."

Neal considered, watching her, his blue eyes alert, the breeze ruffling his sandy hair. For a moment, as she looked at him, she thought of Leah.

"Neal, you don't suppose," she whispered, "Hamid is the one?"

His sandy brows furrowed as he turned to stare down the alleyway. No one was in sight. "Impossible."

"Is it? Why? Bret trusts him with his life, but wouldn't that be the way Hamid would want it?"

"Yes. But we've been through too much together. He wouldn't betray Bret."

She thought of the night on the road when they had attacked the German car. She felt a prick of guilt. No, she quite agreed, Hamid seemed too loyal.

"Where's Bret now?" he asked.

"On his way to the archaeological huts."

"Allison, I think you're right. Something is dead wrong. And Hamid may know what it is. He left for the huts twenty minutes ago."

Her heart wanted to stop. He would arrive before Bret. He could hide. And Bret didn't expect Hamid to be there. He would have the advantage over Bret.

Neal grabbed her arm. "Allison, get in the car. I don't know what's going on, but we have to get out to the huts. There may be others with him."

"How do I know I can trust you?"

"Allison! Didn't Leah trust me?"

"Yes, and someone murdered her."

"Good heavens, you think I did? I wasn't anywhere near the digs when it happened. I was in Jerusalem! That should be your answer."

It dawned on her then. Yes, he had been in Jerusalem. Mrs. Rose Lyman had told her so. She smiled with relief. He grinned and tossed her bag into the back of the car.

They drove away, leaving the shadows of the narrow streets, and were soon on the road toward the wilderness of Jerablus.

She faced Neal, the hot wind in her hair, her eyes anxiously searching his. "How did you escape Jerusalem? How is David?"

"David's still in detention. Rotten luck. But I was never arrested. Remember when I went to warn the Zionist leaders?"

"Yes, but they already had been arrested."

"Exactly. The Turks took them to Jaffa and expelled them from Palestine. But we'll be in touch with David Ben-Gurion when he gets to England. We have an all-Jewish squadron in the making. Just the sort of thing David would be excited about. We have to get him out of Turkish hands!"

"What of you; how did you escape?"

"I returned to Rose's house, but the Turks were swarming about. I waited, thinking Bret might arrive. He needed to be warned, but he didn't come. The Turks left with some prisoners, including David. I didn't see Rose or Benny, and I was sure they would do nothing to you with Uncle Marshall so high in British government. So I struck out on my own."

"How did you get out?"

"On the train from Haifa to Damascus. Then I returned to Aleppo to find Bret's assistant, Hamid. We talked, and I stayed with him a few weeks. Then we went back to the expedition house, the one Leah and I shared." He turned somber. "It was then I discovered a guard had been killed, and my things and Leah's ransacked. Hamid left and returned a few days later. He told me Bret had wired him about Jemal being aboard the train. The information we were seeking was with Jemal, who was on his way to the Germans in Baghdad. I was under Bret's orders—so I thought—to get into that compartment and find the papers."

"That's what Hamid told you?"

He looked at her, his blue eyes sober. "Yes. He's either working with the enemy, or he's been deceived as I was. We'll soon find out."

When they arrived at the Cairo archaeological huts between Aleppo and Baghdad, the blazing sunset was retreating from the deepening sky. Neal stopped the vehicle before the huts were in sight and climbed out from behind the wheel, handing her the keys.

"I'll circle round and approach from the other side," he told her.

"You're expected to arrive alone." His blue eyes contemplated her gravely. "Be careful, Allison."

She watched him slip away into the desert twilight, then drove the final portion alone, trying to calm the beating of her heart. She realized Bret wouldn't know of Neal's presence unless Hamid had informed him—but was Hamid loyal?

As planned, she made no attempt to hide her arrival. She was to appear confident that she was alone, the huts closed and empty for the late summer. Held in the foreboding grip of anticipation, she approached the familiar huts, viewing them as living entities wrapped in secretive isolation.

Naturally, she saw no sign of Bret's vehicle. Hamid, too, had apparently approached on foot—because he was really Bret's enemy? Or just being cautious, waiting? Unless Bret had somehow become aware of Hamid's arrival, he wouldn't know his assistant was also prowling the grounds. If only she could warn Bret. But she must do nothing to rouse the suspicion of the person waiting for her now. Who waited in the growing darkness for her to unearth the book Leah had carefully hidden on another windy Arabian night? Hidden before she kept her appointment with—Neal? Hamid? Jemal? The baroness? An unknown?

Allison's teeth chattered, and she tensed her jaw. "Bret is also here," she told herself and found solace in knowing that his strong form was concealed somewhere nearby, watching her even at this moment. Unless—unless something had happened on the way to thwart his arrival. What if Hamid had lain in wait for Bret?

She wouldn't think of it. If she allowed her fears to mount into swooping birds of prey, she would turn, screaming mindlessly, and run back to the vehicle. She must be brave, she must look to the greater source of her protection and strength, her high tower, her shield and sword.

The Arabian winds were rising with night's approach and stirring the carpet of sand beneath her crunching boots. The sand continued to swirl, forming mounds that reminded her of giant ant hills moving eerily along with ceaseless motion.

Did Bret suspect Hamid? Were they both watching her approach? How vulnerable she must appear to what awaited her.

A feeling of urgency and disquiet rode the moan of the wind. She walked through the tinted twilight, clutching her kitbag, the revolver in her jacket pocket, her throat dry.

Entering the grounds of the lodge, the huts faced her in a half-circle. On the other side of the bowl-like grounds, shadows from the hedge of leafy date palms slithered across the sand and rock that reflected the last rosy glow of sunset. Behind the trees, nightfall settled over the gullylike dry watercourse, where reptiles inched from rocks in the cooler night.

It was here the adventure had all begun, and perhaps tonight it would end. A shiver enveloped her as her eyes scanned the huts, lingering on cousin Leah's old room, then moving apprehensively to the hut of the British agent, Major Karl Reuter.

Behind her the date palms swayed with a rushing sound that ebbed and flowed, to her left was the now-dark dining hall, and next to it stood the larger huts used for lecture rooms. All stood shrouded in silence.

Where was Bret? Neal? Hamid?

The last shade of color died. Night descended, deep and black.

Memories of Leah were everywhere, and Allison's imagination grew with every desert sound. It seemed her cousin's urgent words written in the letter sent to the *Mercy* spoke again to Allison prompting—prodding—her forward toward the darkened enclosure beneath Karl Reuter's back porch to rescue the book. "Come," the book seemed to beckon, "hurry, hurry."

Allison steeled her emotions for the worst. It was dark enough now. The enemy would be watching her as alertly as she also watched. She swallowed and pressed the button on her hand torch. She had just announced her presence. Did Bret see the light? He had promised her he would be here. He wouldn't let her down.

She walked toward the hut, remembering the night she had followed Leah inside, remembering how Leah had fled with Bret behind her, and she, Allison, had been left inside that darkened room. The real enemy had been in there, too. "The third man" she and Leah had taken to calling him. Was it a man?

Leah had hidden beneath the porch. She had heard the murderer's footsteps retreating down the steps and disappearing across the soft sand. She had gone back there again later to conceal Woolly's book.

Allison approached the hut where the unshuttered window watched. With sweating palms, she flashed the beam up the steps to rivet it on the door. It was shut, but was someone inside? Bret? One of the others? Not Neal; he couldn't have gotten ahead of her so quickly. He would be farther behind, perhaps nearing the outside of the dining hall now. He, too, would see her torch glaring brightly, shouting her presence to everyone watching her from the darkness.

Drawing a deep breath, she went up the steps. A gust of wind blew across the yard and through the date palms, shaking the stiff, overweight clusters of dates and whispering around the rough wooden walls of the empty hut.

Allison tried the back door and, finding it unlocked, forced her courage and pushed open the door. Suddenly daunted by the cavern of darkness, she halted, her heart leaping and fluttering like a frightened bird. She would have turned and run but for Bret's image commanding her heart. She couldn't let him down. If she didn't go through with this, he would be left here with the enemy, now unwilling to show himself. Without the tempting bait of the book in her gullible hands, the murderer would slip back into hiding like a cockroach in the woodwork. She also thought of cousin Leah, her blond hair gleaming in the moonlight as she courageously slipped away to keep a duty-bound appointment at the abandoned digs.

Allison stepped over the threshold into Major Reuter's hut and reached for the box of matches that sat on the small table beside the door. She struck one, a flame flared, and her face showed unnaturally pale in its glow. The oil lamp cast its light onto the walls of the bathroom. The tin tub and the old wash basin came to life. The closed-up air smelled hot.

Allison froze. What else did she smell besides staleness, old wood, and furniture? The faint odor of tobacco smoke clung to the curtains. It grew stronger as she moved through the door into the room where the British agent's body had lain on the bed. She felt her way along the wall until she came to the light switch and pressed it down.

In the harsh amber light of the single bulb in the low ceiling, she glanced around the sparsely furnished room. The bed in the corner stood empty. For an apprehensive moment she had imagined she would see the major's body still there, as the bed had been weeks ago, covered with a blanket.

Allison's gaze swerved to the chair she had sat in the night "Colonel Holman" had interrogated her. Someone else had been sitting there, too, perhaps as recently as the last several hours, for on the simple bare wooden floor beside it was a pile of tobacco ash.

She stooped and gingerly placed a finger against it. Some of the gray powder clung to her finger, and she brought it close to smell. A faint fragrance—if one could call it that—was remotely familiar. She tried to remember where she had smelled it before. Then it came back. Helga Kruger's shop in Old Cairo, on the morning she had gone there with Zalika for the medical crates.

She stood, aware that the glowing lights in the small room could be seen throughout the dark lodge and that by now it was obvious she was here. Even now someone might be approaching the hut, thinking the information was here, and that she had uncovered it. She listened intently but heard nothing above a sharp gust of wind that shook the hut.

Her eyes widened a little as she saw a sprawling stain on the scarred wooden floor. She hadn't remembered it from the night she was here with Bret, but perhaps she had been too preoccupied to notice it. As she stooped, there was no mistaking the evidence: The dark splotch was still wet and sticky. Her heart nearly ceased to beat as her eyes followed the spots toward a closed door. The closet. She stood and stared. No. Please, no.

Every imaginable fear erupted like flowing lava from a volcano. Bret had been in here waiting for her. Waiting to protect, but he had been shot before she arrived, probably by Hamid. She envisioned Hamid entering the hut portraying himself as the loyal assistant. What had Bret said about Hamid? That he could trust his back to his loyal friend?

That the blood was still wet proved it had happened only minutes earlier. In this hot environment the stains would dry quickly.

In a moment of despair she sank to the chair, courage and hope fast fleeing. What good would it do to risk everything for the book now? Why not run for her life? She knew it was too late, that she was under scrutiny by unfriendly eyes and that she would never make it to the vehicle without being stopped and forced to reveal the spot where Leah had hidden the book, then silenced.

There was a small chance—Neal was here, too, and she would risk everything that he was not a traitor but as loyal to the cause of England as Leah had been. He knew she was in this hut; he was nearby to protect her now that Bret could not. And he knew that producing the book would lure the enemy from hiding. For Leah, for England, and now for Bret.

A prickling shiver raced up her back, and she had to force herself to turn toward the back porch. No one was there, yet the feeling of being watched persisted and grew stronger.

She rushed through the stifling room, past the bathroom and out the back door into the darkness of the porch. Going down the few wooden steps, she turned her torch into the cavern of darkness that ran beneath. This is where Leah had hid that night. Swiftly now, Allison stooped and crawled beneath the porch, feeling the sand pressing on her palms and knees. She lifted the light to a rough wooden beam where Leah had laid Woolly's book on the Hittites and felt carefully along the ledge until her fingers brushed against the smooth binding. She clutched it to her chest, her breath coming rapidly, her heart beating painfully, and turned to crawl back out.

Someone was nearby. It was no longer merely a foreboding suspicion but a certainty. She remained on her knees, listening to the dreadful sound that came above the wind, the sound that Leah must have heard that night when she hid here.

In the darkness above her, the floorboards creaked beneath the heavy weight of someone's feet. The porch seemed to bow beneath the slow but determined steps—first one, then another, and another. Though she had expected this, she was emotionally unprepared. Someone was standing in the darkness, waiting. The stairs creaked beneath each heavy, downward step, and her mind followed each sound until the sand crunched beneath shoes. She crouched there, clutching the book, staring until a torch flashed on, sweeping the hiding place and coming to her face. She closed her eyes against the stabbing glare, and then it flashed off. Her eyes opened. A match struck, flared, and was followed by a waft of tobacco smoke.

She flashed on her torch and saw his shoes, saw the cuffs of his trousers flapping in the wind.

"Hello, Allison, dear. I've been waiting for you."

21

WITH A HALF-SOB OF RELIEF Allison crawled out from beneath the porch. "It's you! I suppose you know you nearly frightened me to death. You're in the thick of espionage, and I hope you've a steady revolver at hand, because we're likely to need it before this night is over."

She watched the red glow of his pipe brighten in the darkness as he drew on it. The pipe…tobacco…

"Whatever are you and dear Sarah doing here? I suppose you followed me, too, fearing something dreadful might happen to me? What did you tell Aunt Lydia?" she asked.

But General Rex Blaine wasn't speaking, or smiling, or making any light, jovial remarks as he usually did. He stood watching her, a very different man than the portly, retired major-general from the British military in India. She had never seen him look this way before and realized, quite suddenly, that when General Blaine wasn't smiling, winking, and making wry remarks, his face was not affable and harmless. She noticed for the first time the bitter twist to his mouth that she had mistaken for a smile. And the small bright eyes beneath the heavy brows were not those of an uncle but were as cold, deep, and bloodless as the cobras that so fascinated him.

The fear that had left her heart when she saw him now began to intensify. Something was very different about General Blaine.

"Something wrong, Allison?" he asked, unsmiling. "Have I ceased to humor you? You look as though you have just seen me for the first time."

The shock was so devastating that her emotions wanted to reject it, and she clung to the possibility that she was wrong. "Where's Sarah?" she asked breathlessly. "Did you bring her? Is she in the hut?"

"Leave Sarah out of this. Come inside, Allison."

She saw it then, the dark outline of a gun in his hand. She couldn't answer. She stared at him, dazed, unbelieving. She must believe because this was not simply a terrifying nightmare. It was real and more frightening because it wasn't a stranger but General Blaine, a man she had been so sure she knew. General Blaine was the third man.

"Up the steps. Hurry."

She did as he ordered, her legs weak, and in another moment found herself in Reuter's hut. "Sit down, Allison."

She did, her mind working dully. Where was Neal? Where was Hamid? Bret was dead.

General Blaine pulled up a chair and sat down astride it, steadying his gun hand across his arm that rested on the back. He asked very softly, "What do you have in your arms, Allison? So it was a book. Yes, makes sense. *The Hittites*. I only just figured it out. Clever of the agent masquerading as Reuter. Makes me boil to think it was under my nose the night I searched here. Yes, it was I. And I would have eliminated Leah then if you hadn't blundered in. You are a bewildering thorn. I didn't want to do this to you. I was hoping you would stay with Lydia. But you couldn't leave it alone, could you?" he asked angrily. "Major Holden! Oh yes, I just found out about him. Too bad I didn't know at the charity ball. I could have killed him then. But he's dead now. Hamid with him."

No, the thought was too painful.

"Hamid! I thought—" She stopped. He guessed what she was about to say.

"You thought he was a traitor? No, it was Jemal. He's involved, but he's no fighter. He makes a better gravedigger, a spy in Cairo. He detests the baroness because the stupid woman is working for British intelligence."

She gasped. "Helga?"

He smiled disdainfully. "She loathes the superior ideas of the kaiser, of the war machine. She's been aiding the British in Constantinople. She's used her shop in Cairo and these huts as a cover. Jemal's been watching her, but he was slow-witted. He didn't learn of her connection with Bret until recently. Bret! If I had only known—"

Allison tried to keep her voice steady, to keep the panic out of her face. She must gain time. Someone must come; he had to! Neal!

"But why you, Rex? You're British! You hate the Germans."

He smiled wearily. "A clever front, wasn't it? The more I taunted the kaiser and spoke against the baroness, the more convinced everyone became. You'll be shocked to know my parents were German; I was born in Berlin. I didn't come to England until I was seventeen. I met Sarah in India, after I assumed the identity of Rex Blaine. My real name is Willis Brandt."

"Does Sarah know?"

"No. And she won't. She's not involved. When we return to Berlin, I'll have some excuse."

"But why—why are you involved? Even if you were German born—"

He smiled. "Why would I give up dear England once I had had the blessed opportunity to embrace her? Because I despise England! I despise all she stands for—her pride on the sea, her arrogance! Her empire. She never deserved it—it's Germany's time to rule the world. England had her hour, France and Napoleon had theirs—Spain, Rome—it's time for the Aryan race! How I've laughed at the British for their conceited stupidity. I worked for Berlin during all my years in India, and they didn't even suspect."

"What about Major Reuter? Did you...?"

"Kill him? Yes. I knew he was a British agent. We knew when he left Constantinople with the documents. We knew about Neal and Leah Bristow at Carchemish pretending to work for the British Museum. So it was arranged for me to come here with the Archaeological Club. It happened to fit so well that Sarah was involved in archaeology. She never knew I encouraged her to involve herself for my benefit. I did it so subtly she never guessed, nor did anyone else, not even Bret. I fooled him to the end, just as I did you." He sighed. "I'm sorry about you, Allison, but there it is."

"You knew Reuter was an agent, but did you know whom he came here to meet?"

"We knew he was to give the Constantinople papers to someone. But it took us time to learn it was Neal. Neal didn't show—he was alerted by someone when Reuter was killed. Probably his superior. We know now it was Bret. It was my one mistake—killing Reuter before Neal arrived. I should have gotten them both at the same time and waited for Bret, too. Well, it doesn't matter now. We'll have them all before tonight is over. Oh, yes, Allison my dear, we know Neal is here. Jemal will have taken care of him by now. Don't look so fallen. You should have known you couldn't win. You've been very foolish."

"And Leah? You murdered her?"

"It had to be done. Do you think I liked it?"

"Then it was you I heard when she left for the rendezvous?"

"I knew she was in your hut. I decided to let you both look for whatever it was Reuter hid. You were both clever. I must admit it's been a bit tiring keeping tabs on you—first at the charity ball, then at Luxor."

"Was it you who entered the house at Port Said?"

"Jemal. He needed to destroy the letter he sent to Leah. It incriminated him, though she seemed to have overlooked it. The letter mentioned his service at the Constantinople museum. If anyone had bothered to check, they would have discovered Jemal was with the sultan when Kaiser Wilhelm visited the city in triumph last year. I told him to forget the letter, it would prove nothing, but he was nervous and wanted to destroy it."

"How did you do it—with Leah—"

"Simple. I followed her to the motorcar. She wasn't afraid when she saw the affable English buffoon General Blaine. I disposed of her out at the old abandoned digs, never guessing Helga would arrange the jaunt there. When she did, I felt it was to my benefit to be present. I knew they would find the body. I was furious when Leah tricked me, though. She didn't bring the information to meet Neal—she brought Sarah's old notes she had given you on Jemal's lecture, and your Bible. I knew then that you were involved. She would have told you where she had hidden the real information. So I had to watch you until you led me to it—as you finally have."

"Now I remember—that day when Leah came here for the book during lunch—you were late, but I didn't suspect you so it never made an impression. I was watching Helga."

"The face of innocence pays, my dear. And I searched your room when I pretended I needed rest for my back. You remained in Jemal's lecture with Sarah."

"And—and the Kurdish guard at the expedition house? Was it you then, too?"

"No, I stayed here. But Jemal had one of our own follow you and

David. He would have gotten you then except someone arrived and scared him off."

"It was Bret."

He shrugged. "It doesn't matter now. Soon the war will be on and Germany will defeat Serbia, Russia, France—England!"

"You swore your loyalty to the throne of England—"

"Now, now, dear Allison, no use waving the Union Jack before my eyes. It means nothing to me. So enough of this. I've taken too much time already. So that's where Leah put the book, under the porch. Clever of her, wasn't it? I didn't think of it. You're clever, too. I tried to frighten you off—the poisoned water and other things. You should have stayed out of this, stayed on Lydia's ship and tended the peasants you care so much about. I gave you a chance—more than one—to back off, but you wouldn't. Espionage is a deadly game, and people get killed, even little girls with angelic faces. I'm sorry, Allison, but it's got to be this way." He stood. "The book, Allison. Hand it to me."

"Tell me what's in it, Rex. Why is it so important?"

"It's not. It's nothing but a stupid archaeology book. But it would have informed Neal or Bret where the Constantinople papers are hidden."

"What are the Constantinople papers?"

"Secret war documents drawn up between Berlin and the Ottoman Empire against England. They must not fall into the hands of the British minister of war. Not yet. Not until Germany is ready in Arabia."

"Ready? Ready for what?"

"There's no time now." He stood, holding the book. "Get up, we must go."

"Where are you taking me?"

"Allison, you're making this dreadfully hard—to wherever the book tells me the agent stashed those papers. Get up. I'm losing patience."

Allison fought against panic and managed to steady her voice. "You won't get away with it, Rex. British agents are watching this hut. It was planned that I come here like this—because they knew as soon as I unearthed the book you would come out. It was a trap."

His eyes narrowed. "Do you take me for a fool?"

"You knew?"

"Bret's dead. So is Hamid. And Jemal will have lured Neal away by now and eliminated him, too."

"They can't be," she said desperately, tears stinging her eyes. "Oh, Rex! Please!"

A voice interrupted. "Don't beg him, Allison. It isn't necessary."

"Bret!"

General Blaine whirled. Bret was standing in the doorway. Blaine sought to grab Allison as a shield, but Bret fired, and the bullet exploded the lamp. In the darkness, Allison threw herself to the floor, crawling toward the bed. A terrible crash followed the sound of General Blaine's brief groan, then another bullet was fired at close range.

Allison didn't move. For a moment there was silence; then, "It's all right, Allison."

The bathroom light came on, and Bret moved swiftly to her. He gathered her in his arms and held her tightly.

"I thought you were dead—the blood—the closet—"

"I know."

"Who is it?"

His voice cracked with emotion. "Hamid—he got him. Good, faithful Hamid. And I even doubted him. If I only had another chance to tell him—what a ruddy good soldier he was!"

"Oh, I'm sorry, Bret. So very sorry!"

She clutched him, her face lifting from the masculine comfort of his strong embrace. "The book," she whispered.

"I know. I have it."

"Neal?" she inquired, her eyes hopefully searching Bret's.

"Loyal," came the quiet voice, reflecting satisfaction and relief. "He's chasing down Jemal now. Don't worry," he added when he must have felt her tense with alarm. "Neal has what it takes; Hamid trusted him all along."

Despite everything, a slight smile turned her lips. "I—I did, too," she whispered.

"Yes. Courage and dedication run in the family."

"Yes, like Leah…"

His hand tightened on her arm as he looked down at her, and she saw a glimmer of admiration in his eyes. "And you. You couldn't have done better, Allison." His hold tightened a little. "Let's get you out of here."

He led her toward the door, trying to steer her past General Blaine's body, but Allison wanted to pause. A smirk was frozen on his face, and Allison asked quietly, "Did you—?"

"No," Bret said. "He turned his gun on himself. I wanted him alive for questioning. There may be others. Let's go. I have to find the message Reuter left inside this book."

Running footsteps interrupted them, and Allison froze, looking toward the door. Catching her arm, Bret pulled her behind him, lifting his revolver slightly.

Neal called out in a low voice, then cautiously entered, breathing hard and damp with sweat. His eyes briefly took in the scene then met Bret's in wordless understanding.

"Jemal got away," said Neal.

"We'll track him later. There's no time to worry about him now. We have the book. And we have to locate those documents."

"Maybe here at the huts?"

"Not likely, but anything is possible."

"What if there are others about besides Professor Jemal?" whispered Allison, glancing toward the door.

Bret and Neal exchanged glances, as though they knew something more, but neither answered. "Bolt the doors and windows, then search Blaine," Bret told him. "He may have something worth taking to Cairo. I'll check the book."

When Neal returned, Bret had lit the oil lamp.

"What about Hamid?" asked Neal. "Did he find you?"

Allison tensed, looking from her cousin to Bret, expecting to see his pain over Hamid's death. But Bret was once again professional. "Yes, he found me. We got things cleared between us. He reminded me of something I'd forgotten, that Rose Lyman swore you were in Jerusalem with her and Benjamin when Reuter and Leah were killed. I should have remembered," he admitted, "but I didn't."

"It's understandable. You had Allison to worry about on the train. Where's Hamid now?"

Bret's voice was flat. "Dead. Behind the closet door. The matter will need to wait."

Neal said something to himself, angry that Hamid, as well as his sister, had fallen victim to the enemy. Then, in two strides, he was beside General Blaine, stooping to the floor to search him.

Allison couldn't bear to watch and turned away, joining Bret at the desk where he leaned, studying the book beneath the flickering oil lamp. "Find anything?" she whispered anxiously.

"No." His riveting blue eyes met hers above the light. "That coded word he left Leah here on the desk, was there anything unusual about it? The way it was written, for example?"

"Yes." She picked up the pencil and wrote out the word on paper: "HITTITEebg."

Bret studied the word.

Neal came up. "Nothing on Blaine. Not even a coin. He was careful." He shook his sandy-colored head with disbelief. "I'm surprised he was the one. An affable, retired major-general, eager to talk about his old battles in India."

"It was all an act," said Allison. "He was born in Berlin. He despised the British military. He's been a spy for years."

Bret wasn't listening. "The 'ebg' must mean something obvious."

He handed the sheet of paper to Neal. "You're the archaeology expert. What do you make of this?"

Allison was eager to prove herself. "I've always thought the 'ebg' was important."

Bret glanced at her with a brief smile.

Neal studied the word. "If it's a location, it could mean 'Euphrates,' but then the 'bg' doesn't make sense. Perhaps there's some word in Woolly's book starting with those letters," stated Neal. He turned quickly to the back and searched the glossary. "Well, there's no 'ebg.' Anyway, the agent pretending to be Reuter was no archaeologist."

"It needs to be something simple," said Bret. "He wouldn't have had time to come up with anything very complex."

"Too bad it had to be so secretive," said Allison. "He could have just given us the page number. I guess that's too simple."

"You know...," mused Bret, "the three letters are all in the first part of the alphabet. None is past the ninth letter. Suppose 'a' for '1' and 'b' for '2.' Then 'ebg' would be...'527.' Does the book have that many pages?" asked Bret as he leaned against the desk.

Neal flipped the pages. "Not quite, unless you include the index." He looked up. "He's underlined Carchemish."

Allison looked at the underline. "Black ink, the same as Leah's code word." She beamed triumphantly. "And Leah said Major Reuter had visited the expedition house before he came here to meet you in the club. Could the papers be in the house?" She looked at Bret. "And to think we were there the night we escaped Captain Mustafa! But where in the house? We looked everywhere."

Bret looked at Neal, "What page number is listed under Carchemish?"

"There are several, starting with 238. I'll scan them all. There is another underline under the word 'stairs.'" Neal hesitated, as though visualizing the house where he and Leah had stayed. "I don't understand. There are no stairs at the expedition house."

"No, not at the house," said Bret, and his gaze met Neal's. "I'll bet it's the Carchemish Digs."

"You're right. The digs would be safer," said Neal in a low voice. "Why didn't I think of it sooner? Leah told me Reuter had visited the digs just before he came here. She said he showed a good deal of interest in the latest Hittite discovery."

"Why didn't we all think of it?" said Bret. "But we couldn't be sure without the book. And what is the latest discovery?"

Neal had no hesitation. "The palace stairway."

Bret smiled. "That's it." He stood up, snatching the book and closing it with a clap of victory. "Let's go." He ran toward the back door, and Neal, catching Allison's arm, followed in swift pursuit.

Bret had his revolver in hand as he led the way down the back steps into the sandy yard and paused ahead, a dark silhouette, as Allison hurried down the steps into the hot, dark, windy night, her heart beating rapidly.

What if they were followed? Had Jemal really escaped, or had he back-tracked to watch them in the darkness? Was he alone? What if someone else was with him?

22

THE NEXT AFTERNOON, despite the sky's early radiance, something was oddly disheartening about the airless heat. As Allison looked toward the horizon, she saw that the sky was streaked with a foreboding yellow stain. She watched the sky as she sat in a vehicle next to Bret, who drove. Dry lightning did a war dance, and she could faintly hear from across the ranges of wilderness and hills the mutter of a distant storm.

Allison turned to look in the back seat. Neal had driven all night and was stretched out on the seat with his hat drawn low over his eyes.

Bret was grim. "A storm is coming."

Allison shaded her eyes from the sun, which was still shining brightly. But the dirty yellow stain above the desert was spreading.

Bret settled his hat. "Let's hope the Turks are too smart to get caught in this. If they are, we've a chance to do our business and get out unnoticed."

She hadn't forgotten Captain Mustafa or the Turks and Germans. "Coming back here after masquerading as Colonel Holman is dangerous. What if Professor Jemal wired ahead?"

His silence was answer enough.

"I wish you were anywhere but here," he said. "I had no choice but to bring you. I couldn't leave you alone at the huts or chance putting you on the train back to Cairo."

She moved restlessly in the seat, her back aching. "I'd rather take my chances with you and Neal." She remembered the terror of being alone when General Blaine had appeared. She glanced at Bret warily. "What if the Germans are watching the digs?"

Again, his deliberate silence was the only answer.

"Can you tell me what the information is about now?" she asked. "Why is it so important?"

His eyes regarded her thoughtfully. "The Constantinople papers are evidence of something we have suspected for the last year, that the Ottoman Empire will join Germany in war against England."

"Turkey has always been pro-British," she protested.

"So they wish us to think. It's unfortunate that some in our London government wish to continue to bury their heads in the sand until it's too late."

"Are you suggesting the Ottoman Empire intends to side with the kaiser?"

"That's exactly what I mean. The documents our agent came across in Constantinople are proof. They also show that Germany has made secret overtures to Constantinople promising sections of Czarist Russia, territory that Turkey has always had its eyes on. What Constantinople doesn't know is that the kaiser, too, has an appetite for St. Petersburg—along with large sections of France, Belgium, and England."

She stared at him, her stomach doing a flip-flop. "Germany will declare war on England?"

"Eventually. When it serves the kaiser's purpose. Egypt is a bit closer to where we are, isn't it?"

"You don't mean—"

"The German general in Constantinople has plans to conquer all

Palestine. We've long suspected the reasons for the railway being built from Baghdad."

"Yes, Leah mentioned it."

"Remember when you asked me at El-Arish why I was interested in what the Bedouin had to say? He offered news to back up our suspicions. The railway, including the Hejaz, will be used to carry troops and supplies to Beersheba and Gaza for the Germans. And the documents that Reuter took from Constantinople are official proof the Germans intend to invade Egypt by way of the Suez Canal—just as soon as Germany invades Belgium."

She stared at him, amazed and frightened. For a moment she could say nothing. War, not only in Europe but also in Arabia and Palestine—even Egypt.

"The documents," he continued, "are proof to show the hard-headed optimists in London and Cairo. Now do you see why they are so crucial? Egypt at this moment has insufficient troops to hold off any thrust into the Suez by Turkey."

"No wonder the other side wanted to stop Major Reuter," she said. "And to think for a short time it all rested with Neal and Leah."

"And you," he said soberly. "For a time you alone held the key to locating those documents."

She considered this, awed by the thought. Yet here they were, nearing Carchemish. The documents would soon be in Bret's grasp.

"Anything might go wrong," she said.

"Not if we can help it."

"So you've no doubt in your mind the kaiser will go to war," she said, dismayed.

"My personal opinion? I've no doubt. But others in London wouldn't agree with me. For years Germany has been building her army and preparing for conquest."

"Yes," she said quietly, thinking of General Blaine. "To quote Rex,

'It's Germany's hour.' The time for the Aryan race to command a world empire. Time for England to surrender her command of the sea, her colonies, her dreams."

Bret reached over and took hold of her wrist, and she looked at him quickly, as if awakening from a daze. "Forget Blaine."

"About Sarah," she whispered. "She doesn't know he was a German agent. Is there any way it can be kept from her? She'll be brokenhearted."

"That decision won't be left to me, but I'll do what I can. Intelligence will want to keep all this hushed up anyway. And I quite agree she didn't know."

"Did you, Bret? Have you ever had suspicions about him?"

"Actually, no, not at first. Not until we met at Helga's shop in Old Cairo. I looked into matters with the British consul—Arlington. He told me by wire that it was Blaine who had arranged for your aunt's medical crates to be sent from Luxor to Cairo. But Blaine made a dreadful blunder. He didn't think they would be sent to Helga's shop. That was a slip her proprietor made when he thought the crates contained opium he could sell. Instead of sending the crates to an associate of Jemal's, the proprietor arranged for them to be brought first to Helga's shop. So Blaine had to go there. When I saw him and learned he had arrived before you did, I began to suspect him."

"So you followed me to Luxor," she said. "And then to the Hejaz Railway?"

"I expected Blaine to follow you as well, but he didn't. Jemal did. I had to make a choice to stay on Blaine or follow Jemal. Without Neal to help, and with Hamid in Aleppo, I had no one to watch Blaine while I trailed you and Jemal. Helga hadn't arrived yet."

"I'm surprised about the baroness. I had her all wrong."

"She's been an asset to us for several years now. Her dinner parties in Cairo and Aleppo are gathering places for foreign dignitaries and their wives. She's been able to gather a good deal of information for us since she's suspected of having sympathy for Germany's ambitions."

"What of the Berlin-Baghdad Railway? Isn't it being built by German construction companies once owned by Helga's husband?"

"Yes, and it has allowed us to gain information from Berlin, since they report to her on the progress."

"So you followed Jemal onto the train?" she asked.

"I had to. I couldn't allow him to board without being there to protect you. It was a shock to find Neal in that train compartment instead of Professor Jemal." He looked at her. "Remember your suspicion about someone boarding at Damascus who was unfriendly toward you?"

She shivered. "Yes. General Blaine?"

"I think so. He probably convinced Sarah he was coming to find you because he was concerned. By the time she would have found out what happened to you, they both would have been on a ship to Berlin."

"She would have been miserably unhappy."

"Yes, but by then it would have been too late for her to do anything about it."

It was twilight when they arrived at the Carchemish Digs, a huge, oval-shaped site surrounded by embankments as high as twenty-five feet. In the northeast corner the Euphrates River rushed past the site, flowing dark and mysterious.

Allison's first glance at the river in the approaching wind storm conjured up the ancient river's biblical references. She had read in Genesis of the River Euphrates connected with the Garden of Eden and had read of it again in Revelation, where a reference was made to four angels being loosed from the Euphrates to make way for a great army to pass.

As she struggled her way through the ruins over difficult footing, she listened to the river's roar, stirred up by the wind, and looked up into the darkening sky that shrouded the moon and stars. The wind struck in raw, savage gusts that whipped her long hair and skirt. She struggled to keep up with Bret and Neal, who were moving ahead in their eagerness to locate the spot where Major Reuter had safely concealed the documents.

As Neal pressed ahead, Bret paused to wait for her, taking her arm and helping her climb over the mounds of stone and dirt, then clasping her hand and pulling her along at a faster pace.

She could see that the higher embankments protected the Hittite fortifications that looked to be made of crude brick. She saw two gates, one on the south and one on the west end of the digs.

Within the rampart, or the enclosed area of the site, was a much higher mound, its summit reaching perhaps thirteen feet above the mean level of the river. This, she knew from Neal's explanations in his letters, had served the Hittites as their acropolis. It was perhaps a thousand feet long from northwest to southeast, falling off steeply to the Euphrates. The flattened top showed signs of ancient Roman and Syrian buildings, with huge fragments having toppled down, lying on the landward slope.

Allison glanced about at the remains of structures from a Roman-Syrian town, largely built of earlier materials. Some Arab houses were there, too, made from used, ancient blocks.

Bret pulled her over the refuse heaps and structural remains from earlier diggers, as Allison felt the suck of the wind. "If anyone is following us, we'll never hear him," she said above the wind.

"Keep moving."

They came to some main Hittite remains at the foot of a mound where Neal waited, anxiously beckoning them to hurry.

Bret ran ahead, and Allison followed. When she got there, Neal had produced two lanterns. The men were lighting them as the twilight faded. The flames danced up, swaying in the wind, and Allison looked at a large staircase.

"Hogarth, from the British Museum, first began work here a year ago," explained Neal. "He thought it seemed likely buildings would be in the vicinity of a stairway, and he was right. Earlier archaeologists were here before us and reburied some of their finds in their trenches because they couldn't transport them to England. We uncovered a great entrance staircase with some Hittite slabs on each side." Neal led them with the lantern as he talked. "We've been working on this staircase for some time. Reuter knew of it. He came here a few days before he went to the club meeting at Aleppo."

Allison pointed. "There's a lion's head." Artistically, the work was exceptional. She also saw some manner of an idol or a king. They came to the stairs.

"This is the spot," said Bret. "Keep watch, Neal. It will take me a few minutes."

Neal stood in the shadows of the arch, the wind blowing against him, and Allison held a second lantern close to where Bret was working. She kept glancing over her shoulder into the gathering darkness outside the enclosure, feeling a chill edging up her spine. "Hurry, Bret."

"Ah," said Bret. "I have it!"

Allison turned quickly to watch him remove a stone casing in the shape of a box. "There's a lid," she whispered. She stooped for a closer view as Bret removed a large leather portfolio from the casing. He lifted the folder and drew out several official documents from Constantinople. "Bring the lantern closer."

She did, hearing the wind whine about the crevices. "Well?" she whispered hopefully.

He looked at her and smiled. "We have them. Come on, let's get out of here."

Neal was waiting and sheathed his gun in his shoulder holster as they approached. "Got it?"

Bret tapped the portfolio. "All here." He met Neal's gaze. "Take Allison with you to Cairo by train."

Allison was alarmed. "What of you? Why aren't you coming with us?"

"They would recognize me in an instant as Colonel Holman. I've friends among the Kurds, and I'll go there for a time. I'll need to bring Hamid's family word of his death. And I'll need to get this information to my superior. I have to go to London for a time."

Neal looked at Allison, then Bret, and reading their expressions walked away and left them alone in the ruins.

They stood beneath the black sky, and with the wind whipping about them, blowing sand and dust, Allison shivered.

"When you get to Cairo," said Bret, "Return to the *Mercy*. You belong there, you know, in pristine white with a red cross on your breast and dignity and nobility in your eyes. You belong to something far more wonderful than this kind of life."

Her eyes came to his. He seemed to want to say more but did not.

Allison had words of her own, but they, too, died in her throat with the painful beating of her heart. Tears moistened her eyes, and she hoped he didn't notice.

The Arabian winds blew warm and strong and kicked up the sand. It seemed a new song was about to play now that the old one had ended in both tragedy and victory. But the new was not yet one of cheer and hope; it was a dirge that spoke of war to come, of human rage. A new call for valor and sacrifice was also sounding with the rising storm.

"David tells of a Jewish tradition," Bret said. "Upon rising each morning, however dark the day, however hopeless it may seem, they say, `Rise up like a lion, for the service of the Lord!'"

Allison looked at him, and her heart contracted. He did believe.

Their gaze held in wordless understanding, and he gently cupped her face between his hands. As the wind blew her hair, he kissed her tenderly, for a long blissful moment.

"I'll find you again, Allison," he whispered softly. "Wait for me. I'll return from London as soon as I can."

She nodded unable to speak. Then, he released her, and she turned and walked to where Neal waited.

She looked eastward into the black sky. Despite the gloom and threat of storm, a lone, silvery star broke through and seemed to wink its promise that heaven waited behind the darkness. She, too, would wait...until his return. Allison turned and looked back at Bret, a silhouette standing on the stone ruins with the starlight behind him, the wind tugging at his shirt.

"Rise up like a lion for the service of the Lord," she whispered.

Watch for book two of the Lions of the Desert Series, coming in September, 1997!

Author's Note

After researching the history of the time period, I have condensed some of the events that shaped the beginnings of World War I, ending with the capture of Jerusalem in 1917. The history itself is accurate and the mindsets of the different nations are represented through the fictional lead characters in the series.

Listed below are just a few historical facts about events used in *Arabian Winds*, and will carry through to the other novels in the Lions of the Desert Series:

• The arrival of Oswald Chambers to work with the British and Australian soldiers in Egypt is historical (and wonderful!) and will be more fully developed in book two.

• The construction of the Berlin-Baghdad Railway is factual, as is the concern of the British, who feared its use by the German kaiser to bring in supplies and troops in order to seize British Egypt, especially the Suez Canal.

• The circumstances surrounding the banishment of David Ben-Gurion and the Russian Jews from Jerusalem by the Turks is true, and a Jewish spy ring was created to help British soldiers.

• T.E. Lawrence—Lawrence of Arabia—was working at the archaeological site at Carchemish during this time, and eventually went to work at Cairo Intelligence. The archaeological facts about the Hittites are accurately depicted.

The British, German, and Turkish spies, the murder, and the romance are all ideas based on some historical tidbits, but the story is just that—a tale that came to my mind and kept me awake at night!

I've had so much fun writing this book, and have also been personally challenged. I'm looking forward to continuing the story and romance of Allison Wescott and Major Bret Holden in books two and three of the Lions of the Desert Series.

Beloved Reader,

I wish I could meet each one of you personally and thank you for your support and encouragement. I've truly enjoyed your wonderful letters and look forward to hearing more from you. I've also been able to meet some of you bookstore owners and workers at the CBA Convention and it's been a joy!

As I work on the Lions of the Desert Series I want to tell you how much I've enjoyed researching mounds of interesting history about a time period and location (Palestine) that is rich with the evidence of the Lord's hand during World War I. I've been reminded again of how He truly sits as King of history, moving all things, even the mundane, toward the fulfillment of His eternal purpose.

As I looked back to World War I in Arabia, I mused over the future, and was convinced again of how we too are living in a strategic hour. As the Christians who lived in dangerous times past needed to be courageous and strong to stand firm, so we, too, need to do the same in our hour. We don't need to fear, for He is in full control.

With Christian Love,

Linda Chaikin

Write to Linda Chaikin at Palisades c/o Questar Publishers, Inc.
P.O. Box 1720, Sisters, Oregon 97759

PALISADES...PURE ROMANCE

⌒ PALISADES ⌒

Reunion, Karen Ball

Refuge, Lisa Tawn Bergren

Torchlight, Lisa Tawn Bergren

Treasure, Lisa Tawn Bergren

Chosen, Lisa Tawn Bergren

Firestorm, Lisa Tawn Bergren

Wise Man's House, Melody Carlson

Arabian Winds, Linda Chaikin (Premier)

Cherish, Constance Colson

Chase the Dream, Constance Colson (Premier)

Angel Valley, Peggy Darty

Sundance, Peggy Darty

Love Song, Sharon Gillenwater

Antiques, Sharon Gillenwater

Song of the Highlands, Sharon Gillenwater (Premier)

Secrets, Robin Jones Gunn

Whispers, Robin Jones Gunn

Echoes, Robin Jones Gunn

Sunsets, Robin Jones Gunn

Coming Home, Barbara Jean Hicks

Snow Swan, Barbara Jean Hicks (April, 1997)

Irish Eyes, Annie Jones (April, 1997)

Glory, Marilyn Kok

Sierra, Shari MacDonald

Forget-Me-Not, Shari MacDonald

Diamonds, Shari MacDonald

Westward, Amanda MacLean

Stonehaven, Amanda MacLean

Everlasting, Amanda MacLean
Promise Me the Dawn, Amanda MacLean (Premier)
Kingdom Come, Amanda MacLean
Betrayed, Lorena McCourtney
Escape, Lorena McCourtney
Voyage, Elaine Schulte

A Christmas Joy, Darty, Gillenwater, MacLean
Mistletoe, Ball, Hicks, McCourtney
A Mother's Love, Bergren, Colson, MacLean

THE PALISADES LINE

Ask for them at your local bookstore. If the title you seek is not in stock, the store may order you a copy using the ISBN listed.

Wise Man's House, Melody Carlson
ISBN 1-57673-070-0
Kestra McKenzie, a young widow trying to make a new life for herself, thinks she has found the solidity she longs for when she purchases her childhood dream house—a stone mansion on the Oregon Coast. Just as renovations begin, a mysterious stranger moves into her caretaker's cottage—and into her heart.

Sunsets, Robin Jones Gunn
ISBN 1-57673-103-0
Alissa Benson loves her job as a travel agent. But when the agency has computer problems, they call in expert Brad Phillips. Alissa can't wait for Brad to fix the computers and leave—he's too blunt for her comfort. So she's more than a little upset when she moves into a duplex and finds out he's her neighbor!

Snow Swan, Barbara Jean Hicks (April, 1997)
ISBN 1-57673-107-3
Life hasn't been easy for Toni Ferrier. As an unwed mother and a recovering alcoholic, she doesn't feel worthy of anyone's love. Then she meets Clark McConaughey, who helps her launch her business aboard the sternwheeler Snow Swan. Sparks fly between them, but if Clark finds out the truth about Toni's past, will he still love her?

Irish Eyes, Annie Jones (April, 1997)
ISBN 1-57673-108-1
When Julia Reed finds a young boy, who claims to be a leprechaun, camped out under a billboard, she gets drawn into a century-old crime involving a real pot of gold. Interpol agent Cameron O'Dea is trying to solve the crime. In the process, he takes over the homeless shelter that Julia runs, camps out in her neighbor's RV, and generally turns her life upside down!

Kingdom Come, Amanda MacLean
ISBN 1-57673-120-0
In 1902, feisty Ivy Rose Clayborne, M.D., returns to her hometown of Kingdom Come to fight the coal mining company that is ravaging the land. She meets an unexpected ally, a man who claims to be a drifter but in reality is Harrison MacKenzie, grandson of the coal mining baron. Together they face the aftermath of betrayal, the fight for justice...and the price of love.

A Mother's Love, Bergren, Colson, MacLean
ISBN 1-57673-106-5
Three popular Palisades authors bring you heartwarming stories about the joys and challenges of romance in the midst of motherhood.
By Lisa Bergren: A widower and his young daughter go to Southern California for vacation, and return with much more than they expected.
By Constance Colson: Cassie Jenson wants her old sweetheart to stay in her memories. But when he moves back to town, they find out that they could never forget each other.
By Amanda MacLean: A couple is expecting their first baby, and they hardly have enough time for each other. With the help of an old journal and a last-minute getaway, they work to rekindle their love.

Also look for our new line:
PALISADES PREMIER
More Story. More Romance.

Arabian Winds, Linda Chaikin
ISBN 1-57673-105-7
In the first book of the Lions of the Desert trilogy, World War I is breaking upon the deserts of Arabia in 1914. Young nurse Allison Wescott is on a holiday with an archaeological club, but a murder interrupts her plans, and a mysterious officer keeps turning up wherever she goes!
Watch for more books in Linda Chaikin's Egypt series!

Song of the Highlands, Sharon Gillenwater
ISBN 0-88070-946-4
During the Napoleonic Wars, Kiernan is a piper, but he comes back to find out he's inherited a title. At his run-down estate, he meets the beautiful Mariah. During a trip to London, they face a kidnapping...and discover their love for each other.
Watch for more books in Sharon Gillenwater's Scottish series!